Wild, Untamed Passions

"I know you might not believe me, Leigh," Jace said, pulling her into his arms, "but I've never wanted any woman the way I crave you. I'll want more than a night or two from you, much more."

She gazed into his jungle-green eyes and said impulsively, "Surely you know I feel the same way, Jace, and you can have me without all these exasperating games."

His fingers traced her flushed cheeks and parted lips. "If that's true, Leigh, then no more games. But you have to be sure of me and yourself. There will be no turning back."

She took his face in her hands and pulled his head down to hers. "I am sure, Jace. Now, if you don't kiss me, I'm going to scream."

Leigh felt more alive in his arms than she had in her lifetime. She wanted his kisses, embraces, all of him. She yearned for them to be together, tonight and forever, no matter what the dangers . . .

JANELLE TAYLOR

Whispered Kisses

ZEBRA BOOKS
KENSINGTON PUBLISHING CORP.

ZEBRA BOOKS

are published by

Kensington Publishing Corp.
475 Park Avenue South
New York, NY 10016

Second printing: March, 1990

Printed in the United States of America

Dedicated to:
my niece
Robyn Leigh Taylor Harris
and to
my special friends in Athens
Crystie Dekle and Linda Blanchard

Acknowledgment to:
Elaine Raco Chase
Thanks to a talented writer and a good
friend who advised me this
story should be told as a long historical, not
as a short contemporary, as originally written
in 1981. She was right!

Chapter One

London, England
March 11, 1896

Laura Leigh Webster was annoyed by the late invitation with its ring of a summons. She did not mind having dinner with her stepuncle and guardian, Lord Chadwick Hamilton, but she hated to endure another unpleasant evening with his petulant lover Louisa and their friends. Still, she supposed it would be best to just dress quickly and join them. She was going to be going on a safari with these people; she might as well learn to enjoy their company.

As Leigh fastened a locket around her neck, visions of British East Africa floated dreamily through her mind. That wild and exotic land seemed to call to her as the American West had called to settlers. Even though Chad was taking Louisa, Reid, and Cynthia along, Leigh was eager to leave on their journey. Her tasks here were finished for a while, and others could wait until her return. It was time for a taste of adventure.

Leigh had come to London in February to claim an inheritance from her grandfather, William Webster, who had died in December. So far, she had learned a great deal about the family business and her enormous inheritance from Chad, who was her legal guardian until she reached twenty-one in November and who was to continue running the textile empire for her.

Chad had also introduced her to a constant social whirl that was like nothing she'd ever experienced back home in Texas. It was delightful learning her way around London and getting reacquainted with Chad. She smiled as she remembered how infatuated she'd been with her grandfather's shadow when she was fifteen. He'd been quite charming then, too! But if she didn't hurry, she'd get no warm smiles from him tonight! She locked her door and dropped the key into a string purse.

At the hotel's entrance, a waiting carriage approached the fashionably chad female before a doorman returned to aid her. Leigh asked the smiling driver if he was available to take her to Stams Street. The man looked at her strangely but nodded, jumping down to assist her into the carriage. Then he asked for the address again. Leigh spoke it, then spelled it for him, deciding it might be her American accent that had him confused.

They headed off in an easterly direction. It was almost dusk, and lanterns on the carriage were burning to warn pedestrians against stepping into its path. Leigh noticed that streetlamps were being lit where electric street lighting was unavailable. The driver talked to her over his right shoulder, telling her about London. Leigh was too polite to say she had already toured his beloved city. Yet, as she studied the sights they were passing, she did not recognize any of them.

Her ears and nose told her they were nearing the waterfront. She heard the soft ringings of bells as anchored ships bobbed on the rising tide, and squeaking noises as they rubbed against wooden docks. She heard unlowered sails flapping in the breeze, and sailors passing orders back and forth as they prepared for late landings. Then, she saw masts towering above structures for the storing of goods before or after loading. Down a street or two, she glimpsed the cluttered docks surrounding the Thames River and a variety of vessels—small crafts, sailing ships, and one steamer. She leaned forward and tugged on the driver's arm. "Are you sure you know where Stams Street is?" she inquired.

He smiled and replied, "Tae be sure, lass. There she 'tis." He pointed ahead to where a glowing lamp illuminated a sign which read STAMS STREET. He halted and jumped down. As he assisted her from her seat, he smiled amiably and said, "Number six be down there, near tha end, lass. That'll be three shillings."

As he held out his hand, Leigh fetched the money from her purse and paid him. She walked to the shadowy street—more like an alley, she told herself—and glanced down the full length to a walled deadend. She didn't like this situation. No one was about, and it would be dark soon. There must be a mistake. Before she could ask the driver to either wait for her or to escort her to the door, he departed in a rush. The hurried clattering of his horse and carriage drowned out her calls to him.

Her blue eyes wide and apprehensive, she checked her surroundings. The air was cooler and damper at this secluded location so close to the water. Still, no one was in sight. Dusk was closing in on her and the alley. She heard no music, only faint noises of dock work and lapping water in the distance. It appeared too deserted and dismal for a restaurant to be nearby. Perhaps, she reasoned as she tried not to panic, it was

9

a private address and a surprise party was in store.

Leigh walked to the building marked 6 and halted. Sighting the address, a small amount of relief filled her. She approached the heavy door and knocked, the sound ringing hollow and faint in the enclosure. Nothing. She pulled on the handle. It was locked. Balling her fist, she pounded on the thick door. No response.

Concern created tiny lines on her forehead and between her brows. This setting explained the driver's odd look when she had given him the address. She wondered why Chad would ask her to come to a deserted location, then not be there. He was too familiar with London to . . .

Leigh scolded herself for jumping to dark suspicions about her stepuncle and guardian. The Webster estate was worth a large fortune, but she knew for certain that Chadwick Hamilton wouldn't inherit it if something happened to her. In fact, since she had the power to ensure his lucrative and prestigious position, it was to his advantage to keep her safe and well. Besides, Chad was more than fond of her, a fact that his jealous and greedy mistress had trouble accepting.

Perhaps, Leigh mused, Chad was watching her this very minute, testing her courage and wits before they left on the dangerous safari. He did have a devilish, mischievous streak. Or, Leigh reasoned, maybe this alarming joke was Louisa's doing, meant to terrify her into running home to America. No, she refuted. Chad would be furious with his lover for playing such a perilous trick on his ward. Whoever was to blame, what she had to do was correct the error, and fast. This location was certainly dangerous for a woman alone. She needed to leave, now.

But before doing so, she would knock on every door in the forsaken area to see if someone trustwor-

10

thy was around to assist her. There was no response at any of them. Most were marked with names of companies and included their business hours, all ceasing at five o'clock. She noticed the brass lettering on one: Alfred Johnston, Exports/Imports, British East Africa — her destination when she sailed on Monday.

Leigh felt uneasy, as if she were being watched. She wished she had her pistol or rifle for protection. On the ranch, she had confronted dangers before: wolves, thieves, snakes, and occasional rustlers. But she had been armed and usually not alone. Leigh scolded herself for getting into this predicament.

The man spying on Leigh was enchanted by her beauty and baffled by her presence in such a hazardous setting. When she lifted her face to observe her surroundings, he noticed that her features were exquisite, her eyes large and expressive. They were a rich blue shade that matched the campanula and monkshood that his mother had loved and grown in her flower gardens. Her brows and lashes were a dark brown, in startling contrast to her golden-blond hair with its sunny highlights. His gaze slipped over the way her hair was secured into a chignon at the back of her head, tendrils dangling down her neck and near her ears. Those short curls seemed to dance playfully in the breeze as if reveling in their freedom and closeness to such enticing flesh. A deep and vivid blue aigrette was pinned snugly against the flattering hairstyle, a spray that seemed to match her eyes, if his were seeing correctly in the fading light.

His stirring study continued. Her face was oval-shaped and her complexion was tawny from unprotected hours outdoors, a fact he found unusual for a proper lady, since most avoided the harsh sun with

11

parasols to keep their skin like ivory silk. Her lips and cheeks seemed naturally pink and alluring. It did not take long for him to realize she had more than enough charms to stimulate a man's interest and desires.

From his advantageous position above her, he could see her clearly though the light was fading. She was slender, of medium height, and her figure was appealing. Very appealing, he concluded, as he was reminded of how long it had been since he'd enjoyed a woman's charms. Despite his many experiences with the fair sex, something told him he had never had a woman like her before.

He tried to divert his carnal yearnings by examining her clothing, seeking clues to her presence on the docks. She was wearing a gown with a blue velvet bodice that dipped to a point onto a cream brocade skirt. The tulle overskirt was decorated with blue floral sprays and the elbow-length sleeves were lifted and puffed at the shoulder, giving an impression of good posture and pride. A not-too-low neckline called his attention to that satiny area of bare flesh, and his fingers itched to wander over it. A small bouquet of blue silk flowers was attached to cream flouncing on the full bosom and made a striking contrast. Ivory sweepers that trailed the skirt gave off a soft rustling noise as she walked in soundless kid slippers.

He shook his dark head to clear it. He could not understand what a lady was doing here alone. She seemed to be looking for someone or a meeting place, perhaps a lovers' rendezvous. If so, the man was a fool to be late and to sacrifice a moment in those arms! He was certain everyone had left the area, and that number 6 — where she had first knocked — was unrented. He watched and listened.

* * *

Hoping this was merely an accident on someone's part did not lessen Leigh's tension and annoyance. She threw her cloak around her shoulders and headed toward the alley entrance with the main street nearby. At least she would be safer on the lamplit street where a carriage might come by at any time. Until one did or she reached a larger and better lighted street, she should keep moving in the same direction from which they had arrived.

Though Leigh's kid slippers made little noise on the stone street, her gown and petticoat rustled noticeably. She came to a sudden halt, and her panic mounted. Two sailors blocked the alleyway. Perhaps that explained why she'd had the eerie feeling of being watched. One took a long drink from a bottle, then tossed it aside. Glass shattered loudly. The two men laughed and nudged each other, then headed her way.

If they hadn't already sighted the begowned and vulnerable lady, Leigh knew they'd see her—there was still enough light for them to spot her cream colored skirt and blond hair. It was foolish to scream for help and appear terrified and helpless. Yet that was how she felt as they closed in on her, leering, laughing, and joking in a crude manner. From their rumpled clothing and the way they were walking and talking, they had been drinking heavily, and her father had always said a drunken man was dangerous and unpredictable.

Leigh thought quickly. The two sailors were between her and escape. Weaponless, she had only her wits for aid. Perhaps a bluff would work on them and gain her freedom from the entrapping area. She mustn't let them know she was shaking in fear. She had to put up a bold front and hope they were sober and smart enough not to assail a lady—if they could

13

consider her one when she was in this awful location at night, and alone.

Walking forward, Leigh held her shoulders and head high as if unafraid of anything, especially them. She tried to pass between them without speaking. It didn't work; each grabbed at a wrist. As she yanked backward to free herself before they got a good grip, her maneuver put them between her and the alley entrance again.

"How dare you touch me!" she cried. "Move aside so I can pass. I'm late for my dinner with Lord Salisbury," she informed them, praying that powerful name would frighten them into obeying her.

The two sailors looked at each other, then howled with laughter. "Come on, me pretty wench, dinna be puttin' on airs wif us," one taunted in what she thought was an Irish or Scottish brogue.

"Yeah," the other one agreed. "We'll hae us a guid time right 'ere. Ye been waitin' long, me bonny lass?"

Leigh sent them a cold and arrogant glare. "Move aside or you'll be sorry," she warned, taking two steps backward. "Just like that stupid carriage driver who let me off at the wrong address. I suppose he thought it would be a funny trick on a naive American visitor. Neither I nor the prime minister will find this joke amusing." Her mind searched for a plan. She hadn't seen anything lying in the alley to use as a weapon — no brick, board, bucket, or such. "If it's money you're after, I only have a few pounds and shillings with me. I'll give it to you after you let me pass. I can go on to Lord Salisbury's and you can go somewhere to buy another bottle."

One man pulled a bottle from his pocket and said, "We got us a bottle o' guid Irish whiskey. Let's be movin' down tha alley sae nobody'll disturb us. Ye ken have tha first sip after a wee kiss."

14

"Let 'er drink tha whole bottle, Jaimie, whilst I work under 'er skirt," the other man teased. "We been at sea to long to wait. Ye be 'ere an' dressed fur business. We're as guid as any customer ye'll find tonight, me bonny lass. What's yer price? We hae plenty o' money. I'll tak' a tumble wif ye first, right down there."

"She's got two ends, Sean. We ken enjoy 'er at tha same time."

The men's vulgarity riled and frightened Leigh. She glared at them and stated, "I'm not a . . . a prostitute. I was on my way to a party, but the carriage driver left me here by mistake. If you come near me, you'll pay with your lives."

"Mistake, ye sae?" one sailor mocked her dilemma. He looked behind him, then back at her "Nae matter. We need a woman bad, an' ye're 'ere. If ye be guid an' nice, we'll let ye go afterward. If ye dinna do as we sae, ye'll git hurt. Then-n-n," he said, drawing out the word to an intimidating length, "we'll tak' ye tae our capt'n an' he'll sell ye to one o' them sheiks, after he be done wif ye. Which'll it be, lass? Us or a bad dream?"

"If you dare harm me, you foul—" She didn't get to finish her desperate threat before they grabbed for her once more.

Leigh fought like a wildcat, kicking, scratching, pelting her attackers with all her might. She heard her gown rip, and increased her struggles. Her hair came loose and the aigrette was flung to the ground. Her cloak was yanked off and cast aside. She wished she had on her boots, as her slippers did little—if any— damage to their shins. Several nail-tips broke as she clawed at her wicked assailants. They reeked of whiskey, body odor, greasy hair, and horse-flesh. They seemed to be all over her, and

15

winning the fierce battle.

The man spying on the predatory scene from an ajar window above them knew he had to help the young woman. He had hoped to remain concealed until her departure, but those ruffians were forcing him to expose himself. It was obvious the careless beauty was lost and in trouble. She was a superb fighter, but no match for those two wild animals. He had hesitated too long as it was. And there was something more that alarmed him about this brutal assault. He didn't believe those men were really sailors. Their uniforms were not genuine navy issue. Someone had gone to considerable trouble to arrange this. Swearing under his breath, he rushed toward the back stairs, knowing if he was captured tonight it would cost him his freedom and probably his life.

"I'm Lady Leigh Hamilton. Lord Chadwick Hamilton of Webster International is my uncle. I was on my way to meet him for dinner. He'll kill you if you harm me," she cried breathlessly as she fought with the men, hoping to discourage them with fear of revenge.

The crude beasts continued in their attempt to subdue the thrashing female, laughing and joking as if it was a child's game. She pleaded with them to stop, but they chuckled and increased their efforts to assault her. She tried to reason with them, and offered them a reward if they let her go. Nothing worked, not threats, not resistance, not a bribe, not pleas, not reasoning, not appealing to their non-existent consciences!

If she had ever doubted their malevolent intention, Leigh no longer did. They were enjoying her struggles, her helplessness, her feeble attempts to thwart them. Their lewd remarks singed her ears. Their cruel

16

hands pawed at her. One sailor trailed slobbery kisses over her bare shoulder and back while the other one spread them over her face in his attempt to find her mouth. She wanted to retch. She screamed instead, and found hands clamped over her dry lips. Blind terror now ruled her senses.

When the assailant's hands moved so he could replace them with his mouth, Leigh screamed again and kneed him in the groin. He doubled over with pain and nausea, cursing her through ragged gasps for air. The other man swore at her and yanked her around to face him. He lifted one hand to strike her with brutal and disabling force as he called her terrible names and vowed she would be tortured for her action.

Before the blow landed on her jaw, Leigh ducked her head to deflect it and didn't see what happened next. The attacker's wrist was seized and his arm was twisted behind him. Leigh was yanked from his bruising grasp and shoved against the brick wall as she was moved from between her assailant and her rescuer. Dazed and winded, she failed to comprehend the meaning of her sudden freedom and she braced herself for a renewed defense.

A fierce struggle took place between the three men, which she witnessed as her quivering hands shoved her tumbled hair from her line of vision. She noticed that third man was attired as gentleman, and he fought with enormous skill and prowess. Although the odds were two against one, the sailors could not hold their ground against him. He moved with quickness and agility, landing his blows while managing to dodge theirs. Within minutes, her frightened attackers fled for their lives.

Leigh's chest heaved from her exertions and fear. She wished her champion had beaten her attackers

17

senseless so they could be arrested and punished, but she was glad to be rid of them and to be safe. Leigh swayed against the wall and tried to slow her erratic breathing as she accepted the deliverance from peril. She was not a crier, but tears welled in her eyes and her shoulders trembled with relief and exhaustion. It was over, she told herself.

"You all right, miss?" a deep and mellow voice inquired.

Leigh lifted her head and nodded, unable to speak just yet. Her heart was still pounding. She wished she could sit down, as her legs were weak. Her rounded chin quivered, and she clenched her teeth to halt it. She ordered herself not to burst into sobs. She was safe now, thanks to this handsome man. Yes, her mind concurred, very handsome. He was standing in the middle of the alley where an adoring full moon embraced him with her silvery fingers. He was tall, several inches over six feet. His hair was deep brown and his skin was sun-bronzed. She could not make out his eye color from where she stood, limp and tremulous against the wall. She guessed that the stalwart man was over twenty-five. As her wits cleared and she relaxed, she hurriedly scanned him. He wore tapered fawn trousers, a dark-brown—unbuttoned vest, and an ivory—half buttoned—shirt, but no waistcoat or tie or jabot. His shoes appeared dark brown, and freshly shined from the way the moonlight shone on them. It looked as if he had been dressing when he rushed to aid her. Perhaps her screams had summoned him.

He realized she was still shaken, so he kept his tone gentle. "Didn't anyone tell you it isn't safe for a beautiful young woman to be out alone at night, especially in this rough area?"

His head never moved and his eyes never left her

18

face, but she felt as if he was taking in every inch of her like a keen-eyed tracker seeking clues to solve a mystery. She straightened and went forward to stand near him, as if she were a child being drawn to the safety of a parent. In the bright moonlight she made out his features; they were chiseled, well defined. His jaw was strong, but not too square. There was a deep cleft in his chin she found very appealing. His hair was mussed, but looked as if it would be straight and thick when brushed neatly. As if taking a clue from her gaze, he ran his fingers through it like a makeshift comb. There were tiny lines near the corners of his incredibly green eyes that told her he was an out-doorsman, as did his tanned complexion. At closer inspection, his nose was a little large and had a small hump, but it only made him look more rugged and virile.

Her gaze helplessly drifted down his throat as it moved with speech when he repeated his earlier question, to which she still did not respond. As he propped his hands on his hips, the movement drew her attention to them and his waist. He had a marvelous physique. Her gaze traveled upward again. His stance caused his unfastened shirt to gape, revealing dark hair on a hard-muscled chest. This stranger had a curious and unexpected effect on her. Never had reality faded or her wits fled in a man's presence. She felt . . . mesmerized—yes, that was the correct word—by him, by the shadows playing over his handsome face, giving him an aura of mystery and potent enchantment. Her eyes returned to his and she took a deep breath, wondering how much time had elapsed while she had examined him like a prized stallion. Her voice, hoarsened from her desperate labors, sounded harsh when she replied, "I wasn't out alone, sir. I became separated from my family and I didn't

19

know which way to head. I was seeking help. You don't need to scold me like a child. It was a foolish accident, but those men had no reason or right to attack me. Even if they did mistake me for a . . . a prostitute, one shouldn't be abused."

She realized her words sounded ridiculous and rude. This generous and stalwart man had endangered himself to rescue her from a precarious predicament. She must appear foolish and reckless to him, and her impulsive story didn't ring true. She knew that from the reproving scowl on his face. She cleared her throat and explained. "I'm sorry. I didn't mean to sound so brusque and ungrateful. I haven't settled down yet. I didn't get separated from my family. I was to meet them at a restaurant for dinner, but the carriage driver left me here by mistake. He rode away before I realized my error and could halt him. If you hadn't arrived . . ."

The man studied her with keen interest. He liked her courage and belated honesty. He had watched her discover her error, try to solve it, then defend herself against the two rough brutes. She hadn't burst into tears and he was glad, because he wouldn't know how to deal with an hysterical woman. But he wouldn't mind if she melted into his arms for comfort and protection. Even if she had been reckless tonight, she possessed endearing strength. She was exquisite, the rarest flower he had ever seen. Her eyes were a rich and deep blue, and they possessed a sparkle that diamonds would envy. Her hair was as golden as the afternoon sun on a dark river, even if it was falling down from its becoming style. He almost commented on its mussed condition but held silent because he liked its exotic and sultry look, like a lion's tawny mane blowing in the breeze. She was slender, but very shapely, and she fought well when threatened. This was a vital creature who could enflame a man's blood and loins; that he knew and felt for certain, especially with her gazing into his eyes.

"I see," he murmured. "Why did he let you off here?" He noticed the aura of wealth and genteel breeding exuding from her, but there was something strange about this incident. He glanced up the alley, praying she wasn't a ravishing decoy and this wasn't a clever ruse to lure him out of hiding. Surely no one knew of his presence.

Leigh noticed his wariness as she admitted, "I told him to take me to number six Stams Street. That's here, of course, so I must have read the address wrong on the invitation. He should have realized I was mistaken and corrected me, at least waited for me to discover my error. But he raced off as if a pack of starving wolves was after him. I looked for someone to help me, but it's deserted here and I'm unfamiliar with this area. Then, those sailors tried to . . ." She inhaled and shuddered as the full reality of her near disaster settled in on her.

"Here now, you're safe. They won't be back tonight." He pulled a handkerchief from his back pocket and with care dabbed at the blood easing from the corner of her mouth. With her head uplifted, the soft moonlight flowing over her face, and those vivid blue eyes engulfing him with interest and trust, he felt a curious sensation assail him, one akin to tenderness. "You best do this. I'm no good at doctoring and I could hurt you," he said, the contact with her igniting new flames within him. How strange, he mused, for this little wisp of golden glory to enchant him completely.

Leigh took the cloth and wiped at the redness on her chin. He grinned as she wet it with her tongue and washed away the last traces. Her tongue tested the

21

injured area and she winced; she must have bitten the tender skin during her struggles. The cut would annoy her for a few days until it healed. She realized that he was observing her with bold intensity and open curiosity, and she warmed and trembled.

"I know there isn't a restaurant around here, not the kind you're looking for. Do you know its name?" he asked, struggling to restrain the fiery urges that she sparked within him.

"No, I don't. I was only given the address—the wrong one. I hope you didn't ruin your clothes," she remarked, unsettled by this man who didn't look the least ruffled—in appearance or manner—by his confrontation with those crude bullies.

He glanced down at his garments and shrugged. "Too bad that little scuffle didn't ruin them. Then I would have a logical excuse for skipping my dinner tonight." That wasn't the truth, but he had to respond in a polite and careful manner.

Leigh laughed as she offered, "Perhaps I can reward you by dirtying them." She sensed he hadn't been truthful, because he didn't seem a man who did what he didn't want to do. If he had to attend an offensive dinner, he must have a good reason for doing so, and he didn't need to explain himself to a total stranger in a dim alley.

His smile was disarming and his laughter contagious when he sent forth both before replying, "Don't tempt me, woman; I'm a weakling for heady amusement and unusual adventures."

"So am I," she responded rashly, and saw a sensual smile capture his mouth and a matching gleam appear in those compelling eyes. "My cloak and purse," she murmured to cover her slip in ladylike behavior. She glanced around for her possessions. This man had been a perfect gentleman so far, but the attrac-

22

tion between them was powerful and they were in a secluded location. She didn't want him to mistake her gratitude and interest as wanton overtures and become too forward with her. "It's getting late. I'd better go."

He retrieved her purse and cloak, and held them for her. "We'll locate you another carriage with a better driver." He smiled and offered her his elbow to escort her to the main street. *It is late, very late,* he agreed. He was too distracted by this fetching female and intoxicating episode, and she was too responsive for him not to notice and be affected. He had to get moving. He had plenty to attempt tonight under the cover of protective darkness.

As they walked along, Leigh eyed him. His tanned face said he spent most of his time outside. His physical condition said he was an active man. His playful smile had revealed even, white teeth the color of virgin snow but with the power of a white-hot heat to melt it. Yet, it was his eyes, his arresting gaze, that paralyzed her until she felt brazen and weak. They were as green as newborn leaves in the spring. His gaze was alive, merry, mischievous, secretive. His rich voice returned her to reality once more.

"Where are you staying?" he inquired as they halted beneath the streetlamp. If she had been missing very long, someone must be searching for her and might track her here. He had to get rid of her quickly and safely before his presence was discovered and he was arrested and imprisoned. His dark thoughts caused his tone to sound cold and annoyed when he added, "I'm very late for my dinner appointment. Let's get you out of here. It'll have to be back to the hotel because your clothes and hair are mussed. Surely you don't want to go looking like this or tongues will wag like crazy."

23

Miffed, Leigh told him the name and address of the hotel. His change in mood baffled and surprised her. He was speaking to her like an errant child again! Suddenly she was very unsure of herself.

Yet the man beside her was much too aware of her beauty and appeal. To him, she was a formidable magnet who was pulling him into greater peril. He'd already remained too long. A defensive and instinctive urgency to withdraw surged through him — for more than his physical safety. He had no time for this woman or romance. He needed to get out of sight fast, and out of London soon.

Confused, distressed, and enchanted by this enigmatic stranger, she almost whispered, "I'm sorry I detained you so long. If you'll be kind enough to help me find a carriage, I won't trouble you further. I'm certain everyone is worried about me and out looking for me. I need to get to the hotel and repair my appearance." She checked her gown and fretted. "It's ruined, and it's new."

Perceptive to her new mood and his, he softened and flashed her a crooked smile of apology. His accent was definitely British, she concluded. But why was he so mercurial and skittish? He wasn't the type to be afraid of anything or anyone; his brave actions had proven his courage, compassion, and self-assurance. She was positive that his odd behavior had to do with more than the possibly unwanted attraction between them.

His jungle-green gaze met her ocean-blue one, and he lost himself in those swirling pools. He caressed her flushed cheek and teased, "Don't worry about making me late. I would skip tonight if there wasn't something important I need to find . . ." His words halted as he realized he was talking too much to relax her. He lowered his hand and took a few steps away from her to cool his fiery blood. Perhaps it was because he hadn't been near a very beautiful and desirable female in a long time. He had secluded exile and a foe's treachery to blame for that denial. For what seemed like ages, all he had cared, dreamed, and thought about were justice and revenge. Soon, he would track them down and capture them, no matter what he had to do to his prey!

Leigh watched him slip into brooding silence. As she waited before him for a carriage or his mental return, she recalled how his size, strength, and prowess had easily and swiftly discouraged her would-be assailants. Although she was five foot five, the top of her head only reached his shoulder. He was like a towering oak. His lean, firm body moved with ease and purpose. His stance and bearing were ones of self-confidence and vainless pride. She detected a smidgen of arrogance yet, he did not give off an "I know it all" air, only an "I do what *I* think is right." Still, he seemed tense. No, she corrected herself, he seemed alert, like a rancher awaiting the arrival of ravenous wolves or dangerous rustlers after his stock. But why, she mused, when he believed her attackers would not return?

Leigh remembered how glimmers of merriment and tenderness could soften his features in a blink. His face had planes and angles of strength and determination. In fact, his features were bold and striking with a royal or aristocratic hint. He could be very tough or extremely gentle, and she liked that heady mixture in a man—a blend her father had possessed. She sensed undercurrents of powerful emotions that were savagely tugging at him tonight like an unmerciful and stormy ocean at a drowning victim. She wondered what kind of problem was tormenting him and how he would solve it, with fists or wits—or with

25

both. He was indeed the most virile, fearless, handsome man alive. He was even more appealing than Lord Chadwick Hamilton, which was a difficult task to accomplish. She was drawn to him and to the aura of excitement—and even a hint of danger—that exuded from him. Yes, she admitted, he was a stimulating blend of dangers and desires.

Leigh pondered what it would feel like to have those sensual lips covering hers. Recalling the forceful and repulsive kisses which the sailors had placed on her lips and body, she rubbed her mouth as if to remove all traces of them. She shuddered.

"Cold?" he asked, and came forward to put her cloak around her shoulders. He wiggled her purse onto her wrist.

"Those vile beasts kissed me," she murmured.

On impulse, the dark-haired man lifted her chin and gazed into her responsive eyes. "Real kisses should be like this, my damsel in distress," he murmured, then closed his mouth over hers.

Leigh's senses reeled at his touch and taste. His lips were gentle yet persuasive. They were seeking and hungry, yet controlled. She swayed against him and responded by returning his kiss and slipping her arms around his waist. His kiss deepened, and his embrace strengthened. Never had Leigh been held or kissed this way. She liked the wonderful sensations and wanted them to continue. The danger of such behavior escaped her. She was only aware of her desires.

She pressed closer to him, their embrace becoming enticingly intimate. Her heart pounded as his skilled mouth aroused her to greater heights. She was floating in a dreamy land. Not once did she think, or want, to refuse him or to pull away. He moaned against her mouth and tightened his hold.

Though her response became as feverish as his,

something told the man she was an innocent. He leaned away from her and gazed into her flushed face and smoldering blue eyes. She looked so young and pure with those big blue eyes and soft gold hair, but so much a captivating creature on the verge of womanhood. He wanted to learn all about her, not just make an easy and meaningless conquest. She was too unique to treat that way. Yet this was not the time or place to test or enjoy her potent magic. Didn't this blue-eyed angel realize what she did to a man? Didn't this flaxen-haired minx understand how dangerous and inviting her impetuous actions were? Didn't this maiden grasp what she was unintentionally imploring and inspiring him to do? This tempting female and curious situation spelled trouble, big trouble! With a strained voice he almost demanded, "How old are you?"

Leigh's eyes widened in puzzlement. "Twenty, why?" Did he fear she was too young and naive to be desirable? After all, a man like this could have any woman he wanted.

"Name?" he questioned in that same stern tone.

"Laura Leigh—" She did not finish because a noise caught their attention and both glanced in that direction. It was a carriage, but too distant to hail. He had released her and scanned their dusky surroundings with eagle eyes. "Who are you?" she asked.

With a roguish grin, he replied, "Sir Lancelot, naturally." He saw her frown at his jest. Clearly this girl was a virginal innocent and she didn't realize the dangerous flames she was igniting within him. She had that same trusting, but not gullible, air that Joanna had before . . . He dismissed that infuriating line of thought. He had to end this matter and get out of the light. In a serious tone, he said, "Just a friendly warning, Laura, don't ever respond to any man like

27

that if you intend to remain pure in mind and body. You're far too beautiful and tempting to be ignored. Tell your father—"

He sounded almost angry, which was exactly how she felt at his chiding. She interrupted. "My parents are dead, and I'm old enough to take care of myself. In most circumstances," she added when she saw him shake his head skeptically. "I'm a grown woman, sir, not an inquisitive child."

He shook his head again and refuted. "You're wrong, Laura. You are an inquisitive child encased in a woman's ravishing body. I witnessed how smart and skilled and brave you are, but you clearly lack the experience to deal with what could happen between us . . . What almost *did* happen. Be content I didn't seduce you in that alley, or abduct you to a better place for it. Be glad I'm a gentleman; most men aren't," he disclosed with a cocky grin.

Even as she denied his claims, she had the sinking feeling he was telling the truth about himself and her. Embarrassed and dismayed, she reasoned, "If I'm so naive and you're such a gentleman, you shouldn't have kissed me like that! What did you expect me to do? Stand quiet and still like a statue?"

At his amused chuckles, she blushed. "I only meant . . . I was going to say . . ." she stammered before his intense stare and provocative grin. "Oh, you devilish rake! You know what I mean."

"You definitely mean you enjoy my kisses," he mirthfully explained for her.

Flustered and enchanted, she blurted out, "What woman wouldn't? But you're being mean and rude. I don't deserve that. After all, considering what I just endured, my wits aren't clear yet."

"Forgive me for teasing you, Laura, but you're an absolute breath of invigorating air. I suppose I worded my caution wrong. The world can be a jungle and men can be beasts. Be careful of predators like those who attacked you and of cunning ones like me. In fact, if a carriage doesn't come along soon, I might change my mind about remaining a gentleman and making my appointment." He smiled, but they both realized he was only half joking. "If your parents are deceased, who were you to meet at that restaurant tonight? Perhaps a sweetheart, fiancé, or husband?"

After her brazen behavior, she couldn't allow him to think she was wed or even betrothed. "No, Lord Chadwick Hamilton and friends," she answered, feeling it unnecessary to further explain herself to a quicksilver stranger on a deserted street in a strange city.

The man was wary and intrigued. Her accent was American. If she was traveling with relatives, they should be with her tonight. His instincts warned him there was something strange about this incident. What was she doing in London, and with a notorious seducer like Chad Hamilton? That connection disturbed him. Nor did he need another beautiful and reckless woman getting him into further trouble! "I'm very late," he said. "Let's see if we can find you a carriage in a busier place." He seized her arm in a firm — but painless — grip and led her down the street, through another long and dim alley, to the next street. They saw a carriage dropping someone off not far away.

Her rescuer yelled to the driver and signaled him over to them. He assisted her into the seat and gave the driver the name and address of her hotel and paid him. He warned Leigh solemnly, "Don't ever let me catch you in a secluded area like this again. Next time, Sir Lancelot might not be around to save you."

He vanished into the shadows before she gathered

her scattered wits and stolen speech. She was tempted to order the driver to wait for her, to leap from the carriage, pursue the stranger, and question him. She didn't even know her champion's name or where he lived. But he disappeared as mysteriously and suddenly as he had appeared.

The carriage was moving; it was too late to learn his identity and location or to make certain she had thanked him properly for saving her chastity and life. A sigh left her lips as she mused, *Just wait until tomorrow, Sir Lancelot; you can't escape me this easily.*

Chapter Two

Despite her dreamy vow, disappointment and emptiness plagued Leigh on the ride back to her hotel. She might never find "Sir Lancelot" again. She wished he had been willing to escort her home—the ride would have given them more time to talk. At least she might have learned his name.

Leigh straightened her cloak to conceal her torn gown. She combed her hair but did not repin it into its neat chignon. She realized the blue aigrette was gone. It was no doubt ruined, so she didn't need to return to the alley to look for it. She would purchase another when she carried her gown to the seamstress to see if it could be repaired.

The carriage halted at the hotel and she was assisted down by a polite doorman. Leigh was surprised to find there was no message from her stepuncle. She was long overdue to meet him. Perhaps Chad assumed she had decided not to come to dinner or believed his late invitation hadn't reached her. No matter, she wasn't in any mood to track him down. She hurried to her room to change clothes.

Leigh summoned the ladies' maid to help her unfasten the gown. She explained the epsiode to the older woman, who showed genuine concern over her disheveled condition and frightening experience. After the waiting woman left, Leigh washed the dirt from her face, arms, and hands, and soothed the scratches with a healing balm. Nothing could be done for the bruises, which would be darker by morning. She noted several ragged fingernails and fetched a rubbing board to repair them, glad they had not been torn to the painful quicks.

As she worked on her toilette, Leigh's mind wandered. How amazing it was that she was here now in England, an heiress about to embark on a grand adventure. How magical it all seemed, especially after Sir Lancelot's daring rescue.

Of course, this was not her first trip abroad. Before Leigh was sixteen, her family had made several voyages to England, where she had gotten to know her grandparents through more than an exchange of letters and her father's stories. She had loved her grandfather but had not known him well. The only blood relative she had left when her parents died was her mother's sister in Texas.

Leigh's aunt had never tried to rule her life. Jenna had allowed her to make most of her own decisions. But Jenna's new husband hadn't felt the same; he had wanted her to marry and leave.

Annoyance filled Leigh Webster as she reflected on her last few years in Texas. What *if* she were still single at twenty? That wasn't spinisterhood or a disgrace. She had her own income from her grandfather, she could more than support herself. When news arrived of her enormous inheritance, Jenna's husband Carl had wanted to sail with her to "protect and chaperone" her. Leigh had turned him down as politely as possible for her aunt's sake. She didn't want Carl intruding on her new life. Nor did she want that obsessive ranch foreman pursuing her. She found it hard to trust a man who was too handsome and charming, too smooth. Maybe that was why she had trouble fully trusting her guardian.

She had met Lord Chadwick Hamilton—with his inherited title of earl—on the last trip in '90, shortly after Chad had gone to work for William Webster. The two men had become good friends, and her grandfather—after training him—had allowed Chad authority over most of his business affairs. Perhaps, the blonde decided, because his only son was far away and Chad was filling an emotional emptiness.

Following her parents' deaths in '91 and her grandmother's in '92, William had married Chad's mother—Lady Fiona Hamilton. Knowing how the loss of her parents had affected her, Leigh understood why her grandfather had sought love and happiness with a new wife and stepson.

Leigh wanted love and happiness and marriage—but only with a special man, a strong and honest one, a man who accepted her with or without beauty, elite status, and wealth. Perhaps she would meet the perfect mate here, as she hadn't in America.

Leigh knew that special man was not her handsome guardian. Even if he hadn't already been spoken for, she was hesitant about Chad. She couldn't put a finger on anything particular, but . . . *But what, Leigh?*

During her last visit, her grandfather had revealed affection and admiration for Chad, and faith in him. Her father had also liked and trusted Chad, and was glad the young man took the heaviest business burdens off his aging father's shoulders. Chad had charmed her mother, too, and had taken both women on pleasant outings. For a time, Leigh had been smitten by the handsome twenty-six-year-old earl whom her family so liked and enjoyed. But that was six years ago, and people did change.

It worried Leigh that Chad wasn't angry with her grandfather for leaving her almost everything. Most men would be in his place, she thought.

Chad had worked hard for Webster International. William had left his stepson and widow financially and socially comfortable. William had gifted Chad with a townhouse years ago, and he had left his London home to Fiona. From the will, both had been given sufficient — but not overly generous — money for support. Too, Chad possessed a well-paying position as manager of the firm, and Fiona had the beauty and charms to earn another advantageous marriage. Yet, to have so much within his grasp and to watch it go to someone else had to hurt and embitter. *Shouldn't it?* she mused. And what of his mother, Lady Fiona Hamilton Webster?

Leigh wished she knew if Fiona had purposely sailed to British India on January eighteenth to avoid the young woman who was arriving soon to inherit most of her second husband's wealth and possessions. And, she wondered, too, if the widowed countess had wed William Webster out of love. It seemed odd to Leigh that such a stunning, youthful, titled woman would marry an untitled, rather plain man who was so much older and less socially involved than herself — especially one so recently widowed.

Her grandmother had invited Leigh to spend the summer of '92 in England, but Sarah had died before plans were finalized. Leigh had been informed of her grandmother's death, but not invited to the funeral. She had been informed of William's remarriage but not invited to the wedding. Nor had she received any letters or invitations from Fiona since the woman joined her family. It was as if Fiona wanted William all to herself. If this was so, then her grandfather had obviously complied, for his letters to Leigh had become fewer and farther between and were always about Chad and Fiona. Yet he had invited Leigh to spend her twenty-first birthday with him, and he had left the bulk of his estate to her. Chad had told Leigh that his mother planned to be gone for six months. The blonde was eager to learn if Fiona bore resentment against her. Only time could answer those plaguing questions.

Leigh slipped into a simple day dress that buttoned up the front. She brushed and arranged her tawny locks. She was fine, only slightly injured and very vexed. But she was stimulated by the excitement of the evening, by her unknown champion. And, she was hungry and thirsty. Perhaps, she thought, it wasn't too late to have something sent to her room.

There came a persistent knocking at her door and she answered it to find Chadwick Hamilton standing there and looking disquieted.

Leigh motioned him inside. His hair was as black as a moonless night, wavy and silky, and brushed away from his tanned face with flawless features. He was thirty-one and six feet tall, with a physique men envied and women craved. Chad possessed a special gaze and grin that could disarm and sway; perhaps that was what unsettled her. Anyone — male or female — would love to have his overwhelming allure. His lordship's eyes — a rich blue with a tiny hint of hazel — were nearly magical with their power to enchant and entice or to inspire admiration and affection. Chad Hamilton was confident and masculine. Who wouldn't be with his looks, wealth, aristocratic title, and irresistible prowess Leigh mused? But was there a greedy rogue lurking behind that magnificent Adonis visage?

Chad began talking before she could. "What happened to you, Leigh? At seven, I came to make certain you'd received my dinner invitation. When the doorman said he'd given it to you and had seen you leave in a carriage, I returned to the restaurant. When you weren't there, I assumed you had made plans with someone else without telling me. Then I realized it wasn't like you not to send me a message of regret so we wouldn't keep waiting for your arrival. I came back to the hotel and the doorman said you'd returned not long go and were in your room. Why didn't you come inside and join us?"

Leveling her gaze on him, she said, "I did get dressed and leave to join you, Chad. But the carriage driver took me to the wrong address and left me there, on the deserted waterfront. There is no restaurant at number six Stams Street."

The black-haired man looked baffled as he concurred, "Of course there isn't. It's at number six *Stems* Street. Whyever would a responsible driver take a lady to the wharf and leave her there alone? Didn't you notice a street sign and the deserted area and realize you were mistaken?"

She stared into his inquisitive blue eyes and said, "That's the address you wrote in your message, Chad. I knew it seemed strange, but I figured that warehouse was owned by us and perhaps you had a surprise party in mind. It happened too fast to think clearly."

"You were mistaken, Leigh. Is my handwriting that bad?" he asked. "Do you still have the note?"

Leigh walked to the side table and lifted the page. She held it out to him and said, "Look for yourself."

Chad took it and did so, then remarked, "It says Stems Street, Leigh. S-t-e-m-s." He spelled it for her and handed back the page. "I'm sorry you misread it, but I'm glad you got home safely."

Leigh stared at the troublesome word, and saw he

was right. "I thought it said *Stams,* and that was what I told the driver so I guess I'm at fault. But he should have realized I was mistaken. As soon as I got out of the carriage, he took off like an escaping stallion who smelled a branding fire." She went on to explain what had taken place in the alley—excluding the romantic part about her rescuer from her narrative.

"Heavens, Leigh, are you all right?" he asked. He ran his fingers through his dark hair and sighed deeply. "I should have known something was wrong and searched for you sooner. I never would have forgiven myself if you'd been injured. I should have come to the hotel and escorted you to the restaurant, but I was involved with an important business meeting. I never imagined anything like this happening. I assumed the doorman would get you a carriage—and it's only a short ride away. You could have been killed or abducted. This is my fault for not taking better care of you. I'm sorry."

She was touched by his expression and mood. "Why didn't you call the hotel to check on me? They have a telephone in the lobby," she remarked.

"But the restaurant doesn't have one yet, so I couldn't ring you. I thought perhaps you might need a little urging to join us. I know how Louisa and Cynthia make you uncomfortable, and I'm sorry."

Leigh noticed the lines of worry that etched Chad's forehead and creased the skin near his blue eyes and sensual mouth. He had apologized twice. She was vexed with herself for ever thinking dark thoughts about him. Chad had been kind, thoughtful, gentle, and protective. His winning smile and mood relaxed her. "It wasn't your fault, Chad. I don't know how I misread the address twice, but I'm fine. If that man hadn't come along, I don't know what would have happened."

"Who was he? He deserves a reward for his help."

"I don't know. He didn't give his name. He was in a hurry to make an appointment. As soon as it was over, he found me a carriage and sent me home. I was too upset and mussed to track you down and join you, and it was too late by then."

Chad embraced her and said, "At least you're safe; that's all that matters." He gazed into her eyes and vowed, "I wouldn't want anything happening to you. Next time be more careful and observant, my little ward and boss. Please don't let this happen again. You've already scared years off my life."

"I've ruined your evening, Chad. I'm sorry. And I promise I'll be more careful in the future. In fact, I'll carry my derringer with me from now on. Uncle Colin gave it to me. The Wild West can be a dangerous place, so he made certain I had protection. It's small enough to fit into my purse, so I can keep it with me at all times."

"That's a wise idea, Leigh. I wish you had been carrying it and shot both of them. How dare they attack you, or any lady!"

Fury darkened his eyes to midnight blue and furrowed his brow.

"They were drunk and restless, Chad. I'm lucky they didn't harm me, and I had very little with me to steal, just a few pounds and—" Her fingers went to her throat. "My locket!" she cried in panic. "It must have been torn off during the fight. Father gave it to me. I must get it back. Help me, Chad."

"I'll go to Stams Street in the morning and look for it," Chad suggested. "If I don't find it in the alley, I'll post a description and a reward for its return. I'll also report your assault to the authorities. As for your rescuer, since we don't know who he is, we can't reward him. But if he happens to contact you, let me know and I'll handle it."

Leigh focused widened eyes on him. Her heart pounded at the idea of seeing the irresistible stranger again. She concealed her excitement and inquired, "Why should he contact me?"

Her stepuncle laughed, then replied, "You're a beautiful woman, and he saved your life. Surely he'll want to see that you're all right after your misadventure together. In his place, I would. He's also a witness who can identify your assailants. I hope we can locate him."

Chad's gaze was soft and complimentary. He looked appealing in his ivory shirt and blue waistcoat and pants. Irrefutably he was breath- and wit-stealing, and a skilled charmer. Leigh didn't doubt he could talk a starving woman out of her last bite or penny, or talk a disgruntled client out of his anger and into his next order. Chad must have been a valuable asset to her grandfather and the firm. If she wasn't careful, that old infatuation might return, Leigh warned herself. She tried not to gaze into those arresting blue eyes or be captured by his magnetic spell, and asked, "What about your friends?"

He shrugged his powerful shoulders. "Probably finishing dinner about now. If you're certain you're all right, I'll rejoin them. Unless," he hinted with a sly grin and tug at her arm, "you'll change clothes and come along. I wish you would, Leigh. You brighten any room you enter. I won't let you out of my sight for an instant. I'll guard you with my life. Do you want to try it again?"

She eyed his entreating expression. He could be mighty persuasive, but she said, "Not tonight, Chad. I'm still jittery, and tired. I'll have something sent up here. Then I can settle down while I eat."

He looked disappointed, but smiled in acquies-

39

cence. "I'll take care of it before I leave. I'll see you tomorrow. This time, I'll fetch you. No going out alone, understand?"

"Yes, sir," she stated with merry laughter. "Good night, Chad."

"Good night, Leigh, and sleep well."

She saw his blue gaze inspect her from head to foot, as if to make certain she was uninjured. She guided him toward the door, teasing, "Go along, your lordship. Your friends are waiting for you. They'll wonder what happened to both of us. I'm fine, honestly."

"You're sure?" he inquired once more.

"Positive, Chad. But you can do one thing for me," she hinted.

His gaze agreed with his answer. "Anything, Leigh. What is it?"

"Let's keep this nasty episode between us. I wouldn't like to be the topic of such an embarrassing conversation. Please say I had dinner downstairs and you couldn't find me the first time. Is that all right?"

"It'll be our secret," he agreed, a twinkle in his eyes. Then his smile lessened as he queried, "What about the attackers? With your description, they could be located and punished. Perhaps a reward for helping to find them—and your locket—will bring forward your witness to help us."

Leigh considered his words. "Forget about the authorities and those ruffians. Wicked men eventually get caught and punished. But find a way to post the reward for my locket without telling how I lost it. Say it happened when you took me on a tour of the waterfront."

"You're a smart woman, Laura Leigh Webster. Consider it done."

Leigh leaned against the door after his departure.

She was pleased that he hadn't wanted to leave her alone and had twice taken the time and trouble to check on her absence. Chad was a strange man: open and warm and tender in one situation, then arrogant and mysterious and wary in another. Yet few people seemed to notice how complicated and intricate he was, and it was his ability to hide that subtle complexity that troubled her on occasion. Still, Leigh liked the forthright and sunny side of him best, the one he used with her the most. He made life in London so exhilarating for her. He made her look forward to so many experiences particularly their impending two-month safari. It would be, as he claimed, a splendid way to get better acquainted and to relax after the unexpected changes in their lives.

Leigh recalled what Chad and others had told her about Africa. He had explained how safaris were the height of intrigue and pleasure these days for English society, how many people were tempted by colorful tales of fortunes to be claimed there and adventures to be enjoyed. Every time he revealed more about their impending journey, his voice and expression had been filled with contagious enthusiasm.

It sounded so breathtaking to her, the experience of a lifetime, an opportunity not to be ignored or rejected. It was the perfect way and time to expose her strengths, courage, and skills to her stepuncle so he wouldn't worry about her new ownership of the firm.

Since her arrival, she had observed the man who'd be in control of her life and inheritance for the next eight months. Leigh was trying hard to prevent any problems between her and Chad by showing him she not only wanted to be friends but wanted him to continue managing the firm for her. For now, that seemed to work just fine. Yet she could not help but wonder what would happen if they disagreed on business matters once she learned all about the workings of the firm. She was after all, the owner, the final authority, the one with the most responsibility. How would he accept any changes she wanted to make? Would he view them as an intrusion, a challenge, a criticism?

She knew the business empire was an enormous responsibility for such a young and untrained woman, but her grandfather must have had faith in her capabilities and character or he wouldn't have left it to her, only blood heir or not. Besides, she had Chad and other qualified men to help her, and she knew a little about the firm from her father.

In the past two weeks, Leigh had visited the interconnected companies and met their managers and employees. She had admitted to herself and to Chad that she was nervous about owning such a large and prestigious firm. Chad had done nothing to conceal his pleasure with the will's stipulation that he remain as head of the firm which he had helped to prosper, and she was glad she had him at her side.

Leigh was certain she could learn about the business, but she was smart enough to know she would need help. She hoped Chad would provide that assistance and knowledge. But if their relationship — personal and business — didn't work out, she knew she could always sell the firm to him upon her return to England, then decide where to live and what to do. She did have the country estate, and plenty of time to make her final decision. She did not want to return to Texas, for certain, because of her new uncle and the lusty foreman.

She had a responsibility, a challenge, to meet. First she had to learn if she could run the Webster empire, then decide if she wanted to do so. Besides, her grandfather owed her. It had been his idea for her father to go to America and to remain there. It would bring in more money and power, he felt, for Thomas Webster to be situated there. At least that had been her impression over the years. She assumed it was accurate, for why else would they not have returned to England when things were going so well with the Georgia company? If they had, though, her parents would still be alive. She confessed that she felt slightly bitter toward her deceased grandfather, but she must not let such destructive emotions eat at her. How she wished she had questioned William Webster about that matter before his death.

Leigh walked to a window and gazed at the quiet street below. Chad had rented this lovely hotel suite for her stay in London, explaining it would appear improper if she moved into his townhouse, even with two servants there. Leigh had agreed. She could imagine the gossip that would have been created by such living arrangements! After all, they weren't blood kin; they were adults, and Chad was many a female's obsession. . . .

Lady Louisa Jennings', especially. Leigh fretted over two dismaying angles of the imminent trip: Louisa and Marquise Cynthia Campbell. She wasn't jealous of Chad's relationship with the wealthy Louisa; she just didn't like the hateful redhead. Nor did she care for Cynthia, his best friend Reid's companion.

It remained to be seen if Leigh could make friends with either or both women. It did not look good so far. Not that she hadn't made cordial overtures, but the two females were not receptive. Lady Louisa was determined to capture the sensual Lord Hamilton and somehow viewed Leigh as a threat to that conquest. Yet Leigh was just as determined not to let them spoil her upcoming trip. It would be nice if their journey could begin with a truce.

Leigh frowned at the difficult job ahead of her. If she hadn't made any progress with the two women in over two weeks, how could a few more days aid her? How could she win them over without being false and fawning, which went against her grain. *Oh, well, do the best you can, and let it go at that.*

Her meal arrived, as Chad had promised. With leisure and enjoyment, she devoured vegetables and meat and sipped wine. Yet something still troubled her. She retrieved the note from where Chad had discarded it in the trash. As she read it, the word "summons" echoed through her mind again. Perhaps, she concluded, it was the wording of the message: "I want you at a private dinner party of great importance at a very special restaurant, so don't be late or refuse. I'll expect you at 6:30 sharp in your best gown to stun a friend of mine."

As earlier, she wondered why Chad thought she might refuse or object or be tardy. She wished she had asked why the evening had been of "great importance" to him and who was the friend she had been ordered to enchant. She needed to remember to ask him tomorrow.

Glancing back at the note, she read, "Take a carriage out front to #6 Stems Street." So, how had she read "Stams" twice? Too, if Chad had returned to the hotel to check on her earlier, why hadn't the doorman told her when she asked if there was a message from her guardian? Could the note have been altered during her absence? Could Chad have lied to her?

You're grabbing at a dust devil, Leigh thought. Chad stood to lose too much if anything happened to her. He wouldn't inherit Webster International if she died, and he wouldn't want it split in half. It was to his advantage and interest to keep her well and safe, she knew. Even if he did crave the firm, she would have to be alive to keep it whole or to sell it to him.

Leigh recalled her time with her stepuncle. Chad included her in on everything, and he was so protective. Sometimes she found him watching her as if he considered her a beautiful and desirable woman. Yet why did he keep Louisa around if he was attracted to his ward? And why was his lover going on a safari with them? Unless the charming lord was afraid to move on her too quickly because he felt she might think he was after her enormous inheritance. Too, the handsome and virile Chadwick Hamilton was unaccustomed to any woman resisting him, something Leigh had done and couldn't imagining herself not doing. "We shall see, my handsome guardian, what your real intentions are."

Leigh donned her nightgown and slipped into bed. "As for you, my daring Sir Lancelot, if ever we meet again, and I'm certain we will, I'll teach you a thing or two about western women," the intrigued girl from Texas vowed.

In a warehouse at the wharf, Jace Elliott teased his nose with the silk bouquet of flowers that had been torn from the beauty's gown. Her special fragrance still clung to it and tempted his senses to call forth her image. He lifted the blue aigrette and looked at it, recalling how the hair ornament had contrasted against that head of flaxen hair. He reflected on their curious meeting before he laid both items aside and reached into his pocket to withdraw the locket she had lost.

Upon returning to the warehouse—owned by a friend—to complete his interrupted dressing, he had sighted it twinkling at him beneath the moonlight on the alley floor. He felt as if he had found a golden nugget. While retrieving it, he had sighted the silk bouquet and aigrette.

"Laura . . . Laura Leigh . . ." he murmured. He liked her name, and thought it suited her. It was soft and silky, like she herself. Both her name and her appearance evoked impressions of warm sunshine, of mellow feelings, of flowing honey. Her eyes were like tranquil blue waters that enticed him to sail into her heart and soul. She was like the diamonds he had once mined, rough-cut at present, but ready and eager to be chipped into valuable shape and polished to a higher sparkle.

Jace opened the locket and studied the couple encased there. He guessed they were her parents. He wondered what the girl would do when she discovered such a treasure missing. Would she return to search for it? To look for him? She seemed brave enough to do so but level-headed enough to think that unwise. He snapped the locket shut and dropped it into his pocket. Then he smelled the bouquet once more before putting it aside.

So far, his trip to London had been for naught. The man he needed to see was unavailable. The two witnesses to his alleged crimes had vanished, as had Joanna Harris. Even her mother didn't know her whereabouts, or if Joanna was connected to the truth. Yet the woman hadn't seemed shocked by Jace's grim speculations.

But who wanted him framed and killed, he asked himself for the hundredth time, and why? No doubt because the guilty and cunning culprit knew Jace Elliott would never give up his search for the truth and vindication! He must prove the evidence implicating him was false. He had to learn who was responsible for the disgrace and destruction of his father. He had to discover the dark reason behind that deadly plot and the means by which it had been carried out so perfectly.

A vital clue was missing: motive. If he could discover *why*, that would unmask *who* and *how*. This lethal mystery still seemed as hopeless and frustrating as it had over a year ago. But he was determined to solve it, and had sworn on his father's grave to do so.

Jace's wandering mind traveled to his best suspects: Chad Hamilton and William Webster. Yet Webster had plenty of money and business without stealing his father's, and supposedly they had been friends. It was true that Chad had hated him and wanted revenge, but ruining Joanna Harris should have been enough cruelty and vengeance for his old friend. Chad had chosen to make Jace his enemy, and the devilish rake had done the unforgivable to him and Joanna.

Jace's restless mind drifted to the damsel in distress he had rescued earlier. What was her connection to Chad Hamilton? He didn't want to envision her as one of Chad's ill-fated conquests like Joanna had been, so he dismissed her from his troubled thoughts.

His time was limited. He didn't know where to look for favorable evidence, but he wasn't one to wallow in self-pity nor to remain ignorant or in jeopardy and dishonor. He had a terrible problem and he must find a way to solve it. Before he could approach the authorities and be questioned, he had to obtain proof he was innocent of the accusations. Without it, he would be arrested and jailed, then tried and convicted and hanged. But until he returned to England and was questioned, he couldn't be legally charged or pursued out of the country. Too, there was someone powerful trying to impede his case in order to give them time to solve it. With some of the people involved dead, others missing, and none talking, it appeared hopeless.

But nothing, Jace Elliott vowed, was utterly hopeless. Some things just required more effort than others, especially things as important as his freedom, and the exoneration of his deceased father.

He pulled the locket out again and fingered it. He had a strong feeling that it meant something special to him, as well as to Laura Leigh. He felt as if she'd been placed in his path tonight. The locket burned in his grasp and mind like a fiery but obscure clue. Perhaps it was an omen, telling him to get close to this particular female by providing him with the means and motive to do so. Was fate—after almost destroying him—giving him a helping hand? A visceral feeling told him to study that tawny-haired beauty who had a connection to his suspects. But how could he accomplish that as he couldn't show his face in daylight without risking the loss of his head? This prize was the key to getting to Laura Leigh and unlocking her mysterious role in his destiny. Again he irritably mused, but how and when and where?

He knew her name and where she was staying. Perhaps . . .

Chapter Three

The following morning, Leigh went to have her unfortunate dress repaired. The seamstress suggested replacing the snagged overskirt and also said she would stitch on a new silk bouquet. Fortunately she had another blue aigrette that would match the gown.

While there, Leigh paid for and picked up the special garments the woman had completed for her safari. Earlier that day she had purchased a pith helmet and two pairs of walking boots for her impending adventure. While she was away, many of her possessions would be left in London at Chad's townhouse. Others — used on the voyage to and from British East Africa and during her stay in Mombasa — would be stored at the hotel there, as she could carry only so many items with her on the trail.

When she returned to the hotel with her purchases, Lord Chadwick Hamilton was awaiting her with a frown on his handsome face. He helped her with the packages and followed her inside her suite.

The dark-haired earl questioned, "Where have you been, Leigh? I was worried. You promised not to go out alone again."

Leigh smiled and replied, "I didn't mean I would make myself a prisoner in my room, Chad. I was referring to going out alone at night."

He exhaled loudly and shook his head. "What makes you think beautiful, wealthy females are any safer alone during daylight hours?" her guardian reasoned as he stood near the front window.

Leigh watched how the morning sunlight played over his appealing features as she related where she had gone and why. "I was very careful, *Uncle* Chad," she teased. "I'm not a little girl, and I did carry my gun. See," she remarked, opening her purse to show him the derringer before tightening the strings and tossing it on the sofa.

"I only have your word you know how to use it. Besides, a villain could grab your purse to rob you. Then where would you be? In danger again," he answered his question.

"You worry too much, Chad. I'm an expert shot, and I stay alert. Did you find my locket?" she inquired to change the subject.

He looked disappointed as he told her, "No, but I did post the description and a reward. No word from your rescuer of last night?"

"None, but that doesn't surprise me. I doubt he'll appear at my door. If he does, I surely wouldn't let a stranger inside. Oh, yes . . ." she began. "Why didn't the doorman tell me you were looking for me when I spoke to him last night upon my return?"

Chad thought a moment, shrugged, and surmised, "Probably we talked to different doormen, else the mystery would have been solved more quickly. As for tonight, I'll come by for you at half past six. Right now, I need to make a last visit to my office to be certain our arrangements are in order. Unless you have something special you want to do, I think we should all finish packing and rest tomorrow and Sunday. The first day at sea can be busy and tiring."

50

"I remember," she said, recalling her recent voyage from America. "We certainly have plenty to do. It sounds fine to me."

"When Mother returns from India," he suggested, "you can move in with her and get out of this cramped hotel. I'm sorry the house is closed up and the servants were given time off, but we didn't know if or when you'd arrive, and she's to be away for a long time."

"You're very kind and thoughtful, Chad, but this is fine. I wouldn't want to use her home when she isn't there."

"Well, when we all get back, at least you can go through your family's things. I'm sure you'll find items you'll want to keep. Mother said there are letters, photographs, and such that you should have."

She smiled in gratitude. "Thank you, Chad. I'm eager to get them. It's very kind of your mother to let me go through everything."

"Rightfully, family keepsakes belong to you," he replied.

Leigh agreed, but said, "She was his wife for years, and I'm grateful she feels this way." Leigh could not call or think of Lady Fiona Hamilton as Mrs. Webster or as her stepgrandmother. "I'm looking forward to seeing the country estate."

"You'll love it there, Leigh. It's large and beautiful. But Cambridge is too far and our time too short to travel there before our departure. I hope you don't decide to sell it; that estate has been in the Webster family for three generations."

"Of course I wouldn't," Leigh replied.

"I'll see you later, my little ward," he said before leaving. "If you need or want anything, have the doorman bring me a message."

"I will, and thank you for everything, Chad."

51

He clasped her hands in his and gazed into her deep blue eyes.

"This trip will be a wonderful adventure, Leigh. I only wish William and Mother could be with us. He planned it before he died. I'm delighted you're taking his place. It's just what we need."

Leigh perceived the seductive aura about him and wondered if something would arise to prevent his amorous companion from going, as it didn't seem proper in the first place. True, Chadwick Hamilton wasn't blood kin to her, either, but he was her legal guardian and stepuncle. Nor, would they be alone in that exotic setting; Reid and Cynthia, the guide, and their bearers would be present. As if she hadn't noticed his enticing behavior or was unmoved by it, she responded, "I wouldn't miss it for anything. I know it will be marvelous."

He released her hands and opened the door. He had told her before, but he repeated, "Be ready at five Monday morning. I'll be here before dawn to get you and your luggage. We have to be aboard and ready to sail at eight. You are a prompt lady, aren't you?"

They both laughed. "If anyone misses the ship, it will be Cynthia," Leigh remarked. They both laughed at the shared joke, as Reid's companion, the marquise was known to be always late for the purpose of making a grand entrance.

Leigh opened a dresser drawer and withdrew the handkerchief that her rescuer had given to her on the wharf to tend her bloody lip. The laundress had washed and ironed it, and the blonde was awaiting the occasion to place it in "Sir Lancelot's" hand. She hadn't been able to get him off her mind. He kept jumping around inside her head like a persistent flea

52

looking for the right place to bite or nest. Who was he? What was he? Why had he been so changeable and secretive? Would she see him again? If ever she did, it would not happen before she returned to England . . . not for months. What if he was betrothed or wed? What if he didn't live in London and was gone by now? She realized the odds were against another chance meeting.

Unless he saw the message about her locket and was reminded of his interest in her. What if he came to see her, or sent a message? What should she do? He was a stranger, a moody and mysterious one at that, so he could be dangerous. She should forget him, daydreaming about him could lead her into trouble.

No, she corrected herself, thinking didn't imperil one; acting rashly on such thoughts did. She wouldn't go to the wharf with the hope of sighting him, and she would remain in her suite this weekend as promised.

Leigh put aside the reminder of her misadventure with the desirable stranger. She was particularly restless today. She was accustomed to daily chores and exercise, activities that kept her busy and in firm condition. She was unused to servants—maids, cooks, laundresses, seamstresses—tending to everything for her. She did not care for a lazy existence. She wanted to stay active, not become someone waited upon hand and foot, or have so much leisure time that it compelled her into mischief.

For now, the stimulating safari would absorb her energy and thoughts while she mentally adjusted to her new life. Then, perhaps learning the business and settling in here would do so later. If not, she would seek—or follow—her destined path, wherever and whoever it might be.

Whoever . . . Her dreamy mind echoed and filled itself with the image of the man from last night. *Forget him for now, and get busy,* Leigh instructed herself, *or you'll be the one missing the ship Monday. If you do, you'll be stuck here alone until Chad's return.*

Leigh pinched her hand and warned herself against such wicked thoughts. Beautiful dreams weren't reality, she knew.

Leigh began packing until it was time to dress for tonight's scheduled event at Lord Salisbury's. It was such an important evening. Lord Cecil Salisbury was a man of many titles: three-time and current prime minister, four-time and current foreign secretary, Third Marquess of Salisbury, Earl of Salisbury, Viscount Cranborne, and Baron Cecil of Essendon. He was an aristocratic statesman of great wealth and power.

Leigh was looking forward to meeting the prime minister and to having a glorious time. With the fashionable long gloves, she wouldn't have to worry about the scratches and bruises on her arms showing or have to change her choice of gowns. There was a scratch near her throat where her prized locket had been torn off, but her thick necklace of pearls — a gift from Chad — would conceal it. As she readied herself, she hummed and envisioned this special affair.

Leigh glanced around the festive ballroom where dancers were moving to the music provided by the group of musicians in one corner. People mingled with a guest list of over a hundred, chatting genially, joking, discussing politics and hunts, and laughing. Others observed the goings-on with keen interest while sipping wine or stronger drinks. And still others nibbled on delectable after-dinner treats.

Never had she seen such opulence and elegance, or so many exquisite gowns and costly jewels. Everyone was having a wonderful time, including Laura Leigh Webster.

They had dined earlier in an assortment of rooms, a meal such as she had never eaten before. She had sat between Chad and Reid, away from the two women who so resented her presence but who were at least well-bred enough to behave themselves at such an important gathering. Afterward, the music and dancing had begun. She had danced with many men, some married and others available bachelors. Their conversation had been light and cordial and pleasant. Most had given her kind or polite condolences about her grandfather—a man widely known and respected—and queried her future plans. They had chatted about America, England, the queen, and her impending safari. She had received many invitations to dinner, tea, the theater, hunts, and other activities and had responded graciously in each case with a promise to accept the invitation upon her return to London.

Leigh's pulse raced from her merry exertions. Her cheeks glowed from the excitement of it all and from the sparkling wine. Without conceit, Leigh knew she looked lovely in her ballgown of creamy satin with its flowing skirt and short train, both embroidered with golden threads in a floral pattern. The bodice was snug, with abundant pleats to give it the desirable fullness between it and the full bottom which accentuated a small waist that did not require the boned and laced corset to achieve an hourglass look. The short sleeves were puffed, with bows attached to the shoulders. The notable décolletage revealed tawny flesh, and a triple strand pearl necklace was fastened about her throat. Dark gold plumes fluttered in the

55

breeze each time she twirled during a dance. When she was still, they rested fetchingly against her wheat-colored hair that was arranged in multiple curls atop her head. From beneath the golden sweepers of her gown peeked bronze kid slippers. Her grooming had been completed with long cream gloves. She was glad the seamstress Chad had recommended was so talented and knowledgeable about proper fashions and flattering colors.

Chad had complimented her numerous times about her "ravishing" appearance when he came to get her. During the evening, he had beamed with pride and possessiveness when other men did the same. But it was the envious and hateful glares from Lady Louisa Jennings that had convinced her of her success.

As she chatted with a stout lord with whom she had just shared a dance, Leigh saw the curry-haired, green-eyed Louisa dancing with Chad. She was dressed in a green brocade gown with ivory trim that looked enchanting against her ivory flesh. She was wearing a jeweled clasp in her fiery mane. As always, expensive cream almost concealed the abundance of pale freckles that splashed over Louisa's nose, cheeks, and back. Her faint golden-red brows and petal-pale lips were darkened by expensive, imported cosmetics. At twenty-six, Louisa was a ravishing woman. She would have to be stunning, Leigh mused, to be the constant companion of the most desired bachelor in London. As if sensing Leigh's eyes on her, the future countess turned and searched for her. Leigh averted her gaze and focused her attention on her partner once more.

As the evening passed, Leigh was aware of the vexed looks that Louisa gave to any female with whom Lord Hamilton danced or spoke. She noticed how the petulant woman tried to remain near Chad and tried to discourage any woman from approaching him. Leigh tried not to feel glad each time the flame-haired beauty failed in her futile task. Chadwick Hamilton was too much in demand by the fair sex, tonight and every day for women to succumb to the fear of Lady Louisa's temper.

Leigh noticed how dashing he looked in his ivory waistcoat and gold-trimmed trousers — a color scheme that matched her own. She was also aware of what a striking couple she and Chad made.

Perhaps, Leigh surmised with amusement, the women were vying for the position of Louisa's replacement. After all, if rumor could be trusted, Chad had stayed with Louisa longer than any of his past conquests. She had heard that Louisa and Chad were "very close," and she understood what that meant. Everyone seemed to know about the affair, and that disquieted Leigh, who feared men would think she was another of Chad's conquests. Perhaps, one day, women would be able to behave as they wished, but not yet, not without risking their reputations. Leigh knew she wasn't a prude because she didn't feel that physically responding to the man one loved was wrong or wicked in all circumstances but having sex without love was both. At least, that was what her mother had taught her, and she believed it. She knew from experience that life could be short and cruel, and there were sometimes valid reasons why lovers couldn't wed.

But that wasn't the case of Louisa and Chad, or Reid and Cynthia, either. Several of her dance partners had made certain Leigh knew that her guardian was unavailable but that they were eager for her company. From the way Chad's gaze kept returning to and engulfing Leigh, she was doubtful of the assumption concerning her guardian, and that troubled her.

Leigh had danced with Chad several times, and he had introduced her to people whom he wanted to make certain she got to know. During one such time, she found herself in the company of Cabinet member Joseph Chamberlain, Britain's colonial secretary, and a "very good friend" of her guardian's. Chamberlain was credited with pioneering efforts in educational reform and slum clearance, taking steps to improve housing, and working for the municipalization of public utilities.

Years ago, the fervent Liberalist had been called a dissenter and an upstart, and had frightened the Conservatives. He had been past Prime Minister Gladstone's cohort in the House of Commons. He had favored Irish reforms, Home Rule, for a time but had changed his opinions and sided with Conservative leader Lord Salisbury and become one of Salisbury's followers. Currently he was secretary of state for the colonies and had an avid interest in African affairs.

After the introductions and his request for her to call him Joseph, he said, "I'm sorry about your grandfather's death. William Webster was fine man. We dined and hunted together on several occasions."

Leigh smiled politely at the lean, narrow-faced man. She noticed how his ribboned monocle made his right eye appear large and stern. She tried not to stare at it as she replied, "You're very kind, sir. I only wish I had known him better."

"Do you plan to remain in London with us?" Chamberlain asked.

Leigh was warm and weary from her exertions on the dance floor, from her attempts to behave correctly, and from the heady wine. She cooled her glowing cheeks with her fan as she replied, "I haven't made any plans yet, but it appears I will stay if all goes well."

"Of course you will," Chad injected, grinning at her. "What could possibly go wrong or change your mind? Nothing, my dear Leigh." When she smiled in appreciation, he continued. "It would be a crime to allow such a lovely jewel to escape our country. Besides, I'm looking forward to teaching you all about the business you inherited, and to working with you. You aren't a woman who's afraid of a challenge or a change in her life. You're much too brave, confident, and intelligent to let anything defeat or trouble you."

"Come now, Lord Hamilton," she teased. "You know men do not care to have women intruding on their business affairs."

"I don't intend for you to intrude, Leigh," Chad came back. "But working as partners will be most intriguing and delightful, most stimulating. Don't you agree, Joseph?"

The colonial secretary removed his monocle and slipped it into his pocket before he answered. "I'm certain it will be. You may not know it, Miss Webster, but I'm a fighter for the rights and freedoms of everyone, including the female sex. If you're capable of learning how to run Webster International—and Chad seems to have unshakable confidence in you—why shouldn't you do so?"

"She has many talents, Joseph, and I'll teach her the rest. I was thinking of investing in the Uganda Railroad if it looks promising when I reach East Africa. What do you know about it?" Chad inquired, abruptly altering their line of conversation.

The older man responded, "I think the railroad should pay for itself, Chad. Our friend and leader Lord Salisbury has pushed the concept for years. However, it could be a waste of money if defense of the interior is his motive rather than expansion and exploration. Ever since Uganda was made a protectorate in '90, several politicians have been determined to open the way to exploit rather than colonize the area and draw on her abundant resources for the good of the empire. It's my hope they don't use the same methods Cecil Rhodes did to get his clutches on Zambesi. Excuse me—Rhodesia, it's called now. We don't need more trouble in our colonies."

Chad and Leigh noticed the bitterness in his tone. It was no secret that Chamberlain was still stewing over the infamous Jameson Raid last December against the Boers in South Africa. There was something about Chamberlain that made Leigh uneasy and mistrustful. She observed him closely.

"Rhodes did do a lot of good work there, Joseph," Chad said. "He's become a millionaire with his gold and diamond fields. I wouldn't mind succeeding in that grand a fashion."

"Yes, but he's caused a great deal of trouble among the Boers, Germans, and the natives. He's been forced to resign as prime minister of the Cape Colony because of that Jameson business. I'm fortunate he hasn't dragged me down with him, not yet anyway. I warned him to hold back his attacks until it was clear they were plotting against us. He claims he telegraphed Jameson not to make that raid in December, but the lines apparently had been cut and Doc never received his message. If Parliament and the queen don't believe their claims that they went into thwart a revolution, I don't know how this nasty situation will work itself out. He's returned to the colony to ward off new trouble with the Matabele tribe. I dare say that neither matter is settled, and they won't be without more bloody conflicts. Don't tell me that is where you're heading?"

"Heavens, no, Joseph. I'm taking Leigh and friends to East Africa. As far as I know there aren't any warring Zulus or Matabeles in our newest protectorate. Those Zulus slaughtered thousands of Britains on their rampage. I certainly wouldn't place Leigh or *any* of my party in that kind of danger. What I have in mind is hunting and sightseeing. I hear the game and landscape in that area are splendid. Leigh and I are looking forward to our adventure."

Chad smiled at his ward before disclosing, "While we're there, I want to check out a few business ventures: perhaps with ivory, hides, crops, gold, and diamonds. There's also a big tourist trade blooming like a tropical flower. Safaris have become the very thing. Imagine what a luxurious hotel could earn there, not to mention the sale of garments and trinkets from native materials. The possibilities are endless. I could have cloth and skins shipped to our mills here, native garments made, then shipped back to sell to all those impressionable British females who want to bring back a piece of Africa to show off to friends. With the interior being opened up and the railroad moving along swiftly, it's get involved now or be too late. The first man to pluck that exotic flower will be rich and famous. And I must admit it would be exciting to furnish animals or trophies for the Geographical Society and to have my name on little plaques beneath dangerous beasts on display." He chuckled, then winked at Leigh.

"I hear the American Museum of Natural History has been working on African displays," Chamberlain remarked. "I'm certain our Royal Society doesn't want to lag behind the Colonists in any area. Have you made arrangements with them to sponsor your safari?"

"No, I want to be on my own. If something exceptional turns up, I'll contact them by cable from the protectorate."

"Make certain you don't rile the aborigines' protection society. They claim their task is looking after the interests of natives around the world and they gave Rhodes a hard time in his colony. They were afraid the Africans would be mistreated and exploited. I daresay though it is unfortunate, you can't colonize any wild area without a little exploitation. The same goes for the Church Missionary Society; they put their noses into more than religion. They've sponsored several wars there, supposedly for the supremacy of the Protestant religion. They sold war bills for that conflict in Uganda. As for where you're heading, I believe the Imperial British East Africa Company has it fairly well locked up. The natives are allowing the IBEA Company to build forts in their area. They have a treaty with a Kikuyu chief to supply the railroad with meat and other necessities. From the reports I've received, farmers, engineers, miners, builders, lawyers, missionaries, and soldiers are taking over most of Africa—Britain and foreigner alike. It won't be wild much longer," Chamberlain surmised. "Be glad you'll see it before it's spoiled by so-called civilization."

"Is there much trouble with foreign goverments in Africa?" Leigh inquired. "Do you still have border disputes and battles? You and Chad have mentioned a lot of trouble."

Chamberlain replaced his monocle, looked at her, and answered, "Mainly with the Germans and Dutch. They were in on that Jameson affair and other troubles. If we could move them and the Belgians out, we'd control most of Africa from the Cape to Cairo. If it were up to . . ."

The discussion was interrupted as Lord Salisbury paused to speak with the trio a moment. After small and cordial talk, the impending safari was discussed once more. Leigh observed the rotund but well-dressed man with his nearly bald head and a heavy beard. His naturally puffy lids almost concealed gentle and intelligent eyes. He told them they had little—if anything—to fear from the natives, especially the Masai who didn't mind the British takeover. He began to talk about the queen, who could not attend tonight's function. It was clear to Leigh that the man was filled with admiration and affection for her.

"As long as Victoria is on the throne, Great Britain and her colonies will prosper. She's ruled for fifty-nine years, and is still quite young and vital for seventy-seven. Never have I known a more honest woman and ruler. Have you met her, my dear?" he asked Leigh.

"No, your lordship, but I would be honored and delighted to do so if the occasion presented itself. Tell me more about her," she encouraged, aware she was one of Lord Salisbury's favorite subjects. Her mother had taught her that nothing relaxed or pleased a person more than speaking on a favorite topic and having a good listener. But Leigh's interest was not a pretense; nor was her motive guileful. She wanted to know all about Britain and the country's ruler. After all, she was half English and she might live her remaining life here.

"The queen is devoted to her family and her subjects. She is the symbol of middle-class virtues. She represents stability, decency, morality, humanitarianism, and progress. The throne will never be in jeopardy as long as there are monarchs like Victoria to occupy it. I'm glad you've come to our country, Miss Webster, and I hope you choose to remain here. We did have little tiffs with your country over the Somoan Islands and Venezuela, but we settled them nicely," he teased.

Leigh smiled, amused that he hadn't mentioned the Colonists' victorious fight for independence over a hundred years ago. She knew that many of the Britains still believed that America would eventually be brought back into the British Empire, be it by request or force. Leigh knew that would never happen. Yet she had wondered often what would have happened to her parents had Thomas Webster met Mary Beth Leigh during that fierce struggle for freedom: beautiful American patriot against handsome English warlord. She cleared her head of such romantic fancies to respond almost tardily, "I'm glad, too, your lordship. As you may know, I'm half British and proud to be so, and I do think I will be settling here permanently."

A broad smile was almost concealed by the heavily whiskered face, his twinkling eyes were visible. "Excellent. I shall look forward to chatting with you again. When you return from Africa, contact me and I shall arrange for you to meet our beloved Queen Victoria."

"You are most kind, your lordship," Leigh replied. She watched him excuse himself to mingle with other guests.

Chad teased his ward first and then Chamberlain, "You charmed him like magic, Leigh and as for you, Joseph, you two seemed to get along fine. I thought perhaps our prime minister was annoyed with you these days."

"We settled our differences when I sided with him against Irish Home Rule," Chamberlain responded. "As you know, I'm very much in favor of imperial unity these days. But he *is* a little miffed over my alleged involvement with Rhodes and Jameson. Salisbury is a powerful imperialist. He's also a very religious man. His wish would be to conquer the African natives with Christianity rather than with military or intellectual might. I myself doubt that is possible. I fear I must agree with Cecil Rhodes on one point; 'Money is power, and what can one accomplish without power?' Of course such a statement is possible for a man of his wealth and power."

Chad laughed and jested, "You're a clever man, Joseph, a wealthy and powerful one yourself, so you'll be exonerated. If there is any way I can be of help to you in this or any other matter, I stand ready to do so, as always. We leave Monday, but I'll return in late June. We're taking a steamer, one of the newest by Cunard."

"Cecil left South Africa on January fifteenth and docked here on February third," Chamberlain informed them, "so your voyage should require about three weeks. Perhaps a little more if weather is bad."

Before Leigh could ask questions about the voyage, Chad inquired, "Is Rhodes in London now? I'd like to see him again."

"No, he sailed for Cape Colony a few weeks past," Chamberlain reminded. "Word arrived of new trouble with the Matabele warriors and he left to settle it. I'm inclined to agree with whatever measures he must take. With ninety percent of the world diamond market at stake, we can't afford to lose that area, nor can he. When we made it a colony, we staked our claim. Now, we have to defend it."

A brave bachelor approached the group to ask Leigh for a dance. She was anxious suddenly to flee the men who were so engrossed in their entwined interests that she was almost ignored. Though she wanted to learn all she could about Africa and England, an invigorating dance might stir her sluggish body now from the wine and fatigue of listening to so much that was new to her. She slipped into the man's arms and away they twirled.

As they moved in time with the music and her partner seemed at a loss of words, Leigh thought about the conversation. She hadn't known the impending trip would combine business with pleasure, nor that Chad had commercial interests other than the firm. She hoped he wasn't planning to venture out on his own and leave her floundering on the bank like a fish out of water. She needed his expertise to keep her from losing her inheritance. Perhaps he planned to use this trip to teach her how much she needed him. Perhaps he was perturbed that her recent peril had not caused her to fall apart — or to fall into his arms. She didn't like that dark thought. Surely Chad hadn't arranged that episode on the docks to terrify her into clinging to him. Surely he hadn't swapped the notes during her absence. Those were horrible suspicions, she chided herself, and dismissed them. Yet soon she needed to know his plans for the future. From the corner of her eye, she saw Reid Adams and Marquise Cynthia Campbell dancing, and she focused her attention on them.

Chad's best friend and constant companion was thirty-four. His sharp, narrow eyes gave him an intense gaze, and their grayish-brown color added an air of secrecy, of impenetrable eeriness. His nose was long, thin, and rather sharp. His mouth seemed tight, as if he had to force his lips over his teeth to close it. Reid's face was triangular, the point at his chin and straight at his hairline, of medium brown. Despite his incisive features and spare frame, he was very nice-looking in a rugged manner. At six feet, he was lean but strong. From what she had heard, his father had made a fortune in shoe manufacturing but was wasting it on gambling and drinking. The wealthy and successful Reid had turned his hand to shipping, which was how he had met Chad. He was a quiet and serious man, and a strange one, always observing everybody and everything. He seemed a lonely, sad soul, and that touched Leigh's tender heart. But, she reasoned, he didn't have to pretend he was having fun, or force himself to be with the brunette.

Cynthia seemed to be enjoying herself. The widow of twenty-eight was wearing a fiery silk gown that clung to her enviable figure. Cynthia always was ready to join the group for fun and games but she apparently was not in love with Chad's best friend and made no excuses for her feelings and conduct with the ruggedly handsome and wealthy bachelor. Maybe, Leigh surmised, they needed each other for physical and social reasons. The marquise obviously did not care what people said or thought about her — her manner of seductive dress and brazen behavior made that clear. Red plumes waved about in Cynthia's brown hair as they danced, and a necklace of many diamonds glittered around her throat.

Leigh wondered if those expensive gems had come from the DeBeers Mine in South Africa, owned by Cecil Rhodes, whom the men had been discussing earlier. Between words of cordial banter with her dance partner, Leigh wondered if Africa was wilder than she had imagined. From the men's conversation and from earlier talks with her guardian, it sounded as if there had been a great deal of trouble there over the years, trouble she hoped was under control by now. Still, the daring American decided, a certain amount of danger made any adventure more stimulating and challenging.

Leigh watched Louisa Jennings join Lord Chadwick Hamilton and Colonial Secretary Chamberlain. From their expressions and close proximity, the conversation near the far wall seemed serious and interesting, but she could not return to the group because she was in constant demand on the dance floor.

"Make certain you stay out of South Africa during your trip," Chamberlain cautioned Chad. "I can't say how long it will be safe there."

"Probably safer than it is here for someone working against the Irish Home Rule Bill," Chad commented on the nefarious Phoenix Park Murders of a few years past. "People in high places have already been murdered over that explosive cause, and you're viewed a traitor to it. You've helped defeat it twice, old friend, so be extra careful. And don't make any trips to Ireland like Lord Cavendish and Thomas Burke did."

"Don't worry about me. I've never been known to back down on a good fight. But why are you really going on this safari at such a time? William's been dead for less than three months. Shouldn't you stay here and make certain the transition of the firm to you and Leigh goes smoothly?"

Chad waited until Louisa left to dance with Reid, then replied, "Business, old friend, in two areas. I want to see what's available there before it's all claimed by others, and I'd like to get to know my new boss and owner better. If East Africa looks promising, can you help me get financial backing for control and expansion? Rhodes couldn't have done what he did in South Africa without plenty of money from investors."

Chamberlain glanced about to make certain no one was within hearing distance. "Salisbury has his eyes on the Uganda Railroad and East Africa. Whatever I did to help you, Chad, would have to remain between us. You realize we can't use the same men and methods Cecil Rhodes did at the Cape. Another fiasco and I'm finished in government. By the way, who's going to be your guide? As colonial secretary, I know Jace Elliott lives and works there. I hear he's a Great White Hunter of enormous reputation and skills. Many of our friends have used Elliott as their guide, and I've received no complaints against him and his men. Too bad Elliott got into trouble with his father and had to exile himself to stay alive. Quite a terrible crime and scandal. The authorities are eager to ask him a few questions, then send him to the hangman or prison. He's been lucky to avoid them so far. If he ever shows his face here, he'll have a lot of explaining to do to stay alive."

"Do you really think Brandon and Jace Elliott were involved in murder and arson?" Chad inquired.

"That's what the evidence and court said, and Elliott's suicide note revealed the same. It was confirmed to be in his handwriting, so he's clearly the one who implicated his own son. Of course, there are those who believe the old man was insane when he wrote it and believe Jace is innocent. But if he is, why does he refuse to come forward and clear himself? I would venture it's because he can't; he's guilty. I didn't know Brandon Elliott well. He was in the House of Commons, but he was staunchly working for the passage of Irish Home Rule."

"But did Brandon Elliott want it badly enough to destroy the opposition and himself?" the dark-haired man pressed.

"He must have. He killed himself before he could be arrested and tried. During the investigation, evidence was uncovered linking Elliott to those Irish rebels, the Invincibles. It's no secret Stokely was against Home Rule, or that he had hired men to unmask them; he wanted revenge for the wanton way those rebels destroyed his company in Ireland. It could be that Stokely or his men found proof against Elliott, proof that was destroyed during the fire. And a dead man can't talk."

Chad shrugged. "I suppose you're right about Brandon; evidence doesn't lie. But it doesn't sound like the Jace I went to school and sea with. Of course, he could have changed. I've only seen him a few times since those old days together, and he wasn't too friendly. I suppose he's still vexed over my affair with Joanna Harris."

Joseph grinned and teased, "Ah, yes, I do recall that tiny scandal. I suppose that means he won't be your safari guide."

"I've hired a man named Jim Hanes, second best but skilled and reliable. Most of the guides are off doing other things this time of year. Their busy time is during Africa's short rainy season from October to December. We English also prefer getting away to the tropics during our cold, damp winters. I realize we'll hit the long rainy season of April to June, but it can't be helped. It's the best time to take Leigh before we plunge into hard work. Besides, it will be nice to be there when it isn't crowded with other safari groups. We won't have to waste time entertaining or being entertained in other camps. With luck, Jace Elliott won't be around while we're there. But if he is, maybe we can make peace."

"Have you talked to your lovely ward about becoming one of your investors? She is one of the richest women in England now."

"I don't want to ask Leigh for anything this early in our relationship. I prefer for her to get to know me better. And that will be easier to accomplish away from so many distractions. As you can see, she's made quite an impression on everyone, especially the young men. I might even confess, I'm more than taken by her myself. But if she makes an offer, I'll accept it," Chad added.

"Find a way to lock into the gold, ivory, or diamond prospects, and I won't have any trouble obtaining you backers."

"Don't worry, old friend, I fully intend to make my fortune in Africa." Chad grinned, then parted with Joseph Chamberlain.

The large but crowded ballroom had become hot and stuffy, so Leigh sneaked outside to cool and calm herself. She was having a wonderful time, but she needed to rest a moment. She had danced countless times and met numerous people. Yet she wished for the presence of one person who was not there.

Leigh strolled in the garden and gazed at the moon. In a few days, it would be shining on water during her voyage, then over a tropical jungle in Africa. The blonde passed a sparkling fountain, artistically planted floral beds, neatly trimmed shrubs, and imported trees, admiring all. She halted near a gazebo to relax.

Suddenly her lost locket dangled before her vision and a mellow voice from behind said, "I thought you might like to have this back."

Leigh had not heard him approach. She whirled and almost seized the treasure from his extended hand. "My locket! Where did you find it? I feared it was gone forever." Her hand closed around it and sentimental moisture glimmered in her eyes.

His green gaze traveled over her as Jace replied, "In the alley. It glittered in the moonlight. I'm glad I noticed it. Obviously it means a great deal to you." As she gazed at the meaningful possession, lost in poignant reflection, Jace observed how the gold threads in her gown matched her hair. The white pearls and creamy fabric made a stunning contrast against her tanned flesh, silky skin his fingers longed to stroke and roam at leisure. Her waist was small enough for his large hands to encircle and nearly meet in front and back. It seemed like ages since he had last seen and touched her; yet it also seemed that no time had passed since their separation. He realized how pleasant it was to be with her again and hoped no one would interrupt this stolen visit. How he wished he didn't have to sneak about to see her, but that couldn't be helped for now. Her sultry voice warmed him as she spoke.

"It means so much to have it returned. Chad posted a description and reward for it. Thank you. I'll see that you receive the reward. Where shall I send it? To whom?" she asked, meeting his gaze as she begged her body to stop trembling.

Chapter Four

Jace's sensual lips curled into a compelling grin as his fingers toyed with the bow at her right shoulder. "Your beautiful smile and gratitude are thanks enough, Miss Leigh. You look ravishing tonight. Are you having a good time at Lord Salisbury's?" Jace had been watching her through the windows all night, and he was glad she had finally taken a breather from her many admirers. He had observed her with Chadwick Hamilton, and vexation had chewed at him. Of all men, Chad didn't deserve this exquisite prize.

"Thank you for the compliment, kind sir. And yes, I'm having a glorious time. Did you want to make certain I survived that nasty encounter, or did you only want to return my locket?"

He looked into her eyes and said, "I wanted to see you again, and apologize for being rude and rushed."

Leigh felt herself tremble at his nearness and gaze. "I do recall you were both, as was I," she responded. "Thank you again for my locket and my rescue. Friends?" she hinted, and offered him her hand.

He clasped it between his and smiled as he replied, "Good friends, I hope."

Leigh did not extract her small hand from his

larger ones as she asked, "Did you make your dinner appointment and have fun?"

He did not break their locked gaze. "Neither, I'm afraid."

"I hope it wasn't because of helping me."

"Not in the least. But if I'd known I was wasting my time, it could have been spent with you. After your frightening ordeal, I didn't like sending you off alone and still upset."

She laughed to break the tension rising in her body, and teased, "Aren't you the same man who warned me about cunning predators and scolded me like a child . . . for being too friendly with a strange man? I still don't know your name or where you live."

He chuckled and evaded her last words. "Alas, guilty as charged, Miss Leigh. But I hope you forget such foolish and impulsive words." He released her hands and reached into his pockets.

She saw that he was in casual garments, a cotton shirt and dark pants. Obviously he wasn't a guest she had missed seeing all night. "What are you doing lurking out here in the darkness?" she questioned, noticing that he was on alert again and still mysterious.

"I tracked you down to return your locket and these . . ." he replied, holding out the aigrette and silk bouquet. "I was hoping you'd come outside alone for fresh air, but I honestly doubted it. Those eager young men have been keeping you busy inside, but I can't blame them . . . Here."

Leigh couldn't conceal her surprise. "My gown is being repaired and I purchased a new hairpiece. Why not keep them as souveniers of an exciting evening? If I carry them inside, someone might wonder how I recovered them. I asked Chad not to report my attack or to seek you as a witness, because I didn't

74

want people to learn about my carelessness. You do understand?"

"I shall keep them with pleasure, Laura Leigh. It was a most interesting episode." He stuffed both items into his pocket. He could not sneak into the party to see Lord Salisbury, who had arrived in town this afternoon, yet, if he was quick and clever, he might learn something from this female who was close to Chad. But how? Without her room number—which he dared not request—he couldn't visit Laura tonight, or risk searching the large hotel for her room. Nor could he expose himself to request it at the front desk! Too, she might not be alone.

Leigh's eyes roved her rescuer's towering frame and handsome face. She was thrilled to see him again, but she was nervous, as well. They were alone in a moon-lit garden, and he was most enchanting. She noticed how his brows—close to his eyes and over prominent bone structure—gave those green depths a hooded air of sensual mystery. A small hump indicated to her that his nose had been broken long ago but clearly had healed without disfigurement. His angular jaw-line was clean shaven, and she had the urge to run her fingertip over his inviting lips and through the cleft on his strong chin. She mastered that wild impulse by questioning, "You didn't say why you are sneaking around in the shadows? You could have returned this at my hotel and left it with the doorman."

He chuckled, knowing she was apprehensive. He stroked her warm cheek with the back of his cool hand, a very strong one. "Then I couldn't have seen you again. Do you mind my forwardness?"

Leigh wondered if she had misjudged this man. What if he was here to spy on an important person or to commit a daring robbery? What if he was following her for a dark reason? After all, she was a wealthy woman now. Perhaps he was up to hazardous mischief.

"Who are you? What do you really want from me? Why do you keep showing up in the oddest places?" she questioned.

"How else can I pursue a beautiful woman in such demand if I don't trail her constantly to catch her without her horde of admirers?"

"Will you trail me all the way to Mombasa, Sir Lancelot? That's where I'm heading Monday morning with my guardian," she said to test his intentions. "I'm sailing to East Africa with Lord Hamilton and friends to go on a safari. We're staying there two months and the voyage requires three weeks in each direction, so we won't return until late June. As you can see, my gallant champion, you'll have to find another damsel in distress to rescue and track on dark nights."

"Lord Hamilton is your guardian?" he asked, staring at her.

"Yes, he is. And I doubt your sneaky pursuit and my recklessness will please him if he catches us. After all, I don't even know who you are. He is most strict and protective," she ventured to catch his reaction to her impending and lengthy absence and to withdraw more information. She knew that Chad would be furious with her for taking such a risk, but she couldn't help herself.

"I see . . ." he murmured, wondering where that "strict and protective" nature was last night when she was out alone and in danger. "Is the whole family going?" he inquired in a casual tone.

"Of course," she responded, wanting only to let him know she wouldn't be alone with Chad, but not wanting to explain about Louisa, Cynthia, and Reid. She awaited his response to those words.

Jace's heart raced with excitement and anticipation at those unexpected clues. He was to sail at dawn, hopefully after meeting with Lord Salisbury, if he could catch the powerful man alone. If the entire family was going on safari in his area, that meant William Webster would be along, the man who had taken over his father's business because of "outstanding debts" to Webster International. He had tried to sneak a visit with the old man, but the Webster home was closed up tight and the servants were gone. Perhaps, he reasoned, they were staying at the hotel until Monday's departure.

By sailing at dawn, Jace schemed, he would be several days ahead of them, awaiting their arrival. With Webster and Hamilton within his reach, perhaps he could unmask the truth, as they were his best — no, *only* — suspects. He eyed the woman before him and prayed she wouldn't become Chad's mistress before docking in Mombasa. It wasn't above Chad to seduce even an innocent and naive ward!

Jace saw her watching him. He could not help but wonder if Webster and Hamilton had discovered his presence and set up their first meeting for a dark reason. Or perhaps this blossoming flower was being used. For all Jace knew, she might not be Chad's ward at all, as his old friend was rather young and notoriously rakish to be appointed a female minor's guardian! Jace could not imagine any loving father tossing his innocent lamb to such a notorious wolf. Yet Laura struck him as being honest.

This meeting was accidental, as neither she nor those men could have known he'd be here. He had seen her tonight with Chad, and it strangely seared him like a roaring fire. He wondered how much Laura Leigh meant to Chad, and if Chad meant more to her than a guardian. How had an American girl become an Englishman's ward, when Chad had no blood kin except his mother? Would Chad be upset if something happened to Laura in Africa? After all, the jungle was a perilous place for someone who didn't know it. Jace worried that his treacherous old friend had something special in mind for her, else Chad wouldn't have taken on the responsibility. Or maybe there was a cunning lioness beneath that golden mane and tawny body. For certain, she was irresistible and enchanting. But could she be sincere?

Jace tested her interest and loyalty toward Chad. "From what I've heard, your guardian has quite a reputation as a womanizing scoundrel. I hope you don't fall prey to his wiles. You're much too lovely and genteel to be added to his long string of conquests."

"Does a similar warning apply to you, Sir Lancelot?"

An engaging grin captured his face. "I'm afraid my secluded and busy lifestyle does not provide opportunities for me to meet and romance exquisite creatures. I suppose that's why I'm so enchanted by you, Laura Leigh. Believe it or not, I don't usually chase after bewitching strangers, so you must excuse my boldness and understand my predicament. Sadly, my time and therefore my efforts are limited."

"Who are you?" Leigh asked again, more intrigued than ever.

Jace looked her over, then playfully blew on the plumes in her hair. He chuckled as they fluttered wildly, just as his heart was doing from alluring nearness. He grinned and teased, "You'll know soon, my fetching damsel. Let it be an eagerly awaited surprise."

Before she could react, she was pulled into his arms and kissed. The stranger's lips were persuasive and

78

enticing as they parted hers and compelled her response with skill and ease. His effect on her susceptible body and mind was instant and overwhelming, and no refusal was possible. Her senses reeled and her wits vanished as their lips meshed tighter. Tingles raced over her body as an array of sensations assailed her. She yielded to him without restraint, powerless to resist him, unwilling to resist him. A reckless emotion attacked the core of her being and she embraced him fiercely, helplessly surrendering to the magic of this passionate and perilous moment. As if coming from her soul, a fiery heat seared her from head to foot and branded her with his mark of ownership. Their first kiss on the waterfront had been nothing like this.

Leigh had dreamed of this heady moment since first meeting the seductive stranger. His deft tongue teased along her parted lips and darted into the moist and inviting haven. His mouth was flavored with aged brandy, and she savored his intoxicating taste. He smelled of clean flesh and freshly washed clothes, of a tropical paradise whose blazing sun was baking her skin. She seemed to melt like a snow flake beneath its powerful heat. She wanted him closer, and nestled against him. His fingers trailed up and down her back as his mouth traced her features before capturing her lips again. She wanted his thrilling kisses and caresses to continue forever. His body was hard against hers, his lips tender, yet deliberately stimulating, his hands gentle but firm and possessive. Forgotten were her fears and doubts of him, forgotten was reality itself. All she knew was his irresistible embrace. A soft moan escaped her lips before she grasped his head and drew his mouth more snugly against hers. She pressed closer to him, as if daring even air to separate them.

Jace shuddered in fiery arousal. She was like a hungry lioness in his arms, feasting on him, devouring his control. The equatorial heat couldn't compare with that of his body. He wanted to carry this heady moment to the limit. He was tempted to seize her and flee with her to consummate the feelings she inspired within him. He had only enough wits left to know he had to cease this madness.

When Jace drew back, he saw the blaze of desire in her wide eyes and on her rosy cheeks. She trembled with desire, as did he. He read other emotions in her sapphire gaze: she was wary, alarmed, and innocent. But she was strongly attracted to him. That was a good start, if she was important to his enemy, and even if she wasn't. Perhaps Laura was the golden key to unlock the door to this dark mystery. He would know very soon, but for now, he'd knew he must leave before he frightened her, or someone discovered them, or he lost all control. Besides, they would meet again soon, in his territory. Once he had her in his domain and African winds were blowing over them, he would become the predator again and she his exquisite prey. For now, she was a trail too wild to walk . . .

He forced his thoughts to return to business. Unable to meet with Salisbury, and with Chad here at the party, it was the perfect time to search Chad's home and office for clues.

In a playful tone, the provocative Englishman murmured, "I don't want to spoil your fun tonight, so I'll leave you to charm your many admirers. Don't worry, my golden enchantress, our paths will cross again. I promise you, Laura Leigh, I'm no fool or coward. With luck, next time, you'll be the persistent tracker and I'll be your fortunate and obedient quarry. I promise you I won't try to escape or resist your lovely snares."

Leigh was too dazed by his amorous siege, curious words, and swift departure to respond. As she tried to comprehend his meaning and halt her trembling, he slipped into the shadowy bushes and vanished. Her keen eyes searched for moving branches and she listened for footsteps or broken twigs. She strained her ears to catch his location or to hear which direction he was taking, but he moved like a stealthful wolf on the prowl. How, she wondered in amazement, had he learned such skills? A puffy white cloud drifting across a serene Texas sky made more noise coming and going than he had, and a lack of wind rustled more leaves than his movements. This man, she realized, possessed more than one kind of prowess.

Once more the emerald-eyed man was gone, and without giving his name. Perhaps he was playing a roguish and guileful game to entice her interest. Or perhaps he was crazy and dangerous. *Which is it, my handsome stranger?* Leigh mused. *We shall see, as I have no doubt our paths will cross again. Then, I'll solve your riddle.*

She heard familiar voices and panicked. With haste, Leigh concealed herself to prevent being found with passion-pinkened cheeks and mussed hair. She crouched down, peered through the bushes, and listened.

"I need to talk about something important, Louisa," Chad was saying.

The redhead pressed close to him and murmured in a seductive tone, "The kind of talk I want to do can't be done here, although it would be most exciting to use Lord Salisbury's garden."

"Stop that," he ordered as he pushed away her probing hands from below his waist. "I want the truth, you hot-tempered wench. I know how much you dislike Leigh. Did you have anything to do with

81

her attack on the wharf? You were too drunk by the time I returned to the restaurant to give me any straight answers. Then you spent the remainder of the night with Cynthia. That isn't like you."

"Did you miss me in bed, lover?" she teased but did not continue when she noticed his frown. "Don't get upset, Chad. Cynthia and I needed time to finish our travel plans and wardrobes. We're leaving soon, and there are things to do."

"You're stalling. Did you try to have Leigh scared off—or killed?"

Louisa brushed strayed locks of fiery red from her ivory face. "Are you serious?" she asked, glaring at him.

"You're damn right I'm serious! You wrote that message. Did you list the wrong address, then have hired men waiting for her?"

"Did I *what?*" she shrieked at him. "How dare you think so wickedly of me, Chadwick Hamilton! Surely you know me better than that by now. Did she show you the note?"

"Yes, and it said Stems Street. But somehow I doubt she read it wrong twice. How did you pull off such a dangerous stunt?"

"I didn't. But I'm glad the little chit ran into trouble. We haven't had an evening alone since she got here. It would suit me fine if she sailed back where she belongs. She isn't one of us, Chad, and I don't like her clinging to you."

"Leigh doesn't cling to me, Louisa. We're friends. Swear you didn't pull a crazy ruse last night," he insisted.

"You're questioning me like a criminal. What has she done to you, Chad, to make you treat me this way? It's mean and unfair. Everything was wonderful between us until she arrived."

"Swear it, Louisa," Chad persisted, "and you'd better tell the truth. Leigh is important to me. I'm responsible for her."

"Responsible, pooh!" she scoffed and stomped her foot. "I'm not blind, dear Chad. I've seen the way you watch her, and I've seen how she melts over you. Don't play with her, my love, or you'll be in trouble. People won't take kindly to you seducing your innocent ward, even with her permission."

"The problem is all yours, Louisa. Leigh's been trying to be friendly with you. In fact, she's been twice the lady you were reared to be. Learn to get along with her or we'll all be miserable. I've worked too hard at the firm to let your petty jealousy and envy spoil things for me. Leigh and I can get along fine if you stop interfering and misbehaving. If you refuse, I can't allow you to be around her anymore."

"If you weren't so bewitched by her, you'd realize she probably tricked you to seize your attention and affection. If she was attacked, why didn't she want you to report it so those villains could be caught and punished? If she read the note twice, how could she make an error? Why hasn't her champion contacted her or you for a reward or assistance? I bet she lied to you, dear *uncle*."

"Don't be ridiculous," he scolded. "She's too honest."

Louisa laughed. "No woman is totally honest with a man, my naive lover. We have to retain our mystique." Her tone and expression waxed serious. "I know how important she is to your future at the company. I love you and need you. I wouldn't do anything to hurt you, Chad; you must believe that."

"Settle down, woman, I believe you. I didn't tell her you wrote the message, and she doesn't know my handwriting. I figured that news would cause more trouble between you two." He took a deep breath. "I guess it was Leigh's mistake. If not, I just hope she doesn't think *I* tried to pull a dangerous trick on her."

"Don't be gullible where she's concerned; it could destroy you."

"Stop it, Louisa. Give Leigh a chance to become your friend. And stop making Cynthia treat her so badly. I want this safari to be fun for all of us." He grasped Louisa by the shoulders and asked, "What have you got to worry about? You're going with me, and you're sharing my tent, not Leigh. If I wanted another woman, Louisa, nothing would stop me from leaving you."

"You can't, Chad. No other woman can please you like I do."

He chuckled and cuffed her chin. "Come on, Louisa, stop making things so hard for everyone. Prove you have brains inside this lovely head. Be nice to Leigh, show some pride and restraint."

"I can't help it, Chad. Sometimes you make me so mad. You used to change women like . . . most men change shirts, and you let that little chit do as she pleases. Without you, she's nothing, because Webster International is nothing. The will says she can't fire you until she's twenty-one. By November, she'll realize how stupid that would be. She needs you, Chad. I just don't want her to need you *too much*. You're mine, isn't that right?"

"As long as you behave yourself, I see no reason to cease our relationship. It suits us both. Promise you'll be a good girl?"

"Good in public, but very bad in private," she replied, licking on his thumb in an erotically suggestive manner.

"Cool your flames, Louisa. You are one greedy woman."

"And you love it that way. I'll go freshen myself upstairs. You find your little ward and dance with her before I return and have to endure such a painful sight."

"Come along, my fiery wench," he teased, pulling on her arm.

When they were out of sight, Leigh left her hiding place. Now she knew Chad was not responsible for the dangerous mistake last night, and she was relieved about that but worried over his possibly amorous feelings toward her. She wanted to keep their relationship businesslike, but friendly. But would he allow it, she fretted, if he decided he was attracted to her?

Leigh wasn't convinced of Louisa's innocence, which created a new worry. She was annoyed that her guardian had broken his promise and told the offensive woman about what happened, that is, if Louisa hadn't already learned the truth from her thwarted hirelings.

Are you being unfair and ridiculous? Leigh asked herself. *Louisa can be mean, but is she evil and dangerous? If not, why did Chad suspect her, and question her and threaten her?* That worried Leigh, as did telling her guardian about what happened in the garden tonight.

If she told Chad the stranger had returned her locket, it could arouse his suspicions against her, especially after Louisa had planted seeds of doubt in his mind. The redhead was right about Leigh needing Chad for the business. Too, she had to admit that both episodes sounded strange, even doubtful. If Chad did believe her account, the stranger's curious behavior might alarm him. No, she decided, she mustn't tell her guardian the locket had been returned or that she had seen her rescuer again.

Leigh hurried to a side door and slipped into an

85

empty hallway. She went upstairs to the ladies' chamber to check her appearance. She found Louisa still there, arranging her hair and makeup. She smiled politely and took a seat near another mirror.

To Leigh's surprise, the redhead asked, "Would you like to use any of these?" Louisa motioned to the colorings before her.

Leigh responded to the woman's overture, however false and coerced. She lifted a blue powder and asked, "How do I put it on?"

"Like this," Louisa instructed as she brushed onto her lids a green powder that matched her emerald eyes. "Egyptians and Chinese have used such colorful tricks for ages. These were ordered from the Orient. They're quite expensive, but worth the money and trouble. Try this for your lips," she suggested.

Leigh took the small container and rubbed a pink cream on her mouth, then lightly brushed a blue powder onto her eyelids. She was amazed at how it brought out the color of her eyes and lips. She smiled at the redhead and said, "I like it, Louisa. Thank you."

"You don't need help like I do," Louisa remarked, "but you're welcome to use whatever you like from my collection. You're lucky you don't have dreadful freckles to cover. They make a woman look so much like a child. I had hoped to outgrow them, but no such luck."

"On most redheads they're dark and large, but yours are pale and small. They add color to your skin, and I think they're attractive." It was the truth, but Leigh doubted if Louisa would believe her. Oddly, then the redhead grinned and turned to Leigh.

"Then I won't fuss about them anymore. Would you like to try this perfume from Paris? It drives men wild."

Leigh's fragrance had faded, so she tried the one Louisa held out to her. The scent was seductive and pleasant. As Louisa groomed herself, Leigh wondered if Louisa possessed the cunning to plot against her. The ruse last night had required clever planning, expert timing, and accomplices. If this vixen was to blame, Louisa was dangerous, and had to be watched.

Louisa halted her task. "We haven't had much time alone for woman-talk, Leigh. I hope we can get better acquainted on the ship and during the safari. What do you think of your guardian?"

As she sealed the small bottle of expensive perfume, Leigh replied, "Uncle Chad is very nice. He's taking good care of me. This new world is strange and intimidating at times; it's so different from ranchlife. I'm glad I have Uncle Chad and all his friends to help me adjust." She met Louisa's probing gaze in the mirror and said, "You two look very happy together. When are you getting married?" Leigh hoped that calling Chad her uncle would fool the woman into thinking she viewed him as kin, not as an available attractive man. She also hoped that Louisa believed she was pleased they were a couple and would eventually wed. But that she wasn't. Chad deserved a better woman than Louisa Jennings!

Louisa laughed heartily. "Chadwick Hamilton doesn't have marriage in mind any time in the near future. And you? Did you have a suitor in America?"

Leigh seized the opportunity to divert the conversation from Chad. "The foreman on my aunt's ranch courted me. He's very handsome and virile, and all the girls craved him. He has cornsilk hair, eyes like chocolate, and a sunny smile." She let her won dreamy smile fade. "But men who are too handsome and charming make me nervous and wary. If anything is supposed to happen between us, it will one day. Father always told me that fate tracks us down wherever we go. If it doesn't, I'm sure Tyler will. He's determined to win me."

Cynthia entered the room and gaped at the two laughing females. "I wondered where you were, Louisa. What's taking you so long?"

Leigh watched the brunette ignore her presence, approach the mirror, and take a seat to repair her grooming. "Louisa and I were getting better acquainted, Marquise Campbell."

"Please, call her Cynthia," Louisa encouraged. "After all, my dear Leigh, you have far more money than she does."

Leigh flushed and lowered her head as if embarrassed, but she was infuriated. She wanted to make progress toward a friendly relationship with both females before their trip, but how could she if Louisa antagonized her friend?

Cynthia scowled and retorted, "That was mean, Louisa."

"I was only teasing, and you know it. Leigh is a darling girl, and I'm afraid we haven't been very nice to her. We'll change that tonight. From now on, we'll be best of friends. Agreed?"

The brown-haired woman gaped at Louisa as if she were drunk, then her chocolate gaze shifted to Leigh.

"Admit it, Cynthia," Louisa said. "We got off on the wrong foot. You and I were accustomed to being the centers of attention until this lovely child arrived from America. We were jealous of her youth and beauty. There, I've said it. Now, let's forget it and move forward. Agreed?"

Laura Leigh Webster and Marquise Cynthia Campbell looked at each other strangely. Then both shrugged and smiled.

"Good," the redhead commented. "We're about to leave on a wonderful trip, so let's do it in grand style. Such fun awaits us there."

Leigh smiled and said, "Thank you, Louisa. You don't know how much it means to me for us to be friends. Uncle Chad will be happy."

"No, Leigh, he'll be *ecstatic*," Cynthia remarked, rolling her eyes heavenward. "Pass me that lip cream, Louisa. I need repairs badly."

"I think I'll get something to drink. My throat is dry," Leigh told them, wanting to get out of the room as quickly as possible, for her pretense was strenuous work and she was running out of small talk.

The moment the door closed behind the blonde, Cynthia asked, "What in hell's name was that about? Have you gone daft?"

Louisa's green eyes narrowed and chilled. "That little tart! I hate her, Cynthia, but Chad insists we be nice to her. We're going to be so good and sweet that candy will pale beside us. Neither of them will think we have a reason or the skills to harm little Leigh. Chad questioned me earlier about her attack, but I convinced him I didn't pull a mean trick on his little ward." Louisa related the conversation to her best friend and cohort.

"You sly witch," Cynthia accused. "I love it. How can I help?"

"Better than you did last night. Your stablemen did a sorry job. I hope you punished them," the redhead spouted in vexation.

"It wasn't their fault, love. If a tower of strength hadn't happened along and rescued her, her ravished body would be floating in the Thames. At least Sean and Jaimie were dressed as sailors and didn't give us away. I ordered them to stay hidden for a while."

89

"Yes, we were all lucky last night," Louisa agreed, "Since they didn't steal her purse and the carriage driver didn't keep the note, thank goodness she left it behind so that doorman could exchange them."

Cynthia sighed in relief. "Those were good precautions. I'm glad it's over. I was nervous when Chad left twice to check on her."

"Me, too. I only hope that witness doesn't give us trouble."

"What's next?" the eager marquise asked.

Louisa halted her task to answer. "I have to be careful, Cynthia. If there's another *accident* too soon, not only will Chad and Leigh get suspicious but so will the law. She has to be killed, and I have to snare that infuriating rake. How else can I get my hands on all that lovely money? Chad doesn't know my family is nearly broke; Father's managed to keep it a secret, but time's running out. Once my lover learns the truth, he'll be after Leigh with all his might."

Cynthia grasped the woman's hand and gazed into her green eyes. "You know I'll do whatever I can to help you. We're best friends, Louisa, and I love you dearly. Besides, it's wicked fun."

Giggling, the redhead playfully pinched Cynthia's cheek. "I know," she concurred.

"Do you think Chad suspects you poisoned William?"

Louisa sent her an evil smile. "Never. I paid a lot for that special drug, and it worked. His death looked like heart failure, as I was promised. But neither of us suspected the old man would leave everything to that little chit."

"If Chad learns what we're up to, he'll kill us."

"He won't," the redhead vowed with hostility and smugness. "Besides, he should hate the old bird for almost excluding him from the will. William was like

90

a father to Chad. I wonder what happened . . . No matter," she stated. "I have him duped completely, and I'll do anything necessary not to lose him, or rather *that fortune,* even lick Leigh's feet for a while. When everything's in his grasp and we're married, he'll be sorry for all he's done to me. I've made a public fool and harlot of myself to trick him, but it will be worth it one day. Don't fret, my sweet; we'll triumph. Soon we'll be very rich and powerful women, and Lord Chadwick Hamilton can go to the devil where he belongs."

"I hope we don't fail. With the Webster holdings, we can do as we please, just you and me. I only hope my money holds out until we succeed. If it doesn't, I'll have to sell the estate and possibly my jewels to survive. That could give us away as frauds."

"Don't panic, Cynthia, and don't sell anything. Use your skills and beauty to settle any pressing debts. Most men are willing to collect in that delightful manner. We'll be rich and free by June."

"I'm scared, Louisa. Chadwick Hamilton isn't a fool."

"But Chad doesn't know I want Webster International more than he does and that I'll do anything to get it." She ran her tongue over her lower lip. "I wish I knew where Joanna Harris is; I'm certain she and Chad were involved in that Elliott mess. She would make an excellent blackmail tool."

"Speaking of Jace Elliott," Louisa continued, "I always wondered what happened between Chad and Jace, besides Joanna Harris. From what I've been told, they were best friends until Chad returned home alone around six years ago. Rumor said he was in terrible shape, but William took a liking to him and helped him."

"Poor Chad was hit hard by his father's violent

death during the dock strike; he lost everything except his title. You and I know how that can affect a person." They exchanged knowing looks.

"I don't like mysteries, Cynthia, and Chad has many. Secrets conceal a person's weak points. I've questioned him plenty of times, but Chad won't tell me anything. I'm sure he wants revenge for something that happened during their seafaring days. It had to be bad to turn best friends against each other. Every time Jace's name is mentioned, Chad's eyes turn to blue ice. Whatever it was, I bet it's the reason Chad took Joanna and ruined her. I wonder if it has any-thing to do with those dreadful scars on his chest and back," she mused. "He's never seen without his shirt; he even wears a nightshirt in bed or makes love in the dark. But I've stolen peeks and felt them. They look like pagan symbols, and they're so deep. It must have been terribly painful."

"How strange," Cynthia murmured.

"I know Jace owns a coffee plantation in Africa and that he's a safari guide. If those two meet again, it'll be a violent clash. Too bad, because Jace Elliott is one desirable male. I won't mind having him around for months in the hot tropics."

"You've met him?" the brunette questioned.

"Several times. He was home in '92, '93, and '94. You were away each time with that old marquess. Actually I tried to seduce him, but failed. He was a good catch, and made me hot and tingly all over. He returned to Africa just before his father died."

"If he's rich and handsome and you can't get Chad . . ."

"He'd be a good lover, but I'm not the pioneer type. Besides, a criminal in hiding makes a bad marital prospect."

* * *

As Leigh danced with Chad, he glanced at her and remarked, "You smell like Louisa. I never noticed that before."

Leigh smiled and related, "Louisa loaned me her perfume. We had a long talk. She was very nice."

Chad looked surprised and pleased. "Good. I was hoping you two would come to an understanding."

"We have," Leigh assured him innocently.

Afterward, as she danced with Reid Adams, she entreated, "Tell me about Chad's mother. I recall little about her. I met her only once, and I'm sorry she isn't here so we can get acquainted. It would be nice if she could have gone on safari with us as planned."

"Mrs. Webster was deeply affected by William's sudden death," Reid replied. "Her visit to India will do more good for her."

"What's she like? From what I remember, she's very beautiful." The curious female probed for facts about her stepgrandmother.

His grayish-brown eyes smiled as he answered. "Most men and women will agree that Fiona Webster looks very young. In fact, she can pass for my age, an older woman's dream. She's had a tragic life, losing two husbands. But she's a strong woman, like her son. I met her years ago, after Chad and I became friends. You'll like Fiona; everybody does. She's a kind and gentle woman, a real lady. She'll be home in July, and you'll see for yourself."

Leigh noticed how carefully Reid measured his words. She didn't know if it was to make certain he got his meaning across or if she made him nervous, or if he'd had too much to drink. Maybe—she mused—he was always like that. After all, she didn't know Reid Adams well. The dance ended, and Leigh was passed into another guest's arms.

Early Monday, Leigh answered the knock on her door. "Ready to go," she announced with a cheery smile.

"I'm sorry, Leigh," Chad told her, "but our ship needs repairs. From what I've been told, we'll be delayed a week. Go back to bed and get more sleep. We'll talk at dinner tonight. I'm sorry."

Disappointment was revealed in her blue eyes. It was still dark outside, and her guardian looked weary and annoyed. "I suppose it can't be helped."

He tugged on a tawny curl and said, "I promise, we'll leave by next Monday or I'll buy my own ship to take us there. Everything's set, and I don't want my plans spoiled."

Leigh closed the door behind him and leaned against it. "Another week in London. What shall I do with it?" she murmured.

Images of "Sir Lancelot" filled her head as she changed back into her nightdress and returned to bed. *I wonder how I can locate you and discover all your secrets. Surely there has to be a safe way. But how?*

Chapter Five

Tuesday afternoon, Leigh sat in Chad's office and sipped tea. They had spent the day touring the several buildings where her many employees worked. She had watched them labor while making linens and garments, and chatted with some of them. She found it fascinating to watch the raw products made into fabrics, then see the material progress into beautiful and useful items—all with her family name on them! Pride and joy filled her.

"Much of the cotton used comes from Georgia and Texas, doesn't it?" she asked her guardian between nibbles on a sweet cake.

Chad set down his cup and smiled. "Most of it from Texas, and a lot from your aunt Jenna. It's high grade, so we'll be buying from her as long as she continues to grow it."

"That's good news. Thanks."

His blue eyes were lively as he teased, "Why thank me? You're the boss and owner now. You can buy from whomever you please."

Leigh's apprehensions were evident when she responded, "I didn't realize so much was involved. You have to know about materials, and purchases, and shipments, and employees. There's so much scheduling to do where they're all concerned. My head is spinning from all I've heard and seen. I just hope I can learn so much."

The black-haired man chuckled at her fearful tone and expression. "You can, Leigh, but it will take time and training. If you order too much, or ship too late, or anger customers, or machinery breaks down, or workers get unhappy—you have to know how to deal with a crisis. If you don't, you can lose it all, faster than you can imagine. Especially if more than one major crisis occurs at the same time."

Leigh sighed deeply. "I'm glad you're so knowledgeable, Chad, and so willing to help me learn. It never sounded simple and easy when you explained it to me, but it's even more complicated than I realized."

"That's why you hire good men and women to tend certain chores for you. A person can't be skilled in every area. Talented people save you money and headaches."

Leigh poured them more hot tea, and added sugar and lemon to hers. "Do you think they're worried about having a female owner?"

"No. I've talked to most of the area bosses since your arrival, and no one wants to quit the company."

Leigh smiled. "That's because you're still the boss. If you left the firm, Chad, I'd be lost, bankrupt within a month. You aren't thinking about starting your own business in Africa and moving there, are you?" Her blue gaze settled on him.

"If you're referring to that talk with Joseph—as I told him, I'm interested in new ventures, but not in moving on. I think it's wise for a man to have his own earnings and victories; does marvelous things

96

for him. But this place is home and life to me. I'm very happy here, Leigh. I hope you still feel that way after November."

She looked surprised. "Of course I will. I want to learn the business and help out, but I want you to continue running it."

Chad settled back in his chair behind the large desk. "You've seen the books, so you know how well we're doing."

"What about competition?" she questioned.

Chad leaned forward again and propped his elbows on the wooden surface. "There isn't any to concern us. Stokely Limited was burned down close to two years ago, and the head of it was murdered. The stockowners couldn't rebuild because it wasn't insured and the cost was too great. As for Elliott's of London, Brandon Elliott was the one accused of the arson and murder at Stokely, more for political than competitive reasons, or so the charges and evidence implied. We'll never know the truth, because he committed suicide."

"How awful. What a terrible way to lose your competition."

Chad shrugged. "Elliott had recently expanded and renovated, so he was deep in debt. Once it was announced he was to be arrested and he took his life to avoid disgrace, we collected on his debts by taking over his firm. William was the one who loaned him the money; they were planning some joint projects. There's an old saying, 'One man can't have good luck unless another man has bad luck.' Sometimes that's tragic but true. Until some smaller companies expand, Webster International practically owns a monopoly in our market."

"Speaking of luck, didn't you mention we'd had some recently?"

97

A broad smile filled Chad's face and eyes with pride. "We had several special orders come in last week, large contracts, Leigh. Elliott used to fill most of them. Hotels and restaurants wanting new drapes and linens, and fabrics to recover furniture. Those kinds of labor and materials are expensive. We'll make a big profit on them."

"If those jobs are so important and special, do you think we should be leaving the country for so long?" she queried.

"Our manager at Elliott's old firm knows what to do. He'll see that the jobs are handled with skill and speed. He and the clients know I demand the best quality and charge the most reasonable prices. Besides, one of them wants an exotic look to his restaurant, a jungle air, something different and exciting to obtain more business. I told him I would bring back native cloth, treasures, and trophies, at a nominal cost to him since I'll already be in Africa. Tropical plants, wicker and bamboo furniture, African colors and patterns on the chairs and tables, stuffed exotic birds or live ones in cages, native artifacts, clever lighting," he murmured his list. "I can close my eyes and envision it now. It'll be the talk of the town. I doubt there's an Englishman alive who doesn't want to go on a safari. This way, he'll get a taste of the jungle while enjoying a fine meal and drinks in familiar surroundings."

Leigh's eyes and cheeks glowed with anticipation. She liked this sunny side of her guardian. She wished he could be this way all the time. Without Louisa's influence and presence, maybe he could, although that would be dangerous for her, as Chad was much too appealing like this. "It sounds wonderful, Chad. With your help, it can be authentic. Whenever we go there, it'll remind us of our special trip together."

Chad's gaze met hers, and he looked at her a little too intimately and too long. Leigh hadn't meant her words as he seemed to be taking them. She felt herself growing warm and tense with anxiety. "More tea?" she offered, rising to fetch it to end the awkward moment.

It was time to ask Chad a rather troubling question. She had wanted to get to know Chad better before delving into the curious and possibly painful topic of her grandfather's will. Reading the will had told her why she didn't need to fear lethal mischief from her guardian, but not why the man who had become like a son to William Webster had been nearly excluded in favor of a stranger. Yes, she realized, Chad could inherit half of the wealth, but only after his mother's death. She was certain he didn't want the firm cut into pieces or a stranger to walk in and take partial control. If the other heir was a stranger . . . "Who is Jace Elliott," she asked, "and why does he inherit half of everything if I die? Why haven't I met him?"

If Chad was surprised by her question, it didn't show. But a sad look took away the glow from his eyes and too-handsome face. He exhaled heavily before responding.

"Jace Elliott was Brandon Elliott's only son. Brandon and William were longtime friends, and partners in the deal that got us his firm. He made out that codicil right before he died. Why, I have no idea. As far as I know, William hardly knew Jace. Mother, who gets the other half, wasn't told William had changed his will. It came as a shock to both of us. I know this might sound terrible, Leigh, and I loved that old man dearly, but he seemed to feel curiously guilty over Brandon's bad luck and suicide, almost as if he was to blame."

Leigh straightened in her chair as astonishment filled her eyes. "Are you saying Grandfather was involved with those . . . deeds?"

Chad was silent and thoughtful for a time. "I honestly don't know what to think, and that worries me. He seemed to take Brandon Elliott's death too hard, even for a good friend. He became moody and withdrawn, and he refused to tell me or Mother what was troubling him. As far as I know, William had no reason to leave half of his worth to Jace Elliott in the event . . ."

Leigh noticed how reluctant he was to finish that grim statement, and she was glad. She decided not to ask him why he had almost been precluded, as that could hurt and embarrass—or silence—him.

But Chad informed her, "William knew I would inherit Mother's share when she died, so I guess that was his way of including me. William knew, as manager of the firm and with the additional allowance he stipulated, I would have plenty of money for support, and I'm capable of making my own money. Besides, I'm only kin by marriage, so he didn't owe me anything. There is another speculation: William probably assumed Mother would fall in love and wed again. He could have feared her next husband might be tempted to harm you if she inherited everything on your death. It might have been an odd way to protect you. A few people do get crazy and dangerous ideas when this much money is involved. William trusted me, but he didn't tell me everything."

Leigh realized that Chad could inherit Fiona's half only if Fiona inherited it first. In a way, that still meant Chad had gotten little of an enormous estate which he had helped build, and which was owned by his stepfather. Of course, Fiona had her own inheritance for him to receive after she and her family. It was no secret his father had left little behind. "But why Jace Elliott?" she probed.

Chad shrugged. "Perhaps as a kindness to Brandon for losing everything. They were friends, and partners of a sort. If there was an agreement between them to leave Jace half if anything happened to Brandon and you, William didn't mention it, and it wasn't in their contract. Jace wasn't notified about the codicil, and I'm certain he doesn't even suspect what William did. Unless, as I said, it was part of their deal and Brandon told his son. You see, Jace was implicated in his father's crimes and he can't show his face in England. If he does, he risks arrest and prison or hanging. Besides, once you marry and have an heir, the codicil means nothing. You'll have a new will long before you die, Leigh, so this doesn't matter."

Leigh disagreed, but didn't say so. What if her grandfather had changed after his son's and wife's deaths? The business meant a lot to him, or he would have kept his family close to him. No, she couldn't let her past resentment and doubts cloud her judgment. Maybe her father had wanted to be on his own and live in America. "Where is this man?" she asked.

"I haven't seen Jace in two years, and he hasn't lived in England since he was eighteen. He left school and joined the Royal Navy. Afterward, he became an adventurer. William couldn't have known him well as a child or seen him much over the years. Jace lives in Africa, has a coffee plantation in the mountains there. It's possible you'll meet him while we're on safari. If he was involved in the treachery and needs money, it could be imprudent for him to learn what you're worth to him. You can discuss it with him, if you wish, but I think it would be most unwise. As for me, I'll admit I'm baffled and angered, and a little hurt, that William included a stranger instead of his stepson and friend. Yet, knowing the kind of man he was, he must have had a good reason. There's no need to worry, because the codicil will be of no value as soon as you wed."

Leigh was eager to meet Jace and learn the truth. Perhaps this was another reason why Chad wanted to proceed with the safari. "Do you think Jace Elliott is dangerous?"

Chad shrugged and pursed his lips. "I knew him years ago, Leigh, before all this trouble. He did a few bad things in the past, but that doesn't make him guilty of such evil."

"Why doesn't your famous Scotland Yard go after him?"

"Brandon Elliott left a hazy note implying Jace had been in on his crimes, but the police think he was crazy when he wrote it. As far as I know, there aren't any other witnesses or evidence against him. The problem is, he makes himself look guilty by refusing to come and answer questions. He's probably afraid they have more on him, and he's scared he'll be arrested and executed. Of course, he could be innocent but can't prove it, so he's taking no risks. As long as this charge is hanging over his head, he couldn't claim anything he might inherit. But he won't anyway, because you're young and healthy."

"What about his father's holdings? Did Mr. Elliott lose everything to us?"

"Not everything, but his wife sold the remainder and moved to Scotland to escape the scandal.

There's no reason for Jace to come back."

"Except to prove his innocence, if he isn't guilty."

"From what I remember, Jace was a proud and stubborn man. It wouldn't surprise me if he gets brave, or reckless, one day. In his place, I would never stop trying to clear my name and save my life."

"Neither would I. He must not be much of a man to take this lying down. I would scream and kick and fight all the way to the gallows."

Chad laughed heartily. "Me, too. We're a lot alike, Leigh."

She noticed that amorous warmth coming into his eyes and tone again. She halted it by continuing to speak, "Now I can see why he might be dangerous and should be kept in the dark. A bitter and wicked man who thinks he lost everything to us could want it back any way necessary."

He smiled and coaxed, "Don't worry, I'll protect you while we're in Africa. We aren't going near his plantation, so we'll probably miss him completely. If not, the codicil will be our little secret."

One I hope you keep better than the last! Leigh scoffed to herself. She had to know if Chad doubted her grandfather's guilt. "One more thing and the subject's closed, Chad. Do you think Grandfather was involved with Mr. Elliott in getting rid of their competition? Could Mr. Elliott's suicide have been to protect both of them? He and Grandfather had formed a sort of partnership, and that would explain why Grandfather felt responsible for Jace. He may have had a secret reason for planning this safari, such as wanting or needing to see Jace. If so, was it about those crimes, those business dealings, or the will?"

"I just don't know, Leigh," he murmured. "I

103

don't want to think William was capable of such treachery. But does anybody really know what another person feels and thinks, or what he's capable of doing? We all have our dark sides, our flaws and weaknesses, powerful urges to obtain our dreams at any price. These feelings have to be controlled. If not . . ." He paused. "That's how you separate the good men from the evil ones. I won't tell you not to worry about me, because I can be just as greedy and devilish as any man," he teased. "Does that make me sound—"

A knock on the door, interrupted Chad. Peering inside, Reid Adams remarked, "Martha told me Leigh was here, and you two were having tea. When you finish, I need to go over a few shipments. If you're in the middle of something, I'll wait outside."

"We're just talking, Reid, so please come in. Would you care for tea?" Leigh asked, glad for the timely intrusion.

"No, thank you. I'll be eating dinner early, and my appetite's already lagging. What have you two been doing today?" he inquired, his grayish-brown eyes alert, and his gaze troublingly direct.

To lift the heaviness in the office, Leigh quipped, "Showing Leigh how much she doesn't know about this business."

With a sly grin and shake of his head, Chad corrected, "Showing Leigh what she has to learn, but seeing how easily and quickly she'll succeed."

"Sounds as if you two have enjoyed yourselves," Reid hinted.

"A most satisfying day, Reid, my friend, most enjoyable. Leigh and I will work nicely together. She's confident but not cocky. She knows her strengths and weaknesses. Unlike most women, she isn't afraid or ashamed to admit either one. I find that most refreshing."

Leigh retorted with a smile. "You're biased, Chad, because we're family. Actually, you seem more like a brother than an uncle."

The ebony-haired man chuckled and jested, "Actually, Blue Eyes, I'm not either one by blood, and I'm glad."

"You don't like being my guardian?" she asked, trying to tease him out of his amorous mood.

"I love being your guardian. What man wouldn't? But family members make terrible friends, and I want us to be good friends."

Leigh wondered if Reid noticed Chad's flirtatious behavior. She had no choice in the ensuing silence but to say, "We *are* good friends, and I'm glad. I'll leave you two to talk business. I need to wash this hair. Some of those buildings we visited had a lot of dust and fuzz."

"It comes with the area, Leigh. Shall I hire more cleaning women?" he jested, then laughed as she sent him a scowl.

"It wasn't a complaint or criticism, just a reality. I'll find a carriage out front and go back to the hotel. Don't worry," she remarked at his reluctant gaze. "This is a good area and it's still daylight. I'll be fine. I have my trusty derringer with me, and I can shoot straight."

Chad stood and walked her to the door. "What about dinner? Would you like to join me later?"

She touched her blond hair and said, "I can't go out looking like this, and it takes my hair a long time to dry. We've stayed busy all day, so I think I'll rest tonight. Tomorrow will be a busy day, too; I'm going shopping and having lunch with Louisa and Cynthia. You don't mind, do you?" she asked in a carefully polite tone.

"I'm disappointed, but I'll survive. Louisa is occupied tonight, so I'll have to dine alone. You women have a good time tomorrow. Do you need any money?" he asked, reaching for his wallet.

She put her hand to his to halt him. "No, you've given me plenty. I've already purchased everything I need for the trip."

"You might see something special tomorrow," he said, holding her hand gently.

"If I do, I'll have them hold it until I contact you."

"You're a rich woman. You can afford to indulge yourself."

She laughed and told him, "If I spent money all the time like I have since arriving here, I'd be broke in a year."

Chad shook his head and released her hand to stroke her cheek. "I'd never let you go broke or wanting, Blue Eyes. I'm a good guardian and excellent business partner, remember?"

Leigh felt herself almost flinch. This man was unpredictable, and almost alarming at times. "You are, Chad, and I appreciate it. I'll see you soon. Good-bye, Reid," she said calmly, turning to smile at the sharp-featured man who was fetching himself a brandy.

Leigh left without saying anything else.

Reid sank into a comfortable chair and sipped the brandy. He watched Chad return to his place behind the mammoth desk. "What was that all about?" he asked his grinning friend.

Chad leaned back in his chair and glowed. "She's utterly amazing and totally fascinating, Reid. She's beautiful and desirable, unlike any woman I've known, and I've known plenty. She asks questions, she listens, she learns, and she's smart."

106

"Smart enough to fend off a lecherous old guardian," Reid jested.

Chad frowned. "That's the only thing I don't like about her."

"Why, because no object of your desire has ever spurned you?"

"She hasn't spurned me. She just hasn't leaned my way. But she will; she won't be able to control herself. I'm irresistible," he joked.

Reid bent forward, resting his forearms on his thighs. "Maybe she's trying to show you she wants you to be her guardian and friend—but nothing more. I think you're making her awfully nervous."

"You think so?" Chad asked, a worried look on his face.

"Does her conquest really matter?" Reid answered. "We're going to kill her in Africa, frame Jace for it, and have him executed. Once your mother inherits everything, you'll control Webster International, and it will all be yours one day. That is the plan?"

"*Was* the plan, Reid, old friend," Chad corrected, "I have a new one, a better one. If I marry Leigh, I can have it all, and now."

Reid straightened. "Don't tell me you've gotten snared in your own romantic trap. You haven't fallen in love with her, have you?"

"Love?" Chad repeated. "What is love, Reid? I surely don't know. Never experienced it. What I do know is that it's time for me to settle down. I need a proper wife and to sire my own heir. Respectability is demanded for men in our social position. Leigh's personality and character suit my needs, and her wealth and beauty do, too. As soon as the wedding ceremony is over, everything she has will belong to me. Everything."

"This could complicate all our plans. What about Jace and your revenge? I agreed to aid you because he did you wrong and we're best friends. Are you willing to forget justice merely so you can win Leigh? Has she come to mean that much to you in such a short time? Jace is still out there, free and unpunished — and a threat to you."

Chad's eyes chilled at dark memories. "I've worked hard on a clever plan for Jace's defeat. I took away Joanna, his father, and the Elliott name and business. All Jace has left is his life and plantation — a thriving business purchased with diamonds half belonging to me. He betrayed me, stole from me, and left me to die a horrible death. But I can't act rashly. There's only one safe way to prevent losing all I've worked for over the years, and that is by marrying Leigh and getting rid of Jace Elliott. In the secluded and romantic jungle of Africa, I can accomplish both dreams. Jace will never give up trying to clear himself. I can't allow him to survive. And I have no doubts I can win that beauty."

"The original plan was clean and simple: get rid of all obstacles. If you let this girl bewitch you and change things, it could fall apart."

"I won't let it. Leigh is perfect for the life I have in mind. Don't worry, old friend, I'll make certain nothing goes wrong with my new plan. If it does, I promise you won't be incriminated."

"What about Louisa? You know what Shakespeare said about a woman scorned. She'll rant and rave. You could lose it all."

"Louisa wouldn't dare give me any trouble," Chad vowed.

Reid Adams was troubled by Chad's impulsive behavior. His friend was never gullible or erratic. And Chad had never been lovesick; that worried

Reid most, because it clouded his thinking. Leigh was stronger and smarter than Chad realized; winning her didn't seem possible. It wasn't logical or safe to alter matters now. If anything went wrong . . . "Don't fool yourself, old friend. Louisa's in love with you, even if she is bad-mannered and irascible at times. She can make things embarrassing and uncomfortable for both of you. How would Leigh feel then? She doesn't want any trouble here with anyone, not when she's trying to break into our society and business world. If she's as smart as you think, she'll back off to prevent any problems. Then where will you be? You need Louisa on this safari, or the prim Leigh won't go."

"If Louisa presents a problem here, she's not going with us. If she makes any there, she'll be the one Jace kills and will die in Leigh's place. The way that bitch has been annoying me lately, I wouldn't mind getting rid of her for good. One thing for sure, Louisa can't be allowed to suspect her role in my plans. I'll keep her duped a while. As for Jace Elliott, finally I'll have justice and revenge. After I return home and marry Leigh, I'll have his plantation burned. That should lure him back to England to be executed legally. My hands will be clean."

"Why did you warn him when he returned to London?" Reid questioned. "He could have been captured and killed long ago."

"Before he dies, I want Jace to have time to suffer like he made me suffer. Killing him would have been simple and merciful. I didn't like killing Brandon Elliott," Chad admitted. "He was good to me over the years, better than my own father. But Jace forced me to strike where it would hurt the most: at his father, Joanna Harris, the business, his family name, and his damned survival. William shouldn't have left half to Jace instead of to me."

"Why didn't he, Chad?" Reid asked, "Do you think he suspected something? Did you kill William like you killed his wife?"

Chad was shocked by his friend's words. "No! I loved that old man, until he betrayed me after his death. William never knew I was responsible for his good fortune. We were like father and son. He helped me reclaim my social position, earn a fortune, whiten the family name my crazy father had blackened, and gave me self-confidence. I don't know why William left everything to Leigh, or made that insane codicil." Chad paused, lost in thought. "But you're right; he must have suspected I was responsible for Stokely and Elliott's bad luck. That's the only reason he would have left half of everything to Jace. But that bastard will never get his hands on anything of mine again!"

When Chad's frown increased, Reid added, "Leigh hasn't been here long, and she knows how you feel about this firm. If you go after her this soon, she'll think it's only the business you want."

"You're right. I'd better cool my ardor before I make a mistake with her, especially after Thursday night. I have a feeling Louisa was entangled in that mischief. I had a talk with her. She won't try anything stupid again because she doesn't want to lose me."

"If you suspect Louisa is to blame, why let her near Leigh? Louisa doesn't know about the will, so she probably assumes you'll get at least half if her rival meets with death. You and I know how much she wants you, old chap. But if Leigh dies and Jace doesn't, you'll never get that other half from him."

Confident, Chad responded, "Louisa will behave herself, and I need her a while longer. We'll both

110

watch her closely. As for Leigh, I have plenty of time for that delightful conquest."

"The slower you work, the better. She's a female to be wooed, not one to be swept off her feet and seduced. If you try to conquer her that way, my friend, she'll think she's no different from the rest of your prey. But what if your new plan fails? You could endanger it all."

"If I can't ensnare Leigh with love and marriage, I'll be forced to go back to my original plan. But, even if I'm forced to get rid of her, I don't want Louisa for a wife or as the mother of my children. One thing for certain, Reid, Laura Leigh Webster is a very special woman."

"And one marked for death, my enamored friend," Reid added, "if she doesn't fall under your spell. I never thought I'd see the day when Chadwick Hamilton became the love-smitten conquest. Keep your wits clear, old chap. She's a very valuable asset, so treat her that way. I'm glad you sent your mother away until this matter is settled. If anything goes wrong in Africa, she could be implicated."

"You're right. Mother has already made her sacrifice for me by marrying William so I could become his son. Now, maybe she can find a new man to wed, a rich and virile and titled one this time."

"What if the man she falls in love with is none of those things?"

Chad laughed mirthfully and shook his head. "Don't be fooled by my beautiful mother, old friend. Her angelic face and manner mask the same dark side I inherited from her. She had plenty of lovers while married to my unfortunate father, but she was always discreet. I'm certain she cooled her hot blood elsewhere while married to William.

111

Don't feel sorry for Fiona or concerned over her happiness. Mother can be a worse bitch than Louisa; she's just smart enough to conceal it. Where do you think I learned all my charm and skill?"

"You sound as if you hate her," Reid said.

"Heavens, no. She's a wonder, but I've never trusted her completely. She's too secretive with me. Frankly, I think this new plan is best. I wouldn't want Mother tempted by all that money and power. That would be a lethal mistake. For her sake, I hope she'll be satisfied with the payment I promised her for marrying William."

"But that was for half of everything when he died. Leigh got it all. If you marry her and take it, where does that leave Fiona?"

"Hopefully in some rich stallion's bed, and very soon so she'll forget that rash promise. Maybe she'll be too busy and wealthy to remember. While I'm in Africa seeking revenge, I plan to have a marvelous time and see what business ventures are available. Once Jace is destroyed and Leigh is mine, the dark past will be over, Reid. Only sunny years will lie ahead. Merciful heavens, I can hardly wait."

Leigh sat on her bed with her legs folded, brushing her damp hair. She fretted over Chad's behavior this afternoon. It annoyed and worried her. She had to find a way to control him or it would spoil everything. Her restless mind went to the stranger from the wharf. He was handsome, virile, charming—*perfect*. But she had not seen or heard from him in four days. He knew where she was staying and he had vowed to pursue her. What had happened to him?

Leigh tossed the brush aside and fingered the books she had purchased for the voyage to Africa: books by Dickens, Hugo, Twain, Hardy, Kipling, Melville, and Conrad. She loved to read, and she especially needed distraction tonight. She chose *Far from the Madding Crowd* by Thomas Hardy. After what the store owner had told her about it, perhaps she would discover something interesting and useful about men, women, and romance. For certain, she needed to learn more about dealing with all of them! She curled on the bed, opened the book, and began her "lessons."

Wednesday was a beautiful spring day, and things had been going well between Leigh and the two women. It was obvious to Leigh that Louisa and Cynthia were making a conscious—though false—effort to be nice to her. They had shopped for hours but purchased little. However, Louisa had made it a point to buy two rather daring night-gowns and to tease naughtily about how much Chad would like and enjoy them during the trip. The two friends had joked about how much luggage they were taking with them, how it would require ten extra bearers to carry their clothing and Oriental cosmetics.

Louisa had questioned Leigh at length about her Texas "beau," the ranch foreman Tyler Clark, and both the redhead and brunette had offered their matchmaking services with an eligible English no-bleman if that romance failed. Leigh had misled them to prevent more jealousy. Leigh had tried to learn more about her guardian, but Louisa had changed the subject each time as if to quell any interest. Over a lingering lunch, the two English-

113

women had talked of Fiona Webster's beauty and charms with envy, and about the safari with enthusiasm. But they had consumed too much champagne and their banter soon sunk to a risque and embarrassing level. The lunch had ended with Louisa making a toast: "To our new friendship and to a marvelous safari. May the best woman bring home the best prize." They had clinked glasses, then did the same with Leigh's before downing their contents. Leigh had taken several small sips then departed.

The following day, Leigh rested, read, and attempted to keep "Sir Lancelot" off her mind. It was difficult, because he kept sneaking into her head every few minutes. The man certainly knew how to rouse a woman's intrigue with his little waiting game.

Leigh remembered how his wavy hair fell over his right temple and how it curled under at his nape. She envisioned those mysterious and enticing green eyes with their hooded brows. He was so tall and strong, so masculine and virile. She recalled how his touch and nearness made her warm and trembly. She adored the little valley between his nose and upper lip, and the deep cleft in his proud chin. He had wonderful hands, powerful one moment and gentle the next. His smile was devastating to her senses, and she longed to see it again. And his voice, that smooth, suggestive English accent, it washed over her, enflaming her very soul. How she craved to hear it once more.

The mysterious stranger had seemed such a likable, easygoing man. He was humorous and fun, and he certainly knew how to get to a woman. Yes, she admitted, she was anxious to see him again, and soon.

Friday night, the group of five had dinner with a client named Sir David Lawrence and enjoyed *The Taming of the Shrew* at the theater. Afterward, they had coffee and dessert while discussing the performance. For the first time, Chadwick Hamilton had kissed Leigh's cheek after biding her good night.

Late Sunday night, Leigh lay in her bed with anticipation and suspense as her covers. The steamer was repaired. They were set to sail at eight in the morning. That meant being up and dressed by dawn, but her anticipation was so great she couldn't get to sleep. She was packed and ready, a second time, yet, she was reluctant to leave London.

She knew why: the green-eyed ghost who haunted her sleeping and waking moments. Late June was far away, and her return didn't even mean their paths would cross again. For all she knew, he'd gone his merry way to play his game with another woman. It had been over a week since she'd seen him in the garden, and he knew she was leaving tomorrow. Or did he believe she was already gone? Perhaps that was why he had made no attempt to see her.

No, she argued with herself. *If he's tracking and pursuing me as he claimed, he knows exactly where I am and when I'm sailing.* Before she faced the wild perils of the jungle, she had wanted to experience sweet passions again.

115

Chapter Six

Mombasa, British East Africa
April 13, 1896

The voyage was almost over and the steamship would be docking soon. It had required three weeks for the trip from London to Africa. The weather had remained clear and calm, preventing any rough seas or more delays, and Leigh was glad. It was three-thirty, but it did not get dark until after eight in this area astride the Equator. Passengers were in their cabins or staterooms, grooming themselves to leave the ship and preparing to watch the sights as they neared shore.

The ship had steamed down the English Channel into the Atlantic Ocean to skirt France, Spain, and Portugal. It had passed through the Strait of Gibraltar between Morocco and a British colony on the Rock, a wondrous sight, reaching to a height of thirteen hundred and eighty feet. The peninsula had been owned by the British since the eighteenth century and was a symbol of British naval strength.

They had sailed through the beautiful and tranquil Mediterranean Sea that separated Europe from Africa. They had neared Egypt and the Suez Canal, which crossed the Isthmus of Suez, connecting the

116

Mediterranean to the Red Sea. In 1888, the canal had been opened to all ships and nations in wartime or peace, and no acts of hostility were allowed in its waters, though it was considered to be still hazardous.

Leigh had stayed on deck during the time it required to pass through the area. She had heard how many ships had failed to make this crossing, but plans were being made to widen and deepen it even more. As it was so important to international trade, she knew everyone would be delighted when that was done. As for their voyage, the canal had saved them four thousand miles over the cape route.

They had entered the calm Red Sea to reach the Gulf of Aden. At Cape Asir, they had sailed southward in the Indian Ocean along the African coast. Before nightfall, they would dock at Mombasa.

Mombasa, her mind echoed in anticipation. It was one of the oldest cities in Africa. By the ninth century, ships filled with silks, spices, carpets, porcelain, and other luxurious goods sailed on the northeast winds from India and Arabia to this area during the winter to spring season. From spring to winter, opposing, favorable southwest winds carried ships from Mombasa to transport ivory, skins and hides, rhino horns, slaves, oilseeds, kanga and kikoi cloth, mangrove poles, coral, tortoise and cowry shells, ambergris, and wild coffee. The territory had reached its golden age as a center of coastal commerce during the seventeenth and eighteenth centuries, and was still dominated by that activity.

As she completed her grooming and packing, Leigh reflected on what she had been told about British East Africa, particularly Mombasa. The traders had come first, the Arabs and Chinese and others with their caravans — seeking the wealth of ivory, animal hides, and slaves. By the fourteen hundreds, Mombasa was a substantial town with a premier position on the coastline, along which was a chain of Omani Arab trading posts, ruled by the Sultan of Zanzibar. Mombasa was a prosperous city that many nations craved but Britain now ruled.

The area had changed hands many times over the centuries. The Portuguese had sacked and claimed Mombasa in 1505, and dominated the coast and trade route to India for many years. But the Omanis had wanted East Africa, and the two opponents had battled time and time again for its possession. Then, the Dutch, Persians, Belgians, Italians, Germans, French, and British had moved in, and the greedy scramble for portions had begun in 1879. In '84, the "Dark Continent" had been divided into "spheres of influence" at a Berlin conference, to which no Africans were invited.

The missionaries had arrived next to "Christianize and civilize" the natives. Many battles had resulted in the struggle for religious supremacy. Many of them had been—and so remained—financed by the Church Missionary Society of London. One such battle in Uganda had culminated in that area being claimed as a British protectorate, and later the area she was to visit.

Other battles had come about as the results of political and racial differences, such as the Zulu war in '79 and the Jameson Raid against the Dutch Boers last year. Her studies had taught Leigh that Africa could indeed be a dangerous place.

During the voyage, she had listened to many conversations. Most passengers—who were heading for Rhodesia—viewed Africa as an exotic paradise, with its tropical climate, abundance of big game, splendid landscape, and a large supply of cheap native labor. Others claimed it was a harsh, unpredictable, and perilous land that could devastate any reckless man and could drain the very life from him. Leigh had decided she would draw her own conclusions after she visited East Africa—one day to be renamed Kenya—and completed her safari.

Leigh smiled, thinking how pleasant the trip had been so far. Louisa Jennings and Cynthia Campbell had been on their very best behavior, and Chad had cooled his excessive ardor toward her. Even Reid had been friendlier and fun to be around. There had been dances, and dinners, parties and teas, interesting conversations, and lessons in skeet shooting to absorb her time and energy. She had enjoyed that sport, as it had allowed her to practice for the safari.

The ship's horn blasted in the quiet air, alerting the few departing passengers they were near port. Quickly Leigh fastened her last case, locked her door, and hurried to the deck to view the sights.

Leigh was wearing a pale blue day dress and carrying a parasol to shield her eyes from the bright tropical sun. She sighted Chad and the others at the railing and went to join them. "It's so exciting," she said to him, as he turned to smile at her.

"We finally made it. I can't wait to get into that jungle."

"Me, too," murmured Louisa and possessively took his arm.

There was a sparkling glare from the water's surface, and the air was hot as it blew into Leigh's face. She raised her parasol to shade her squinted eyes. Despite the ocean breeze and the thin material of her dress, she felt beads of moisture forming on her face and body. She had never been in the

119

tropics before, but she had been told the coastal temperatures were warm all year. The coolest season in this equatorial area was in July, about eighty degrees. The warmest month was March, when it reached nearly ninety. But the nights were supposed to be pleasant, dipping only into the sixties. Of course, rain showers were frequent from April to September.

The steamship sailed past stretches of wheat-colored sand that drifted into prolific undergrowth of succulents and mangrove. The coral coast with its idyllic reef lagoons and sylvan beaches beckoned to Leigh. The cautious vessel sailed into the narrow channel toward the small island where they would drop anchor. From there, they would be transported into Mombasa. The British flag could not fly over this landing area, because it was the property of Simba—the Sultan of Zanzibar—and Britain paid him fees to use it.

Chad pointed out a variety of boats that were preparing to meet them and vie for their business. "Look . . ." he gestured to Fort Jesus, a symbol of past domination during the time the Portuguese had tried to destroy the Arab grip over trade here.

Leigh's eyes returned to her destination. She gazed at the emerald setting that was outlined against an azure sky, and beyond the blue ocean. Her pulse raced with suspense. She saw mango trees and coconut palms, almost dazzlingly white flat-topped homes, coral block structures with red or white roofs, Arab *dhows* with billowy sails, and Moslem mosques that told a history of trade and intwined cultures.

"We'll go ashore first," Chad announced, "then our possessions will be unloaded and sent to the hotel. I've paid a man to take care of that task for us. Come along, ladies. Let's find carriages and take a better look at this town."

Chad selected the Arab *dhows* to give them an entertaining boat ride. When their group reached the landing steps, individual rickshaws were rented to carry them from the island into town to their hotel. They crossed a wooden bridge and traveled down a dirt street.

Leigh was amazed by how fast the men could run while pulling an occupied rickshaw. Their pace was steady and swift, as if hurrying to get in as much business in one day as possible. The runners appeared to be in excellent condition, but the day was hot and the distance was long for such a gait. As she traveled, she wondered how they held up under such a burden in this climate. Yet the ride was surprisingly smooth; it was fun, and gay laughter spilled forth. All Leigh's senses were alert, but the unfamiliar and intriguing sights flashed by too fast to suit her. She couldn't wait to savor them at her leisure.

The town was large, spread over a wide area. Streets went in all directions. Many were shadowed by two- and three-story buildings and homes of coral block or stucco with high-pitched *makuti* roofs. Huge, ornate doors — some inlaid with silver designs — sealed off the interiors from courtyards brightened by the hot sunlight. Windows had shutters to hold back the intense light and intricate grills for protection. Many homes had verandas and balconies on upper levels.

Shops were everywhere, of every description, size, and purpose. Stalls lined some streets where colorful fabrics from India, China, Arab countries, and other lands were for sale. She glanced at the costly silks and satins. At other stalls or along the street,

121

native cloth such as *kanga,* bark cloth, and *kikoi* were on display. Within a few feet, artistically woven baskets, fresh fish, unknown foods, and other goods were offered.

Leigh noticed items made from ivory, coral, tortoise shell, cowry, gold, silver, brass, ebony, hides, and rhino horns. Merchants sat amongst sacks and piles of aromatic tea, coffee, spices, fruits, and nuts. In the rickshaw, she passed Moslem women, veiled in black *chadors* and the traditional *bui-bui* garment as they strolled the streets making their purchases. She saw people in an assortment of clothing and accessories: African tribesmen in their bright garb and fascinating jewelry, bearded Sikhs in black turbans and white *kanzu* robes, British in their white or khaki clothing, and others in their own country's raiment. There were peoples of all walks of life and from all nations: Arab, Indian, Persian, African, European, Asian.

It was a crowded, busy, and enchanting sight. She inhaled odors she did not recognize, mostly from the strange foods being cooked and sold. She took in deep breaths when she passed spice sellers, and savored those delightful smells. She enjoyed the heady fragrance of tropical flowers, some being sold near the streets, and her nose told her that breads and pastries were being prepared close by. She savored the wonderful aromas.

Some areas were noisy and cluttered where men were hawking their goods and services, and people speaking several languages were haggling noisily or bartering briskly over prices. Others, where owners were content to relax and await customers, were quiet and calm. She heard laughter and snatches of conversations. The predominate language was Swahili, a mixture of Bantu and Arabic, but it also borrowed heavily from other languages, including English. Swahili was the common link between this melting pot of races.

Leigh heard the creaking of carts and the heavy fall of oxen's hooves as goods were taken here or there at a leisurely pace. She heard the clinking of metals as brass containers were examined. She heard merchants yelling at her group to halt and inspect their wares. She heard wind whistling past her ears.

By the time they reached the hotel, it was six-thirty. Chad had selected one away from the noisy coast and bazaar area in a section of lush greenery and quiet seclusion. The rickshaws halted before the entrance, and Chad paid the runners.

"Jambo, rafikis. Karibu, bwana, bibi. Oonitwa nani?" the hotel doorman greeted them. When no one responded and Chad said they didn't understand, he repeated in English, "Hello, friends. Welcome, sir, ladies. What is your name?"

As Chad conversed with the man and the others gazed about and chatted, a large cart arrived with their belongings.

Chad grinned and remarked to the man in charge, "You said you were prompt. A job well done, my man. I hope you were careful."

"Plenty careful," the man responded, grinning broadly in anticipation of a fat tip from the well-dressed Englishman.

Hotel helpers were given instructions about the luggage and crates, and they went to work moving the baggage to the appropriate rooms. The crates for the safari were to be stored in a separate room: the cleverly invented Kodak box cameras, a gramophone and records, silver, crystal, china, table-cloths, wine, special blends of tea, and other "necessities" to make their journey comfortable.

123

"Everyone get settled in and refreshed," Chad told his group. "Then, we'll meet downstairs for dinner at eight. I'm hungry as a lion."

In her suite, Leigh paced the floor, tense from the episodes during dinner. Louisa had been in a foul mood, Chad had been too attentive to Leigh, and Reid and Cynthia had been strangely silent. Louisa's mood had worsened when Chad had danced with his ward, then ignored the sullen red-head for most of the evening. Leigh had escaped at the first available moment, but only after teasing Chad into dancing with Louisa to calm the woman. Chad seemed surprised and annoyed that their guide, Jim Hanes, hadn't arrived by the time their native meal ended. Leigh was eager to begin their safari, to get into the lush jungle and out of the hotel where she felt cooped up.

Leigh fretted that if Louisa's behavior didn't improve, Chad was going to end their relationship any moment! If he did, the Texas girl worried, Chad might aim his sights on her!

A pouring rain began. Leigh hurried to the door that opened onto a private balcony overlooking a lush garden below it. The torches were extinguished by the heavy rainfall, and smoke escaped skyward until it was obscured by the water. Heavy drops pelted loudly on the tropical plants with their large leaves, beating upon the fragrant hibiscus, bougain-villaea, and frangipani and sending delicate blossoms to the ground. Yet the breeze accompanying the heavy shower was like a caress upon Leigh's face and body. Fireflies no longer danced with the flowers in the garden, but the distant sounds of music and birds and tree frogs drifted to her ears. It was dark, because the silvery moon was hidden behind clouds. She leaned against the doorjamb and closed her eyes as she inhaled the scents and listened to the sounds of nature.

Leigh's dreamy mind floated toward another topic and affixed itself there: the mysterious stranger in London. She had thought of him constantly during the voyage and she chided herself for scheming how to locate and ensnare him, and for avidly searching every face and deck of the ship with the hope he was aboard. He hadn't been, and he could be anywhere in England by now, could be anywhere in the world. Yet the thought of never seeing him again brought on intense feelings of loneliness and anguish.

How, she questioned herself, could she feel so strongly about a man she barely knew? She had not seen him in a month, exactly a month today, yet, she could picture him as clearly as if he were standing before her this moment: that windblown brown hair, those secretive green eyes, that bronzed face, that muscular body. He kept intruding on her happiness and concentration. How could such brief encounters have had such a stunning effect on her? If only he weren't so unforgettable, so alluring, so magnetic!

If only you knew his name, her troubled mind retorted, *where he lives, what he does for a living . . . if you'll see him again.*

Leigh traced her fingertips over her parted lips and called to mind the kisses he had placed there, kisses that had stolen her breath and wits and caused her to behave intimately and passionately. "Who are you? Where are you?" she whispered in torment. "You can't leave things this way between us. You can't. And, if you're married, I'll kill you

125

for tempting me and teasing me."

One thing Leigh found amusing—or ironic—was the fact that she now viewed Louisa in a different light. Since meeting the elusive stranger, she now understood how fiery passion could consume a person and how frustrating and alarming it was to desperately desire someone you couldn't win. And how maddening it was to be just another conquest to a man you loved, a man to whom you had given your all. Perhaps it did make a woman act impulsive, brazen, jealous, and even rude at times. Maybe she did understand Louisa—and love—a little better now.

Love? her mind echoed, and she deliberated that condition. No, Leigh reasoned, she couldn't be in love with that emerald-eyed rogue who haunted her day and night. She did not know him well enough for that to be true. But, she admitted, her feelings were traveling in that direction. She was physically and emotionally attracted to him, yet she knew, love required far more. It also required knowing, respecting, and liking a man.

Leigh smiled as warm memories filled her head. Her mother had told her of those matters when she was only fourteen and had her taste of first love. Her mother had tried to explain the difference between infatuation, physical attraction, and real love: emotional facets Leigh had not fully understood until now. "Thank you, Mother," she murmured.

Leigh left the doors open to listen to the rain while she tried to quell her tension and prepare for sleep. She doused the lamps and climbed into bed. "Africa," she whispered. "You're actually in Africa."

* * *

The next three days passed in a blur. On Tuesday, the women were confined inside because of the heavy rains and mud. Chad and Reid sought their guide without success. Leigh spent the day reading. Dinner passed smoothly and genially, revealing that Chad and Louisa had settled their differences last night, much to Leigh's relief.

On Wednesday, they took a ride in a *dhow* to a small island where they enjoyed a picnic at a beautiful lagoon. Afterward, they strolled around town to see the sights and to shop. Leigh and Chad, with Louisa's assistance, selected and purchased many items for their client's restaurant in London, and everyone seemed to enjoy themselves.

Thursday morning, the women were told to relax again at the hotel while Chad and Reid checked out business ventures in Mombasa. At dinner, Chad told them that their guide, Jim Hanes—who had gone inland last week—had not returned to his office yet. All they could do was wait, and have fun. But he did reveal plans for a special evening the following night: a party at Alfred Johnston's home, and on Chad's thirty-second birthday.

Friday morning, Leigh sneaked out to go shopping for a birthday gift for her guardian. She was not away long, and for a good reason. During the entire time, she felt as if she were being watched. It wasn't unexpected for strangers to receive attention and stares, but the gaze she sensed was evil and intimidating. She had searched the buildings and crowds but couldn't find anyone suspicious spying on her. Uneasy, she had returned to her suite to put away her packages and to drop her derringer inside her purse.

At two o'clock, Chad came to Leigh's suite with an unexpected gift for her. After unwrapping it, she glanced at him and murmured, "It's exquisite."

"An exquisite necklace for an exquisite neck," he replied. "It's very old and valuable, but it belongs to you. It was part of the Webster estate, and Mother thought you should have it. I found it in the safe the day before we sailed, and I was saving it for a special moment. Wear it tonight if it matches your gown," he coaxed.

"It will, and I shall," she responded happily to the treasure. "I have something for you, too." She fetched his two gifts and said, "Happy birthday, Chad," and handed them to him.

He opened the first one and withdrew a two-foot blade. As he examined and admired it, she explained, "It's a *simi,* a bush knife for rituals. I thought you could hang it in your office as a souvenir of our safari . . . Now open the other one," she coaxed eagerly.

He did so, and she related, "It's a carved statue of Ngai, the Kikuyu god who lives atop Kere-Nyaga, the tall mountain here. Isn't the workmanship wonderful?"

"They're both magnificent, Leigh. Thank you," he said, and kissed her cheek. "I'll always treasure them. They're the best birthday gifts I've ever received. No, the best gifts for any occasion, because you selected them with the best motive of all: friendship."

Leigh smiled, but tensely. Chad was standing too close, was smiling too warmly, and was gazing at her too tenderly. Yet, for once, his mood seemed genuinely affectionate and sincere. That worried her even more than his overt flirtation. "Where is

128

Louisa?" she asked to bring him back to reality.

Chad realized he was making her jittery again, so he slowed his pace. "Taking a nap. She's expecting a long and busy evening. Why don't you rest, too? We'll leave at seven." Chad took his gifts, thanked her again, and left.

Leigh was dressed in the sapphire- and cream-gown she had worn the night she had been attacked on the London wharf. Thanks to the delay in departing, it had been repaired in time to bring with her for special occasions.

Her tawny hair was swept up on the sides and secured atop her head with the new blue aigrette. The remainder of her wavy mane flowed down her back like a golden river. She lightly dusted her lids with the blue powder Louisa had sent to her room, and smeared a thin coating of pink cream on her lips.

Leigh lifted the necklace that Chad had given to her. She had never seen her grandmother wear it, but she had been around the woman on very few important occasions. The blonde was delighted that Chad and his mother had passed it along to her, but was surprised Fiona had parted with the unusual treasure.

Leigh studied it with keen interest and admiration. On a delicate gold chain was attached an irregular-shaped piece of labradorite, an iridescent blue feldspar whose surface alluded to a dreamy underwater world. With very little imagination, one could easily pick out gently undulating algae and a sunken ship that had found its final resting place on the sandy floor of a deep blue ocean. She fastened the necklace around her neck.

When the correct time arrived, Leigh left her suite. As she descended the steps, Chad came forward to meet her. His blue gaze swept over her, then alighted briefly on the necklace.

"Does it go all right with this gown?" she asked.

"It makes me think of peaceful oceans, and sunken treasure ships, and magical sirens. You look absolutely stunning tonight. Every man in the room—single or married—will be aching for your company."

She laughed softly. "You do wonders for a woman, Chad. Thank you, for the compliment and the keepsake." As they hesitated at the stairs chatting, Louisa came to join them.

"Ready to go?" she hinted, watching Chad observe Leigh in a disturbing manner. "You look lovely. That necklace is beautiful."

Leigh fingered it and said, "It belonged to my grandmother, so I inherited it when Grandfather died. It's exquisite, is it not?"

"You're lucky those ruffians didn't steal it when they accosted you. Isn't that the same gown you were wearing that night?"

Since Leigh knew that Chad had revealed the episode to his flame-haired lover, Leigh had also related her experience to Louisa during the voyage and asked her to keep her secret. "Yes, but it was repaired in time to bring it along. As for this treasure, I wasn't wearing it that terrible night. Chad passed it along to me only this afternoon."

"How fortunate for you that he brought it with him. It's perfect with the gown. And I like your eyes and lips."

"Thank you for loaning the cosmetics to me. You'll have to tell me where to order them when we return home."

"Why don't you simply borrow mine until November," the redhead suggested, "then I'll give you a whole supply for your twenty-first birthday. And Chad can throw a huge party for you. Won't that be fun?"

"Sounds wonderful to me," Chad declared. "You ladies ready?"

Both said, "Ready," and they exchanged glances and laughter.

The estate at the edge of town was elegant and large: a white stucco, three-story mansion nearly surrounded by the lush greenery of wild Africa. There were about seventy guests: a mixture of Britains, with a few Arabs, French, and Indians. All were either close friends or local business acquaintances of their host, Alfred Johnston, who had invited her group the moment he heard they were in Mombasa.

Music was being played in several rooms, and champagne and wine flowed. Treats had been placed here and there for guests to nibble on after the sumptuous dinner had been completed. Floral fragrances wafted through the mesh-covered windows that kept out mosquitoes and other insects. Everyone was dressed in his or her finest garments and the rooms were vivid with the array of colors from the ladies' gowns and jewels. Men's talk and pipe smoke drifted through the cleverly decorated areas, and women's laughter floated through the air with them.

Leigh had danced many times, and sipped a little champagne. She was admiring a painting when her host asked her to join him for the next dance. She walked to the appropriate room and slipped into his

131

arms. They chatted in a cordial manner as they moved about the room. Alfred Johnston was an interesting man whose company she enjoyed. She recalled seeing his name on a warehouse door at the wharf that terrible night. When she mentioned it, he explained about his export/import business.

As he spoke, she studied him. He appeared to be over fifty, with salt-and-pepper hair, and a lean body. His face was pleasant and darkly tanned from the tropical sun. He was around five feet ten inches tall, and a good dancer. She liked his heavy English accent, and notice how educated and intelligent he seemed. From what she had observed during the evening, he was happily married, and was well-liked and respected in the area. He was also very wealthy and good-humored.

Their conversation moved to the impending safari. He enlightened her on the jungle, wild beasts, natives, and African history. He warned her about harmful vegetation, insects, and snakes, and how to avoid them. She noticed how his dark eyes glowed with love and pride for his adopted land. His mood and manner were infectious, making Leigh even more eager to get her journey underway. If only their guide would arrive!

As her second dance with him ended, he suggested, "Why don't you come into my special room and view the artwork there?"

Leigh accompanied Alfred to the rear of the mansion and into a large room whose walls were covered with magnificent paintings and artifacts. Small tables held other treasures that he had collected from Africa and around the world. She looked around, fascinated.

"Each one has a special story and adventure behind it," he hinted.

"Please, sir, tell me all of them. Or as many as time allows," she entreated eagerly. "What about this vase?" she asked, pointing to one with Egyptian symbols and pictures painted on it.

Before Alfred Johnston could relate any stories, a Hindu servant summoned him. "Stay here and look around if you wish. I'll return later and fill your ears." He excused himself and left the room.

Leigh walked to a painting of a group of lions and gazed at it.

Jace Elliott halted at the doorway and stared at the woman's back. At last the people he was awaiting had arrived. He had begun to worry that he had been tricked into leaving London. For weeks he had stewed over this mystery and fretted over Laura's involvement in it. He had met the most beautiful and desirable woman ever seen, only to discover she was his enemy's ward, or so she claimed. He had met her under curious conditions that made him suspicious. The men who had attacked her were certainly not sailors! Then she had mentioned a safari during their second meeting, a safari with the man who wanted to destroy him.

Of all places in Africa, he reasoned, why would Chad come to his territory? How had this enchanting creature come to be his foe's ward, and why had he brought her along? That bastard was up to something, and Jace needed to learn what his former friend had in mind. He suspected he was being lured into a deadly trap and this female perhaps the means to blind him to the pitfalls ahead.

He would have to thank Alfred again for including Chad's group tonight and for agreeing to lure Laura away from the guests and her guardian. He wanted their reunion to occur in private. If he was going to learn anything from her, he had to take her off guard. Jace never doubted for a minute that Chad had come to Africa for revenge and that this female was part of Chad's plot. But, he mused, how and where did she fit into his foe's treacherous scheme? And was she a willing participant? The suspense had chewed on his nerves. "One never knows whom one might meet in Africa, does one, Miss Laura Leigh?" a husky voice asked from behind her.

Recognizing it instantly, Leigh whirled and gaped at the man whose vision had haunted her for over a month. He was leaning negligently against the doorjamb and grinning broadly. His brown hair was combed neatly, and he was attired for this occasion in a dashing white linen suit. The tapered coat and pants evinced his muscular physique, their snowy color enhancing his dark tan and matching his teeth. His eyes were like flaming emeralds, and she felt consumed by their roaring blaze. Her pulse and heart raced, and her breath was stolen. Joy flooded her and washed away her wits. Unable to move again, she stared at him. "I didn't think I would ever see you again," she murmured as her softened eyes seemed to caress him.

"Didn't you now, my enchanting damsel in distress?" he teased, coming forward and halting within inches of her. His engulfing gaze never left her wide blue one. "I had no doubts whatsoever that we'd meet again, and again, and again," he vowed in a tone which caused Leigh to warm and tingle. "But you made me wait too long," he added.

Chapter Seven

"I don't understand . . ." she murmured, her wits scattered by his unexpected presence and close proximity. He looked so handsome in his well-made suit, and he smelled wonderful. His smile was dazzling with those white teeth set amidst a darkly tanned face of handsome features. "I don't even know your name or where you live. I don't even think I thanked you properly for your gallant rescue that first night."

"But you did thank me, remember?" he hinted, seductively passing his tongue over his sensual lips as his fingers grazed hers lightly.

Leigh grasped his meaning and warmed even more at the recall of the stolen kisses they had shared. She trembled at his touch and stepped backward without even knowing it. "No matter. I wish to make certain I've done so properly. What are you doing here?"

"Trailing you, of course," he teased, stepping forward again.

"Isn't that what *I'm* suppose to do this time?" she came back too quickly. She watched his gaze travel over her, and hesitate at her throat. She saw his green eyes narrow and chill.

Harsh memories rushed into Jace's head. "That was the original plan. What took you so long to get here?" he demanded almost harshly. "I was about to give up on you and go home."

Leigh noticed that the playful mischief in his gaze had shifted to an emotion she did not understand. There was a sharp edge to his voice now, and that disturbed her. She wondered why hostility and cynical accusation seemed to exude from him. She sensed a tightly leashed anger and tension coming from the man. How mercurial he could be, she decided in annoyance. Baffled and alarmed by this egnimatic stranger who evinced a streak of danger, she replied, "Our ship was in need of repairs and we were delayed for a week. Now, if you'll excuse me, I'll rejoin the party." She tried to sweep by him, but he gently caught her forearm.

He faced her. "Won't Chad be angry if you fail to enchant me? With a little effort, Miss Leigh, it could be an easy and possibly enjoyable task. Try it. I know Chad will be pleased since he wants me here so badly. Don't fail twice in a mission."

Leigh looked at him in utter bewilderment. Since he was dressed for the occasion and was inside the house, he must have been invited by their host. He seemed at ease, not cautious and alert as he had been those other two times. Why had he come to Africa, and how had he wrangled an invitation to this party? And what was all this about Chad? She stared at him, then said, "I don't follow you."

He threw back his head and filled the room with a hearty laughter which belied his fury with William Webster for giving his mother's most prized necklace to Chad's ward—or for selling it to Chad to use as a seductive token. The items in

136

his father's safe had been special family possessions, belonging to Jace. The old man had no right to those sentimental and ancestral treasures, or to get rid of them without giving Jace the opportunity to reacquire them himself. No doubt it had been part of the settlement for those faked debts! Then, for Chad to use Laura's lovely neck to flaunt it in his face tonight was too much of a challenge, something that demanded repayment. To make matters worse, according to the hotel desk clerk, Webster hadn't even come with them to Mombasa. Now Chad was trying to hire him, *him*, to lead their safari! No doubt his ward was the bait to entrap him, since Chad had a mistress along. But, Jace mused, was her role a willing one? He had to be firm to provoke information from her. "I don't understand. I don't follow you," he mocked her claims. "I warn you, Miss Leigh, don't tempt me to alter my first impression of you. That could be a dangerous mistake," he threatened.

Leigh gaped at the man as if he were insane. She was too stunned to jerk free and run from the room. Why, she wondered, was he threatening her, taunting her, playing crazy games with her?

"I thought you were only a beautiful woman in trouble that night in London. For your sake, I hope that's true. If you're under Chad's spell, I'd advise you to break it and sail home on the first ship to America. This is no place for a delicate creature, and Chadwick Hamilton is a voracious beast who will devour a careless victim like yourself. Did you tell him about our meeting, or did he already know I was in London? Did he arrange our little encounter near the docks? Were you supposed to snare me for him?"

137

he questioned deviously.

That burst of words clearly told Leigh the two men were not friends. As for his other questions, she was completely confused. Dismay, and a little fear, flooded her seawater eyes. She yanked her arm from his light grasp and glared at him. "I don't know what you're talking about, sir. How could I tell my guardian about you when you've never told me your name—or anything about you? He's going to be furious that you followed me here and that you're being so hateful. If you want to stay out of trouble, then steer clear of me. I don't want to hear any more of your accusations."

Leigh brushed past him and headed for the door, then she halted and turned. Something strange was going on, and she needed—wanted—to discover what was afoot. With bravery and boldness, she approached him and said, "Yes, I do want to know. What *do* you mean and why are you so angry?"

He focused that challenging gaze on her and asked, "Were we supposed to meet that night in London? Did Chad want us to meet and get acquainted? Were you supposed to lure me here for some reason? I know how sly Chad can be, and I know he wants me here with you."

Leigh mistook his meaning. She recalled Chad's words about "stunning a friend of mine." This stranger had been dressing for dinner when he had rushed to rescue her. He had gotten angry when she mentioned Chad's name and her dinner appointment. Could he have suspected that Chad was throwing them together, and he didn't like it? Had their first meeting been arranged to make this man interested enough in her that he would come along with them? That would be ridiculous and dangerous. Yet she questioned, "Are you the man I was supposed to meet that night? Does Chad want you to come on safari with us? Tell me exactly what you're accusing me of doing."

It was Jace's turn to be unintentionally misled by her words. She had taken a long time to come up with an answer, a bad one. "Come, Laura, don't play more games with me. I'm here now. We both know that meeting on the wharf was no accident, and your mention of this safari wasn't, either. The woman I rescue *just happens* to be Chad Hamilton's ward. This ward *just happens* to mention they're leaving Monday on safari. Her guardian *just happens* to want me along," he scoffed.

"Tell the truth. It was a clever ruse to catch my attention, to get me here with you, wasn't it? How did Chad know I was hiding there?" Cold lights glittered in his verdant gaze. A tight sneer controlled his mouth and a tic appeared along his chiseled jawline. "Well?" he demanded. "Did you lose your courage after getting a look at me? Was old Chad angry after you seemed to fail in your assignment?" he almost snarled. "I'm here now, so what do you two want with me?"

Leigh shook her head to clear her wits. "I wasn't trying to meet you, and I didn't tell you I was coming to Africa so you would track me here. I was trying to discourage your interest because you seemed devilish and smug, and maybe dangerous. I take it you know Chad?"

He obviously didn't like her response. Leigh saw his furious gaze return to her necklace and linger there, growing colder and narrower by the minute.

For an instant, she thought he was going to snatch it off her throat. Yet, when his gaze returned to hers, it was relaxed and enticing!

In case she might be telling the truth, Jace decided to soften his approach. "What else will you take from me, my tawny lioness?" he asked in a lazy voice.

His abrupt change took her by surprise, and she found herself gazing into those hypnotic green pools. She broke herself from their spell and queried, "Why should I want anything from a total stranger with such a quicksilver manner?"

"Well, I don't suppose you want to come to my hotel room and retrieve your possessions. I can see you've already replaced them, or Chad did it for you," he stated in an insulting tone.

Leigh's cheeks flamed with vexation. "That is quite enough, Mr.— Whoever you are! I told you to keep them. I don't need any reminders of that horrible night."

"You really shouldn't have worn such an elegant gown that night after agreeing to that little ruse with those . . . so-called sailors. I wondered why they gave up so quickly and easily. I imagine they weren't paid enough to get beaten up by me, just enough to catch my interest and attention. Tell me, Laura, how far would you have gone with them while awaiting my rescue? What if I'd already left my hiding place and wasn't there to be ensnared by your little game?"

Leigh wasn't one to react violently to situations, but at his implication her hand lifted before she even realized it.

He seized it in midair and pinned it behind her, bringing their bodies into intimate contact. "Temper, temper," he teased. "Such potent fire in those entrancing eyes. So beautiful and devious. Not such a delicate lady after all. Chad has taught you well about wild perils and sweet passions. Sometimes it's too dangerous and costly to walk a wild trail, Miss Leigh. You should retreat before it's too late."

"I don't know what's behind all this, but I don't like it, or *you!* When I returned to the hotel that night, I checked the dinner invitation. It said Stems Street, not St*a*ms, so the mistake was mine, not Chad's. Stop accusing him and me of trying to entrap you. Our first meeting was an accident, and *you* arranged the second one! First, you entice me to chase you, then, you threaten me to go away. I don't understand you, and I don't like your behavior."

Her defense of his enemy annoyed him. Yet he was captured by the innocence in her eyes and tone. Maybe it had been fate's design. Her eyes seemed to freeze into chips of blue ice, warning him of her rapidly rising fury.

"Take your hands off of me this instant. If there's a problem between you and my guardian, your quarrel does not include harassing and insulting me. I won't respond to your absurd accusations further, except to say I honestly was attacked that night in London. No tricks were involved on my part. If you don't release me this minute, you brute, I'll scream very loud," she warned.

"And spoil Chad's plans for all of us?" he taunted, appearing not the least troubled by her threat. He started off using the crazy coincidence to provoke her into revealing something — anything — useful, then summoned a crafty ruse. When she twisted in his arms and looked ready to call out, he added, "Not to mention the humiliating scene it would create in Alfred's home. You'll ruin the party and start a lot of nasty gossip. Naturally I'll announce it's a lover's spat. After all, we met secretly twice in London. If Chad didn't sic you on me, he'll be most vexed and intrigued by that news. Shall we tell him?"

Leigh ceased her struggles but panted in frustration, "You rattlesnake! At least explain what's going on inside that head of yours! Why do you dislike and distrust me? What have I supposedly done to you? In fact, who are you?"

He grinned as he lessened his grip on her. "I don't dislike you, Laura. In fact, I feel just the opposite. You know who and what I am, my cunning enchantress. And you know exactly what I mean."

Exasperated, Leigh sighed heavily and shook her head. "Think what you will, but I don't have the vaguest idea. Besides, if you think you're being tricked, why did you come to Africa? That's an awfully long and expensive journey to undertake merely to scold me. Unjustly, I might add."

When her blue eyes looked dewy and she drew in a ragged breath of air, he suspected again that Chad was using her without her knowledge and consent. "It was no trouble, Laura. I live here. I sailed home the morning after our talk in the garden. That is what you and Chad wanted, isn't it?"

"You live here!" she exclaimed in surprise. "Who are you?"

"Jace Elliott, coffee grower, safari guide, and whatever else you'd like me to be, Laura." He watched her eyes widen and her face pale, and heard her sharp intake of air. But it was the curious array of emotions—alarm, hesitation, disbelief,

142

confusion, even fear—in her large eyes that caught his complete attention and interest.

"You're . . . Jace . . . Elliott? Brandon Elliott's . . . son?" When he nodded both times, she licked her dry lips and stared at him. Part of it made sense now. She understood why the mention of Chad's name that night on the dock had altered him. She grasped why he had been hiding, and why he had been so cautious and alert, and why he had been so certain they would meet again soon. He had risked capture by coming to her aid. But why did he think she and Chad knew he was there? Why did he consider Chad an enemy? Was there something between the Elliotts and Websters that she and Chad did not know?

Naturally he would be resentful toward William Webster's granddaughter, especially if he didn't know about the will's stipulation. But, she fretted, why was he playing romantic games with her? For revenge? No, she reasoned, he had responded to her before learning who she was. But, she argued with herself, why had he endangered himself to meet her in the garden at Lord Salisbury's? What did he want from her? As she eyed him closely, her mind hinted, *So, this is Jace Elliott, the man who inherits half of everything if . . .*

"What were you doing sneaking around in London? I thought you were wanted by the law and couldn't—" She halted as he released her and let her sway against the wall behind her.

Jace had noticed her reaction to his identity. "So, you do know who and what I am; you just didn't realize Sir Lancelot was Jace Elliott, isn't that right? Why didn't Chad tell you the truth before involving you?"

"Involving me in *what?* You've made so many

143

charges and innuendoes that I'm confused. Pl.... explain."

"For God knows what reason, old Chadwick wants me to lead your safari. Of course I do have a reputation as the best guide here, but why does he really want to hire me, Laura? Why did he order you to lure me out of London? So I'd be here when you all arrived? Why?"

Astonishment glittered in her eyes. "Where would you get a crazy idea like that, Mr. Elliott? Jim Hanes is our guide. We're waiting for his return so we can head inland. He's late, but he'll arrive soon. Even so, why should that request annoy you to such extremes?"

"Why indeed, his beautiful accomplice?" Jace mocked.

Leigh was irritated. They were just beginning to make headway in this mess. "Is there a reason why you keep calling me beautiful and accusing me of things I don't understand?"

"Because you *are* beautiful, too beautiful and tempting. If I agree to head up your safari, how will you thank me this time?"

Leigh flushed in a mixture of embarrassment and anger. "You're impossible, insufferable, crazy, rude, and bitter. Why on earth would we want you around us day and night?"

"That's what I keep asking myself, woman. Chad and I don't get along at all, so why did he send for me and want to hire me? And why is he using his tasty ward as bait for his little trap?"

"Chad sent for you? Why? He told me he had hired a man named Jim Hanes. He's been to his office twice since our arrival to check on the delay. You're mistaken, or downright lying."

"If you'd like to see his written offer, it's in my

144

hotel room. Or, you can go ask him right now. It's a fact, woman."

She stared at him. "Chad would never hire you," she argued.

Jace took in her reaction, and Chad's arrival outside the door. Apparently, Chad had elected to pause a moment and eavesdrop. "Why wouldn't Chad hire me, Miss Leigh?"

"Because you're a wanted criminal," she replied, not daring to tell the truth this time. Surely this was the last man Chad wanted around them. Obviously he was lying to glean information. Yet, if he and Chad never saw each other, what did Jace mean about their not getting along? More important, did Jace know about the will? She dared not ask. "We wouldn't go into the jungle alone with you."

To steal this golden treasure would avenge what Chad had done to Joanna, Jace speculated. If she vanished in the jungle, what would his enemy trade or do to get her back? Jace knew he needed to be with them and, for some reason, Chad was giving him an opportunity. He had to take it and uncover that motive. "The only way I'll agree to work for Chad is for you to personally make the offer," he bartered.

Leigh's mouth dropped open and her eyes enlarged. "If that's what is required, Mr. Elliott, you'll *never* work for us. I wouldn't ask you to take us if you were the only guide in all of Africa."

Jace revealed a smug grin and responded, "Then I suggest you inform your guardian and group that there will be no safari. Without me, you can't go inland. Jim Hanes has a busted leg, and there's no one else available. That's why you need me."

"We *don't* need you. We'll buy maps and go by ourselves."

Jace shook his head. "You can't."

"You can't stop us, Mr. Elliott," Leigh argued.

"Yes, Leigh, I'm afraid he can," Chad stated from the doorway. "He can and he will, if we can't persuade him to be our guide."

Chad closed the door and joined them. The men stared at each other for a time. Leigh felt the animosity that permeated the room. Her curious gaze shifted from man to man. It was clear to her that they were not mere acquaintances, as Chad had implied.

Chad spoke first. "Jace Elliott does have the power to prevent our safari if he refuses to become our guide. It's the law here. The Imperial British East Africa Company and the Colonial Office won't allow safaris without a special license and an approved guide."

"What about Jim Hanes?" she argued.

"As Jace told you, Jim has a broken leg. He's in Nairobi. There isn't anyone else around to hire. Either we convince Jace to take the job or we miss our adventure. While I was at the Colonial Office, they told me Jace was expected in town any day now. I left a letter for them to pass along to Jace, offering him the job. I was hoping, after he met you, he would be persuaded."

Leigh recalled Jace's accusations. "Did you arrange that mix-up with the dinner invitation so Jace and I could meet in London?" she asked. "How could you allow those ruffians to terrify me? If Jace hadn't come along that night, I could have been injured. Were you hoping I would ensnare Mr. Elliott for you?"

Chad looked shocked. He glanced at Jace, then

146

back at Leigh. "He's the one who rescued you when you were attacked?" he asked, looking totally surprised. "Why didn't you tell me?" To his enemy, he questioned, "What were you doing in London, Jace? That was mighty foolish, don't you think?"

"Don't tell me you're worried about my safety old friend," the green-eyed man scoffed.

"Then, you didn't arrange that incident?" she pressed to Chad. "You said you wanted me to meet someone important and 'stun' him."

"Of course I didn't. I wanted you to meet that client of ours who wants the jungle effect for his restaurant. We were going to discuss business over dinner. He had to leave London, so there wasn't another opportunity for you to meet him before sailing. I didn't know Jace was in London, and he was a fool to take such a risk."

"But you told me you believe he's innocent," Leigh protested.

"What difference does that make? He can't prove it."

"Thanks to someone's clever frame," Jace sneered.

Chad ignored Jace's last words. "I heard about your misfortune with the coffee crop," he said, "so I know you must need money. Why don't you accept my offer? I didn't arrange your meeting with Leigh in London. I didn't know you were around, and I didn't know about Hanes's accident until we got here. I was hoping you'd agree after meeting my niece. This adventure was planned for her enjoyment."

"Laura Leigh is your niece? She doesn't favor Fiona, so I guess that means your father had a bastard child hidden away who died and left you the responsibility of Laura." To her, he scolded,

147

"You said Chadwick Hamilton was your guardian, but you never mentioned he's your uncle. Which Leigh was your father? Did we know him, Chad?"

Suddenly she realized that Jace Elliott didn't know who she was. She recalled that night on the dock which explained why he had kept calling her "Laura" or "Miss Leigh." It also put a new light on his earlier words and behavior . . .

When she held silent and pensive, Chad inquired, "Didn't you tell him your name in London?"

"She gave her name as Laura Leigh," Jace answered, "but I didn't give mine. You know how it was, Chad—see but don't be seen."

Chad also comprehended Jace's astonishment at discovering exactly whom he had rescued. *But,* my friend, he mused, *you're in for an even bigger surprise.* "Allow me to make the proper introductions. This is my ward and stepniece, Laura Leigh Webster, William's granddaughter from America." Leaving that stunning news to sink in, Chad turned from Jace and said to Leigh, "You know by now this is Jace Elliott, the Great White Hunter and best guide in Africa. And we need him to take Jim Hanes's place."

Jace stared at the beautiful woman, who now seemed nervous. "You're a Webster? Why didn't you tell me?" That cast a new light on matters, one he liked even less. It vexed Jace to learn she had Webster blood and to recall she was traveling with this flirtatious scoundrel. "So, you two are family."

Chad grinned at Jace's reaction. "By marriage only."

"If she's a Webster, how can she be your ward?"

148

Jace probed.

"I'm Leigh's guardian until she reaches twenty-one in November," the raven-haired man revealed. "She arrived in February after William's death in December. She inherited Webster International and his estate."

Jace couldn't conceal his surprise and interest. Lord Salisbury hadn't cabled this news to him, but he knew why: his friend didn't want him getting desperate and daring. It was obvious now why the Webster home had been closed up and empty. "The old man is dead?"

In a solemn tone, Chad replied, "Yes. I'm surprised you didn't learn about it when you were in London recently. Leigh is William's only blood heir. I thought this trip would do us both good before we settle down to business. Leigh and I haven't seen each other for a few years, so it seemed an excellent way to get reacquainted without a lot of distractions. Don't you agree?"

Jace didn't like the fact they were old friends . . . and family. Maybe she was a better actress than he had feared, or maybe Chad had worked his potent charms on her. But what did they want from him? If their meeting had truly been an accident but Leigh had recognized him and told Chad of his presence, perhaps they had lured him out of London on purpose. Perhaps Chad had feared what he would uncover there. Perhaps he had come here to end their war. No, he had to be wrong about Leigh; her behavior was convincing. If anything, Chad was using her.

"Why not let bygones be bygones, Jace? Take the job. We need a guide and you need the money. It's a good deal for all of us."

All three mused in silence for a time. Jace's

spirit was troubled. Lord Salisbury had left town immediately following the party, so they hadn't gotten to talk. He had hoped Webster would be with Hamilton. He knew how greedy both men were. A savage hunt was exactly what those two men would enjoy! Now, with Webster dead, all he could do was work on Chad to obtain the evidence he needed to clear himself.

Jace had been lying in wait for them. When they were late arriving in Africa, he had worried they had changed their minds or lied about their safari. Then the railroad had asked him to guide a work party to their next site. Since he'd used the new train to cover most of the trip out and back, it hadn't taken long. He had planned to track them through the jungle and to find a way to join their group, but Jim's accident had worked in his favor. If indeed, Jace silently scoffed, Jim *did* have a broken leg. That was something he needed to check on. He didn't like surprises, and he had been given plenty tonight.

Jace wondered if Chad was hoping he'd fall for Leigh, trail her to London, and get captured and hanged. Jace also wondered how much Leigh knew about him and his past with Chad, and why she hadn't told him her last name that night. Yet, upon reflection, he grasped how the oversight had occurred and never been corrected.

He pondered the situation. Now that Leigh Webster owned everything, including the holdings cleverly stolen from his father, where did that leave Chad and Fiona? Would Chad and his mother inherit it all if anything happened to Leigh, especially while in Jace Elliott's care? If so, Chad could get rid of both of them while in Africa. That speculation disturbed and angered Jace. If

Leigh's innocence was genuine and there was a lethal plot against her, the blonde would be safer in his care while he exposed and defeated it than she would be if he refused and they returned to London.

Jace continued to sort the pieces to this puzzle. There was another road Chad could travel: marry Leigh and take everything. Jace had witnessed how his enemy watched the girl, so why bring a mistress along to mess up his seduction? Unless the redhead was a decoy to fool Leigh or to distract him. Without a doubt, Chad had a special reason for bringing Leigh Webster here and for throwing all of them together. Jace was going with them, but he couldn't appear eager to do so. He had to let Chad *convince* him.

Leigh was trying to decide why these two men hated each other, and why they would even consider working together. Male pride? Revenge? A challenge to prove who was the better man? Why hadn't Chad told her more about Jace? And, why would Chad risk having the resentful and intimidating man around them? Was her guardian trying to discover how much Jace knew about the Webster/Elliott connection and the curious will? How strange that her rescuer was Jace Elliott of all men! The best part was that he hadn't known who she was until tonight.

As for Chad, he was delighted to have his plans proceeding perfectly. He didn't like the fact that Jace and Leigh had met in London, but Leigh would never be attracted to a criminal. And Jace, Jace would view and treat her as William's blood, as kin of the man who had taken everything from him. No, he decided, he didn't have to worry about anything happening between those two.

151

"Well?" Chad broke the heavy silence in the room. "Don't be stubborn and foolish, Jace. I'm willing to pay twice what you normally receive so this trip won't be wasted. Even if we wait around for another guide, we could be in danger out there with a less qualified man. I'm responsible for Leigh, and I don't want anything happening to her. Take the job," he urged.

"It would never work, Chad. I'd be the absolute authority out there, and you couldn't stand that. There are rules and regulations to cover sporting licenses, and you can be reckless and impulsive. The IBEA Company has laws governing the protection of animals in the Serengeti district, and that's where we'd head first. They regulate the use and possession of all firearms. They don't allow any skin, rhino horn, or ivory hunters; or permit natives to hunt during closed seasons; or allow sportsmen to take more game than the license permits. There's no wanton shooting from boats; or shooting female animals, especially with young; or excessive killing just to get the best trophies. If you break the laws here, you can be arrested and fined, and your guide can lose his license. As I recall, you've never been one to like or obey rules."

"I read the laws and regulations posted at the Colonial Office. I promise we won't break any of them, and you'll be in full control. That little accident that got your nose broken wasn't entirely my fault. If there's one thing you must know about me, it's that I keep my word."

Jace recalled Chad's "word" in '92 vowing revenge: "One day when you least expect it, old friend, I'll make you pay for what you did to me in South Africa, and pay dearly." Chad had kept that dark promise. But, Jace mused, was the un-warranted revenge completed? He doubted it, and shook his head as if refusing the man's job offer. He knew Chad wouldn't give up easily. "Forget it, Chad. I'm going home in a few days, as soon as I finish some business with Alfred."

Leigh glanced at Jace's nose, wishing she knew the story behind that, as well as all the others between them. She said, "He's right, Chad. Let him go. It wouldn't work to hire him. In fact, I think it's best if we sail home as soon as possible."

"We haven't spent all this time and money to be defeated now. You don't want to spoil everyone's trip, and you've been looking forward to this journey. We're here now, so why turn back before we've been inland? If we only ride to the end of the rail line and see the sights, it'll save our investment. I promise, if Jace won't come to work for us, I'll find someone else." Lightheartedly he added, "Besides, I am your guardian until November. The rest of us are staying, so I can't allow you to sail alone. It's dangerous and improper. Remember what happened in London when you went out unescorted."

Look who's talking about being proper! Leigh almost scoffed. Legally Chad *was* responsible for her. Until November, she was required by English law to obey him. She could refuse and leave; she could even return to America. Chad wouldn't really stop her. But that was silly and rash, and it would cause trouble between them.

She summarized the situation in a calm voice. "I sailed from America alone and unharmed, so you know I can take care of myself." She glanced at Jace and shrugged. "We can't go on safari without

Jace Elliott. Obviously he isn't interested in or willing to help us. He also doesn't like any of us, and we'd be under his control out there. But you're right. We're here, so let's stay and enjoy ourselves. We're also clever, so we'll think of a way to salvage this trip."

Chad's unfathomable gaze locked on Jace's impassive one. "Is no your final answer, Jace?" When the man did not respond, Chad asked, "Leigh, will you leave us alone to talk privately? There's something Jace and I need to settle, an old problem."

"Of course," she replied, then glanced at Jace and left the room.

Chad spoke first. "We were close friends for a long time, Jace." He saw Jace frown, but he continued. "We both know we can't ever be friends again, but we're grown men. It's time we started acting like adults and at least formed a truce. Despite what happened between us, we're even now. Our private war can be over if you let it die."

"Even?" Jace scoffed, his green eyes glittering with hostility. "You call ruining Joanna and helping Webster take everything from my father getting even? You call those cruel deeds simple bygones? You had no reason to seek revenge against me. I told you I searched for you, and I tried to repay your losses. You had no reason to use and hurt Joanna, to turn her into your harlot. One day you'll pay for that, you sorry bastard. Where is she?"

"I don't know," Chad answered honestly. "I haven't seen or heard from her since she left me." He exchanged glares with Jace.

Jace knew Chad hadn't gotten rid of Joanna

Harris, because he had received several letters from her over the years. Yet someone had to be mailing them for her from ports around the world, which prevented him from discovering her whereabouts. Nor had Joanna ever told him what had happened between her and Chad. Maybe that was Chad's unfinished business with him, to make sure he and Joanna didn't get together again and talk. Jace craved answers to those secrets. If only he or Salisbury's detectives could find her and . . . "Did she leave you or was she discarded like all your other used-up conquests?" Jace refuted coldly.

"She's the only woman who ever discarded me. It didn't work out between us, so she left London. I'm surprised she hasn't gotten in touch with you. As for your innocence years ago, you're a liar and a betrayer. Jed and the others told me you never searched for me. You sold our claim and left South Africa with all our diamonds. You left me to suffer and die at the hands of those savages."

"You're a blind fool, Chad. I told you in London when I found you alive that they were lying. If you'd bothered to check it out, you would have discovered I tried for weeks to track you down and rescue you after your capture by those Matabele warriors. There wasn't a trace anywhere. I assumed you were dead. I didn't know you had survived and escaped until I saw you in London. After I left South Africa, I was too deep in the jungle to get any news from home. When I did, Father never mentioned your return home; he probably figured I knew about it. I told you the truth that day, but you refused to believe it. We were best friends. We did everything together. Didn't that count for anything? How could you believe I would betray you over some shiny stones? Did we

155

ever really know each other? Or have we changed this much since the old days? Best friends to worst enemies. How sad and stupid. You shouldn't have destroyed Joanna and my father to get at me."

As on that day long ago, Chad didn't want to believe Jace. If he did, it would make all his actions and losses his own fault, something a man like Chad couldn't accept. Too, he needed the driving obsession of Jace Elliott to give him strength and purpose. He felt if they ever made real peace — which was undoubtedly impossible after all he had done to Jace — he would become the weaker one again. He had loved Jace like a brother; in fact, deep inside he still loved him. But by brutally cutting Jace from his life, he had found power, and he never wanted to lose that intoxicating feeling. Besides, after all he'd done, it was too late to turn back now.

"Joanna was the one who came after me, Jace." Chad informed him. "Believe it or not, but I thought I was in love with her. After we were together for a while, we both realized it was a mistake. She left town because she was ashamed of what she had done. As for your father, I liked and respected him. Brandon made that business deal with William, not with me. They were planning some joint projects together. When your father . . . died, what did you expect William to do, lose his large investment by not laying claim to it?"

Chad ruffled his neat hair and exhaled loudly. He was feeling desperate to trick Jace. "Look, I doubt you were embroiled in that mess with Stokely, and I guess you've suffered as much as I have. I've never had another friend like you. We shared a lot. Frankly I still miss what we had together, but I know it's lost forever. You're right; it was a sad and stupid mistake. Can you blame me for hating you after what I endured and was told? Not by one man, Jace, but by several. Friends or not, you have to admit you looked guilty. Why don't we let our dispute end here? We don't have to like each other for you to take this job. Dammit, man, I was the one who warned you to escape that day."

"Warned me?" Jace hinted skeptically. "You stood there and gloated over the trouble I was in. You made sure I learned every grim detail from you. If I hadn't bound and gagged you and hidden you in that warehouse, I doubt I would ever have escaped."

Chad shook his head, but grinned. "As much as I hated you, old friend, I wouldn't have exposed you. Death would have been a merciful end. I wanted you alive to suffer like I had. Every time I looked in the mirror, I was reminded of your desertion. If there's one thing those Matabele warriors taught me, it was that dying releases a man from pain. You want to know how many times I prayed for death, Jace? Plenty, just like I knew you would." Chad sighed heavily. "But that was six years ago. You can't go on hating a man forever. I'll never forgive you for what you did to me, but I understand how greed can blind and control a man. Let's leave it at, you made a mistake. I'm a rich and respected man now. William left me plenty of money and a good position; I was like a son to him. William was a good man, Jace. He turned me and my life around, and I'm sorry he's gone. As for our trouble, I don't need to spend any more time and energy on the past. Let it finally be over for both of us," he lied.

Jace stared at his former friend. It was a pretty and colorful picture that Chad was painting, but Jace wasn't buying that cheap canvas. "A truce, is it?" Jace murmured.

Leigh knocked on the door and opened it. She tried not to look at Jace Elliott, who seemed to be the center attraction in the room. "Chad, it's late and most of the others have left. We should be going. I've kept Louisa and the others out, but she's getting impatient."

"Let her," Chad replied. "This is important."

"I'll tell them you'll join us shortly," Leigh hinted.

"Wait, La—Leigh." Jace directed his gaze and questions to her. "Tell me, Miss Webster, do you honestly want to go on this safari? Do you understand what you're getting yourself into out there? Are you willing to face the dangers, the discomforts, the cramped tents, the lack of privacy, the demands of such a long trek?" He noted every changing expression in her eyes and on her face.

Jace held up his hand as he continued, "Spiders as big as my hand. Vipers that can strike you dead within hours. Huge snakes that drop on you from trees, encircle your body, and slowly squeeze the life from it. Hungry bugs that crawl and feast on your pretty hide. Insects that suck the blood from you or bury themselves under your skin or nails while leaving their nasty germs inside you: the tsetse fly, the malarial mosquito, tunga fleas, and hookworms. Crossing rivers infested with man-eating crocs and irritable hippos. Jungles teeming with hungry lions, rogue elephants, and more." He paused in his melodramatic performance. "Then, there's quicksand, plants that can slay you as easily and quickly as a black or green

158

mamba, natives who eat pretty blondes just for good luck, and the pure hardship of such a journey. Is that how you want to spend the next two months? Or, are you only being a good little girl and meekly obeying *Uncle* Chad?"

His last question provoked Leigh to uncommon recklessness. She thought she grasped Jace's motives: to discourage her, to make her the one to cancel the safari. In an angry tone, she related, "I'm not a coward or a weakling, Mr. Elliott. I was half raised on a Texas ranch. I've battled snakes, wolves, rustlers, insects, and other perils. I've worked in rainstorms, sleet, and snow, and beneath a blazing sun. I've been on cattle roundups that had plenty of hardships, dangers, and little privacy. I've forded rivers as perilous as any you have here. And no amount of easy walking can compare to sitting in a saddle from sun-up to sundown, so I can put up with discomforts. I haven't cried, or been terrified, or felt too weak to make it, and I'm not afraid of spiders. I can ride, shoot, track, walk, and work as good as the best man."

Leigh saw a mocking grin slip across Jace's arresting face and settle in those laughing green eyes. His mood and expression seemed to say he was flinging down a gauntlet before her and daring her to retrieve it. Challenged and vexed, she rashly continued. "I'm willing to bet anything, my physical and emotional stamina are as good as yours. I don't scare easily, and I'm strong and smart. I don't take foolish risks, and I obey orders. I doubt your jungle can demand more than I can handle. If it does, I'm certain our guide can come to my aid with a few lessons. I've camped out many times, but we slept in bedrolls on the ground, no nice tents. So this trek will be a simple luxury."

When Jace's expression altered to one of respect, she added, "There is nothing I would *honestly* enjoy more than going on a safari. I have no doubts I can withstand its minor hardships. The problem is, I doubt I could cope with your irascible nature and mercurial personality. In fact, I'm positive you would spoil the trip for me. If the safari depends upon my personal plea for your assistance, then forget it. Good night, Mr. Elliott. I'll see you outside, Chad." Leigh closed the door and joined the others to explain the delay.

Chad and Jace chuckled. "She's quite an amazing woman, my little Leigh," Chad remarked. "Well, did she convince you?"

"If a man must use a woman to get his way," Jace ventured, "at least select a beautiful and tempting one, right? What's the real bargain with your fetching ward? A peace-offering, old friend? She's beautiful, intelligent, and wealthy. I think I'll accept your retribution and sacrifice in exchange for a truce and the job."

Chad's grin faded instantly. He replied before thinking, "don't be absurd. Leigh isn't a peace offering for Joanna. She's mine, or will be soon. She'd never respond to the likes of you, not with those criminal charges hanging over your head."

Jace came to full alert, and noticed how Chad glared at him for eliciting that slip. Chad had bewitched and ensnared Joanna easily and quickly. Would Leigh Webster be any different, any stronger, any wiser, more honest? To compel the man into further slips, Jace teased, "Well, I'll be damned. You want her for yourself. Is that what this little safari is all about? You want to get her away from all her admirers in London so you can

160

charm and seduce her and get your greedy hands on her inheritance. You want to show her what a big and brave man you are in the wild. Aren't you afraid I have more charm and skill than you do? Aren't you afraid of me winning Leigh and stealing everything you desire? That would make us even, old boy."

"Don't play games with me, Jace." Chad warned. "I'll admit I want Leigh, but only because she's a special woman. I've changed since that trouble with Joanna. Leigh wants this trip, and I want to give it to her. Name your price."

Something still wasn't quite right, Jace concluded. "Don't take me for a fool, Chad. You have a mistress on this trip, remember?"

The two men knew a lot about each other. It was almost as if they had slipped back briefly into their old days together.

Chad took the only path he saw out of his tangled territory, to pretend he'd been unmasked and was being honest and desperate. "Only because the plans were made before Leigh caught my eye. I couldn't change them without making her nervous. She's a lady, so she wouldn't have come here alone with me, guardian or not. She's different, so I have to move slowly and carefully with her." He fused his gaze to Jace's and vowed, "I'm confident enough to make a wager with you. I'll double your salary if Leigh isn't mine before this trip is over. She'll marry me the day we return to London." He chuckled and coaxed, "Come on, Jace, for old times' sake. We don't have to forgive each other or forget our past, but this will settle things between us. I'm not afraid to risk everything. Winner takes all: the money, Leigh, the pride of victory, final revenge, and Webster Inter-

161

national."

Jace took the fetching bait. "You always were a betting man, Chad, and one for taking crazy risks. I can recall times it got us into deep trouble, but we surely had fun getting out of it." Jace felt uneasy at the good memories and feelings that statement evoked. "What makes you think Leigh would want either one of us? Besides, you can't bet something you don't own."

Chad felt that he had Jace hooked on his deceitful line, so he held on tightly to reel him in. "Leigh will be good for me. I need her."

Mirthful laughter spilled from Jace's lips. "Why, because old man Webster left everything to her? You need to marry her to get it all back? I know the feeling of great loss too well, old friend."

Riled, Chad argued, "What difference does it make to you why I want to marry her? You need money, and I have plenty."

"Plenty of hers, for the time being." Jace eyed him and asked, "What happened to you in South Africa, Chad? That's when you changed, not after Webster got a hold of you."

"I grew up, Jace, but you've remained a sentimental, rough boy. I'm rich and powerful and well respected. I run one of the largest companies in England, maybe in the world. But you, you're still scrounging to survive, and partly with my earnings. You play the big game hunter, but you're scared when it comes to a real challenge. If not, you'd have exonerated yourself long ago. You're stuck in this uncivilized jungle forever, and your name's as black as night. So which one of us is smarter and braver, and better off? You a coward now?"

"This time I'll win. My usual price is twenty-five

thousand pounds for two months. If you win Leigh, you won't owe me a single pence. If I win Leigh, you double it and owe me fifty thousand. Well, old friend, do we have a truce and a deal?" Jace asked, as calmly as if he were saying good morning to a mere acquaintance. He wasn't afraid to make such a bet, as Chad could never win Leigh, not with the plan Jace had in mind . . .

Chadwick glued his gaze to Jace's challenging one. All the old hatred and craving for revenge stormed his body. But, he plotted, no matter what happened, he couldn't lose. If anything did occur between Leigh and Jace, he could always go back to his original plot to kill them. "Agreed—victory to the man who wins Leigh Webster during the safari. As soon as payment is made, we swear to stay out of each other's lives forever."

"If we both fail, you still owe my twenty-five-thousand salary."

"Agreed. Anything else?"

"Before we sign a contract, remind Leigh of her bet with me and make certain your ward will live up to her end of the bargain."

"What wager did Leigh make with you?" Chad asked.

"You heard her moments ago. She bet *anything* she was as good in the wilds as I am. I plan to collect on her bet and yours. She has to hire me and she has to wager something of value."

"What if she refuses to bet with you?"

"Use your charms to convince her, or the deal's off. Make it appear her wager is the reason I changed my mind. If she believes I'm agreeing to please her, it'll remove the edge you already have with her. That's only fair. I'll get her answer tomorrow." At the door, Jace turned and said, "By the way, happy birthday, old boy. Now, we're the same age again." Jace left by the back door to avoid Leigh.

A guileful grin broadened Chad's mouth. Jace's arrogant demand had given him a clever idea. He would make certain to leave enough space between their wagers and signatures to fill in one other term without Jace's knowledge, one he could use against his old friend if this bargain soured . . .

Chapter Eight

"I didn't mean a real bet!" Leigh exclaimed. "Is the man crazy?"

"That's how it sounded to us, Leigh," Chad replied. "Are you afraid he was right about it being too hard on you?"

"What about Louisa and Cynthia?" Leigh reasoned in annoyance. "Nothing was mentioned about it being too hard on them."

"They've been on hunting trips with me and Reid several times. It'll be difficult for those spoiled beauties, but they'll do fine; they always have. What about you, my Wild West ward? Do you have any frontier spirit? You seem confident, skilled, and determined to me. What will you prove by refusing to bend a little? We both know he's being stubborn and demanding, but that's how he is. Are you going to let Jace Elliott believe you're a cowardly weakling? All you have to do is ask him to be our guide and bet him a thousand pounds you'll win. What difference does it make, Leigh? I'll furnish the money, and help you succeed. What have you got to lose but a wonderful safari?"

At her pensive silence, Chad continued. "Besides, this will give you the opportunity to get to know Jace, and us the chance to observe him. We need to discover if he's aware of that strange codicil to William's will, and if he knows the reason behind it."

"Is that why you proceeded with the safari Grandfather planned?"

Chad looked surprised. "No, Jim Hanes was hired as our guide, and I assumed we wouldn't even run into Jace. This is a big territory. Jace just happened to be in town when I needed a replacement, so it seemed a cunning idea to solve two problems with one task. Think about it, Leigh, and don't refuse too quickly. A safari and answers."

Leigh strolled to the balcony door and gazed outside. She knew why Jace was not at his plantation; that night, in the garden at Lord Salisbury's, she had told him about this safari. She needed facts about Jace and Chad, so she hinted evocatively, "What if Jace paid Jim Hanes to fake an injury so you'd turn to him for help? What if he knows about the will and is luring us into the jungle to get us at his mercy? That may sound crazy, but half of Grandfather's estate is still enormous."

Chad had to dispel her mistrust of Jace, as Jace was a threat only to him. Chad knew his ex-friend was not a criminal and would never harm Leigh, even if she was a Webster. For his scheme to work, he had to dupe and control both of them. "If Jace wanted to harm you, Leigh, he could have done so on the waterfront or before he fled England. While nosing around, he probably learned about our safari and rushed home to chase the beautiful woman he had rescued earlier. He has to be intrigued and charmed by you. If he's tricking us, which I doubt, it's only to embarrass me in the wilds. Now that I've seen and talked with him again, I can't imagine Jace harming you for any reason. I just don't want him learning of that codicil and thinking William was making re-

166

quital. That could lead to trouble."

As if believing every word, Leigh murmured, "You could be right, Chad. Jace didn't know Grandfather was dead until last night. He seemed dismayed, as if he had wanted or needed to see Grandfather. Perhaps about those crimes in London, or maybe he was hoping Grandfather would finally and unselfishly clear him." Doubts about both her grandfather and rescuer pained her deeply. One thing she had learned about the mercurial hero was that he couldn't conceal honest shock, or do it as easily and skillfully as he masked most of his feelings. She liked that.

"With William and Brandon dead, we'll never know the truth."

"I hate thinking such thoughts, Chad," she said, "but this whole affair is so odd. Jace couldn't have been playing games with Laura Leigh Webster because he didn't know who I was. But what is he thinking now? What was his connection to Grandfather? Lordy, what is he planning with this gambling game?"

"Just delightful sport with an enchanting woman," Chad teased.

Leigh recalled Jace's warning: "Don't tempt me to alter my first impression of you. That could be a dangerous and costly mistake." Jace had told her she was "too beautiful and tempting," but for what purpose? For revenge? For killing her to get back his losses to her grandfather? *Stop being so suspicious of everyone, Leigh,* she admonished herself. First, she had suspected Chad of deadly mischief. Next, she had suspected Louisa of it. Now, she was considering Jace as a threat. It was terrible to think the worst of everybody around her. She could not observe these people intelligently and clearly if she was so biased against them. Besides, she deduced, normal people didn't go around killing and plotting against another person all the time, and they couldn't all be crazy or evil. Her imagination was running wild. She was being foolish and unfair. But there *were* a few puzzles to solve.

One was Jace Elliott. She was intrigued by him and strongly attracted to him. Going on safari with that secretive male was the only way to unravel his mystery. Too, she didn't want to be bested by Louisa and Cynthia. She wanted this delving journey for many reasons.

She finally turned to Chad and asked, "How did you convince Jace to take this job?"

He chuckled. "I didn't. You did."

Baffled, she asked, "What do you mean?"

Chad needed to test a worry of his: Leigh's possible attraction to Jace. "I think he's smitten by a beautiful and charming woman, and hungry for all she has to offer. If he is, he might open up to you."

Leigh's blue eyes widened in astonishment. "You want me to romance that unpredictable, insufferable beast," she murmured, "so I can spy on him? That would be just as offensive as the attack on me in London."

At her heated response and expression, Chad relaxed. "Heavens, no! Jace Elliott is a wanted man. I don't want you getting tangled up with the likes of him. I meant, make friends, or pretend to do so to see what you can learn about his connection to us."

"Is that what *you're* doing, Chad?" she queried.

"I would love to, but it wouldn't work. Jace Elliott wouldn't tell me anything important unless there was a motive behind it."

"Are you two old enemies?"

Chad knew that Leigh was smart and alert, so he had to tell her something. Surely she had perceived the animosity between Jace and himself; it was better if he answered her rather than his rival. He wouldn't mention Joanna Harris, and was certain Jace wouldn't, either. "We've had problems in the past, but it was a long time ago. Jace and I were schoolmates and shipmates, but our friendship soured. He's always been a cocky and reckless man, so we parted ways six years ago. He continued his worldly adventures, then settled here. I returned to England and went to work for William. We've only seen each other a couple of times since '90, and those brief meetings weren't pleasant. The last time was in December of '94 when I warned him to escape from London before he was arrested," he disclosed.

That news took her unprepared. "You warned him? Why?"

Chad shrugged and said, "Because I was the first one to see him when he docked that day. Either he didn't know about the crimes, which is what he claimed, or he didn't know he'd been exposed. He was coming to tell his father about the loss of his coffee crop to disease. That's the money Brandon was planning on borrowing to pay off his debt to your grandfather. In case you don't know it, a coffee crop takes three to four years to mature. That's why Jace needs money. He lost everything in '94 and had to replant the next season. Now he has to survive until his new crop is ready. So you see, my lovely ward, we'll be doing him a favor to hire him. Maybe it will change his mind about liking us."

"Obviously you never believed he was guilty or you wouldn't have warned him to flee that day. You can't totally hate him. Doesn't he realize you helped him and now you're trying to help him? Again?"

"He doesn't *want* to realize it, Leigh. Jace has done some pretty wild things in the past, but murder and arson are not like him. It was an impulsive action to warn him and, to be honest, mostly I was taunting him. Even when friendship hits rough seas, you never forget there used to be calm ones. I won't lie and say I forgive him or want to be friends again, but I don't mind having him around for a while. We are adults now."

"That's a very kind and wise attitude, Chad," she complimented him. She sighed deeply, then revealed, "I suppose I can entreat him to lead us, and make that silly bet with him. As you said, what difference does it make? I won't lose."

Chad practically beamed with the joy of what he considered a victory. "Thanks, Leigh. I'll tell Jace and the others our safari is on."

Less than an hour later, Jace Elliott knocked on the door to her suite. She opened it, frowned to vex him, and said, "You don't waste any time claiming a victory, do you?"

Jace chuckled and walked inside. He seated himself on a small sofa, leaned back to make himself comfortable, then crossed his legs. "Nope," he replied. "I didn't want to give you time for second thoughts. You do have a stubborn streak, woman. You leave me no choice but to force you to chase me."

Leigh frowned again, closed the door, and went to lean against the balcony doorjamb. She stared at the grinning man. For once, she wasn't at a total disadvantage; she knew who he was and that he wouldn't vanish into the night. He was certainly all male, and he looked enticing in his jungle khakis. His brown hair was windblown, and his emerald eyes sparkled with smugness. He looked utterly relaxed for once. But why shouldn't he be? she mused. He was in his element, and he had won their first battle.

It seemed to her, Jace's personality and character had been molded by the terrible events and perilous surroundings of his existence. He was cold, forbidding, and demanding one minute; then, tender, reasonable, and compassionate the next. He was a strong, proud, intelligent man, but he was filled with bitterness and resentment. There was a hint of touching tragedy and an aura of magnetic mystery about him. She knew the reasons for a few of his miseries, but she was positive the man had more secrets. She wondered what he had been like before his troubles.

Her gaze roamed the contradictory male who sat watching her. He was self-assured, but slightly arrogant on occasion. She liked the fact he wasn't a quitter, as his daring visit to London had proven, and she was glad he wasn't self-pitying. She liked his sense of humor, when she wasn't the butt of it. He radiated fiery sexual prowess, but he hadn't used his charms cruelly or meaninglessly, at least with her. Yes, she admitted, he had teased, tormented, and tempted her. But, she confessed, he hadn't taken advantage of her, not yet anyway.

She decided that Jace Elliott could be as wild and hazardous as the territory in which he lived and worked. He could be as steamy and alluring as the lush jungles he clearly loved. And his knowledge of this land, its people, and survival skills made him a valuable guide.

Jace was aroused by the way Leigh was studying him. He watched conflicting and changing emotions sail through her seawater eyes. He recalled how she had greeted him last night, and how she had responded to him in the alley and garden. Sunlight flowed into the room and dreamily bathed her in its golden glow. It danced off her tawny locks, caressed

171

her face, and outlined her shapely hips and legs beneath her thin dress. Her eyes seemed so blue, and her lips so inviting. He knew how her mouth tasted, how she felt in his embrace, how her smile affected him, how she smelled. She touched him in ways he hadn't been touched before. He wanted all of her, and for keeps. In self-defense, he coaxed, "Why don't you have a seat so we can get on with our business?"

His words and voice broke the spell over Leigh. Not wanting Jace to think her afraid of him, she went to sit beside the enchanting beast. She looked at him and commented, "At least I'm not in the dark about you anymore. I assume you were in London to gather evidence to prove your innocence. That does explain your odd behavior during our meetings. I could tell you were tense and wary. I found it odd, and disquieting. Did you make any progress?"

Jace shifted his position to face her. He rested his left arm along the top of the sofa, his fingers near her head. In a pleasant tone, he remarked, "You're very perceptive, Miss Webster, but I'd rather not discuss my personal troubles today, if you don't mind."

"Certainly not. It really isn't any of my business, is it? I always feel at ease going into a secluded jungle with a wanted man."

"To put your mind at ease, I'm not guilty." He grinned, then laughed before saying, "Of course that's what all criminals-on-the-way-to-the-gallows vow, isn't it?" He laughed again, a rich and mellow sound in the romantic quietness that surrounded them. He waxed serious. "You have no reason to believe me or to trust me, Miss Webster. I'm sure you don't have a high opinion of me, and that's understandable, given what you think you know about me and how I've behaved to you. First, I want to apologize for my offensive and rude conduct, and my unjust accusations. I'm sure Lord Chadwick Hamilton has painted me midnight black to you, but, honestly, I'm not that bad."

His apology and manner were unanticipated, and pleasing to her. She relaxed and smiled. "To the contrary, Mr. Elliott. He says you're old friends who parted ways years ago, and he doesn't believe you're guilty of those charges. True, he doesn't like you, and I don't know why, but he doesn't hate you, either. As for me, I'm grateful that you risked so much to come to my rescue that night in London. Not every man in your perilous situation would have been so brave and unselfish. I honestly hope you work out your problems. But I am curious. Why were you tracking me in London? It was terribly risky to come to Lord Salisbury's to return my locket. And why did you change your mind about becoming our guide?"

Jace liked her calling him "brave and unselfish." He didn't believe what Chad had told her, but apparently *she* did. He wondered if Chad—whom Jace was positive still hated him—had told her such lies so she would agree to hire him as their guide. His old friend was resolved to tricking her into marriage before November, when he would lose his control over her. Leigh Webster had also lied to him, at least when she changed her story in the alley and hadn't given him all of her name. Yet he surmised it was because she had been afraid of him. "*You* changed it for me, woman," he answered belatedly. "After witnessing your courage that night in the alley and upon hearing good things about you last night, I am most intrigued by you. I suppose you're qualified to survive anything I—or the trail—hand out to you. If not, I'll be the one to profit from it. But," he hinted, "I'm curious about a few points myself."

Leigh was relieved they were talking cordially

rather than quarreling or playing with words. This wasn't the grim meeting she had anticipated and dreaded. "Such as?" she encouraged.

"Why did you tell a stranger about this safari, and why didn't you tell your guardian about our second meeting?" he probed.

Leigh glanced away for a moment, then returned her gaze to meet his. "Actually, you made me nervous, and a little frightened. I didn't know who or what you were, and you were popping into and out of my life at random with vows to pursue me. For all I knew, you could have been a kidnapper, or crazy. Since you were behaving so mysteriously, I was trying to discover how news of my lengthy departure would affect whatever plans you had for me. It makes me nervous not knowing people's motives. I assumed you were simply playing devilish games to spark my interest."

She grinned at him and murmured, "Then again, you could have been dangerous. I must admit, I was shocked to see you here. When you started making all those wild accusations, I didn't know what to think. Believe it or not, Mr. Elliott, but there was and is no plot to ensnare you. Of course, all alleged plotters vow innocence, so it's up to you to decide if I can be trusted."

Jace laughed heartily. He was impressed by her bluntness. "I promise you I'm not dangerous or crazy. Frankly, Miss Webster, I do believe you. But I am having trouble trusting your guardian, with good cause. You didn't say why didn't you tell him about that night in the garden?"

Leigh flushed slightly. She was hoping he would forget that question. "I didn't want to worry him. If he learned my rescuer was stalking me, it could alarm him. Too, he might think it odd that we had met twice and I still didn't know your name. After all, that mix-up with the dinner invitation seemed a little incredible. I didn't want him to think I had made the mistake intentionally to . . . skip dinner."

Jace accepted her explanation, wondering with a smile if she had wanted to miss that dinner. That boded ill for Chase! "One last question before we move to the reason for my being here: Why did you wear that necklace last night?"

"Necklace?" she echoed, then recalled his reaction. "Why do you ask? It belonged to my grandmother and matched my gown. I inherited it when Grandfather died. Chad passed it on to me."

"When?" He asked another question, rather than responding to hers.

"Yesterday. Why?" she probed again, knowing it had meaning.

Her honesty and openness pleased him. "It belonged to my mother," he revealed. "It was her favorite piece, a very rare and unique one. I suppose Webster took it when he took everything else belonging to my family."

She didn't like the sudden chill in his eyes and tone. "That isn't fair, Jace. They were in business together. When everything went wrong, it must have been part of the financial settlement. It's beautiful and valuable, but I'll return it without payment or questions. I know it must be very special to you. I'll fetch it now."

Before she could rise, Jace stayed her. "Please keep it. It'll cause trouble with Chad if you hand it over to me."

"It's mine," Leigh told him, "so I can do as I please with it. Chad is my legal guardian until November, but not my boss, and he doesn't try to be one. I insist you take back your mother's necklace."

With the hand resting along the sofa top, Jace

175

twirled a tawny lock around his forefinger. "I'm glad he gave it to you rather than to his mother or another woman. Besides, it looks perfect on you. I insist that you keep it as a kindness to me."

Leigh settled back on the sofa and relented slightly. "Only if you promise to ask for it back anytime you want it."

"No matter if Webster earned it legally and I have no just claim to it?" he pressed. "It is quite valuable and beautiful. Most women wouldn't be so brave and unselfish," he said, using her earlier compliment.

Leigh frowned at his first choice of words. She wondered if there was a reason why Chad had given her the necklace, in this place and at this time. It could have been to provoke Jace into working for them, or perhaps Chad had found it in the safe and didn't know its history. "I'm not most women, Mr. Elliott. Besides, I have more money than I can spend in five lifetimes. The necklace is an Elliott family heirloom, so rightly it belongs to you. Let's get one thing straight, Jace. I didn't know my grandfather well, but I'm sure he wasn't responsible for your father's misfortune. It was a failed business deal, nothing more."

Jace realized she was now using his first name, and he liked the way it rolled off her tongue. He also noticed that she wasn't convinced by what she had just told him. That, he found intriguing. He cautioned himself to move slowly and cautiously with her in that area. "Let's get on to our business, Leigh. What shall we wager?"

She had vowed she would never do this, not even if he was "the only guide in all of Africa." But she was provoked, challenged, trapped. "As Chad explained, I believe the demand is for me to beg you to be our guide and to make a bet with you. All right, Jace.

176

Will you please be our guide? Is one thousand pounds enough to wager?"

Jace grinned in relief. "Indeed, you *are* brave and unselfish. I like the way you yield without cowering. Yes, my enchanting lioness, I'll be your guide through the African wilds. Nothing would please me more than getting to know you better. As for your wager, I'm sure a thousand pounds was Chad's suggestion. He craves money and power, but I don't. All I need is enough money to live on, and I earn plenty for that. You did say, *anything* last night," he reminded her.

Leigh looked baffled, worried. She studied this moody and mysterious man who had been thrust into her life and heart. She wanted to get to know him better. In fact, she wanted him, period. "If you don't want to bet money, what do you have in mind?"

"Winner's choice, Miss Webster," he announced.

Leigh stared at him. "That covers a large territory, Jace."

"Anything your heart desires that I own or can get." He added mirthfully, "Legally, please. I'm in enough trouble with the law as is."

Leigh's heart fluttered. "Anything? As you warned me once, that could be a costly and dangerous mistake."

"But you must confess, it will be exciting, and profitable for one of us. My offer stands: anything I own," he asserted with an air of nonchalance. He waited to see if he would receive any clues to Chad's guileful trip. Was Leigh aiding Chad's plot? She looked so innocent and honest. Joanna had appeared to be both but had proven she was neither. He could be wrong about Leigh, too, but prayed he wasn't. "Well?" he hinted. "You don't plan on losing to me on purpose, do you? So what difference does it make?" he teased.

A big difference, she concluded. "I don't plan on losing, period. If I do, what prize do you want? Part of Webster International?"

"No, I'm happy in the coffee and safari businesses. If textiles interested me, I would have joined my father's firm years ago."

"Then, what do you want from me as a prize, if you win?"

"Need you ask?" he murmured with an engaging grin. He moved closer to her and captured her gaze with a stronger hold. He lifted her hand and turned it over to kiss her palm, then each fingertip. He was glad she did not look or pull away. Jace felt her tremble, and he was aroused, too. Her hands were soft but chilled—a sign of tension. Her respiration had increased—a mark of nervousness and desire. He doubted Chad affected her this way.

He loved just being near her. She was easy to talk with and comfortable to be around. This woman wasn't false or flirtatious. She was exquisite, a prize to win and value and defend, a prize he craved. He admitted to himself how strongly she affected him, and how much he wanted her. She was someone to share everything with, when the time was right. But he had to be certain she was as genuine, direct, and honest as she alluded to being, which would take time and effort. From observing his parents' and other couples' relationships, he knew physical attraction wasn't enough to bond a man and woman together, not the way they should be.

"Even if it was unintentional, you've tempted and tormented me, Leigh, so you have to know what I want from you." His fingers trailed over her cheeks and lips as he disclosed in a husky tone, "If someone wants to really enjoy it, a special treasure can't be

178

taken by deceit or force. It must be surrendered willingly or it's meaningless. Ever since that night in the alley, you've haunted me day and night like a golden ghost. In my present predicament and exile, I have little opportunity for romance. Since time is short, I'm afraid I have to be impulsive and forward. The plain truth is, I want you, woman."

Leigh was stunned. He certainly was direct! His jungle-green eyes were alive with passion and the thrill of heady adventure. Lordy, he was tempting, and she was too susceptible. His fingertips stroked her cheek. She was moved by his touch and words, yet she was uneasy. Why didn't he want to win his father's firm or the equivalent in money? Did he think winning those would be easy after seducing her? Did he want—need—vengeance against the Websters and Chad first? Did he see her as a path to victory? Surely he sensed how vulnerable and receptive she was to him. Leigh pushed his distracting hand into his lap. She had to think clearly, if that was possible with him so near. "That's a mighty big wager on my part, Mr. Elliott. Of all women available, why do you want me—an inexperienced girl—as your lover? Besides, I couldn't even stay behind as your mistress and ruin my reputation. Chad would be so furious he would resign and leave me in a barrel of trouble. I can't become your lover on a crazy bet."

She misunderstood his meaning, and Jace knew he must let her do so for a while. If he demanded a future marriage, she might panic, and a marriage might be impossible for a long time given his situation. Yet he had to discover her feelings today. "I want you, Leigh Webster, not another woman," he stated simply. He locked their gazes. "Once this safari is over and we've become good friends, I want you to spend your last night here with me, all night. I would

179

love to wager more time, but I know that's impossible. What prize do you crave, Leigh?"

Her gaze slipped over his muscular, virile frame. Her keen eyes took in his attractive features, that alluring smile, his potent appeal. At least he was honest about his interest in her, but could she agree to one passionate night in his arms and bed when she wanted so much more from him? Yet that one night could lead to something more valuable and permanent if she lost the bet. No, she couldn't lose, so why not agree? What should she play for: the plantation, money, or him? She knew how he valued his freedom. His grin was so smug. He was demanding her all, so why shouldn't she do the same? She heard herself say, "The price will be you, Mr. Elliott, total possession."

It was Jace's turn to be stunned. "That would make our wagers the same," he ventured. "There wouldn't be a loser or a winner. Of course, I'm not complaining, but Chad surely will."

"No, our wagers are not the same," she corrected him. "If you lose, you exonerate yourself, marry me, and move to London." She witnessed the disbelief in his gaze as she continued. "If I win and Chad deserts me, you'll be there to run the firm for me. Surely you learned the business from your father, so it shouldn't be a problem. As far as my guardian knows, our wager will be for a thousand pounds. Another thing, you must give your word of honor you won't do anything intentional either to make me lose this bet or to help me win it. Agreed?"

Jace wondered what she was up to with this provocative and incredible proposal, even though marriage had been *his* original idea. But why wed him, a near stranger and alleged criminal, when she had her choice of men? Was she trying to lure him into danger in England? That was the only way to exonerate him-

180

self. Did she think he would refuse her terms and say to forget the wager? He tested her feelings for, and loyalty to, his foe by saying, "If you lose, I get you for a night and get even with Chad. If you win, I still get even with Chad. Either way, I'll profit. But how will you benefit from winning? What debt do you owe me that has to be paid with a sacrifice? Clearing myself can't mean this much to you, even if I saved your life. And you can have this quarry anytime you want him, my daring predator."

Leigh ignored his generous offer. "Why do you need to get even with Chad? What happened between you two?"

"It's an old quarrel, a private one. Why don't you ask him?"

"I did," she confessed. "He's as quiet about it as you are. Why the big secret, Jace? How bad could it be?"

"One day I'll tell you all about it, but not now."

She persisted. "But I need to understand so I won't get entangled in this mess. How would you get even through our wager?"

"Either way, Chad would lose you." She looked puzzled. "Don't fool yourself, Leigh. He wants you as badly as I do, but not for the same reasons. I guarantee you'll be better off with me."

Leigh fretted over the fact he had revenge in mind, and that she might have misread him and his "reasons." If Jace was willing to marry her or become her lover immediately, why withhold something so important? The past had to be significant, since both men were so affected by it. Since neither would talk, both had to be involved equally.

Jace couldn't tell her yet about Joanna's conquest or Chad's wild charges of treachery and betrayal. Added to the trouble he was in already, it would darken his image too much. If the truth came out, Chad would try his damndest to convince her Jace only wanted revenge because of Joanna. Jace knew if he held silent, Chad would, too; the man wouldn't confess freely and paint himself black. He glanced at the alert blonde. Leigh needed to get to know him and trust him before she would accept his claims of innocence on all accusations. "You need a husband this badly for some reason, or is this a joke?"

"No, I don't need a husband for any reason, but your freedom is the most valuable possession you own, just as what I'll have to gamble is mine. Since you insisted on my plea for your guidance and this bet, I have to strike where it hurts the most."

At her playful attempt to unsettle him, he chuckled. "How could it possibly hurt me to marry the beautiful, enchanting, and wealthy Laura Leigh Webster, a woman I desire like crazy? Too, it would keep Chad from getting you. It's a great deal. But the truth is, I want you far more than I crave revenge."

Leigh knew she had wagered rashly. She could not understand what had gotten into her. At any moment she had expected him to halt this madness, but he hadn't. Yet, if he could clear himself, he would have done so by now, so she had nothing to fear.

Jace tested her. "It's a very tempting wager, Miss Webster: me against a glorious African night with you. But if I lost, I might not survive in London for you to collect your winnings. Then, we both lose. Yet that's a risk I should be willing to take."

Leigh paled and stared. "You aren't serious?" Jace grinned. "You can't be." His grin broadened, then he chuckled. "This sport has gone far enough. Let's get down to real business."

Jace laughed at her anticipated reaction. "Coward," he taunted. "Already admitting your defeat? Or simply regretting your reckless demand? Tell me, Leigh, which do you fear most: winning or losing? And why are you so set on me clearing myself? Don't you think I've tried? Don't you realize how dangerous that can be?"

"You don't strike me as a quitter, and you've taken that risk before. That is why you were in London recently, wasn't it? Maybe I can help. Maybe I can hide you while you search for evidence."

He was intrigued, and suspicious. "Why would you do that?"

"You saved my life, Jace, and you also took another risk to return my locket. Most of all, I like you and I think you're innocent. I want you cleared so you can get rid of your bitterness and stop being a prisoner here. That has to be frustrating."

He was moved deeply. "Why does any of that matter to you?"

She laughed and jested, "How else can you track and pursue me?"

"It hasn't been a problem for me yet," he retorted merrily. "How much did Chad tell you about my trouble in London?"

She related what she knew about it. "As you can see, not much, so what did he leave out?"

Jace exposed a few facts to see how she took them. "I'm not guilty, and neither was my father. We were cleverly framed. Who, how, and why, I don't know. The two witnesses are gone, but the evidence is still on file. The authorities have enough proof to arrest me and question me if I step foot in England, but not enough to pursue me here and charge me. If I turned myself in, I would be stupid, because I have no alibi, and no proof I wasn't involved. Circumstantial evidence would do me in. Frankly, I don't intend to die for crimes I didn't commit. Somehow I have to prove

183

my father was framed and murdered and prove I wasn't involved. I can't do that dead or in prison."

"Or from Africa, Jace. Who stood, or stands, to gain from destroying you and your father?" Leigh asked in a serious tone. "Who hates you that much?" His response was one she didn't want to hear.

"Your grandfather and Chad Hamilton. With Stokely burned out and killed, my father blamed and destroyed, and me helpless—they got everything, a near monopoly, lots of money and power. And Chad got revenge. Then, Leigh Webster was thrown into my path."

"That explains why you were so suspicious of me and our meeting. After sneaking into London, you rescue a woman to learn she's connected to the two men you've come to investigate. Then, she mentions a trip to your territory. I'll admit it sounds odd. But those are pretty wild charges against my family, Jace."

He agreed, and wondered why she wasn't furious. "No wilder than the ones I'm accused of, and you did ask for the truth. My father didn't kill himself, Leigh. He didn't commit arson and murder. He didn't write that letter to me, at least not willingly. I have to learn the truth and punish whoever is responsible. I honestly think it was William Webster and Chadwick Hamilton."

To her, he appeared sincere at this moment. "How could they possibly have done such an evil thing?" she refuted. "You can run a man out of business without murder and arson. Or you can burn out a rival like Stokely and foreclose on another one's debts, as Grandfather could have done with Brandon Elliott. You're talking about cold-blooded murder, possibly two of them. My grandfather wouldn't do that. Besides, they were friends, and partners in new ventures."

"Who told you that?"

"How would you know if it's true or false? Chad said you'd been gone since you were eighteen, and you've only visited a few times. Did you know my grandfather? Did you have any connections to him?"

Jace didn't grasp the purpose of her last two questions. "I received letters and cables from my father. Sure he was in debt to Webster, but they weren't partners. As for being friends, I'll admit my father liked and respected Webster, and thought he felt the same about him. He also believed he could trust him; that's why he accepted the loan. As for me, I didn't know Webster or have any dealings with him."

His answer left Leigh even more confused about the codicil, if Jace was being honest. It also made her doubts about her grandfather resurface. "What if there was someone else who wanted Stokely out of the way, or your father, or both?" she speculated. "Or what if that person simply needed someone to blame or an explanation for the death of one of them? Perhaps the guilty person simply used your father's note to keep you away so you couldn't unmask him. There are other possibilities and suspects, Jace. Don't you think you've been away too long to know about them? Aren't you allowing Grandfather's takeover and your feud with Chad to color your judgment? Chad told me you were planning to use the earnings from your last crop to pay off that loan. Was it destroyed by foul play?"

"Nope, just disease." He was impressed by her wits but her words didn't change his mind.

"Then they aren't responsible for your father being unable to settle his debt with them. Surely you don't expect a businessman to write off a bad investment because of a client's tragic death. If you hadn't lost

185

your crop, the loan would have been repaid."

"Not for another year. I was hoping Webster would be here now so I could question him about that loan and what happened."

"I'm sorry he didn't get to make this trip. It could have been good for both of you. Chad said he was very depressed after your father's death. It's a shame you didn't get to see him before he died in December. I'm sure he could have explained everything."

He sensed more in her words than she was telling. "Why?"

Leigh didn't detect any revealing reaction to her probing. "So you could get rid of these suspicions. It isn't good to hate and be bitter for so long. Why won't you or Chad tell me what happened between you years ago? If you believe he would go to such lengths for revenge, it must have been something awful."

"I'll tell you the whole story while I'm collecting my bet. I wouldn't want what happened so long ago to color your judgment of me, and it would. I am going to win, Leigh, be assured of that." He sighed deeply and flexed his taut body. "I didn't want to get into my troubles today, but we've been discussing them at great length. We can't solve anything, especially here, as you said earlier." He smiled and said, "Perhaps I will entice your help one day. Let's get back to a matter we *can* solve. What you're asking is to my benefit, so you'll have to select another prize. How about my plantation?"

He was refusing to wager himself and she wondered if that meant he only wanted her virtue as a vengeful prize. Since she wasn't going to lose, why not let him enjoy that stimulating fantasy? "That would leave you with nothing after I win," she stated, allowing the other matter to drop for now.

"You're risking a lot, so I should, too. Although marriage to you is quite tempting, woman, I can't honestly gamble with something I don't know I can do. We both realize I might never be able to clear myself, and I couldn't move to London. I love Africa; I belong here. Do we have a deal?"

For some reason her grandfather had felt he owed this man. With cunning and daring, she could settle that curious debt now. She had an enormous amount of money and property, so she could venture part of it. Chad had said he needed money . . . "In all seriousness, no more games or tests, I'll wager one-third of all I own. If you win, you can use your earnings to hire investigators to clear you while you remain safe at home."

Jace was astonished; he knew what the Webster empire must be worth. "I'd rather have you for a night," he bartered.

"How can you turn down so much money and the power it carries? Chad said you lost your crop and it takes years to nurture another one."

"Because I want you more, even for one night. Besides, you can't use Webster's money to buy off my resentment toward him. His debt to me has nothing to do with you or with us. I'm not in a financial bind, Leigh. I did lose my last crop, but I had enough to replant and enough to live on until it matures and is sold. Until then, I get more offers for work than I can accept. I don't need or want Webster charity. I earn my own way in life. But thanks for the offer."

Surely one night with her couldn't be that valuable to him. Unless he knew exoneration and marriage were impossible. Or he knew Chad would spurn her after she slept with him and that would be his revenge. Whatever his motive, Jace had a clever plan in mind. To uncover it, she had to play along. "Before I

187

say yes or no, what are the terms and rules for victory or defeat?"

Jace stood and walked to the balcony door and sank into deep thought. All she had to do was break one rule to lose, and that was inevitable. No matter her wits and skills, in the jungle this Texas girl was a tenderfoot. He turned to face Leigh. Her expression was inquisitive and tense. Yep, he decided, she couldn't win, but money wasn't what he wanted from her, nor would his pride allow him to lose on purpose. Even if she didn't know it, he had integrity! "This sport will be fun for both of us, Leigh. We'll put our deal in writing: my plantation against one night with you."

"That isn't what I said."

"I know, but this seems more like an equal bargain to me. I can earn another one if you should happen to win mine, or I could stay on as your loyal manager. Then, if you wanted to play predator, you'd always know where to find me. You could visit your new home and business anytime you pleased. As your employee, I'd be at your beck and call day and night. Forget the money, Leigh, because I can earn all I need with coffee and safaris. I don't crave one-third, one-half, or all of the Webster empire. Money comes and goes all the time, but not a woman like you. With that wager, I'd be too tempted to lose. It isn't fair to entice me to cheat, Miss Webster."

Leigh knew she would never accept his home as payment so she didn't mind his wager. But by accident or intention, if she lost . . .

"Well?" he prompted. "Do you agree? Green Hills Plantation against the intoxicating seduction of Laura Leigh."

She swallowed hard. "How will the winner be chosen?"

"First, for each terrified scream or time you complain or lag behind, you owe me a kiss. Rule two: each time you get into trouble or danger, you owe me an extra night. Rule three: if you cancel the safari or prove unable to complete it, you owe me any prize I choose to select, which will be your presence in my home for one full year. Rule four: when you lose, you pay your debt immediately and in full."

She was astounded by how easily and swiftly he listed those "rules," as if by rote, especially number three. Of course, she had nothing to worry about concerning that particular one. She would never call off the safari even if he harassed or provoked her at every bend, and she would complete it even if she had to drag herself through the jungle on her belly. But she would tell him to leave it out because she could not live with him for a year, not as his mistress. To taunt him, she murmured, "Aren't you afraid you're tempting me to lose, Mr. Elliott? At least to get into mischief."

He grinned. "If you'd be honest with yourself, you'd know you want me as much as I want you, woman, but you wouldn't intentionally lose. You're too proud and honest."

"Are you certain?" she teased. "Besides, all those rules apply to me. What about you? And how is the winner chosen?"

"Fair enough. If I prove too weak or tired to make a full day, you get a kiss. If I get into trouble or endanger your life, you get five kisses. If I quit the safari for any reason, you get an extra prize."

"Awfully vain, aren't we?" she murmured, laughing.

"Nope, just trying to simplify things for you. If I lose, you win my plantation. If I don't hold up, take your choice of an extra prize."

Leigh wondered if his adding "an extra prize" was his way of offering himself if he lost. "Suppose I don't want to trade kisses with a smug rogue like you. Why not let rules and points select the winner? The one with the largest number wins. I should get ten in advance. After all, I am a delicate woman in strange surroundings, so I should be allowed some tiny advantage over a big, strong man in his element."

He chuckled at the heavy southern drawl she affected during her last sentence. "Points are boring, Miss Webster, unless one gets extra prizes. The winner is the one who breaks the fewest rules. One other stipulation . . ." he added, his tone and gaze serious. "You have to promise not to endanger your health and safety by trying too hard to win. No pushing yourself beyond your endurance or taking risks. In exchange, I won't make this trip harder than normal. Agreed?"

"That's only fair. I know my limits and I promise not to recklessly exceed them, even to beat you. If neither of us earns points or we tie, it's a draw and the bet is nullified. On rule one, a terrified scream does not include a shriek of surprise."

"Be assured I know the difference. You can also rest assured I won't do anything intentional to lose my home or to let Chad appear a better man in the jungle, even to win a valuable prize like you, woman. Let's get our deal into writing. If there's one thing a man or woman should honor, it's his or her word. I can be awfully dangerous if crossed, Miss Webster, so think this over before you agree and sign a contract. I wouldn't want to force you to live up to your bargain, but I will. You'd better get some rest. It's going to be a long and demanding year."

"The safari is for two months, Jace, then you get one night with me *if* I lose," Leigh stressed. "I won't

190

cancel the safari or be unable to complete it, so forget the year part. And I won't get into trouble or danger, so don't count on earning extra rendezvous, either."

"We'll see," he murmured, his green eyes alive with intrigue.

"Yes, Sir Lancelot, we certainly will," she concurred.

Chapter Nine

At dinner, Jace Elliott went over the hunting and gun control laws mandated by the Colonial Office for this English protectorate. He continued with the regulations issued by the Imperial British East Africa Company under the title of "Sporting Licences" for a fee of twenty-five pounds which was valid for up to twelve months. He related the 1886 "Schedule of Duties" for controlled items and he stressed the use of quinine to prevent malaria and the danger of drinking unboiled water.

Jace told them his head man—Wanjohi, called "Johi"—was gathering supplies and hiring bearers. When all questions were asked and answered, Jace excused himself, explaining he needed a good night's sleep because he had plenty of tasks to complete before they left Mombasa on the twentieth. Today was April seventeenth.

Chad grinned and said, "That wasn't a strain at all. It looks as if Jace and I will get along fine. Anyone dissatisfied with him?"

All four shook their heads.

"I told him about the supplies we brought along," Chad then said. "He's to check them out tomorrow. You women decide on what you need in the jungle,

192

then have the rest stored in our supply room. We'll pick them up as we're leaving town. I hope you're all ready and eager to have fun, because I am. I can't wait to get into that jungle."

"Me, too, Chad," Louisa concurred.

Cynthia looked as if she was having anything but fun. Reid acted as if the safari didn't matter one way or the other to him. The blonde rose from her chair and said, "If you don't mind, I'll read a while and turn in. It's late and I'm tired."

In her suite, Leigh sat on the sofa in deep thought. She tossed her tawny locks over its back and leaned her head against the soft surface. Her dark-blue eyes stared into space. Jace and Chad's behavior had her confused. She wanted to know what had started the vengeful war between old friends. She knew that Jace had to be wrong about her grandfather and Chad. During the safari, Jace would grasp his error. Afterward, surely he would focus on unmasking the real culprit, and she would help him. If he could get his dark past behind him, perhaps he would seek a bright future with her. He had admitted he was drawn to her, so she had to increase that pull.

Yet all evening Jace had treated her as a client, nothing more. He had hardly glanced at or spoken to her. But, she decided, that could have been a pretense for the others. Their bet hadn't been mentioned, and Leigh wondered if the other women and Reid knew about the so-called thousand pound one.

The safari would get underway in three days, and her wager with Jace would begin. Despite their bargain, this afternoon he had left her side without making any attempt to embrace, kiss, or seduce her. Jace Elliott had her totally baffled and frustrated.

Leigh jumped up and paced the room. She had

learned a great deal about the enticing man since meeting him. She was glad Jace had been open about a few matters. And she had learned more about herself and her emotions. She loved being with him. She felt good in his company. She believed he was innocent, that he was a unique person. She liked and respected him. She was experiencing more than the budding of friendship. She desired him. She was falling in love with that green-eyed seductor.

Leigh was anxious to see what the next day and the safari would bring. Louisa had asked Leigh to give her and Chad time alone, and Leigh had agreed. She had told the redhead she was going to see the old Portuguese fort. Louisa had hugged her and thanked her.

Leigh had been awakened early that morning, as she had each day. While darkness was deserting the foreign land, she had heard the echoing calls of the *muezzin* from the small towers attached to mosques summoning the faithful Moslems to prayer. It was a custom unchanged since the Islamic traders had first settled in this land. She had listened to the melodious calls of the "Crier" from the minarets, then dozed for a time. Later, she had risen, dressed, and eaten breakfast alone.

She checked her string purse to make certain her derringer was inside and loaded. She sneaked from the hotel and hired a rickshaw to take her to the old fort. As Leigh was rushed along, she quickly glanced at the scenery much as she had done on her arrival, noticing the same sights, smells, activities, and sounds. When the driver halted, she paid him and asked him to return in an hour to fetch her.

Fort Jesus, the sixteenth-century fortress, was located near the natural harbor where her ship had docked to unload its passengers and cargo. It was spread over a large area, and a stone wall encompassed the fortress, other buildings, and the grounds. The fort was unlocked, but no visitors and natives were around today. In size, shape, and appearance, the main structure reminded her of an English castle. The yard was enormous and, despite their age, most buildings were in excellent condition. Tropical trees and vegetation had been allowed to remain intact here and there, giving the fort a mysterious and sultry aura.

Leigh tried to imagine it in olden times—noisy and filled with soldiers, weapons, and supplies. She tried to envision the fierce struggles that had taken place here for control of this crucial seaport. It must have been a terrible loss for the Portuguese.

She strolled about the area, always keeping a tight grip on her purse. Leigh felt safe venturing out alone, but she still did not drop her guard for an instant. Afterward, she planned to visit the bazaar before returning to the hotel. That should give Louisa enough time alone with Chad. Perhaps Jace would return from his business dealings by tea time and they could get together again.

The sun was past its noon level, and her early-fed stomach told her it was nearing mealtime. Her driver was to return at twelve-thirty to fetch her, so it wouldn't be long now.

A man in Arab garb raced to her. Seizing her hand and pulling on it, he entreated, *"Bibi, memsahib,* come! Boy hurt. Need help. *Mbeia sana,* very bad. Please to come help. My son fall, dying."

Leigh hurried out of the fort with the anxious man, along its right side, and down a path toward

195

the water's edge. In the distance, she saw a *dhow* bobbing on the liquid blue surface where sunlight dazzled, then a still body near a large rock. It looked as if the boy had fallen from it, perhaps while playing. His garment was twisted about him. His arms and legs were positioned unnaturally. Leigh's feet slipped and slid as she followed the nervous man to see if she could give aid.

Before reaching the victim, Leigh noticed the prone figure was too large for a boy and his position was odd, as if skillfully arranged. Her guard lifted with speed. As the man in front of her was turning, she fumbled with her purse to loosen its string. She yanked the derringer from inside and pointed it at the deceitful man. She saw how his dark eyes had narrowed and chilled; their gaze and his expression were evil. She felt cold menace in the hot air.

When he lunged for her armed hand, she fired. The jolted weapon sent a bullet into his thigh. He staggered and looked shocked. The prone man sprang from his position and headed their way.

Panic filled her. Leigh backed up and warned, "Stay back or the next shot will be in your chest." She knew she only had one bullet left, but she hoped these foreign men weren't familiar with this type of gun. Obviously she was right, because they halted, then glanced at each other as if plotting their strategy.

From atop the path near the fort corner, Leigh heard a voice. "Leigh, are you all right?" Jace Elliott called out. "I'm coming." He moved as quickly as the terrain allowed, shouting, "Stay calm. I'll be there in a minute."

The two men exchanged words in their language. The second one helped the first—blood flowing down his injured leg—to rush toward their waiting boat. He shoved it into the water, and off the *dhow* went the moment wind filled its sail. Leigh didn't fire at them again; she could not kill a man—even an attacker—in cold blood.

Jace reached her, eyed the gun and vanishing boat, then asked, "What happened? What are you doing here alone?"

Apparently he had put the clues together rapidly and accurately. She explained to the breathless man what had happened. A scowl lined his handsome face. "Don't scold me again, Sir Lancelot," she teased to lighten the situation. "Ever since that night in the London alley, I carry my trusty derringer with me for protection. My uncle in Texas gave it to me, and it works perfectly. What are you doing here, Mr. Elliott?"

"I was finishing some business with a man nearby. I saw you leaving the fort with a strange man. I figured something was up. When I heard that shot . . . You could have been killed or abducted."

Leigh savored the worried look on his face. "But I wasn't. I can take care of myself, most of the time."

"I can see that," he agreed, still frowning. "You shouldn't go out alone, Leigh. The Sultan of Zanzibar probably heard there was a beautiful woman with golden hair here and sent his men to capture her for his harem," he jested, planning to check into the matter.

"You should tell him I would make a terrible slave. I'm willful and stubborn, according to some people I know."

"This isn't a joke, Leigh," he said in a serious tone.

"I know, but it's over now. It's nice to know my Sir Lancelot is always around when I'm in danger. How is that so, Jace?"

Jace caught the provocative tone in her voice. "Probably because you're always into mischief. You're a very desirable woman, so men everywhere will be after you, including me. You realize this means you owe me an extra night with you. According to rule two, if you get yourself into danger or trouble, I get an extra reward. I wonder . . ." he murmured huskily. "Are danger and trouble the same or do I earn two extra nights for you getting into both?"

"You are a greedy rogue, Jace Elliott. We aren't on safari yet, so this incident doesn't count. Besides, I solved it, remember? Did you connive with those men to help me lose my bet with you?"

Making a X over his chest, he vowed, "I cross my heart those men don't work for me and never have. I'll get the Colonial Office to investigate the matter. We can't have ruffians attacking our visitors and scaring them away from our beautiful land. This is all your fault for going out alone. Don't do it again," he cautioned.

"I'll be good, my legendary guide," she teased. "Can I ask you a question that you'll promise to answer honestly?"

"Such as?" he replied, his brow lifting inquisitively.

"Did you pay Jim Hanes to fake an accident so you could replace him?" she inquired, as they headed up the hill.

Jace didn't halt his step. "Right to the heart of a matter, eh? No, Miss Webster, I had nothing to do with Jim's being unable to guide your party. If anyone did, point your finger at Chad."

"Can I ask another question?" she continued, ignoring his charge.

"Go ahead," he remarked, halting to lock his gaze to hers.

"How could you get a safari together so quickly?"

He chuckled. "I started Johi working out the details the minute I received Chad's message on Friday. I handle lots of safaris, so I'm well trained and prepared. I never intended to refuse his job, but I wanted it to look as if I needed plenty of persuasion. I didn't want him to realize how eager I was to spend so much time with his ward. Does it surprise you that I would accept his curious offer just to be near you?"

That wasn't the expected response. "Yes, I was surprised," she informed him, "No, shocked. Why would you go to work for an enemy? You don't appear a man to put himself into a disagreeable situation without a good reason."

He grinned. "I have a good reason, an excellent one."

"Like what?" she pressed.

Tapping the tip of her nose with his finger, he said, "You."

"I doubt I'm the reason—or the only one, at least." Leigh refuted. "Why won't you tell me about the trouble between you and Chad?"

"Haven't you heard the old saying, 'Let old wounds heal?' If you pick at them, they fester again. Chad and I have made a truce, so what difference does it make?" He started moving again.

"Is that a polite way of saying it's none of my business?"

"You're a smart woman," he replied. When she frowned, he added, "I promise I'll tell you everything after the safari."

"Won't it be too late by then?" she parried.

"Too late for what, Leigh?" he countered, halting once more.

She didn't stop. As she moved past him, she tossed over her shoulder, "To be saved from a mysterious rogue like you, of course."

"Do you want to be spared such a . . . an adventure?"

"I haven't decided," she admitted with frankness.

At the corner of the fortress, he asked, "How long have you known Chad?"

Their gazes fused. "Since I was fifteen. I met him when I visited my grandparents in '90. Why?"

"How well do you know him?"

She watched his alert gaze roam her face for clues. "Not well at all. I spent time with him on my last visit. And, after I arrived in London in February, we spent every day and evening together getting acquainted. Too, I had frequent letters from my grandparents about him. I am familiar with his reputation with the ladies, if that's what you're referring to, Jace. If you know him, why ask me about him?"

Jace leaned his back against the stone wall that surrounded the old Portuguese fortress. "He's changed since our old days together."

Although she hadn't known the old Chad, to keep Jace talking, she questioned, "Are you sure?"

"Yes." He straightened to depart, ending the conversation.

Leigh caught his arm to stop him. "Wait, Jace; we aren't finished. What evidence does the law have against you?" Noting his surprised look, she continued. "Please, just pamper me with an answer. It will help me understand both of you to know the

200

truth."

His gaze slipped over her. She appeared sincere. He inhaled deeply and replied in a sketchy manner. "Two witnesses who claim my father was at the crime scene. A knife with his initials. A lantern from Elliott's of London used to start the fire. Papers in his desk tying him and me to Irish rebels. He and Stokely were political rivals."

"But how can they tie you to those crimes?" she asked.

"Are you forgetting about the note from my father implicating me? They proved it was his handwriting, and they knew I was in town. I don't have an alibi; I was asleep in Alfred's warehouse, getting ready to work my way home on one of his ships to save money. I sailed the next dawn without knowing what had taken place just miles from the wharf. I had been visiting my father. That's when I learned about his loan from Webster. I told him I'd pay it off when my crop came in. It didn't; coffee rust destroyed it. Lordy, I can still remember the day I sighted those yellowish, oily spots on the leaves. By then, I'd studied and learned enough to know what had to be done: all bushes had to be chopped down and burned to prevent its spread. That created a total loss of my investment, and years of labor and waiting."

He stretched his suddenly weary body. "Fortunately, I had enough money left to replant the next spring; young shrubs have to be put in the ground before the rainy season. That allows them to sprout and get strong enough to endure the dry season. As soon as I burned the diseased crop, I sailed for London in December to break the bad news to Father. I docked to learn Father was accused of arson and murder, had committed suicide, and had

201

implicated me."

His voice was bitter as he continued. "Chad was the one to expose my dilemma to me. I knew from the way he was gloating that I was in deep trouble. I didn't hang around to be questioned and arrested; the evidence was too cunning and damaging to refute from jail, and I didn't know what else they had on me. I returned to Africa and threw myself into saving my plantation. I knew I had to let things cool down before I could begin my own investigation. Since a coffee crop takes three to four years between planting and harvesting, all I had was time on my hands and frustration to burn off. Once a crop's in the ground, its care is limited to the trimming required to give bushes a robust, balanced framework and to stimulate growth. The coffee cherries should be ready next year, if another disaster doesn't strike. In this business, disease, rainfall, and temperature control your success."

Leigh realized he was rambling, but she let him talk as he pleased. "How can you stay away from your crop so long?"

"I have an excellent overseer named Kambu, and the Kikuyu village nearby furnishes me with plenty of good workers. To support myself, I work as a safari guide for rich and bored Englishmen. But I got tired of feeling helpless and risked a trip to London. Satisfied?"

"Nope. How did you get to Africa? Why did you stay here?"

He smiled. "I love this land; it's wild and beautiful, and full of promise and excitement. I hate being away from it very long. After I finished school in '82, I joined the Royal Navy and sailed the world over. When I had enough of their tight rules, I took off for bluer seas, until Africa caught

202

my eye. I lived and worked in the southern area for a while. Then, I became a member of the Uganda Railroad expedition. It was on that trip that I lost my heart and soul to this land. I learned my way around while doing lots of different jobs."

"Why did you go into the coffee business?"

"I wanted to succeed on my own, not live off an inheritance, and I don't like the textile business. In '91 I happened upon an excellent deal with an Englishman who wanted 'out of this damn jungle and back into civilization.' I used the money I'd earned to purchase his home, land, and crop. It's near Kiambu, northwest of Nairobi, near the rail line they're building. That'll be a big help with shipments and save me lots of work and time. Satisfied now?" he laughingly questioned.

Leigh grinned and remarked, "A little."

"Tell me about yourself. Start with how you got your name."

"Leigh was my mother's maiden name. Laura was her mother."

"That's mighty stingy information. What have you been doing in London? Where are you from? Tell me all about yourself."

Leigh realized he wanted to change the subject and decided to go along with him. She went over her history, then quipped, "Satisfied?"

With a broad grin, he murmured, "A little."

"Tell me more about yourself, Jace. And tell me why," she probed, "are you and he enemies now?"

"I told you that's a taboo subject for now. Ask me again in two months."

"That isn't fair."

"Life never is, Miss Webster. Who knew you were coming here?"

"Only one person. No, two: Louisa and the rickshaw driver." Leigh hadn't forgotten that Louisa had sent the note in London that had resulted in her attack. Her suspicions returned.

"Chad's . . . sweetheart?"

She tried to sound light when she said, "That's right. She wanted time alone with him, so I gave it to her. Why?"

Jace sensed how much the redhead wanted his enemy. "If this wasn't a chance attack, somebody planned it," he hinted.

Leigh reasoned aloud. "Louisa didn't. She couldn't have. She doesn't know anyone here, and she only learned about my visit last night. There was no time for a plot, Mr. Elliott."

Her mention of a ruse alerted Jace. He worried that the redhead had told Chad about Leigh's plans today and that his foe had plotted this perilous mischief. Or, Louisa could be Chad's accomplice in a plot against Leigh. But that didn't make sense, *if* Chad truly wanted to win and wed this golden creature. Under English law, if anything happened to Leigh, Fiona—and eventually Chad—would inherit the Webster empire. So, if Chad couldn't win or didn't want to wed Leigh . . . That thought sent Jace's mind to reasoning frantically. Perhaps Chad needed someone to frame or a logical explanation for the timing of Leigh's death—so close to William's. It didn't make sense for Chad to risk losing her to him. Yet that wager had been created to provoke his interest. He wanted more facts; but he held silent for now.

Leigh intruded on his silent fears. "If you don't mind, please don't tell the others about this trouble," she coaxed.

"Don't want to worry or alarm them?" When she nodded, he asked, "What is my silence worth?"

"Do you always expect payment for everything?" she quipped.

"Why not? That's why I took this job."

"I thought you took it to please and pursue me," she jested.

"You did, did you?" he mirthfully retorted. "You're right. There are plenty of other safaris."

Jace's engaging grin had a weakening effect on her. The tropical sun caused his eyes to squint, and it danced in his windblown hair. He was too tempting. When he made no attempt to kiss her or to even move closer, she said, "I should be getting back to the hotel. I told my driver to return at twelve-thirty. He's probably come and gone by now. Care to find me another carriage, Sir Lancelot?"

"Why don't I see you back? I am responsible for you," he murmured.

"Only in the jungle, my alert guide. But thanks."

At the hotel, Leigh was surprised to discover Louisa had moved into a private room on her floor. Passing the redhead in the hallway, the woman told the blonde she wasn't feeling well due to her monthly flow and that she didn't want to disturb Reid and Cynthia. Leigh didn't believe her, but she said nothing to challenge her.

"Why did Chad want you to change rooms?" Cynthia asked.

"He wants me to go after Jace to help him win a bet." Louisa explained. "He was a fool to reveal it to me, because now I know he's serious about winning his little ward. He pretended their bargain was a joke when he asked for my help, but I know better. He didn't make that damned wager just to provoke Jace into coming to work for him. Chad Hamilton would never risk losing that much money to any man. I'm supposed to make certain Leigh doesn't fall under Jace's spell. Chad said that if Leigh is convinced there's something between me and Jace, she won't give our guide a second look."

"As soon as I have my traitorous lover believing I'm doing everything I can to aid him," Louisa spouted with a sneer, "I'll make certain Leigh won't turn to Chad and tempt him even more before I can get rid of her. But, for now, I have to distract Jace, just like Chad wants me to do. Besides, that handsome devil keeps thwarting my plans for little Leigh, damn him! When I met that Arab, I had to pay him double, because his friend was wounded and he threatened to expose me. She actually shot one of them before Jace showed up again to help her. I would have stolen her gun, but that might have aroused her suspicion before she left the hotel. I was hoping to be finished with her and return home. That hot jungle doesn't tempt me at all, not with Chad rutting for her. If I don't break Jace's concentration, I'll never get rid of Leigh and win Chad. Besides, Jace Elliott is up to something. I can feel it. I think he wants Leigh, too."

"I hate Chad for using you this way Louisa. You think Jace will respond to your note to come here tonight?"

"What man wouldn't enjoy a taste of me?" the redhead teased. "Do me a favor, Cynthia; find out why Jace and Chad are enemies. I'm sure Reid knows. Wheedle that information from him. I don't like mysteries."

"Anything for you, love," the brunette promised, alarmed over this new obstacle to their plans.

"Since Jace is wanted by the law and he lost everything to the Websters, it will be easy to frame him for Leigh's death. We have to be more careful than ever, Cynthia. Chad craves Leigh, so we have to make Jace look guilty in his eyes, too. Once Leigh is gone, Chad will settle for me. Then, I'll take everything and destroy him. Damn the bastard! He doesn't have me fooled. Still, it will be nice to get Jace Elliott beneath me before he dies."

There was a knock at Leigh's door. She was annoyed for she had sent a note to Chad explaining she wouldn't be joining the group for dinner because she was tired and turning in early with a book. If it was her guardian, she would get rid of him quickly. She was moody tonight. Jace hadn't contacted her all afternoon, had dropped her off like baggage after their misadventure. As for the curious exchange between Louisa and Chad, that had her worried. If Chad lost interest in Louisa before the safari . . . "Yes?" she hinted as she opened the door.

Jace swept past her with a tray of fragrant food. Leigh whirled and stared at him. He placed it on a table and grinned at her. She closed and locked the door, then went forward to join him. "What is this?" she questioned, glancing from him to the food and back again.

"You *are* hungry, aren't you? You didn't join us and the man downstairs told me you hadn't ordered dinner yet. Why?"

Leigh was perplexed. "Frankly, Mr. Elliott, I wasn't in the mood to be with anyone tonight. This is very kind of you, but—"

"But what?" he interrupted.

"I wanted to be alone. I have some thinking to do."

"About what?" he probed as he arranged the table.

Leigh joined him and responded, "About many things."

"Such as," he continued in a persistent manner.

"Such as about our brazen guide," she retorted.

Jace halted his work to look at her. She was attired in a fetching gown and wrapper of sapphire silk. He halted himself from asking, out of jealousy, if Chad had given it to her. "Why would you possibly want to think about me?" he jested. "I'm dull."

"You are anything but dull, Mr. Elliott."

"Why is it you get formal with me when I make you nervous?"

"I hadn't noticed," she said, taking the chair he pulled out for her. "I'm starved."

He leaned over her shoulder and asked, "Then why didn't you come downstairs for dinner?"

She tried to ignore his warm breath on her cheek. He smelled of heady spices, and she tingled all over. She was vexed with this tantalizing man who tempted but didn't give. "I didn't realize I was so hungry. This is wonderful. Thank you."

"You're welcome." He leaned against the wall nearby. Her tawny locks flowed down her back, and the color of her garments intensified the blue of her eyes. Her skin looked so soft, and he yearned to caress it.

"Are you planning to stare at me while I devour my food?"

"Naturally. I have to make certain you eat every bite to keep up your strength, and I love watching you do anything."

After Leigh forced herself to eat most of the delicious meal, she hinted, "I finished, sir, so your task is done."

"Is it?" he questioned with an evocative look.

"Did we have other business to discuss?"

"What did you expect after this alluring note?" Jace teased.

The blue-eyed blonde looked at the paper he was waving beneath his nose. She eyed his smug grin, twinkling eyes, and merry expression. "How could I resist such an intoxicating summons?" Without releasing her captive gaze, he repeated its startling message from memory. She listened as he repeated its startling message from memory. " 'Come to my suite late tonight. We'll go over old times and make new ones. Tell no one. I'm eager to see you.' It's signed with a flowing *L*. I'm glad to see you've become the aggressive predator so I can be the helpless quarry for a change."

Leigh jumped up and snatched the note from his hand. He chuckled as she stared at it with wide eyes and parted lips. He knew it was from Louisa Jennings, but it suited his needs.

Leigh was jealous and angry. "I didn't write this nonsense! This is Louisa's handwriting. I recognize it from the sneaky message she sent that night we met on the dock. I know she wrote that note because I overheard her say so. How dare you think I would—"

"I didn't," he injected, halting her revealing outburst.

"But you said . . ." She stopped and stared at him.

He chuckled and shrugged. "It was a good way to see you privately, woman. If Chad demands satisfaction, I can show him this note and explain how

209

my error was natural since I never expected his lover to send for me. I have to use every trick I know to entice you."

Leigh was perturbed. "I didn't know you and Louisa were old friends."

"We aren't. She chased me every time I went home for a visit, but I never let her catch me." He caressed Leigh's flushed cheek and revealed, "You should be aware of my taste in women by now."

"You and Louisa never . . ." Leigh blushed and turned aside.

Jace captured her arms and prevented her from leaving. "No, Leigh, I've never had anything to do with that woman and I never will. My only interest is you."

"Then why did she send you this seductive note?"

"Tell me," he coaxed. "What does Chad hope to gain by throwing both of you at me? Am I supposed to go after his mistress or his ward?"

"What does that mean?" she demanded.

"It's supposed to get you seeing clearly, Leigh. You're blind to him. An old enemy comes here and makes me an offer I can't refuse. He dangles his irresistible ward before me when he wants her like crazy himself. He orders his lover to seduce me. What am I supposed to think?"

Exasperated, she snapped, "How should I know? I don't understand any of this. Are you after me to spite Grandfather and Chad?"

"I swear that isn't true, Leigh." He pulled her into his arms and murmured, "A woman as beautiful and desirable and wealthy as you will have men chasing her all the time. I know this must sound like a seductive ploy, and you might not believe me, but I want you for no other reason than you enslave me. I've never wanted any woman like I crave you.

When I'm cleared, I'll want more than a night or two from you, much more, Leigh."

She gazed into his eyes, lost in that jungle-green terrain. His flowing voice washed over her like an inviting ocean. His nearness and touch were more intoxicating than aged brandy. His words ensnared her. Impulsively, she revealed, "One minute you act so loving; the next, you treat me indifferently. It's like you're playing with me, tempting me and intriguing me, then ignoring me. Surely you've had enough experience to know I feel the same way, Jace, and you can have me without all these exasperating games."

His fingers roamed her flushed cheek and parted lips. "If that's true, Leigh, then no more games. I'm sorry I made it look that way to you. I was only trying to move slowly and carefully to keep from scaring you. It's been damned hard, but I wanted to give you time to get to know me, to like me. I know you're innocent, and I know you're attracted to me, but that doesn't give me the right to take unfair advantage of you."

"How can you take advantage of me if I'm willing?"

"People do things in the heat of passion that they regret later. I don't want you to ever regret anything you do with me. I wanted us to become friends first, then hopefully a lot more to each other as time passes. With these criminal charges hanging over my head and my family name blackened, I have nothing to offer you but a brief time with me. I can't return to England with you, and I can't ask you to permanently exile yourself with a wanted man. I can't even allow you to let people discover our feelings and ruin your reputation. If you doubt me, my feelings, or my intentions—it's wrong for

211

anything this important to happen between us. You have to be sure of me and yourself. Once we accept each other, there's no turning back."

Leigh understood that this proud man wouldn't consider marriage until he was exonerated. That might never happen, and she had to have him. "I am sure of myself, Jace, and now I'm sure of you."

"Think it over Leigh, carefully and completely."

Leigh was glad he was being cautious and frank. She lifted her hands and grasped his face between them. Rising on her tiptoes as she pulled his head downward, she murmured, "I have, Jace, many times. Now if you don't kiss me, I'm going to scream or expire."

Leigh sealed her lips to his, as Jace embraced her. His mouth feasted at hers, just as hers was greedily devouring his. They pressed tightly together and savored this heady moment that both had long awaited and craved.

Jace wanted to prevent as much embarrassment and pain, and to give as much pleasure as possible this first time. He had to control his own desires, and sate them only after she claimed her own. Yet he discovered mastery over his body difficult. She was so warm and eager and responsive. He had dreamed of this night many times, but hadn't expected it to come so quickly or easily. At last he knew he was the man she wanted, and no other.

Leigh felt more alive in his arms than she had in her lifetime. Never had a man affected her this way. She wanted his kisses, embraces, his touch, and all of him. Her body felt as hot as an iron in a branding fire, and she wanted his possessive mark upon her body and life. She yearned for them to become as one, tonight and forever. Even if their affair was dangerous, she had to taste his sweet passions.

Still kissing her, Jace lifted her and carried her into the adjoining room. The covers were already tossed aside. The lamp was burning low and casting a soft glow in the room and on the golden beauty in his arms. He eased her feet to the floor. Deftly he unfastened her wrapper and let it slide to her ankles. Then he unbuttoned her gown and let it do the same. As his mouth roved her face, ears, hair, and neck before locking with hers once more, he removed his shirt and tossed it aside.

Their bare flesh met when he embraced her. Leigh trembled at the glorious sensation, and Jace shuddered from the way her breasts felt against his chest. Her fingers trailed over his neck and shoulders, and she admired the strength and soft firmness of them. Jace's hands roamed her silky back and teased down her spine.

He guided her to the bed and kissed her eyes shut while he removed his shoes and pants. He didn't want to panic her with the sight of his nakedness. Jace joined her on the bed, savoring the sight of her. With great care and skill, his hands traveled over her body, exploring it and mapping it as he had done to this territory. She was so soft and supple, he couldn't wait to taste every inch of her sweet flesh. Her tawny mane spread over the pillow and shone in the lamplight. He stroked it and buried his fingers in it. She didn't seem afraid, but he knew she must be nervous. He moved slowly, gently, not wanting to make any mistakes with this special woman.

Leigh was consumed by desire. She couldn't seem to get him close enough to please her. His lips and hands worked magic on her, and she felt enchanted. Surely she could lie here with him like this forever.

213

Her breasts were firm, and their peaks hard. She quivered each time his fingers or lips touched them. It created such a tormentingly sweet sensation. When his hand ventured lower, she tensed at the shocking ecstasy he created. A moan escaped her lips. Leigh's hands wandered over his bronzed back, up his neck, into his mussed brown hair, and across his powerful shoulders. "Oh, Jace," she murmured and clung to him.

"Just relax and let nature do all the work for you," he whispered into her ear, his warm breath making her tremble. "It'll be uncomfortable for a moment, love, but I'll try not to hurt you." As Jace moved atop her and gently spread her thighs, he kept talking to calm her. "Ever since I saw you that night in London, I've been crazy to have you. When you responded to me, I thought I'd go mad if this didn't happen soon." His lips labored lovingly at hers. He kissed her eyes, the tip of her nose, and every inch of her face. His teeth nibbled at her ear, and his hands caressed her breasts.

Leigh was nearly mindless with the aching need that stormed her body without mercy. "Please, Jace," she urged him to continue.

His mouth captured hers and he kissed her feverishly as his manhood tenderly sought new and rapturous surroundings. He hesitated a while to allow her to adjust to these new sensations. His hands clasped her face between them and his mouth meshed with hers. She was embracing him and responding urgently, so he realized the discomfort had passed. He moved with leisure and caution. He felt her open further to him. Once more she was offering herself freely, totally, and ardently.

Leigh was delighted it hadn't hurt as she had expected. Perhaps that was because Jace was so tender. She wasn't totally ignorant about sex and men. She had overheard information, and her aunt Jenna had told her many things during long and private talks. Maybe the difference between gossipy horrid tales and her blissful experience was the fact she wanted and needed this man with all her being.

The flames within Leigh and Jace blazed fiercely from the sparks of their love and desire. They caressed, kissed, and labored in unison. Soon, the wildfire burned out of control. The tension inside them was nearly unbearable. Their passion was overwhelming. They neared the wondrous conclusion of their first journey together.

Jace knew she was approaching the pinnacle of arousal. It was time to carry her into the valley of pleasure and satisfaction. Up the last hill he raced with her, hesitating only a moment at the heady precipice, then pushing them over its beckoning cliff. He locked his gaze to hers at the moment their ecstasy began. As it continued to surge through them, his mouth covered hers and he rode her to their final location. There, his lips did not cease their labors. He kissed her almost breathlessly until she relaxed beneath him. He lifted his head and smiled, a warm and tender one. In a husky voice, he admitted, "That was the most marvelous experience I've ever had. You sure you're all right?"

She laughed and hugged him. "Never better, Mr. Elliott."

"It's too late to be formal with me now, woman," he teased.

"I suppose so, Lancelot. I must confess, I like this rescue even better than your first one," she replied, mirth filling her eyes.

"I enjoyed both of them, all of them." His fingertips grazed her bare chest. She didn't look embarrassed or ill at ease. He was glad, and relieved. She was his now, all his.

"Is that a possessive or victorious gleam in your eyes?"

He chuckled as he rolled to his back and carried her along with him. She snuggled against him. He sighed with contentment. "Both. You're some woman, Laura Leigh. I'm glad I risked everything to visit London. If I hadn't, I wouldn't have met you."

"Yes, you would have," Leigh innocently refuted. "Even if we hadn't met there, we would have met here in Africa because of the safari."

Jace listed his reasons for thinking otherwise. "But it would be different. If I hadn't been in town lying in wait for you, I would be far from Mombasa and where you're heading. If Chad had sent for me to work for him, I doubt I would have responded." He stiffened and corrected. "That isn't true. I *would* have come eventually to see what he was up to. I have to make certain he isn't responsible for framing me and Father. Don't get riled," he coaxed when she tensed. "I shouldn't have brought up my suspicions. I don't want to spoil this wonderful evening."

Leigh was tempted to ask Jace again about the trouble between him and Chad, but she didn't, because she didn't want it to seem as if she had surrendered just to open him up more. "I agree, so let's drop it for now. Besides, you're right. If we hadn't become friends first, we wouldn't be lovers tonight."

He leaned away so he could meet her gaze. "We *are* friends, aren't we, Leigh? You do trust me and believe in me, don't you?"

"Of course I do. If not, we wouldn't be lying here

216

like this."

"I had to ask. I'm as new at this kind of relationship as you are. It'll take some adjusting."

"And what now, my competitor? My wager is worthless, because you've already taken your prize. Shall I bargain something else?"

He teased her nose with a lock of her hair. "No way, woman. As you said at the fort, the safari hasn't begun yet, so this doesn't count as part of our deal. One night with you only whets my appetite to win more. Lots more, if I cheat."

"I told you not to include rule three because I can't stay here for a year, but you wouldn't cheat, would you?"

"No, but I'll work harder than I ever have in my life to get what I want. That's you, Leigh, for as many nights as possible."

"Perfect, because I want you just as badly."

"Even if you cross out rule three, you can have me any time, any place, and any way you want me. Well, almost any place or time."

Leigh's eyes brightened with the smile that captured her lips. "That's a fetching offer, Jace." She knew she would never cancel the safari or fail to finish it. But dare she break rule two to gain more nights with him when her departure might prevent her from keeping her word? What would she do if Jace let her win his home in an attempt to hold her here? To accept payment gave her a reason to stay in Africa . . . No, she couldn't take the plantation.

"You realize we have to keep this a secret until you're twenty-one and free in November. If Chad even suspected there was something between us, he would intrude. He would pack you up and haul you home."

"He can't do that," she argued. "I don't belong to

him."

"This is a British protectorate," he revealed, "and Chad and I are British citizens. William Webster's inheritance falls under English law. You can't take control or sell it until you come of age. Until then, Chad is your legal guardian and you have to obey him. I'm afraid he can force you to leave Africa; British law is on his side for now. He has awesome power over you and your estate until November. If I interfered, I would be in worse trouble than I am now. If I carried you off, the law would come to my plantation to fetch you and arrest me. I'd be sent back to London to face all charges against me. How would it look to everyone if Jace Elliott stole the granddaughter of the man who took everything from him? Like a mean trick on you. They would spirit you back to England to clear your head."

Jace scowled and said, "I bet that's his clever plan, the sorry bastard. He brought you here to bewitch me. Then, when he whisks you home, he hopes I'll follow, get arrested, and hanged."

"What's gotten in to you, Jace? That isn't true. Grandfather planned this safari last winter. When he died and I went to London, Chad asked me if I wanted to come along to get better acquainted. It sounded exciting, so I agreed. Even so, how could Chad know I would make you act so rashly? Besides, you said he wants me. So why would he risk losing me to you, his enemy?"

"He probably thinks you'd never fall for a rogue like me," Jace speculated. "And he does have the power to keep us apart. If you refuse to obey him and side with a criminal, he can have you declared insane, and you'll lose everything to him and his mother. We're trapped, love, so keep quiet so you can stay near me. I wish you could live at my plantation until November, so we'd have more time together." .

"If Chad has that much control over me, how could I?"

"By letting him believe you're sailing to Texas to visit there until November. He'll be delighted to have full control over Webster International for months. Once you have your birthday here, then you can do as you please. I don't like you being in his control."

"I can't be your lover for months, Jace; that isn't right. I have to return to London with Chad after the safari. I have so much to do there. Can you sneak back to England? We could work on clearing you. By November, we can be free to do as we please."

"I can't risk another trip this soon, Leigh. Chad has to know how enchanted I am by you. He'll have the authorities on the lookout for me. And if you return with him after the safari, he'll be after you day and night to marry him so he won't lose everything. That would cause me to go crazy with worry and jealousy. You don't want me to get impatient and reckless, then do something foolish. Stay here and be safe until you're free of him. I'm sure we can find a way to trick him."

Leigh sat up and wrapped the edge of the sheet around her nude body. "Chad doesn't want to marry me. He has Louisa. If he was after me, she wouldn't be here now. Romancing a woman is a mite difficult with a clingy lover along."

"Not for Chadwick Hamilton. He always works on a new conquest before he discards his old one. If there's one thing I'm certain of, it's that he wants you badly. He brought Louisa along so you wouldn't get suspicious or refuse to come."

219

Annoyed, she asked, "How do you know?"

Jace moved to the edge of the bed. He recovered his pants, worked them over his feet, then stood to pull them up and fasten them. Leigh observed him, admiring his firm buttocks and the way the muscles in his back rippled as he dressed. He sat again to put on his shoes. She wondered if he was thinking of a good response to her question. She could not become his mistress and he hadn't mentioned wedlock.

Lifting his shirt and facing her as he donned it, he finally replied. "I know Chad. I know how he treats women. I know he's selfish and greedy, cold and calculating. I know he wants to woo you, win you, and wed you to get at your inheritance. If you fail to believe me, Leigh, you could be in big trouble. Chad usually gets his desires, one way or another."

The cold bitterness in his voice concerned Leigh. To glean more information, she ventured, "You knew him years ago, Jace. Maybe he's matured and changed over the years. He doesn't strike me that way."

Jace stopped buttoning his shirt. He stared at her, then said, "Because you're a woman, and Chad knows how to dupe them."

Leigh frowned. "I don't dupe easily, Jace. I know Chad has some character flaws, but everyone does. He's been kind, thoughtful, generous, and protective of me. We've spent a lot of time together, and he's been nothing but respectful and helpful. He hasn't tried to influence me. I know he's attracted to me. But nothing can come of a one-sided desire, and I'm certain Chad realizes I don't feel the same way about him. He has flirted on occasion, but he's never kissed or hugged or charmed me. Is

220

it so unusual or unthinkable for him to be tempted by all I am and have?"

Jace caught the jesting tone in her last question, but he knew it was a serious one. To keep from losing her with stubbornness or scaring her over potentially lethal perils, he had to relent a little. Besides, he would be around to safeguard her on the safari, and afterward. "I hadn't thought of it that way. You're right. What man wouldn't be tempted by you? I certainly was."

She jested, "I hope you meant, *am,* not was."

He grinned. "Am, was, and will be forever."

Leigh rose, dragging the concealing sheet with her. She leaned against his hard body and murmured, "Good, so stop worrying about Chad. During or after the safari, we'll figure out what to do about us. Even while we're separated, I won't forget you or give up on capturing my handsome prey. You did tell me to become a persistent and aggressive predator, and I am. I won't let Chad intrude on our plans. I promise, nothing he says or does will change things between us."

Jace drew her tightly against him. His mouth covered hers as he prayed, *I hope not, my love, or I'll kill him this time . . .*

Chapter Ten

Monday morning, Leigh headed to the lobby to mail a letter to her aunt in Texas. Her heart soared with a happiness, an event she could share only with Jenna. It would be hard to mask her feelings to the others, but she knew she must. November was—

As she passed a door leading into a lovely garden, her thoughts ceased abruptly. She saw Jace standing in a romantic setting talking to a beautiful, light-skinned African woman. She halted, then stepped to the nearby open window. She peered around the edge and observed them. Something in the way they were standing and looking at each other told Leigh they knew each other well.

Leigh did not like spying on her new lover, but she could not help herself. She felt a chill wash over her. She knew he was teasing the female. Jace grasped her chin and shook it in a playful manner. She captured his hand and held it as she spoke to him. His rich laughter reached Leigh's ears. She wished she could hear what they were saying. The woman was exquisite. Her sarong garment revealed a shapely figure. Her black hair was braided, then twisted around her head like a royal circlet. She never took her brown eyes from Jace, and that riled Leigh, as much as the fact Jace was smiling at another woman.

The blonde watched Jace pull money from his pocket and give it to the woman. They talked and laughed again. As they headed toward the doorway, Jace's arm was around the female's waist. Leigh heard him say, "Don't be like that, Ka'arta. I'll be home soon and we'll solve any problem we have. Love isn't the question; marriage is. It scares a man."

Almost in a run, Leigh rushed back to her room. She did not know what to think about what she had witnessed. It sounded terrible, but she could be mistaken. After last night with him, she had to be mistaken! Leigh cautioned herself not to jump to hasty conclusions. She would ask Jace to explain the incident. If only they hadn't appeared so close and his words didn't plague her so . . .

At lunchtime, Leigh's body and nerves were taut. She could not allow this incident to prey on her mind. She had to find Jace and get an explanation. She didn't care if he was upset with her for spying on him and questioning him. Misunderstandings were stupid and costly. She left her room and headed for the stairs. Just as she reached the first corner, she heard Jace's voice and came to alert. She did not round the bend, because she heard another voice: Louisa's.

"Hurry inside, Jace," the redhead was telling him, "before someone sees you. This will be like old times. Chad is out for the—"

Leigh couldn't hear more because the door to Louisa's new room closed and the lock clicked loudly. She fumed at this new discovery. Jace had said he would have nothing to do with that redhead, then sneaked into her room. After a cozy rendezvous with another beauty! Two curious episodes in one day were too much for her to accept as innocent. It was clear now why Louisa had found a way to have privacy. But who was the first woman and what did she mean to Jace Elliott?

Leigh concealed herself around the corner and waited to see how long Jace would remain inside Louisa's room. If it was only a talk to set the woman straight about his lack of interest and about her wanton note, it wouldn't take long. If Chad caught Jace fooling around with his ward and his mistress . . .

Leigh didn't like the suspicions that thought inspired. She leaned against the wall. Time passed and her tension mounted, along with her painful doubts. She tried to keep her mind blank and alert. She had to give Jace the benefit of trust. The way the rooms and halls were arranged, only someone coming to her suite would pass her. If that happened, she could pretend she was taking a stroll. Louisa's door didn't open again. Jace didn't leave.

When over three hours passed, she returned to her suite, dejected and infuriated. No talk, she concluded, personal or business, could take that long, only "old times," as Louisa had said in her sultry voice. Even if he was trying to romance clues about Chad from the redhead, this was a cruel betrayal.

"Damn you, Jace Elliott," she murmured.

Obviously Jace had lied to her. Worse, she had allowed him, encouraged him, to do so. He had

224

seemed so sincere, so honest, so . . .

"So what, you stupid girl?" Leigh scoffed in anger. "In love with you? How easily and skillfully you tricked me, you sorry bastard. All those accusations about Chad were only a cunning ruse to turn me against him. You see, Mr. Traitorous Elliott, there are a few things you don't know. Such as, Chad has nothing to gain by getting rid of me, but you do. In fact, because of that reckless wager I made with you, you stand to win a lot, either by snaring me in your clever trap or by slaying me. You know you can win with the wager, but do you know you can win without it if anything happened to me? No doubt you only want to use me to spite Grandfather and Chad. Curse you and your rivalry! If it's revenge you're after, two can play at your game," Leigh vowed.

A horrible thought came to mind, and she voiced it in alarm. "Oh, God, what if you two are in collusion? What if Louisa was the reason you were in London? What if Louisa is working on Chad for you, trying to help you pin those crimes on him? What if you enticed her to lure Chad here? Merciful heavens, what if you and Louisa are after me because of the will? Louisa sent that note in London; you were at the waterfront. Louisa knew I was going to the fort; you were there. Coincidence? How else could those men have set a trap for me? Or did both attacks simply play into your greedy claws, you jungle beast? No, that can't be true, not the way she greeted you!"

Leigh vigorously brushed her hair, checked her clothes, and left her room. She walked past Louisa's door with her head held high. She was only half glad Jace didn't bump into her leaving his wanton love nest. She went to Chad's room and knocked persistently on the door. When it opened, she stalked past him and took a seat. Her mind was in a turmoil. She was tempted to tell her guardian that his lover was being unfaithful with his enemy. Her dislike and distrust of Louisa had increased with the redhead's daring conduct. But exposing the tryst was none of her business. In time, Louisa and Jace would expose themselves; villains always got cocky and made mistakes.

"No more secrets, Chad," she stated in response to his quizzical expression. "No more stalling, half-explanations, and none-of-your-business or it's-private excuses. I don't like what I'm feeling and thinking about you and Jace. I want to know what happened between you and Jace Elliott years ago, and I want to know right now. I don't like feeling trapped between you two. Tell me, or I'm going home."

"What in heaven's name brought on this fit?" he asked.

"Hints from both of you without clear answers. In London, you acted like Jace was a near stranger. I come here and discover he isn't. You two hate each other, but you offer him a job and he takes it. How can you make a truce without having waged a war? And a war makes bitter enemies. I can't relax until I know the truth."

"What did Jace tell you to upset you like this?" he probed.

"He's as secretive and bitter as you are, Chad. Why?"

"Are you afraid of him?" the handsome man asked.

"Why should I be? You said he doesn't know about the will, and I certainly haven't told him anything. You also implied he was innocent of

226

those charges in London. Why should he be a threat to me? Yet I get the impression you think he is. I find that odd and distressing. I keep recalling his accusations at Mr. Johnston's party about being your bait and accomplice, about you using me to get at him, to spite him."

"Jace and I talked everything out that night, Leigh. It was mostly a terrible misunderstanding between us long ago. We both thought it was best if we didn't mention it again, because we both acted like bastards and we didn't want you to think badly of us. If I tell you what he did, you'll think he's awful. If I tell you what I did, you'll think I'm awful. It was a crazy and stupid situation."

"*What* was?" she persisted, her expression stubborn. "Tell me!"

Chad inhaled deeply and took a seat near her. To satisfy and fool her, he would reveal part of the truth. "Jace and I have known each other since our early teens. We went to school together and after, we joined the Royal Navy together. We shared plenty of adventures around the world. Later, we hired on as sailors on private ships, choosing whichever one was heading where we wanted to go. We've saved each other's lives and shared each other's good and bad days. We wound up in South Africa in '89. The diamond fields caught our attention. We gathered a fortune. Then I was captured by warring Matabeles. I was tortured and enslaved. When I escaped, I was told Jace hadn't tried to find me, that he'd taken our diamonds and left Cape Colony. I was sent back to London to heal. That's when I met William Webster. My father had been killed while settling a dock strike that was crippling William's shipments.

William felt compassion for me. He befriended me, hired me, and trained me. But that's off the subject. When Jace came to London in '92, he was shocked to find me there. He had believed me dead. I accused him of treachery. We fought, did spiteful things to each other, and made enemies. Once a friendship is mistreated, Leigh, it's over forever."

"How did Jace explain what happened in South Africa?"

"He claimed innocence. He said he searched for me for weeks and presumed I was dead. He came here to work and live. He purchased his plantation with the profit from part of my diamonds. To be honest, he offered to repay me for my losses, but I was too proud and bitter to accept. He visited again in '93 and '94, but we couldn't forgive each other or make a truce. Both of us had done too many bad things to the other. After his father died, I figured Jace had suffered as much as I had. It seemed foolish to go on hating him. By then, I had myself and my life back together. Trouble was, Jace believed William and I were out to get him. I tried to tell him there was no way we could have framed him, but he wouldn't believe me. We went from best friends to worst enemies. That was sad and stupid on both our parts," he murmured, using Jace's words. "Now that William's dead, part of Jace's resentment is gone. The other night, I took the blame for our past trouble, so he agreed to drop the matter. It's only a business deal, Leigh; he needs money and we need a guide."

"What if you were right, Chad? What if he did leave you to die and stole your diamonds? What if he's still dangerous?"

"We were young and reckless in those days, Leigh. If he did betray me, it was on impulse. Jace and I had our share of them, and they got us into plenty of mischief."

Leigh added up the time span. It was seven years since the two friends docked in Africa. Twenty-five was not "young" and "wild." Nor were they reckless children during the ensuing years, during which they had battled bitterly.

Chad continued. "Frankly, as much as I hate to admit it, I don't believe he did leave me to die. At the time, I was too weak in mind and body to think clearly. By the time I saw Jace again, I had convinced myself those men at Kimberley had told the truth. Looking back now, they always were troublemakers. I think they lied because Jace had quarreled with them several times, verbally and physically."

Chad took in a deep breath. "Don't you see how terrible this makes me look, Leigh? I should have trusted him. I shouldn't have spited him. He had good reason to retaliate. Just like he has good reason to be suspicious of me today. He'll find out differently while we're on safari. Maybe that will soften him toward both of us. I have to make peace with him to protect you. Once he sees that I'm sorry, he won't want to spite me again."

"Please don't think badly of me," Chad urged. "I was very ill. I had been terrified and abused for months. I had lived under the threat of torture and death every moment of every day I was their prisoner. I came home broke and weak, to learn my father was dead and my home was lost. I hate to admit it to you or myself, but I was at the pit's bottom, Leigh, ready to break. William saved me from myself and a dire fate. He gave me back my strength, my pride—my life. I loved him, Leigh, and I miss him. You're a lot like your grandfather. That's why I know we'll make a good team. I owe you, because I owe him. And I'm very fond of you."

He stood and paced the room. "Jace should have been patient and understanding; he should have given me time to get ahold of myself; he knew what a terrible ordeal I had endured and what I had been told. He knew my father had been killed while I was enslaved, and that I'd lost everything. Once we got into a fistfight and I was hurt badly. He was arrested, and I let him sit in jail for a month where he had it rough with the guards and other prisoners. He never forgave me."

Chad halted and met her gaze. "I told you he wasn't the reason I came here. Maybe I was fooling myself. Maybe somewhere in the back of my mind I wanted to make peace with him. We had been a big part of each other's lives. Maybe I thought it would prevent him from ever wanting to harm you. He is bitter over his family's losses to William, so it was a good precaution for him to get to know you and like you. He has to get himself and his life back together, as I have, Leigh. Only then will the past be over."

Leigh had remained silent and alert. If Chad had endured such a "terrible ordeal" in Africa, why would he come back?

As if reading her thoughts, he absently remarked, "Maybe I had something to prove to myself by coming here. Maybe I needed to pit myself against the jungle and its perils again; maybe that's the only way I can accept what happened years ago. Sometimes I still have nightmares about it."

That sounded more like the truth than anything Chad had told her. Yet there were contradictions in his words. "Are you sure you want to go on this safari, and with Jace Elliott?"

"They are the only two unresolved problems in my life, Leigh. I'm thirty-two. I want to settle down in the near future. I have to get rid of all my ghosts before I can be free and happy."

Leigh eyed her handsome guardian closely. For the first time, Chadwick Hamilton looked young and vulnerable to her. He looked like a man who had suffered greatly in the past. She had nothing firm to hold against him, and what he had told her did explain the feud between the two men, though she needed more details. She smiled and said, "Thank you for trusting me with this information, Chad. I can see that mistakes were made on both sides. Perhaps this trip will settle everything for everyone. I hope so. What do you say to a glass of wine and an early dinner? I skipped lunch and I'm starved."

"If you'd like to question Jace and tell him what I've told you, I don't mind. I just don't want you upset and scared."

"Let's make this another one of our secrets. Jace might get nervous if he discovers I know the truth about his past."

"Whatever you think best, Leigh. Let's go eat. I can use a drink. This was hard. Even Louisa doesn't know the truth."

"I'm sorry, Chad, but I had to know."

"I should have told you that day in my office. I was afraid you'd think I'm a sorry bastard for being so weak and rash."

"I don't think any such thing, Chad Hamilton. We're friends."

"Please don't let me do or say anything to destroy that bond. If something troubles you, come and discuss it with me. I won't keep any more secrets from you. You don't know how much you mean to me, Leigh. These past few weeks have been good for me. I didn't realize a woman like you existed."

When Leigh tensed, Chad frowned and said, "I'm sorry. That was a little too personal. Let's go eat before I get into trouble again."

Leigh and Chad took a small table in the tranquil garden. Verdant trees and lush vegetation made a semicircle of their secluded area. A cooling breeze swayed the greenery around them. The sun was setting, creating colorful streaks on the horizon. Fragrant flowers blossomed in the private location and sent forth heady smells. Musicians played softly in the adjoining room. It was quite a romantic setting. Chad and Leigh both noticed but pretended not to.

A waiter took their order for two wines. When he returned, Chad toasted her. "To a most unique woman, my beautiful ward."

Leigh smiled and replied, "To my special friend and guardian."

As they dined, Leigh asked, "I'd like to ask one more question, Chad. Why did you give me that necklace on Friday?"

Chad realized Jace must have told her about it. "Actually I brought it to give to Jace. It belonged to his mother. I figured, if we ran into him and he caused trouble, it might soothe his ire against us. Then, I decided that was foolish. William earned it legally and fairly, and it was your property. I had no right to make it a peace offering. I wasn't truthful with you about it, Leigh, and I'm sorry."

"Jace was furious when he saw it on me that night. When he came to my room to discuss our wager, he told me why. I offered it to him, but he refused to accept it. He seemed to think it was odd that I was wearing it that night. Now that I know about the trouble between you two, it makes sense."

"If it hadn't matched your gown, you wouldn't have worn it and he wouldn't have gotten suspicious. I didn't know what you were wearing, and I didn't know he had arrived and would be at the party. It wasn't a trick on my part, Leigh, honest."

Leigh didn't doubt his speculations. "I believe you, Chad, but I'm sure Jace wouldn't."

"Why don't we forget about Jace tonight? He's only our hired man. If things can't be worked out, I'll call off the safari. I don't want you unhappy or frightened, Leigh."

Leigh recalled the contract she had created and signed with Jace Elliott. If she let Chad call off the safari, Jace would win his bet with her. If she refused to honor her wager, he would show it to Chad. Her guardian would wonder why she had made such a rash and intimate bet, and she would be humiliated. Then, Jace would delight in exposing her wanton deed to Chad and others. If not for the paper, it was her word against his. She had to go on the safari and she had to win. Afterward, she would refuse his plantation — purchased with part of Chad's blood, sweat, and pain — and sail home, a place where Jace couldn't pursue her. If he still wanted to do so.

"What are you thinking?" he probed her pensive silence.

She lied convincingly. "About the safari. I want

233

to go, Chad. I want to best that arrogant beast. You promised to make certain I didn't lose. It's not the money, it's my pride at stake. I'm holding you to your word. Don't let him make it extra tough to break me."

Chad grinned and suggested, "If you get weak or have a problem, let me know. I'll find a way to help you. I'll take the blame so you'll be in the clear. We make a good team, Leigh. I'm looking forward to many years with you."

His tone and gaze told Leigh what kind of years he had in mind. Jace was right about one thing: Chad did want. her. Was it the money, she fretted, her, or both he craved? She was a desirable woman, so why couldn't it be only her?

"Would you like to take a stroll?" Chad hinted, after their dinner was finished. "The garden trail is lovely this time of night. It's well-lit with torches."

Feeling brave and bold and spiteful to Jace and Louisa, Leigh smiled and said, "That sounds very nice, Chad. But what about the others? We were to meet them at eight for dinner. They'll be down soon."

He shrugged. "I'll tell the waiter inside to give them a message that we've already eaten and left for a walk."

"Somebody will be angry," she teased in a playful tone.

"That's too bad. I can't spend my life trying to appease a willful woman. After the safari, Louisa and I will part ways."

"Have you told her?" Leigh queried, secretly glad.

"Not yet. I don't want to spoil our adventure. Louisa and I have been a twosome for a long time. I owe her that much. I don't want to hurt or

234

embarrass her. It'll be kindest and best to let her go back home. I'll even let her make me the villain in our parting."

Leigh wondered if he was being honest and if he'd done that before, considering his notorious reputation with women. "You're a good man, Chad. She is in love with you."

He laughed. "Louisa doesn't love anybody but herself, Leigh. Don't let her fool you. I'm nothing but a conquest to her. She enjoys being with . . ." He halted and sent her a roguish look. "How shall I put this without sounding vain? I am considered a good catch. She likes to be seen with me. And she'd like to marry me for my position and money. I'm afraid that isn't enough for me. I want love and respect."

"You amaze me, Chad. Being considerate of old flames is a rare trait."

A genuine smile flickered over his appealing face and settled in his blue eyes. "For some reason I'm changing, and I think it's because of you, Leigh. You're a good influence on me."

"Thank you, kind sir," she responded, returning his smile. He *had* changed during the evening. He was relaxed and open. Maybe Chad was in love with her and Jace wanted to hurt him with her conquest.

"Ready to go?"

"Lead on, Chad; you can be the guide tonight." While they walked, Leigh prayed that the forceful gaze she sensed on them was Jace Elliott's. This should teach the traitor she wasn't to be duped and used. This behavior should make him doubt his effect on her. This would show her if that effect was real . . .

* * *

Jace *was* watching them, and he was furious. He was also baffled. Leigh was matching Chad's every flirtation. What, he wondered, did she have in mind with this crazy ruse? Was she trying to get information? If so, it was perilous to tempt that man. He would tell her so later. He had set one woman straight today, and it looked as if he had another task awaiting him tonight. It hadn't taken long to get his point made with the redhead, after which he had sneaked out the window.

He had sent a cable asking Lord Salisbury to check into the men who had attacked Leigh in the London alley. Leigh had supplied the names she had heard them call each other and their descriptions, and a clue about their smelling of horseflesh. He had suggested all employees of Louisa, Cynthia, and Chad be investigated. If any men with those names and faces worked for either one, he would be notified. A friend in the Colonial Office was checking on her attack herein for him. With luck, it would be the same culprit, giving him only one villain—or villainess—to thwart.

Jace didn't like Leigh being alone in the garden with Chad. He headed downstairs to intercept them.

Leigh walked beside Chad. She realized she could not allow him to kiss her or to touch her, not even to test his magic against Jace's or to punish Jace. She let Chad know not to make advances by the way she talked and acted. They spoke of business and the London restaurant they were decorating. They talked about her days in Texas. "It's late and I need rest. Let's head back

236

now."

"That was a pleasant walk, Leigh. You're enjoyable company. We should do this every night for exercise and to get better acquainted."

"Sounds nice to me, Chad."

Jace met them at the next bend in the tropical path. Torchlight danced on his bronzed face and brown hair.

"Hello, Jace," Chad said. "You finish the preparations today? Our departure is still on for tomorrow, isn't it?"

"Yep. We leave by train at ten. Did you tell everyone to be ready? The train doesn't wait for anyone."

Leigh and Chad glanced at each other and laughed at a private joke. "No such luck, Leigh," Chad teased, "so be good."

"What's so amusing?" Jace inquired, feeling jealousy bite him.

Chad explained. "Cynthia is always running late. This time, she'll get left behind if she tries to pull one of her grand entrances."

"If you two gentlemen will excuse me," Leigh said, "I have to make certain my things are ready so I can get a good night's sleep."

"Good night, Leigh. Sleep well. I'll see you at breakfast."

Jace was vexed by the way his rival bid his woman good night and by the way Leigh totally ignored him in Chad's presence. He hoped it was nothing more than a means by which to conceal their affair, but he feared it wasn't. Leigh gave off a chill that alarmed and confused him. He didn't say good night to her; he would do that later in her room . . .

After she was gone, Chad informed him, "Leigh

237

came to my room late this afternoon and demanded to know about our quarrel, Jace. I had to tell her something, or she was going to call off the safari and sail home. She was upset." He related what he had said to her. "If you don't believe me, ask her yourself."

"After hearing how wicked I am, she still wants to leave tomorrow?"

"Don't be suspicious. It was the truth, and we both know it. I didn't mention Joanna. I thought it was a disadvantage to both of us. Don't you agree?"

"For now," Jace replied flippantly.

"Getting worried about losing your pay and our bet, old chap?"

"Not in the least," Jace replied with confidence.

"You should, because I'm going to win," Chad told him with just as much confidence. "Leigh is mine; I'll make certain of it."

Jace shrugged and grinned. "See you at nine, old friend."

Chad watched Jace vanish into the shadows. For some crazy reason, he was feeling mellow tonight. Seeing Jace didn't sting as usual. And Leigh, she had his heart pounding and his body flaming. As for Louisa, he dreaded to see her, even to sate his aching loins. He didn't even want to talk with his close friend Reid. What, he mused, was wrong with him?

Leigh headed for the front desk and asked for a new room for the night, explaining she couldn't sleep well in the bed in her suite. Hurriedly she fetched what she needed and went to the room where she hoped Jace could not locate her.

When—because she had no doubt he would sneak to see her—he found her suite unoccuppied, let him think what he would, she decided. Until she learned the truth about the incidents with the beautiful native girl and the sultry redhead, she did not want to see him in such a dangerously intimate setting.

By eight the next morning, Leigh was packed, dressed, and ready to depart. She joined the others downstairs for breakfast. Chad was in a happy mood. Louisa was quiet for a change. Reid and Cynthia seemed bored. Jace was gone.

"Jace is waiting for us at the train stop," Chad told them. "Since he does so much work for them, they're letting him pay to have the train take us near the end of the line. The railroad isn't halfway to Nairobi yet. He's having all our supplies and baggage loaded and we're to be out front at nine with any remaining luggage. He's arranged for a man to fetch us."

The depot was nothing more than a small business office of the Uganda Railroad and an area from where supplies to continue the rail line were unloaded from cargoes and transported to work camps along the winding route into the adjoining protectorate. Everything and everyone was aboard within twenty minutes. The whistle blasted loudly, and the engine began to take them to their destination.

Leigh sat in the last car, the only one with seats and windows. She was to the rear, while the others were near the front. She wanted a last glimpse at

Mombasa and the ocean as they moved inland. Jace was riding up front with the engineer. She wondered if he had come to her suite, last night to find her missing. If he had, did he believe she had spent the night with Chad?

Leigh turned to watch the large seaport outlined against a vivid blue ocean, and realized how glad she was she'd come to Africa. The light structures with their red or white roofs, numerous mosques, and jungle greenery were striking against glittery sapphire water and cerulean sky. Soon, ferns and trees of several varieties ended the breathtaking sight. The engine picked up speed and traveled smoothly along the rails. It rolled through picturesque hills; passed plantations of coconut, mangoes, and bananas; and provided magnificent views.

The forest halted for a time. Stretches of small shrubs, baobab and acacia trees, thornbush, grasses, and other unfamiliar vegetation surrounded the short train as it chugged along. Here and there she spotted waterholes where animals were drinking. Everything intrigued her. She saw gazelles bound away at the noise of the engine, leaping gracefully. She saw huge elephants at the edge of the forest they had departed. Wildebeest and zebra mingled in herds as they grazed contentedly until the engine also startled them into speedy flight. She noticed several lions stalking the fleeing herd of brown and striped prey. Nature, she decided, could be very beautiful, and also very brutal.

Onward they traveled. They traversed a narrow gorge where tumbled rocks revealed how they had been blasted out of the path. They entered the Taru Desert. It was flat, sunbaked, and looked as

240

endless at the western plains. The only signs of life were bunches of browned grass, stunted trees, twisted scrubs, and an occasional thornbush and acacia at its beginning. The earth was a dry blood-red, much like Georgia soil, and it seemed to coat everything. It was a cruel and challenging landscape. She could not imagine how the workmen had endured the oppressive heat, choking dust, and hardships while laying tracks through this forbidden area.

The heat had increased, and the train did little to create a refreshing breeze. Leigh felt her clothes and body growing damp. The air was dry and dusty. She knew she looked a mess with red powder on her skin and garments. She knew, because she saw the others covered in it.

Leigh observed how the rails stretched out like glittering silver snakes beneath the tropical sun. She remembered Jace telling them at dinner that this desert had been the great barrier to Swahili/Arab caravans in search of slaves and ivory. She was relieved the train would take them beyond the Taru and that they didn't have to cross it on foot to begin their safari. The Taita Hills loomed before them. Soon, she realized, the Serengeti Plains would be to their left: their first destination.

The others enjoyed a picnic packed by the hotel, but Leigh wasn't hungry. All she wanted was water to soothe her dry throat. She was glad Chad remained with Louisa, despite his glances at her.

The landscape altered its face once more. They entered grasslands with thorn trees, flat-topped acacias, and scrubs, then woodlands. Soon, greenery surrounded them again and sand-colored rocks loomed in the fertile hills. The train slowed and halted.

With strength and agility, Jace pulled himself into their car. "I thought you women might like to refresh yourselves here. We'll stop for fifteen minutes, then be on our way again. We have an hour to go. Our bearers will be waiting for us. We'll load up and walk until dusk. There won't be any privacy at our next stop, so take advantage now," he informed them, not once looking at Leigh.

"Can we bathe and change clothes, Jace. We're filthy," Louisa whined.

"Sorry, Miss Jennings, but we don't have time. The train has to back its way to Mombasa before dark. It's fifteen minutes break, no more." When he briefly glanced at her, Jace noticed the cold glare in Leigh's eyes and wondered—worried—about it.

When the redhead and brunette began to complain, Chad scolded, "Remember, Jace is the boss out here. Don't be childish; do as he says."

"There's a river nearby. Use it if you want to wash your face, but be careful of hippos and crocodiles. Call out if you get into trouble."

Leigh was furious with Jace and Louisa. From the way they behaved, nothing was between them.

The two women walked toward the river first to scrub their hands and faces. Leigh vanished into thick bushes and excused herself. The men did the same in another direction, then headed for the river.

When Leigh reached the water, she noticed it was as red and dirty as she was. The others had already discovered that fact and returned to the train to use their canteen water. Leigh gazed over the landscape as she knelt to wet a cloth. It came back soaked, but red. She sighed deeply, then washed as much of the dust as possible from her

242

face and hands. She blew her nose and cleaned the stifling dust from it. Quickly she brushed her hair, knowing how awful it must look. As for her clothes, they looked ruined. If this red dirt was truly like fiery Georgia mud, the red soil would never wash out completely.

As Jace observed Leigh at the river, he recalled his meeting at the hotel with Louisa. "I don't want this to happen again, Miss Jennings," he admonished her after she had made her desires clear. "It could cause trouble for everyone. I work for Chad. Even if I were interested in your curious offer, I wouldn't mess with the boss's property. I suggest you cool your interest in me and behave yourself."

"Why?" the redhead had asked, trying to caress and kiss him. "I have plenty to offer, jungle man. Chad won't care what I do. He has his lustful eye on his little ward. If she looks his way, I've lost him. Frankly, I'd like to drop him before he discards me. Being tossed aside for another woman is most damaging to one's pride, Jace."

"If you feel this way, why did you come along?" he had asked.

Louisa had grinned, shrugged, and replied, "Chad is a good catch, and Leigh might not be able to steal him from me. Women have to worry about such things as their futures. Besides, with that nasty problem at home, you're unavailable for more than a little sport."

"I'm unavailable for anything, woman, so cool your ardor. I don't want any trouble." Afterward, he had slipped out her balcony door. He gazed at the woman who had stolen his heart. Red dust clung to her blond hair and colored it to a curry shade. "Your hair's as red as Louisa's," Jace said

243

from behind her, choosing the wrong comparison.

"I'm not complaining," Leigh retorted in a cool tone, provoked by his remark. She finished her task and glared at him.

Jace teased, "Don't want to break rule one, eh?"

"I'm not going to break any rules, Mr. Elliott."

Jace knew for certain he hadn't been mistaken about her suddenly cold mood. It was best to be direct and settle the manner now. "I tried to see you last night. You didn't return to your room."

"I assumed you would," she revealed, "so I rented another room for the night. I had skipped lunch, so Chad and I had an early dinner. I wanted to make sure I began this promising trip well rested."

"Are you upset about what Chad told you? He's wrong about me."

She looked at Jace oddly and wondered why Chad had revealed their private talk to his enemy. "You wouldn't tell me what happened, so he did. I had to make certain you two wouldn't involve me."

"If that news made you so miserable, why come here?"

Forgetting it was a joke, she scoffed, "And lose our bet by breaking rule three? I keep my word, unlike some people I know. Did you say good-bye to all your women in Mombasa?"

Jace was baffled. "I don't have any women there or elsewhere, only the one standing here and confusing me with this sudden coldness. What have I done wrong, Leigh? Don't I get a chance to defend myself?"

"Don't you mean, tell more lies and practice more deceits? Who was the native girl you're obviously so fond of at the hotel? I saw you two in

244

the garden, and it looked so sweet to me."

Jace thought a minute, then laughed. "Her name is Ka'arta. She's my housekeeper's daughter. She was in town for monthly supplies. She and Johi have a hot romance going, but he's getting nervous about marriage. I've known her for years, Leigh, since she was a young girl. She wanted me to speak with Johi and settle him down. Jealous?"

Leigh realized his explanation fit with the words she had overheard. "What about Louisa and your 'old times' she mentioned?"

He sighed heavily. "I explained that note to you."

"The first one, yes. But what about the second one, Jace? You haven't mentioned spending all afternoon in her room. I was coming down the hall and saw you enter and I heard how she greeted you." In a thick southern drawl, she repeated those tormenting words. "Three hours later I gave up waiting for you to come out and explain."

Jace laughed once more, this time in relief. He related what he had said and done with Louisa and how he had departed unseen. "I swear it's the truth, Leigh. I know how those incidents must have looked, so you had a right to be angry and jealous. Just as I did about Chad. I saw you two having that cozy dinner and romantic walk. It took all of my willpower not to come down and whip both of you."

"I know you saw us. At least I hoped that was your fierce stare I detected," she confessed with a mirthful grin. "I believe what you told me, but I'm still vexed with that wanton redhead. I don't blame Louisa for desiring you or for being afraid of losing Chad to another woman. But the vixen shouldn't be so deceitful!"

"You sly wench," he jested. "You had me worried and scared."

"You had *me* worried and scared. But it was mean to spite you."

"When you didn't return to your room . . ."

"Nothing happened between me and Chad."

"I know, because I know you. Acting is harder than planning."

"You're right, thank goodness. I was a little dull-witted."

"Let's go before the others get suspicious of us. We'll talk later."

Louisa and Cynthia were in their seats while the others strolled around to flex their bodies. "I thought Jace ensnared her Sunday night after that foiled attack," Louisa whispered. "He certainly stayed in her room a long time and left in a happy mood. He couldn't have seduced her, or she wouldn't have been after Chad last night. Damn the greedy bitch. She wants to play with both of them, the little tease. It looks as if little Leigh isn't so sweet and gullible after all. No one plays me for the fool. I'll teach her a lesson or two. She won't get either one of them, and neither of them will get her. Once we're in that jungle, she's dead game, Cynthia; I swear it."

Reid Adams wiped more red dust from his sharp features and touslled his brown hair. "How is the chase going?" he asked.

Chad smiled dreamily and replied, "Better than expected."

Reid observed the black-haired man and realized Chadwick Hamilton was under Leigh Webster's spell. He glanced at the returning and genially chatting Leigh and Jace, then thought, *You're fooling yourself, old boy. Jace has her hooked already. When you realize you've lost to him, love her or not, you'll kill them both.*

Chapter Eleven

The train halted. Leigh's suspense and anticipation increased.

"*Jambo,* Bwana Jace," Jim's men greeted him.

"*Jambo,*" he echoed and smiled broadly. He asked if everything was prepared.

"*Ndiyo*" came the affirmative response.

When Jim Hanes's men questioned his whereabouts, Jace told them, "Hanes *aliumia mguu*": "Hanes hurt his leg." Jace had hired a few of Jim's men who had been awaiting their boss's arrival in Mombasa. The fact the other guide had made the necessary arrangements for a safari caused confusion in Jace's mind about a possible deceit. Of course, it could have been done to throw off suspicion.

"*Safiri saloma. Subira,*" the train guard told them, which meant, "Have a safe trip. Take it easy."

"*Hakkuma mattata. Kwaheri. Asante, rafiki,*" Jace responded, which translated, "No problems. Goodbye. Thanks, friend."

Everyone gathered nearby while their baggage was unloaded. Leigh could not count the number of bearers, but it looked to be around sixty. The dark-skinned men efficiently packed their burdens and hoisted them abovehead. The train blasted its whistle and began to back away from the large group to return to Mombasa.

Leigh observed her lover as he gave orders and made plans. Jace was attired in a four-pocket jacket in khaki, with matching pants that displayed huge bellows pockets on his muscled thighs. He was wearing brown boots, and he placed a felt hat on his head. He had used it often, and it had lost much of its strength and shape. A holster with a Mauser .44 caliber pistol was secured about his waist.

Her gaze shifted to the other men in their party. Chad and Reid were dressed nearly alike in khaki pants, dark boots, water-resistant pith helmets, and Bombay shirts. The shirt of cotton had first become popular in British India because it was soft, airy, and comfortable. Chad's was blue and matched his eyes, while Reid's was khaki. Both men looked rugged and handsome, and very much at ease.

Leigh glanced at the whispering women. Louisa and Cynthia were also attired in similar garments: they looked sleek and relaxed in their khaki drill skirts and well-made jackets. They quickly donned their "topees"—pith helmets—to ward off the sun.

Leigh was wearing a six-gore skirt in Egyptian cotton with a matching shirt. It was tailored to fit, yet its bottom flare allowed graceful and easy movement. The skirt reached the tops of her brown boots. She, too, put on her helmet to combat the fierce sun overhead.

Leigh longed for a bath. It was hot, and she was still covered in red dust, as were the others. She moved forward when Jace motioned to them to approach for final instructions and departure. He had already assigned them weapons, as guns were under governmental control in this land. Chad received a Lancaster shotgun; Louisa and Cynthia got

Ross automatic rifles; Reid was handed a Krag-Jorgensen carbine; Leigh got a Winchester '94; and Jace took the Mauser carbine.

As each examined the weapons, he said, "We'll swap around during the safari so you'll get familiar with all of these guns. We'll head for the Tsoyo River first, then the Tanzania border. We should reach the Tsoyo tomorrow night, if nothing goes wrong and you all keep up. I sent a runner ahead to have boats waiting to pick us up. We'll make our first main camp near the border. I want to remind you not to drink unboiled water or to forget your daily quinine tablets. Don't bathe your feet in mudholes or go without boots. We have troublesome chiggers, ticks, and hookworms that'll drive you crazy. If I give the order to halt and stand still, do it immediately. You never can tell when we'll encounter an irritable beast. I've gone over the laws, rules, and regulations about hunts, so stick to them. Anyone breaking or abusing them gets sent back. Understand?"

After they all nodded, Jace added, "Walk between the bearers and keep up. Don't interfere with their pace; they're carrying heavy loads. If anyone gets tired or hurt, step aside and send word up the line. If you hear or see anything in the bush, don't panic and fire. Most animals and natives usually ignore the passing of large groups. If you have your canteens and weapons ready, let's go."

Jace slung his carbine over his left shoulder and took the lead. His friend, helper, and hunting-gun bearer—Wanjohi—trailed close behind, chatting swiftly in his tongue. Leigh was next in line. Ten bearers followed her. Chad and Louisa came next, with more bearers between them and the other couple. The remaining bearers stretched out behind Reid and Cynthia. It amazed her that the men could carry so much weight, along with bows and spears.

They walked through the remaining woodlands, occasionally sighting or hearing an animal in the bush. Jace skirted most of the hills, making the trek easier for them. They passed a village where friendly Taita people observed them with interest. Grasslands soon appeared. Jace had told her this area provided the quickest changes in climate and scenery than any other in East Africa.

As they moved along at a steady pace, Leigh studied the man ahead of her. Johi was around five eleven, slim and sleek. Except for small eyes, his features—nose, mouth, chin, and ears—were large. The Kikuyu African had short, curly hair as black as midnight. His shiny flesh was dark brown. There was an undeniable rapport, respect, and deep friendship between him and Jace. From what her lover had said, they had been together as a team for a long time, and the skilled Kikuyu was one of Jace's most valuable assets in the wild. Attired in his native tuniclike garb of multicolored *kikoi* cloth, the African carried a spear and his neck was adorned with several beaded necklaces. His Mannlicher carbine was slung over one shoulder, and a bow and quiver of arrows hung over the other. Around his slender waist was a canteen of water on a rope. None of the objects or combined weight seemed even to be noticed by the alert, agile, and reserved assistant.

Two hours later, Jace halted them near a towering termite hill to rest and to allow the group to examine it and take pictures with their new Kodak box cameras. The bearers laid aside their burdens and sat down to relax. Most, with their weapons across their laps, sipped water from makeshift canteens of gords or ostrichs's eggs. If they were amused or fascinated by the English gentry, it did not show.

Leigh stared at the vivid red insect home that was over twelve feet high, the color making a startling contrast amidst the lush green base. She sipped water from her canteen, then replaced it over her shoulder. She was surprised when Louisa asked to take her picture with their guide. Leigh stood beside Jace and before the tall hill. Her heart pounded with the need to touch him, to kiss him, to—

"I'm finished," Louisa said for the second time.

Leigh glanced at Jace, who grinned at her distraction. She removed her helmet and mopped perspiration from her brow. "It's hot."

As she twisted her hair to stuff it beneath her topee, Jace warned, "I wouldn't do that, Leigh. Mosquitoes love soft, damp napes."

"Thanks for the information, Mr. Elliott," she said merrily.

As they headed off again, Jace found the privacy to ask Leigh, "Were you complaining about the heat back there? Rule one . . ."

Leigh could not help but say, "Guilty as charged, sir."

At her playfulness, Jace smiled in pleasure.

On the grasslands, they saw many animals in the distance: wildebeest, gazelle, zebra, lion, giraffe. Most browers and grazers were eating contentedly while their predators reclined in the shade of acacias and buckthorns, no doubt plotting their next attack. The group didn't halt to take pictures, because Jace said they would see plenty from their first campsite.

He pointed out a large pack of gregarious baboons and told Leigh interesting facts about their tightly knit order. He passed a caution down the line when he sighted an enormous cape buffalo. "There

252

are five big trophies men want from here: elephant, rhino, lion, leopard, and buffalo. Each one is dangerous to track and kill. That cape buffalo there has a foul temper when disturbed. Never underestimate a wild animal. They're clever and deadly."

They skirted a waterhole where wart hogs were wallowing. The African swine had large tusks that curled over their snouts, a horselike mane over their foreheads, and disfiguring protuberances on their faces. The well-trampled and muddy ground revealed that it was visited often and by many animals, as Jace pointed out to her. He motioned to a *kopje,* an outcropping of rocks or earth mounds.

"The natives use *kopjes,* unusually shaped trees, and waterholes as landmarks and maps. If you know the signs, you can't ever get lost."

They traveled a long distance before the sun lowered itself on the horizon and allowed the day to cool. Jace had given them sufficient rest stops. During one he had whispered to Leigh, "You're strong and well-conditioned, woman. Perhaps I should start worrying about losing my plantation to you."

"Perhaps you should," she had replied. "But we do have a long way and a long time to go."

"Yes, but you've already broken one rule."

"Not really," she had corrected. "You failed to warn me that true conversational remarks could get me into trouble."

Finally Jace halted the group to make camp where several men were preparing them with a meal. While his workers labored, Chad approached Leigh and asked how she'd fared today.

"Fine. It was hot and tiring, but fun."

Louisa joined them. "Isn't this wonderful, Leigh?"

"It's beautiful, Louisa. Aren't you glad we came?"

"Without a doubt. I can't wait to get my first

trophy."

Something in Louisa's gaze and tone struck Leigh as odd. Or, the blonde decided, maybe she was too skeptical now of the hot-blooded vixen who lusted for Jace and Chad. "I don't care about taking trophies," Leigh responded. "I just want to see everything."

They were called to eat. The servants had set up tables. China, crystal, and silver would adorn them at their main camp; tonight, it was eat from metal plates and drink from metal cups. They were served roasted meat, cooked vegetables, hot bread, and wine. Leigh, Chad, and Louisa sat at one table on folding chairs. Cynthia, Reid, and Jace sat at another. Johi ate with the other men not far away. Chad had wanted music during their meal from the gramophone he had brought with him, but Jace had resisted unpacking too many items along the trail. Chad had conceded, as he likewise had over the table settings.

Tents were put up while they dined and relaxed, although it was unusual for Jace to give that gentle order on the trail. He told them he was making an exception tonight so the women could splash-bathe in the folding canvas basins and change clothes. A fire burned in the center of camp to ward off a nighttime chill and predators. Lanterns hung here and there to provide light. Supplies were stacked away from the main area, and the bearers made their camp around them to prevent loss to sneaky thieves and damage by wild animals. The eating tables were close to each other, so conversation was shared by all.

"I should warn you women about wearing perfume," Jace said. "It attracts worrisome insects, and it gives us away to our quarry."

254

"Surely you don't expect us to go around dirty and smelly?" Louisa protested with a pout. "Don't be cruel to me, Jace."

"You'll have plenty of places for real baths, Miss Jennings," Jace answered coldly.

"Don't be so spoiled, Louisa. We're all enduring the same. Cynthia and Leigh aren't complaining. You knew what to expect."

Louisa frowned, suspecting Chad's remark was meant to point out Leigh's accomplishments to Jace. "I'm only teasing, Chad."

"Really?" he taunted with a wide grin.

"How far do we travel tomorrow?" Reid interrupted abruptly.

Jace caught his ruse to prevent a quarrel. "We'll reach the river by mid-afternoon. We'll make good time in boats. You should be hunting in a few days. I suggest we turn in after dinner. The first few days are the hardest, getting into shape and adjusting to the trail."

"Sounds wonderful to me," Louisa murmured.

Jace stood and stretched, and kept his gaze off Leigh. "Don't be alarmed by noises at night," he informed them. "Many of the animals hunt and roam during darkness. They usually stay clear of campfires, but it's best to stay inside and to lace your flaps. If there's a problem, shout and I'll come. We have plenty of guards."

Everyone separated for the night. The tents had been spaced for privacy. Louisa joined Chad, and Cynthia joined Reid to the right of their large camp. Leigh entered her tent to the left, as did Jace nearby. The tables were left standing for breakfast, but the dinner remains were cleared to prevent attracting wild animals. The bearers and Johi took their mats beneath the stars, and the camp was quiet.

Leigh sensed a presence. She turned on the bedroll and tried to pierce the darkness. It was very late. In the distance she heard a leopard scream, a sound soon joined by other nocturnal creatures. The scent she detected was familiar. She smiled to herself. "Jace," she whispered, and felt him touch her arm.

He reclined beside her. Pulling her close, he whispered into her ear, "How did you know it was me? I thought you were sleeping."

She captured his head, turned it, and replied into his ear, "Your special, wonderful scent, and I *was* asleep. Isn't this reckless?" she asked, her heart pounding with excitement and her body flaming. Now she knew why he had made his exception about tents tonight.

"Johi will warn me if anyone stirs."

"You told him about us?" she asked, embarrassed.

"No, but he knows I'm here. He sees and hears everything."

Leigh was glad she had bathed as well as possible in the small canvas basin. Despite his caution earlier, she had put on perfume, hoping he would sneak into her tent. She planned to wash it off later.

As Jace nuzzled her neck, he murmured, "Make sure you remove this wonderful odor by morning. I don't want tsetse flies biting you and causing sleeping sickness, or mosquitoes causing malaria." As his hands drifted down her neck, he discovered a bare shoulder. Boldly his fingers closed over her breast, then passed over her stomach. "What's this?" he asked, querying her nudity beneath the cover.

"I was hoping you would visit tonight," she admitted. She brought his head toward hers and sealed their lips. She had been starving for his kisses. Her

mounds with flat tops and a sprinkle of nuts; *irio,* a mixture of mashed beans, peas, and potatoes; and *sukuma wiki,* something like southern greens.

Leigh thought the *ugali* looked like Texas buttes with rocks scattered atop. The easy-to-cut impala was unique, with neither a domesticated stock taste nor a wild game one. She liked the *irio* with its mildly spiced blend, but she did not care for the *sukuma wiki,* which was a little "bitey," as her father used to say. The others drank wine with their meal, but Leigh enjoyed hot tea with hers. The group was quiet for a time as they feasted on the delicious fare. For dessert they were served fried plantains that tasted like wild bananas.

Chad lifted his glass and said, "To us and the fun ahead." The others lifted theirs and sipped the mellow red liquid.

The seatings were the same as before because Jace couldn't figure a way to split up the couples without it looking curious. He wanted to be with Leigh, but that wasn't possible. He knew his time with her was limited if his sly plan failed. If it did, when the safari ended, they would be parted until November, at which time she would be free to return to him. Those would be hard and long months of separation and secrecy. But, he had already taken action and was committed. Once the daring scheme was in motion, surely she would agree to it. Anyway, he was already in trouble, so what was a little more? The results were worth any risk.

"Can we bathe in that lake tomorrow?" Louisa asked.

"It isn't healthy, Miss Jennings. I'll locate a nice area at the river. We don't want anyone getting sick or injured, do we?"

"That will be fine, but it has to be tomorrow. I

can't stand this awful feeling a day longer."

"I'm sure you must feel the same," Jace hinted to Leigh.

"I'm not complaining, but it would be wonderful, Mr. Elliott."

He laughed and teased, "You women and your vanities."

"You want us to look good for the men in our lives, don't you?" Cynthia quipped, sounding a little testy. "It's so hot and stuffy here."

"It'll be cooler tonight. You'll be glad you have a tent, clothes, covers, and . . . someone to keep you warm. It can get rather chilly."

"Inside or outside?" Cynthia purred, glaring at Reid, who had refused to give her the information Louisa wanted about Chad and Jace.

Everyone thought it best to ignore that remark, even Reid.

"Why don't you turn off that music, Chad? You'll scare every animal out of the area. I want a good trophy tomorrow."

"What's bitten your behind?" Chad asked rather sharply.

The brunette stood, glared at the handsome male, and said, "I'm just exhausted, sweaty, and sore. Those insects have eaten on me all day. I itch all over. I'm going to bed." She left.

Chad met Reid's gaze and asked, "Something wrong?"

"She's a spoiled and vain woman. You know how those creatures get when they have to endure a little hardship. She wants to be pampered as she is back home. Hot baths, soft beds, teatime, clean clothes," he hinted.

"I agreed with Jace not to halt for tea at four. It would have taken too much time and work. We needed to reach camp before dark. What did she expect on the trail?" Chad scoffed.

Reid shrugged. "I doubt she gave it much thought."

"If she's going to be an annoyance, you want to send her back?"

"I doubt that's necessary. She'll adjust. If not, we'll spank her."

"If not, she's going back to Mombasa to wait for us there."

Louisa spoke up. "Don't be mean or hasty, Chad. She'll be fine. I'll go talk to her. She's probably just scared and doesn't want us to know. That episode with those water beasts was dreadful for her."

Leigh and the men watched the redhead disappear into Cynthia's tent. "Louisa could be right," Leigh remarked. "It was scary for a while. Our lives were in danger, weren't they, Mr. Elliott?"

Jace grasped her innuendo about his breaking rule two. "Everything here can be perilous, Miss Webster, if you're careless. It *was* dangerous, but you weren't in any danger of losing your life."

She heard hyenas in the distance, a sort of mingled laugh and bark. A lion roared in another direction. An elephant sent forth a trumpeting threat to something infringing on his territory. The wood crackled in the fire. Nocturnal birds and insects had awakened to begin their rituals. Frogs croaked in the river, their pitches varying with their sizes and kinds. Crickets rubbed their hind legs together to make their own special music. The moon was like a tiny slice of silver, and many stars were obscured by clouds. The night was inky black, and the jungle was impenetrable. Lantern- and fire-light flickered on the faces of the group and on nearby objects, creating eerie shadows. Everything seemed so different at night, so mysterious and slightly intimidating. Objects took on strange shapes, as in bad dreams. Death lurked in the wilderness. She was glad Jace was near her.

As they were turning in, Jace managed to ask Leigh, "Do you want me to sneak over tonight?"

"Unless you want to break your rule one by being too tired and weak, I'll see you when it's safe," she teased.

Leigh leaned against Jace and returned his kiss. It felt wonderful to be in his arms, and heady to be alone. They embraced tightly, pressing their eager bodies together. Flames consumed them. Their kisses and caresses became urgent and stimulating. But as he was about to remove her shirt, danger approached the tent.

Chapter Twelve

Johi unlaced the tent's secret flap and tugged on Jace's leg to warn him to make a hasty flight. Having sensed the man's presence in the darkness, Jace clamped his hand over Leigh's mouth to keep her silent.

"Leigh, are you awake?" Cynthia suddenly called out. "Can I sleep here tonight? I can't disturb Louisa and Chad, but Reid and I are quarreling."

"Stall a moment and I'll be out the back," Jace whispered into Leigh's ear. He released her and left without a sound.

"Just a minute, Cynthia. Let me find the lantern and light it." Leigh mussed her hair, clothes, and cot before striking a safety match that filled her tent with a soft glow. She was amazed at how quickly and silently Jace escaped exposure. She unlaced the flaps and lifted one. "What's wrong?" she asked, yawning as if awakened.

"Reid is furious with me for behaving so badly at dinner. We quarreled, and he's pouting. I had to get out."

Leigh noticed how the brunette was scanning her tent. "You're welcome to bunk with me, but you'll need a cot or sleeping roll. Maybe he'll settle down by morning."

Jace joined them at the entrance and asked, "Is something wrong, Miss Campbell? I heard voices and saw you two standing here."

Cynthia's brown-eyed gaze went from Leigh to Jace, then back again. "This is silly. I shouldn't have disturbed Leigh, or you, Jace. I'm sorry. I'll go back to my own tent. Reid will just have to sulk and endure me. Good night." The woman strolled away from them and returned to her tent, glancing back before entering.

"What was that about?" Leigh murmured, relieved they hadn't been exposed. If Cynthia had arrived a minute later . . .

Jace scowled in annoyance. "I think someone suspects us. We should be careful for a while, Leigh. We don't want Louisa and her cohort catching us and telling Chad. He would spoil everything. Go to sleep, love. We'll talk tomorrow."

Leigh watched Jace enter his tent not far away. She closed her flap and laced it, shaking her head in frustration. She did not like Louisa and Cynthia spying on her. Apparently the women wanted to cause trouble with Chad. Now that Leigh knew how much power and control her guardian possessed, she did not want to antagonize him. Learning that she was cavorting with his enemy would certainly cause problems for all of them. It would be so nice when November came and she was free of restraints. Jace was right, she decided; they had to be careful for a few days.

Leigh looked around her tent as she tried to figure out how Jace had fled. There were no marks on the ground, and nothing looked out of place. Then she noticed an area near one support pole where the right and back sides were laced snugly, from the

270

ground to two feet up. She wondered if all tents had secondary openings in case of trouble out front. Tomorrow she would see. If not, that meant Jace had given her a special tent. Suddenly she fretted over how he had known he would need such a precaution. After all, he had ordered tents and supplies before their love affair began . . .

In another tent, Reid asked, "Where have you been?"

"I had to be excused," Cynthia replied, stripping naked and reclining on her cot. She left the cover aside, but it was dark.

"This late? In the jungle? You aren't that brave or rash."

The brunette giggled. "Is that jealousy in you, Reid? Do you think I sneaked a visit with our handsome and virile guide?"

Reid folded his arms across his chest and gazed upward into the darkness. "If you did, I'm certain he wasn't receptive."

"Why, because you never are anymore?" she snapped.

"Can I help it if we don't excite each other these days? Is that what's the matter with you? Frustration? You were a bitch tonight. Maybe we should seek new partners when we return home."

"That sounds like an excellent idea. We haven't pleased each other in a long time. Is she already picked out, Reid?"

"Why should you care?" the man retorted. "You've never loved or wanted me or any man as much as you love Louisa."

Cynthia gasped. "Don't be absurd. We're best friends."

"That's why you're so cold and hateful, because I refuse to give you the information she wants. Chad's past isn't her business."

"If it involves what's going on here," the irate female argued, "it most assuredly is her affair. Don't tell me little Leigh has you enchanted, too. You're wasting time and energy and emotions, Reid. Chad would never let you take Leigh from him."

Reid wasn't provoked as intended. "I don't want Leigh."

"If not that blond witch, then who? You're hungry for someone."

"Just because I no longer find you desirable and pleasing doesn't mean I'm aching for another woman, like you are."

Cynthia warned in a cold tone, "Stop it, Reid."

He chuckled. "Can't you take a joke, your ladyship?"

"Not when it isn't amusing, lover. You and Chad are alike. He'll be sorry if he discards Louisa for that little chit."

"How and why is that, Cynthia?"

"Are you both blind? Our guide has captured her eye."

Reid's voice altered noticeably. "How do you know?"

"I don't, but I would bet my life and money on it. I would say a hot romance is in the making. Chad will lose this time."

"Lose what?" he inquired, coming to full alert.

"Lose everything if he isn't careful. He'll never get Leigh, and he'll lose Louisa if he keeps lusting for his ward and her wealth."

"Who says Chad wants to get Leigh?"

Cynthia laughed merrily. "Wouldn't you, in his place?"

"No, I wouldn't. Chad doesn't have to marry her to control her and the firm. Louisa is much better for him, and he knows it."

"Does he, Reid?" she challenged. "I think he's a little luststruck. He seems as bored with Louisa as you are with me."

"Only because both of you are acting like shrews. All you're accomplishing is to make Leigh look like a dream. If I were Louisa, I would behave myself. If she does, she has nothing to worry about."

Cynthia was surprised. "Are you certain?"

Reeking with confidence, the man responded, "Absolutely. Now, be quite and go to sleep. I'm tired."

Johi reported to Jace's tent and revealed the conversation he had overheard in the couple's tent. "Good work, Johi. Keep your eyes and ears open. Something is going on, my friend."

For two days, there were no perils or problems, or any time for Leigh and Jace to speak privately. Someone was always underfoot. The women were allowed to bathe in a safe area of the river, soothing Louisa's and Cynthia's nerves. The group went walking, looking, and hunting. Pictures were taken. Chad shot an impala for their dinner. At night, Leigh and Jace kept their distance from each other.

On the third day, the safari party left camp early. As they walked along, Leigh asked Jace, "Are there really spiders as big as your hand, huge snakes, and wild cannibals?"

Jace chuckled and said, "Big spiders and snakes, yes. But man- or woman-eaters, not really. That was to test your courage, Miss Webster. I was glad to see you don't frighten easily."

"Didn't you discover that in London?" Chad inquired, grinning.

"That I did, Chad," she replied. "Look," he said, halting them.

A herd of giraffes was browsing beyond them. "They prefer young trees," Jace told them, "so they do a lot of damage. They can peel the leaves from thorny acacias without hurting their tongues, but it hinders new growth. Between them and elephants, they can strip all buds. Sometimes it takes an area a couple of years to recover."

The five towering creatures ceased their feeding to check out the approaching group. Leigh observed the nimble, tall animals. Their hides were exquisitely patterned. Their tails flicked at pesky insects. Their ears wiggled to catch the sound of danger. Deciding they were in peril, the herd loped off at a long, easy stride on slender legs.

The lookout for a troop of baboons barked an alarm and the dog-faced creatures hurried into the underbrush while protesting the intrusion. Countless birds that filled treetops with colors, movements, and songs took hasty flight to land elsewhere until safe to return. Monkeys chattered loudly and scampered for cover, from which they observed the passing humans. An unseen lion growled. An elephant trumpeted. Bushes quivered to expose the escapes of frightened critters. Other small beasts scattered before their approach. The party continued their leisurely walk, searching for rhino today.

"Your Sporting Licence allows each of you to take five big game heads and four zebras, plus smaller eating game," Jace reminded them. "Make certain you select wisely, as there won't be a second chance.

If we take more than is legal, we're the same as poachers. Remember the laws and regulations at all times, and keep them."

The license had cost twenty-five pounds for twelve months, and each member of their group had one. Yet Leigh didn't plan to use hers. Hunting for food was all right, or shooting in self-defense, but she did not care to kill for sport. She only wanted to explore this land.

In a quietened tone, Jace informed and instructed, "The black rhino is a grazer or browser. Usually you find some in the same area with giraffes, and normally in pairs. With luck and from the signs, one is nearby, hopefully a solitary bull. From here on, be quiet and move with caution. If you spook one, he'll charge. They don't see will, but their hearing and smell are excellent. You're only allowed one each because so many have been killed off for their horns."

"Why?" Leigh inquired.

"People in the Middle and Far East believe the rhino has magical and medicinal traits. The Yemen make knife handles from them. One horn fetches thousands of dollars, so poachers love 'em."

"What's the difference between a black rhino and a white one?"

"Not color, Chad. It's the shape of their mouths. Black rhino have hook-lips. They're prized the most. That's what you'll want."

At the edge of a clearing, an elephant had stopped to scratch his side on a tree. The rubbing sound seemed loud in the quiet setting. The tree moved, despite its thick size. The bulky animal was mud-splattered to discourage insect attacks. The huge creature shook his head, causing his trunk to sway back and forth. It looked around with gentle eyes, and flapped its oversize ears to cool itself.

Jace lifted his hand and motioned for caution. "When he stops waving his ears, take care. That means he's nervous. He can run over you without stopping and crush you flat."

Slowly and gingerly they slipped into scrub woodlands. "A rhino always charges in a straight line," Jace whispered, "so don't get in front of him. You'll never escape that deadly horn. I've seen men run clear through, then mutilated and trampled. Don't hurt yourself by running into a thicket to escape or hide; it offers no barrier to him. He'll crash through thornbushes as if they weren't there, but you'll be snagged and trapped. At first sight, you'll think he's clumsy, but he isn't. He can stop and turn faster than you can blink. He's unpredictable and fearless. Even the Masai, who'll grab a man-eating lion by the tail, fear only the rhino. Do I make myself clear?"

"More than clear," Louisa wailed. "I'd rather be in camp."

"Just do as I've said and you'll be fine," Jace coaxed. "This first shot is Chad's. Reid, you're backup man. If you both miss, it's me and Johi. Once we challenge him, somebody has to take him down. Then, the kill has to be marked on somebody's license. The women will hang back with the bearers this time. They're all tribal huntsmen and safari trained, so they know what to do. I've talked to you plenty for the past few days, so keep in mind what I've said."

Grasslands loomed before them. Several giraffes roamed near flat-topped acacias, stretching their long necks to feed in the high branches. Near a cluster of thornbushes, Jace pointed to a browsing rhino, a black one. They halted and came to alert.

The grayish-brown brute was larger than Leigh

imagined. An attendant egret and several tick-birds perched on a back that displayed lumps along the spine. His skin reminded her of unskillfully tanned cowhide that was old and crinkled. His flared ears resembled soup bowls. His large nostrils increased in size with each breath of air taken, which was hot and dry today. His small, beady eyes had numerous wrinkles surrounding them. Two horns protruded on his snout. One was short and straight, the other long, thick, and curved. Jace told them it was razor sharp for battling and digging.

The sky was clear. They were engulfed by a green-and-gold landscape, the area smelling like prairie grass during autumn. Still air was filled with tension and suspense. Chad quivered with anticipation and studied the beast. The three women hung back with several bearers and observed the sight. Jace unslung his weapon, then motioned Chad and Reid forward. Johi followed without a sound.

The cantankerous animal did not hear or smell them as Jace closed the distance from upwind. The grassy surface smothered the sound of their boots. Birds walked up and down the rhino's back, pecking at ticks in the heavy skin folds. The birds were also the alarm-givers for the rhino. Jace had revealed— that on sighting or hearing them—the birds would dart upward, give shrill cries, and head toward the hunters as if to reveal their hiding place to their host.

With his gaze glued ahead, Reid stepped on a rock, causing him to stumble. The carbine was jostled in his grip. Red-billed ox peckers took noisy flight, straight for the men. The rhino's head jerked upward from his grazing. Unchewed grass hung from his misshapen mouth. His fuzzy-edged ears twitched, and his spread nostrils sniffed the air. It only took a moment for the animal to come to full alert.

When the rhino jerked his head upward twice and tossed the grass from his mouth, Jace shouted, "He's on to us. Scatter! At fifty feet, we all fire if he isn't down. It's your game, Chad. Keep alert for a mate, Johi. There's too many tracks here for one."

Jace's voice caught the animal's attention. It lowered its head and charged in her lover's direction, determined to gore the man. Leigh screamed, then clamped her hand over her mouth to prevent further distraction. Terror filled her as the beast ran swiftly at her love.

"Here, you bloody bloke!" Chad yelled.

The animal came to an immediate standstill, whirled in her guardian's direction, and charged straightforward. Its pace was fast and menacing. Chad took aim but waited, and waited.

"Shoot!" Louisa shrieked in panic, but Chad held his fire and stance and ground. "Don't be a fool. Kill him! Now!"

The animal came to an abrupt halt, located the noise, and raced toward the women. All except Leigh screamed. The hunter/bearers prepared for the attack. Leigh lifted her weapon and took aim, not realizing her gun was no longer loaded . . .

"This way, you monster," Chad shouted. "You're mine." He yelled until he succeeded in attracting the animal's attention.

Again, the enormous and strong creature changed directions. At fifty feet, Jace shouted, "Shoot, damn you. Stop playing!"

That time, the rhino wasn't distracted and kept up his charge at the handsome earl. Both man and beast were committed to life or death in a moment. The black-haired man fired, just as Jace shot its front leg to halt its lethal intent. Chad's bullet struck home first, and the beast stumbled and fell, dead near his feet. Chad sent out a whoop of joy, lifting and shaking his gun overhead in victory.

Jace hurried to him. The men exchanged challenging looks. "That was damn foolish, old friend. Don't wait so long next time. Another minute and he would have had you on the end of that horn."

Chad sent him a broad grin. "No way. You would have taken him down before he reached me. I know what a perfect shot you are. I wanted to get him close. I didn't want to take a risk of ruining him. What a prize," he murmured. "Louisa! Come take my picture with him."

The redhead rushed forward and flung herself into Chad's arms. "You scared me to death. I don't like such sport, Chad. You're reckless."

Laughing, he argued, "I was never in any danger. Was I, Jace?"

"We'd have gotten him, but it was close. Too close, Chad. I warned you about showing off and being stubborn."

"You shot him in the leg to slow him," Leigh remarked. "You might have saved Chad's life," she pointed out to everyone. To make certain she didn't insult her guardian, she added, "That was mighty brave, Chad. I would have been scared stiff."

"It was awfully exciting. My head's spinning and my heart's pounding. What a surge! I feel ten years younger."

"And I feel twenty years older, my love," Louisa murmured.

Chad laughed and said, "It wouldn't be the first time Jace saved my life, would it? You remember in '89 when I riled that native in the Somoan Islands by chasing his girl? I thought she was inviting me into her hut for the night. Her man and his friends started beating me senseless. They dragged me down the beach and tried to drown me in the ocean. I came up spitting dirt and water to find Jace all over them. He had to whip three men to rescue me. Broke his nose. What a fight. Those were some good old days, weren't they, Jace?"

"Yep, and you're still a reckless bastard," he quipped, grinning at that amusing memory and rubbing the small bump on his nose.

"But we always won every battle, old chap, and they were fun."

"What will we do with him?" Reid asked, motioning to the dead rhino and ceasing the merriment.

"One of the extra men will take his head downriver to be prepared," Jace revealed. He called the bearers forward to remove the head, load it on a carrying board, and transport it back to camp.

A successful hunt completed, they headed back to camp. They reached the area by five o'clock, with plenty of daylight left. As the white men celebrated with wine, the natives sang and danced as they carried the board with rhino head round and round the campfire in a victorious ritual. Everyone watched and enjoyed the ceremony.

Passing Leigh to fetch a map from his tent, Jace murmured, "You broke rule one today, woman; you screamed. That puts me a point ahead, and you owe me a kiss. I'll collect when it's safe."

Leigh had strolled around the day after Cynthia's surprise arrival at her tent, to find no other shelter with a secret escape route. She wanted to know if Jace had used that special tent with other women in the past, or if it had been made just for her. If so, it had been mighty cocky of him.

Jace spread a map over one table. "We'll head for the Ambroseli Plains next, then Kajiado, and on to Nairobi and the Aberdare Range. We'll take the Tana River to the coast, then back to Mombasa. Every visitor should see the Great Rift Valley. After we reach Nairobi, it'll mostly be sightseeing until we reach the river. There's plenty of game along its banks. The trek should take about two months."

"Sounds great, Jace. This is about the only place in the world we haven't seen together. You ever thought of going back to Australia?"

"Nope," Jace replied, wondering at Chad's mellow mood.

"I still remember all those opals our ships picked up there and took to London. We should have invested in one of those mines. It would be worth a fortune today."

"You and Jace were in Australia together?" Louisa hinted.

"Many times. When we were in the Royal Navy, our ship transported convicts to the colonies there, then goods back to England. The scum of mankind, right, Jace?"

"That's right. Tasmania was said to be the ideal dumping ground for incorrigible prisoners. Port Arthur was a penal colony, one of the most notorious prisons in the world. Frankly I hated taking even convicts there. They were used like slave labor—if they survived the harsh conditions and brutal treatment. The guards used vicious dogs to hunt down escapees. They had this lookout on a place called Eagle Hawk Neck."

"You remember Paddington?" After Jace nodded, Chad informed the others, "It was a legendary slum district in the eighties. The balconies were made from the iron ballasts in ships. You didn't walk through there alone at night, did you, Jace?" The two men exchanged looks, grinned at a shared reflection, and shook their heads.

"What are the plans for tomorrow?" Reid asked as he poured everyone more wine.

"I thought we'd hunt zebra. The following day, if you'd all like, we can visit a Masai village. It's quite interesting."

"That sounds wonderful, Jace," Leigh said with anticipation.

"If you don't mind," Cynthia said, "Louisa and I would like to rest tomorrow. We aren't accustomed to so much walking. Then, we'll be eager and ready to head for that native village."

"Doesn't matter to me," Chad said in a casual tone. "What about you, Leigh? You coming with us or resting?"

Leigh wanted to be with her love. She wanted to study both men. And she didn't want to be stuck in camp all day with those women harassing her with questions. "I want to see everything, so I'm going with you men."

She felt Louisa's cold stare on her, but she didn't care. Jace and Chad smiled at her. "Tell us about native superstitions. Do tribes really eat blondes for good luck?" she asked, laughing merrily.

"Some do, I'm sure," Jace replied after chuckling. "These people believe in witches, too. They're associated with the night, with hyenas, snakes, and other detested creatures. They're said to inherit or learn their skills to harm or slay people. Some of the tribes believe the soul—called *Kra*—of a departed leader lives in a sacred stool, and each successor joins it there at death. No crime is worse than for another tribe to steal one or destroy it, because the souls of past rulers are then lost forever. There's even a secret society that forces warriors to commit suicide if they abuse their tribal positions. The Kikuyu believe that

282

to spit on a person is a friendly gesture, the highest honor you can receive, a gift of himself. So, if a Kikuyu spits on you, don't insult him by striking him or wiping it off."

"You must be joking," Louisa scoffed, frowning.

"Nope, it's the absolute truth; I swear it. Ask Johi. He's Kikuyu. Johi is my right arm. He knows this land and these animals better than anyone. A guide would be lost without an assistant like him. He's one with nature and he has this big map inside his head. He knows what the natives and animals feel and think."

Leigh noticed the affection and admiration Jace felt for Wanjohi. She saw the dark-skinned man grin broadly, exposing snow-white teeth and twinkling eyes. Each man was different, yet they were alike in many ways. Each had his own customs and personality, but each respected the other's. It was apparent they worked well together, and complemented each other. Perhaps Johi would talk more later.

Leigh also realized how special Jace really was. Clearly being a safari guide took a unique man, one who loved outdoor work, who craved excitement, who loved challenging danger. He was a man who stayed calm in perilous situations. He could endure the worst conditions. He was a skilled tracker and gunman, and he knew how to be a leader. He was smart enough to know how to handle people on hunts. He was well prepared with supplies and with entertaining stories and enlightening facts. He knew how to make people relax, to be careful, to leave his land victorious.

"Tell us more, Jace," she encouraged as they dined. "We want to be prepared when we visit that village."

Between bites and sips, Jace related more of Masai

customs, "Spirits of dead ancestors have to be praised, mentioned, and supplicated regularly. The descendents believe their welfare is affected and controlled by them. Dead chiefs are especially important. Possession of their spirits gives the current ruler power, and it's said to give the tribe fertility and a sense of well-being. They also believe that spirits of dead warriors inhabit objects and animals, particularly cheetahs. Some tribes won't kill cheetahs, even if their lives and stock are in jeopardy. We don't want to offend any of them, so we won't hunt cheetahs, either. I don't want any of you to break tribal laws and get snatched during the night for revenge. No treasure, even a jeweled ritual knife, is worth torture and death. Johi and I know this territory, but there are places where we could never locate you. When we visit the Masai village, keep your minds pure and your hands to yourselves. We don't want trouble."

Jace and Chad exchanged a long and silent look. Jace went on. "As with most whites, most natives believe in a remote and omnipotent high god who's reached by sacrifice, prayer, and ritual."

As Leigh captured the hints in Jace's revelation, the conversation drifted to their hunt today and it was gone over in great detail.

"After our social call on the Masai," Reid asked, "what will we hunt for next?"

"Leopard. There should be some in the forest a few miles away." When Jace noticed how much the men and two women were drinking, he cautioned, "Don't forget, no drinking on the trail. It dulls wits and reflexes. It also makes the sun seem hotter. You'll sweat more and could pass out. Drink only in camp, and not too much."

"I think we're being scolded for excess," Louisa

teased.

In a pleasant tone, Jace remarked, "I don't care what you do in London or Mombasa, Miss Jennings. But out here, I'm responsible for all of you. I know what's best, so you have to obey my rules."

Chad locked gazes with his old friend and nodded. "Jace is right, Louisa. The jungle is a dangerous place. If we don't do as he orders, we can get into big trouble. Believe me, I know."

Louisa caught a clue in the men's expressions and moods, and asked, "What do you mean, Chad?"

Chad glanced at the redhead, then at the alert Leigh. "It's one of those memories I'd like to forget. It was a long time ago, and I was reckless and greedy, a young man seeking the wrong challenge and adventure to prove his prowess."

"Like you were today, my love," the woman jested in return. "We have plenty of time to get your trophies, so don't get greedy and take any more risks like that. I was terrified."

"Next time, keep quiet. You had that rhino charging all of you. If I hadn't turned him, one of you women could have been gored."

Louisa pouted sultrily and commented, "I wasn't the only one who screamed. Cynthia and Leigh did, too. We were scared and taken by surprise. We'll do better next time. Won't we, ladies?"

"It broke the tension and gave us experience, Chad. We'll be fine from now on," Leigh concurred with her self-appointed rival.

Talk continued for a while, then everyone parted for the night.

In her tent, Leigh mused on what she had learned today. She was glad the two men were getting along. If they did patch up their torn friendship, she and Jace would be free to drop their secrecy. She missed him terribly. She was with him every day, but it wasn't the same; their closeness was absent. She longed to spend the night together again, but it was too hazardous.

In Jace's tent, Johi revealed the news about Leigh's weapon. The guide asked, "How did it get unloaded? You always check the guns when we return to camp. Did you see anything suspicious?"

A man of few words, Wanjohi responded, "No. She does not hunt or kill. It is dangerous."

"I'm sure Leigh didn't remove the cartridges. Somebody tampered with her gun. Sharpen your eyes even more, Johi. I don't like this."

"She was in no danger. We are good shots."

"We know that, but someone else doesn't."

"She fired in practice last night," the black-eyed man added. "Perhaps she did not reload. I saw no one with her weapon."

"I forgot about practice after we reassigned weapons. I guess you're right, Johi. I won't mention her carelessness to her, but from now on, I'll remind everyone to reload after shooting."

"That is wise."

Louisa strolled around the camp after the others had left for the day. Chad's rhino head had been placed in a boat, covered to avoid attracting heavenly scavengers, and sent back to Mombasa for preservation by a man there. She stared before her. The bright sun seemed to incredibly whiten the snows atop the distant Kilimanjaro. Every morning, they all stared at the awesome sight and wished they could visit it. The base of the towering mountain always looked periwinkle in the early-morning and late evening haze. The sky was a clear blue, and the jungle before it was a lush green. "It's really very beautiful, Cynthia. It reeks of power and danger."

"Since when do you enjoy admiring scenery?" the woman jested. "That's all little Leigh does, gush over every sight and sound."

"We're here, so we may as well enjoy something. Let's walk to that waterhole and talk. The servants can't see or hear us from there. I have something for you to do."

The two women took their weapons for protection and excused themselves from camp. The bearers left behind were either off on their own or busy with chores. At present, some were doing the party's laundry in the river, leaving only two men in the camp.

At the waterhole, Louisa found a spot where tall grass and scrubs concealed it from the campsite. No animals were about this time of day or with the clear river nearby for drinking. Louisa stripped.

"What are you doing?" Cynthia asked with wide eyes.

"Going swimming. It's already hot this early. I'm miserable, and the men are at the river."

"It's dangerous," the brunette warned.

"Not with you standing guard. Is your weapon loaded? That was very clever, how you removed Leigh's bullets the other night. Too bad it gained us nothing. I wish that rhino had attacked her."

"Thank you, but I meant that, Jace said the water is unhealthy."

"That's just Great White Hunter talk, scare tactics to keep us under control. Just like those bitter tablets. I can't stand them."

Cynthia was worried. "You're taking them, aren't

you?"

"When I'm in the mood to punish myself, which is rare."

"Louisa, you're being foolish. Please obey the rules."

"I do, but my own. Relax, I'll be fine." She wadded into the mucky water and took a short swim. After, she let the hot sun dry her flesh before pulling on her clothes. "That's better. Now, listen carefully. Here's what I want you to do."

In Cynthia's tent later, Louisa giggled and said, "You distracted them perfectly, my dear friend and accomplice."

"Yes, but I got scratched up tangling myself in that underbrush. Of course, they never located that necklace I supposedly lost. Did you find anything important?"

"I didn't search Jace's tent. He's too smart and could tell if I went through his things. No matter. I found what I needed in Leigh's tent, and Chad's. I never could look with them around all the time."

"Well?" Cynthia prompted as the woman tended her injuries.

Louisa stopped removing thorn tips and dabbing on balm to reply, "I found plenty, more than I expected. Chad had his contract hidden well, but I located it. The sorry bastard," she muttered, then revealed its contents to her astonished friend.

"So there is more to their wager than he led you to believe."

"He certainly stands to lose more than money," she scoffed in bitterness. "There is no way he'll allow Jace to win and take everything. That means my treacherous lover has to get Leigh, not just prevent

Jace from doing so. This isn't a game or a joke, Cynthia."

"But Reid assured me Chad wants you, not Leigh."

"He lied, just like Chad lied. They're in this sport together."

"I don't understand. Why would Chad bring you along and sleep with you beneath Leigh's nose if he wants her? That's crazy."

"I'm confused about that point, too. I'm certain Leigh would have come with him, even if you and I weren't along. I wonder what he needs with me."

"To distract Jace?" Cynthia suggested.

"No woman could distract Jace with a wager like that at stake. Perhaps there's something we don't know about Webster's will. Perhaps Chad and his mother *won't* inherit if anything happens to Leigh. Perhaps the only way Chad can get anything is to marry that little witch."

"But Leigh is William's only heir," the brunette reasoned. "As his widow, Fiona would have to inherit, and Chad would get it later."

"Not if William has an illigitimate heir somewhere, or he left everything to a friend. The old man was sly, and he might have caught on to Chad's evil before he died. You have to admit, my lover has been acting strangely since the old man's death and Leigh's arrival."

"If Chad can't inherit, he's worthless to you."

"Not if I let him get Leigh first, then get rid of her."

"You can't be serious! Help your lover win another woman?"

"If that's the only way to succeed, I have no choice."

"We don't have time for more games, Louisa.

289

After we get home, neither of us can conceal our dire straits much longer."

"We can do it long enough for Chad to get his hands on that fortune. We've come too far and done too many things to lose now."

"But what if you help him win Leigh and you're wrong?"

"That's a chance I might have to take. I haven't decided yet. This information is too fresh. I have to give it more study. For now, we have to quell this romance between Leigh and Jace." Louisa revealed what she had discovered in Leigh's tent: the contract with Jace.

Cynthia was shocked. "You mean their wager is a farce? It isn't for one thousand pounds as Chad thinks? She actually bet one night with him against his plantation? How could any man risk so much to spend a night between her legs? How does she plan to find time to make her payment, especially if he wins more than one night?"

"Obviously little Leigh isn't as pure and innocent as I imagined. We know she can't win his plantation. I think she wants to lose to him. That gives her a reason to justify yielding her maidenhead to him. You know how prim virgins are; they have to pretend that surrender isn't their idea. That's why she agreed to all those silly rules." Louisa gave her friend a brief summation of the rules in the contract. "No doubt she'll find ways to break rules one and two and pay him along the trail, because it won't be possible to pay him later. We're sailing as soon as this safari ends. Of course she wouldn't break rule three because she could never pay off that loss. Chad would never let her out of his sight for a year. She probably wants to enjoy Jace here, then work on Chad back home. The greedy bitch!"

"What if she's fallen for Jace Elliott and hopes he'll marry her after she gives him her virginity?" Cynthia speculated.

"She's not that crazy. Jace is a criminal in exile."

"If Chad has to win her and can't, we're all, except those two, losers."

"Until I decide what to do, we'll have to make certain Leigh earns more points than Jace. That should worry and distract our guide."

"What if you tell Chad about their secret deal? He'll yank her home so fast her head will spin for weeks."

"No. I don't want him to panic and mess up things. If he was really worried about Jace winning, he would be pursuing Leigh more energetically. Part of what Chad said must be true; his little wager was to provoke Jace into working for him. I think he's after Jace for revenge. If our guide gets killed, Jace isn't a threat to Chad's plans for Leigh. It's clever, get rid of his foe and get the girl."

"Of course, that must be his plan. He's so devious and cunning."

"Not as much as we are, Cynthia. For now, we'll be very generous and help Chad, without his knowledge naturally. Until we know more, we have to keep Leigh and Jace apart."

"You want me to have a fight with Reid and move in with her?" Cynthia suggested.

"That's too obvious and suspicious. We'll just keep them on edge and in doubt. I'll work on Jace; you work on Leigh. Maybe Chad will let something slip. I'll keep a sharp eye and ear on him. If Chad has to win Leigh to become Webster's heir, I must know soon, as that would change my plan. If not . . ."

"But what about the other part of Chad's bet with Jace? The part about winning five thousand dollars each time they sleep with Leigh? Surely one or both men will try to collect on it, many times."

"I'm surprised Jace Elliott let Chad include such a lowdown term. Obviously Jace isn't as honest and honorable as we thought."

"If Leigh's as hungry and eager as it appears from her wager, one of those men could earn a lot of extra money if he's clever."

Chapter Thirteen

The first sight of the *Manyatta*, the Masai village, was a surprise. It was surrounded by a fence that looked like a giant circle of tangled thornbushes, and was twelve feet high. Jace explained that it was called an *engang* and its purpose was to keep out lions and to keep in their cattle.

Once inside, Leigh saw numerous huts with flat tops and made of earth and dung. The dung was thickened and strengthened with straw, and plastered to a round framework of strong branches. The odor was strong but not unbearable. Groups of cattle were everywhere, having been brought inside for the night. Young boys tended the "supreme providers" with great care, even with affection and respect.

The Masai depended on cattle for meat and blood and milk. They halted to watch several men at work with a cow. A leather thong was tied around its neck, and it was held motionless. One man knelt and fired a blocked arrow into the animal's jugular vein. Blood was caught in a gord. Some of the men drank the red liquid hot from the task. Others mixed it with milk, then consumed it. Leigh noticed how the bleeding halted immediately. The cow seemed unhurt, and not the least troubled by the deed, but she felt a little nauseated.

Jace had told them many things about this nomadic tribe of lion-killing spearmen. They settled in an area as long as the grazing was good, then moved on when it wasn't. They never camped near waterholes, because the earth was trampled and barren, and predators were a threat. Water was hauled by women to camp, and none was wasted, not even for bathing and drinking. That was done at rivers.

Flies were numerous and busy inside the enclosure. But Masai did not kill them or even shoo them away, believing spirits of ancestors could inhabit all living things. Their god was called Enkai, and the lives of these drinkers of blood were filled with rituals and customs.

Until his middle teens, a Masai boy tends the herd, while the girls milk cows and serve as the warrior's concubines. Between sixteen and twenty, a boy is circumcised in a grand ceremony. During this training period he is given warrior raiment and weapons, and his head is shaved. A few years later, he becomes a full warrior. Only then can he marry and grow hair to be braided into a certain style.

The Masai warriors — *moran* — were very tall and slender, a handsome race with sharp and bold features. The garb of some consisted of animal skins draped toga-style; others wore a cloth wrapped around their hips. Their hair was plaited in an elaborate style, its top held against the forehead with a cord beneath the chin. The black hair was heavily greased with animal fat and dusted with red ochre. Their storklike legs were decorated with designs running from groin to ankle by scratched mud. Most of them had simple beaded bands around their necks, wrists, and ankles. Their bodies displayed a reddish-orange cast from the ochre mud smeared and dried there. Most had large loops in earlobes stretched to an amazing size.

The girls who served the warriors did so before the age they could conceive, a fact Leigh found distressing. When puberty ended, the young girls were circumcised, too, and declared ready for marriage.

The women looked much different from the men. Their shaved heads shone in the sunlight. Large collars of beads and coiled wires were worn about their necks. To Leigh, the weight seemed as if it would be uncomfortable, but the dark-skinned women didn't appear to notice. They even slept on special wooden headrests to protect their jewelry. Most were attired in *kikoi,* a colorful sarong like garment.

The people greeting them were friendly and courteous. The Masai were said to make formidable enemies but very good friends. They were proud, old-fashioned people who retained their ancient and pastoral existence. They did not seem to mind the British takeover of this land, or dislike the white intruders.

As Jace conversed with the tribesmen, Louisa declared, "I am not eating or sleeping here, Chad. We'll probably all get sick and die."

Chad pulled Jace aside and told him, "None of us want to spend the night here, Jace, or join these people for dinner. I'm afraid our diets and customs vary too much. I think you understand. Let's visit a while, then move on before dark."

Jace was disappointed, but didn't argue. He had hoped to get Leigh alone tonight, after Johi used a "magical native potion" in the others' wine, but he had realized bringing along wine would seem curious. "We'll talk a few minutes, then find a place to make camp."

The Masai insisted on dancing for them. A group of near-naked warriors carrying seven-foot spears gathered before the whites now sitting on brush mats. The men bunched tightly, gave a loud whoop, then jumped into the air in unison, except for one. Their greased, ochre-coated bodies undulated to a drum beat, then leapt upward again. A Masai chant was sung by the dancers. The drumming grew louder. The jumps moved closer together and higher. The man who did not leap with the others murmured a different chant, a longer one. The dancers all sang the same two words over and over.

It reminded Leigh of descriptions she had read of American Indian war dances and chants and their affect on the pioneers. But this was wonderful, not terrifying. It was primitive, hypnotic, and fascinating. She was enchanted by sight and sound.

"What are they saying?" she asked Jace.

He chuckled and replied, "They're telling about their adventures."

"Men's bawdy tales?" Louisa hinted.

"Something like that," Jace answered with a grin.

Louisa leaned toward Jace and murmured, "Actually it's very arousing, don't you think?"

"No, I don't, Miss Jennings," he said, calm and formal.

"Well, I do," she responded, undaunted.

Chad was talking with Leigh. "Isn't this marvelous? Aren't you glad we came? Everything's going perfectly."

"I'm having a glorious time, Chad, and all is well," she said in a tone certain to get her meaning across.

Moving closer to the blonde, Chad whispered, "I am being good."

"Yes, you are, very good. It isn't too hard, is it?"

He sent her an engaging grin. "Surprisingly not at all. Who knows? We might stay longer than planned. Would you like that?"

"What if the others get tired or bored?" she

inquired.

"They can leave anytime they like. They aren't captives here." He lowered his voice even more. "We might have more fun without them. Just me and you, and our guide."

"That wouldn't be proper," she said, trying to discourage him.

His gaze softened. "Under one circumstance, it would."

She laughed. "Stop teasing me, Chad." The drums and dance ended, and so did her dismaying banter with her guardian.

After their return to camp, it rained hard all day and night, and the bearers took cover in the jungle. A meat-and-vegetable stew was prepared by the servants beneath a canvas and brush shelter, then carried indoors and served to everyone. The others rested and played games, while Leigh snuggled up with a book. No one went outside in the storm, except Jace, who sneaked to Leigh's tent.

As he unlaced the secret opening, she quickly put out the lantern to prevent telltale shadows on the canvas walls. "Isn't this dangerous, Jace?" she whispered, even though the rain was loud and heavy around them. She waited for him to seal the entrance.

"Yep, but I couldn't wait any longer to get my arms around you. I've missed you, woman. You don't know what pleasure I get from kissing you and touching you. It's driving me wild."

"Me, too," she confessed as he joined her. "You're soaked. Why don't we get you out of these dripping clothes?"

Jace trembled with desire. "I didn't come here to seduce you, love. I can settle for kisses and hugs and talk."

"But I can't. I want you, and you've seen to it that I need you."

"What a clever man I am," he teased, kissing her.

Leigh's arms banded his body and she nestled against him. "I'm getting you wet, love. Sorry," he murmured against her ear.

"I don't care." She unbuttoned his shirt and removed it. As Jace took off his boots and pants, Leigh slipped out of her garments.

Jace pulled the bedroll to the floor, knowing the single cot couldn't hold their combined weights. He drew her down beside him. They kissed deeply as they cuddled.

Leigh thought it would spoil the romantic mood by questioning him about the secret entrance and by revealing Chad's overture, so she held silent. "This feels good. I like having you near me."

"I *love* having you near me, woman. These past days have been terrible. Half the time I'm scared to look at you for fear of exposing my feelings. The other half, I can't keep my eyes away. What have you done to me? I've never felt so helpless and frustrated. I can't wait to win our bet and get you all to myself. Which reminds me, you owe me a kiss for breaking rule one."

She laughed softly. "You only have one point, my irresistible guide, so don't get cocky yet. If it's payment you demand, I'll gladly comply." She sealed her mouth to his and tantalized him with her tongue.

Jace's hands rubbed up and down her sleek back as she lay half across him. Her tawny mane fell around his head and tickled him in spots. With her so near and steadily consuming his being, revenge and exoneration—all wild perils—seemed far away or nonexistent. He was caught up in a beautiful dream where only sweet passions dwelled with them. He groaned as his arms tightened around her waist.

Leigh's fingers wandered into his brown hair, and damp curls clung to them. She kissed away the raindrops on his face, then drifted down his neck to do the same there. Even the furry covering on his chest was wet, and her fingers played there a while, making tiny curls. His flesh was cool, slick, and firm beneath her roaming hands. She needed and wanted to explore him and felt brave enough to do so. It was as if the driving rain pelted against her tent like a primitive drumbeat, creating a mesmeric force that compelled her to perform this ancient ritual of love.

Leigh's lips journeyed along his chest. Her tongue circled the small but taut peaks on his virile landscape. Her hand drifted along his sides, over his stomach, and into a thicker covering of soft fur. It, too, was damp. She moved her hand lower still, savoring the evidence of his desire for her. Her courage did not desert her, as she was too enchanted by love's task to be sway from this new adventure. She felt Jace stiffen in surprise, heard him moan in delight, and felt him relax once more. With leisure and care, her hand traveled up and down the lengthy domain where heat and strength met her.

Jace didn't know if he wanted to lie still or wriggle in pleasure, or if he could even control his actions. Leigh seemed in a provocative mood tonight, as if she boldly sought a treasure. She was a novice at love, but she was learning fast. He felt tense and afire. His head was dazed by hunger, and his body ached with it. As her hands and lips worked at mapping her easily conquered territory, he shuddered in arousal.

When he thought he could last no longer, Jace rolled Leigh to her back and assailed her breasts with his greedy mouth. His hands and mouth began an intoxicating expedition of their own over her beckoning ground. He called on all the knowledge, experience, and skills he possessed to stimulate and pleasure her, and himself.

When they joined together, it was nearly shattering to both. They labored with love, yearning, and urgency. Their victory came within minutes, so high was their arousal and need.

In the dreamy aftermath, Jace held her against him. "Every time I take you, it's like the first time, the best time. How is that?"

"It's the same for me. I think nothing could be better, but it always is. It's like a hunger that's never satisfied for more than a while. I suppose it's because you whet my appetite and keep me starving for you all the time. That's a mean and naughty trick, Jace Elliott."

"No more than the trick you play on me, woman. You tempt me day and night to lay permanent siege to you, knowing I can't."

That statement worried Leigh. Was this all he had in mind for them? Because he was a wanted man? Or because she only affected him sexually? She wanted more, much more, from him.

"Unless," he murmured, kissing and nuzzling her ear, "you trick Chad and sneak to my plantation."

"You know I can't, Jace. Chad would never agree to a voyage to Texas just months before my birthday."

"He will if he thinks you trust him and you're turning your affairs over to him," Jace refuted. "You don't have to tell him you're returning in December. I don't want you going there as long as he has such power over you. And we can use more time together."

It was tempting, but would it work? Should she even consider more time without wedlock? She loved this man, but how well did she know him? He was eager to keep her here until November, but why? He couldn't

300

get revenge on Chad without exposing them, and Jace would not hurt her that way. What would her love feel and say when she was free to make her own choices? Would he offer marriage even if he couldn't exonerate himself? Was this a test of her feelings for him? "It's crazy, but who knows what will happen?"

His fingers stroked her hair and bare skin. "You're right. I might decide to hold you captive and enjoy you for a very long time."

"I could always escape."

"Not through the jungles around my place. It's very secluded."

Leigh's fingers teased over his parted lips. Her teeth nibbled playfully on his cleft chin. "That sounds intimidating, Mr. Elliott. Who is around to help me if you turn into an uncontrollable beast?"

Soft chuckles sounded in his throat. "No one. My housekeeper, workers, and friends would never take your side against me."

"What if we wind up on the same side and I don't require help?"

"That's what I'm scheming for, woman. How did you guess?"

"Do you hear that?" she whispered, sitting up beside him.

"Hear what?" he asked, coming to alert.

Without hurting him or leaving a mark, she bit his shoulder. "Nothing is what. It's stopped raining. Someone might check on us. You'd better go." She kissed him as if saying farewell.

"Before proving my stamina and desire?" he jested, pulling her back to the bedroll. His mouth fastened to hers, as eagerly as if he hadn't taken her in days . . .

Leopard was on their schedule next. As they walked,

301

Jace instructed the group on the species. "The leopard's a solitary animal, except during mating season. He hunts in the bush and woodlands, but he loves to climb trees to sleep and to bask in the sun. He normally hunts at night, but he'll carry his kill into a tree with him to keep other predators from stealing it. He mostly stalks smaller animals, like waterbuck, but one of his favorites is baboon. If you haven't seen pictures of him, he's tawny with black markings, almost like little squares. He's big, mean, and powerful. He's bloodthirsty, fast, and cunning. And vindictive. He'll attack without provocation, and kill for the sheer pleasure of it — one of the few animals with that trait. Sometimes he doesn't even devour his victim, just leaves the body lying there. Naturally we can't stalk him at night, so we'll try to find one sleeping or chasing baboons."

They had left camp two hours ago. Leigh was feeling strange. She was lightheaded and thirsty. She felt tense, but very drowsy. She surmised it was the climate, or lack of sleep.

As the women excused themselves in the bush, Louisa watched her closely, then asked, "Leigh, do you feel all right? You look dreadfully pale and your cheeks are like red roses."

Leigh drank from her canteen. "I'm tired and stiff. I read too late last night and didn't get enough sleep. I won't do that again, rain or not. It's terribly hot today." She mopped at the beads of perspiration on her face and neck and swatted at insects.

"No hotter than usual," Louisa refuted. "Why don't I suggest we return to camp? I'll tell Jace I'm exhausted and feeling sick."

Leigh was annoyed, because it sounded as if the redhead was trying to prevent her from being the reason to break a wager rule. She assumed Chad had

302

revealed the thousand-pound bet with their guide and had ordered the redhead's aid. It rankled that Chad couldn't keep promises and secrets. More sharply than intended, she said, "I'll be fine after this break. Don't worry about me, Louisa."

They crossed a veld, which was open country where grass and scrubs grew. They were heading for a thorn-bush area, then a thin forest with plenty of baboons: leopard country. They had seen many animals but hadn't stopped to hunt.

The farther they traveled, the weaker Leigh felt. She did not want to alarm Chad and Jace, or to lose another point. Not that she didn't intend to make Jace her future, but a deal was a deal. It had to be won fairly. She staggered, and caught a tree to steady herself. The bearers nearby called out to the leader, a few feet ahead.

Jace halted and looked at Leigh. As surreptitiously as possible, he had observed her at each stop. She had a tight grip on a tree limb and her head was lowered. If only she were closer so he could have kept an eye on her, but the women were journeying behind with the bearers. "Leigh, what's wrong?" he asked, going to her side.

Chad joined them. "Are you ill, Leigh?" He tested her cheeks and forehead for fever as his blue eyes examined her.

Her pretense was in vain. She leaned against a tree and said, "I'm just tired and hot. We've been walking a long time. I'm used to riding horses, not traveling afoot. Can we take a break?"

"Certainly," Chad said before Jace could. "Sit down and rest. Drink some water. You're sweating. That makes you weak and shaky. Jace, how about a fire and bracing tea? It might help."

"No, please don't fuss over me. Just water and rest,"

Leigh implored weakly.

Chad held the canteen, as Leigh's hands were quivering. He knelt beside the blonde, who leaned her head backward and closed her eyes. He glanced at Jace, looking worried. He saw that Jace was concerned.

"We'll rest here, then head back when Leigh feels up to it."

"I think that's an excellent idea," Chad agreed. He passed his canteen to Leigh, because she had emptied hers.

They lingered over an hour. The others strolled and took pictures. Jace and Chad stayed near Leigh, who dozed. Johi watched all of them.

Finally, Leigh opened her eyes and said, "Let's go. I'm fine."

Chad studied her. "You look better. You were mighty pale."

"Whatever it was, it's gone now. Why don't we continue?"

"It's too late in the day. We should return to camp," Jace said.

That night, Jace could not check on Leigh because Louisa stayed with her, at Chad's insistence. Jace hoped her spell earlier in the day was nothing more than fatigue and heat. He knew he should have let her get more sleep the night before. He wouldn't overtire her again.

As Leigh claimed her canteen and weapon for today's trek, she whispered to Jace, "That's two points I owe you."

"Even though it was my fault you were too exhausted to go on?"

"You got as much sleep as I did, so that made us even yesterday."

"Not really. I'm accustomed to this climate and terrain. You aren't." He took her weapon and checked it. "But I'll accept the point. I might need it to win. You aren't cheating, are you?"

"Me? Certainly not," she said, then grinned.

This time, they didn't even make it to the veld before Leigh experienced the same symptoms. The group halted once more.

"Why don't you go ahead with the hunt?" Chad suggested. "I'll stay here and guard Leigh. I don't want her traveling like this."

"I'll stay," Reid said. "You're the one who wants the leopard."

"You take the kill and glory. I'm worried about my ward."

"Why don't we all rest for a while?" Jace said. "If Leigh can't continue, we'll carry her back to camp."

"No," Leigh protested. "I don't want to spoil everyone's fun."

"She's right. Go get us a leopard, Reid."

"If that's what you want, fine with me. I feel lucky today."

After the others departed, Leigh took a nap. Chad laid his gun in his lap and watched her. He wished he could curl up beside her, make love to her, then sleep himself. His fingers stroked her damp hair as she slept. He smiled, then frowned. He didn't like the way Jace and Leigh were becoming friends. He wanted to get her away from the man and back home. If she made it necessary to end the safari, he could work on her in London. The trip had been good so far. They had gotten closer. Without Jace's distraction, his task

305

would be easier, and Jace couldn't pursue her in England. If so . . .

He would gladly pay off her wager with Jace, and he wouldn't mind paying Jace an added bonus for canceling the safari. He caressed Leigh's cheek, then bent forward to kiss it. As she shifted her position, he slipped her golden head into his lap. For a long time, all he did was stare at her. She was exquisite. A marriage between them was perfect, even if he had to give up his revenge on Jace to prevent anything or anyone from stopping it.

That thought shocked Chad. Yet he realized it might not be wise to take any chances of ruining things. He had punished Jace many times, and Jace would surely lose Leigh and the wager. There was nothing to implicate or connect him to the Stokely and Elliott crimes, so perhaps he shouldn't press his luck. The same was true of killing Jace or having him slain. With so much within his grasp, it was crazy to threaten it. A curious relief surged through Chad. Once he had this woman and all she offered, he would possess enough to make him happy for the rest of his life.

Cynthia was staying with Leigh tonight, so once more, Jace could not get at his love. He was nervous. It couldn't be a trick, he decided, so what was happening to her? Johi was keeping a watch on the two women, so Jace knew they were innocent. As for Chad, he seemed too taken with Leigh to injure or endanger her. That left . . .

In their tent, Louisa prepared for bed. "What do you think is wrong with her, Chad?" she asked.

"The climate, like Jace said. If she keeps this up, I

306

might have to take her home. I can't risk her well-being for a little fun."

"Why can't she stay in camp while we finish the safari?" the redhead ventured. "There are plenty of servants here to tend her. She doesn't need a doctor, does she?"

"I doubt it, but I'll keep an eye on her."

So will I, my cunning lover. Louisa had seen the way Chad had behaved for the last two days. It filled her with fury and hatred.

Leigh reclined on her side, toward the canvas wall. She pretended to be asleep to avoid conversation with the dozing brunette. She felt anxious and alarmed. The ailment had attacked her twice. It wasn't normal. Was it unfamiliar food, water—or insects? She certainly had enough bites to irritate her. Or, she mused, it could be someone's doing. But how? Everyone ate the same food, drank from the same bucket, and suffered from the same pests. Louisa had calmed down. Chad desired her. The others were strangers. And, Jace . . .

Jace what? She contemplated in torment. *Loves you? Desires you? Wants to win the bet? He already has three points. If you get sick and can't complete the safari, what then? Could he be playing unfairly with you?*

Their leopard trek continued. They traversed the savanna without trouble. This was an area of intense and gripping drama, a place of the swift and cunning, of violent death, of wild beauty. Zebras mingled with wildebeests for protection from predators. One brown creature wasn't lucky today, they remarked, seeing a female lion hanging on to the nose of a wildebeest,

307

trying to drag it to certain death. Another lioness struck at the animal's vulnerable throat, strangling it to death. Soon the feast began and later the scavengers would finish off what the sated lions left behind. Other lion prides were on *kopjes*—rock or earth mounds—dozing or watching the scene before them, deciding when and who to attack for their next meal.

Jace explained the seasonal migration of the wildebeest, which began in June. The vast herd was joined by zebras, gazelles, and cape buffalos; and all were stalked by lions, cheetahs, hyenas, and vicious wild dog packs. Jace talked of how many creatures didn't survive the annual journey, many trampled or drowned while crossing the Sand River on the trip to and from Tanzania and British East Africa. Their carcasses fed crocodiles and other predators.

As they entered light woodland, impalas exploded into flight, leaping high and fast to escape the intrusion. A herd of elephants with lifted trunks moved toward another feeding area. Gray infants were nearly undetectable in the midst of towering creatures with large legs. Birds and animals scattered in fear before them.

Leigh frowned as her head swam in a bleary sea. It was happening to her again. She was confused, angry, and alarmed. They were far from medical help, if it was required. She did not know if this annoyance was caused by nature or man.

"If his whiskers are down, he's relaxed," Jace was saying. "When they bristle upward, he's angry and nervous, so be careful. Once we—"

"Chad!" Louisa called out, "Leigh's in trouble again." Louisa caught the blonde's arm and steadied her. "Sit down before you fall."

Leigh was too shaky to argue. Chad and Jace rushed to her and dropped to their knees, both questioning her with concern.

"I'm just a little dizzy. I'll be fine in a minute. It's the heat."

Chad and Jace eyed her and argued, "No, it isn't."

"You go ahead," Chad turned to Jace. "I'll stay with her again. She can't continue like this, and there's no need to lose the whole day. We'll camp until you return this afternoon. Reid hasn't gotten his leopard."

"Why don't I stay with Leigh?" Jace suggested. "Johi can take over for me, and the bearers are all skilled hunters. If she needs doctoring, I'm the one best qualified to treat her here. After she's regained her strength, I'll carry her back to camp. We've already lost three days with rain and stops. Johi can help you get that leopard. Just do as he says, and no taking risks."

Chad knew Leigh would be safe in Jace's hands, and that Jace couldn't make any romantic progress with her in that condition. Chad didn't want it to look as if he wanted to get her alone. To prevent suspicion, he agreed. "That sounds fine to me, Jace. I would like to get one of those creatures before we leave this area. You sure she'll be all right and you can manage alone?"

"I think so. She only needs to adjust to our climate."

"Why can't Louisa and I rest here and go back to camp with Jace and Leigh?" Cynthia asked.

"Jace will have his hands full tending and carrying Leigh." Chad answered. "He doesn't need two complaining females atop his task."

"We wouldn't be any trouble, and we can act as guards."

"If trouble arose and you two panicked as you did during the rhino hunt, Leigh could be injured. No, both of you are coming with me and Reid. No more arguing. We'll see you back in camp this evening. Let's go, everybody. I hear a leopard growling my name," Chad jested.

With Johi in the lead and the bearers behind the foursome, off they went to hunt for the day.

Jace was surprised that Chad allowed him to be alone with Leigh. Yet the woman was in no shape to be wooed or seduced, and Chad wanted that fearless trophy. Slinging his weapon over his shoulder, he lifted his love and carried her into the shade of an acacia.

"Leigh, can you hear me?" he asked. His keen eyes studied her. She was ashen and trembly but her cheeks were red.

"Yes," she replied, her dry tongue feeling thick.

Their gazes locked, ocean blue with jungle green. "When you feel strong enough to walk, I want to get you into the jungle so I can check you over for injuries. If you don't feel up to it soon, I'll carry you. Do you know if you have any odd bites? Or any festering cuts?"

"Only a few mosquito bites. Nothing strange."

"I need to get privacy to remove these clothes and check you over thoroughly. If a tsetse fly or malarial mosquito got to you, I need to know, now. You have been taking your quinine tablets?"

"Yes, and I haven't played in any bad water. I'll be fine. Is this a trick to get me alone and naked?" she teased, feeling drowsy.

"I wish it were, but it isn't. I haven't seen any symptoms like yours around here. Is there an illness you might have inherited?"

"None that I know of, Jace," she replied after drinking from the canteen he lifted to her mouth, his canteen.

When Leigh felt steady again, Jace shouldered both their weapons and canteens. He placed one arm around her waist and guided her into the jungle.

He found a safe spot and halted them. Leigh took her canteen and drank again, her thirst seeming unquenchable.

"There's no polite way to say this woman, but strip."

Leigh's head whirled and her knees buckled. "I can't."

Jace laid her on the verdant ground, working anxiously to undress her. He examined her from head to foot, and found nothing unusual. When she pulled him to her and entreated him to make love to her, he protested. "That isn't fair, Leigh. You're ill. I'll let you rest here, then carry you back to camp. If you aren't better by tomorrow, I'm getting you to a doctor."

"I'm completing this safari," she argued. "Even if I have to remain in camp every day, I'm not canceling it."

Jace was scared. He didn't want to lose her permanently. "This isn't a trick, Leigh. Forget the bet. My only concern is you."

Dazed, she argued, "Oh, no, you don't, Mr. Elliott. The safari and wager are on. I owe you four points, so you'd better collect them before we lose count and time. I'd better pay up as we go."

Leigh was so insistent and seductive that Jace lost his head and made passionate love to her. The tropical world where colorful birds sang, playful monkeys chattered, and exotic flowers bloomed was wildly enticing. It was as if they were secluded from everyone and everything in the lush green haven. Primitive instincts took control.

As they lay nestled together, she murmured, "I'm fine now. I was merely faint from hunger for you."

"That's a condition I wouldn't mind you keeping, woman." Despite his jesting words, Jace was convinced something was wrong with Leigh. He needed to get her back to camp so he could search it for clues

311

while the others were gone. If he didn't find anything suspicious, he would need to decide what to do about her illness. He couldn't be selfish and keep her with him if her life or health was in jeopardy. He also wanted and needed more time with Chad, to open up the man about those crimes, but he had to think of Leigh first.

As Leigh slept on her cot, Jace searched Chad and Reid's tents to find nothing enlightening. He was disappointed because he wanted to discover a reason for her condition. He walked to the eating tables outside, lifted the canteen lying there, and drank from it. Within moments, his head was spinning like a leaf in a brisk wind. He sat down and shook his head to clear it. When the spell passed, he noticed the canteen on the table was Leigh's, as each person had one with initials scratched on it. He recalled they had shared his canteen during the return trip, but she had drank from hers before her last dizzy spell and nap.

Jace sniffed the contents to detect no unusual odor. He went to his tent and poured the remaining liquid into a cup. He rinsed her canteen and hung it on the post where all canteens stayed when not in use. Johi filled them each morning from water boiled by a servant, filled Leigh's with the same water everyone else drank. What had been slipped into hers? By whom and why?

Jace searched the two men's tents again. He hadn't missed anything. He was vexed with himself for doing so, but he entered Leigh's tent to search it while she slept nearby. He knocked over her spare boots, and a small bottle rolled to the ground. He bent and fetched it. White powder was inside. Jace used his handkerchief to take a sample. He returned the bottle to its

312

hiding place. He wondered if she did have an illness she had kept from him and this was medicine. He would try to find out from Chad — without letting his old foe know just what he had discovered.

The others entered camp while Leigh was bathing in the river, and Jace kept guard at a respectable and concealed distance.

Chad approached Jace as he sat on the ground cleaning his pistol. "How is she?"

"Like new. Do you know of any family illness she may have inherited?" Jace inquired, looking at his old friend.

Chad shook his dark head. "Did you ask her?"

"Yep, and she answered the same. Leigh says she doesn't have any suspicious bites or scratches. She's taking her quinine; I counted her supply to make certain. She slept most of the day. When she got up, she was fine. Maybe it's just the heat and climate. We'll watch her closely. If she continues like this, we'll have to head back."

"I understand. The important thing is Leigh, not the money."

"I'm glad to hear you say that, old friend. Since neither of us has made any progress, our bet doesn't really matter, does it?"

"You'll still earn the twenty-five-thousand pound salary."

"What about her bet? You covering it, too?"

"Naturally I'll pay the thousand pounds, but it isn't her fault she got sick. No matter, you won it fairly, if she can't finish our trek."

"I can see this situation doesn't upset you. I suppose you wouldn't mind getting her away from my temptation so you can woo her."

"What does that mean?" Chad asked.

Jace smiled. "If she stays here, I'll be after her as soon as she's well. Leigh Webster is one exciting and beautiful woman."

"Too bad you can't follow her back to London," Chad taunted, "if we have to leave early."

Jace stood and stretched. "Ah, yes, those charges against me. You could assist me there, old friend."

Chad looked intrigued. "How could that be?"

"By helping me discover who framed me and Father, how it was carried off, and why it was done. Got any ideas?"

Chad looked at the brown-haired man. "Are you claiming innocence, or just trying to clear yourself?" he challenged.

"You knew Father well enough to know he wasn't involved."

"True," Chad admitted. "But then who do you think did it, and why?"

"You and Webster," Jace responded in a calm tone.

Chad frowned at him. "When are you going to stop thinking like that? I would never kill Brandon and Stokely to get at you. I liked your father; he was good to me over the years. He was the kindest and gentlest man I knew. After that South African affair, there were bad feelings between you and me, but I'm not that wicked. My quarrel was with *you*."

"You hurt Joanna to get back at me," Jace reminded.

"That had nothing to do with our trouble. It just happened."

"It wouldn't have if I'd been home."

"But you weren't. Besides, it would have happened between us anyway. Joanna wanted me as much as I wanted her. When you find her, ask her, and you'll see I'm not lying." Chad sighed heavily. "I only let you

314

believe it was for spite because our affair upset you so much. You're the one who came to our home and attacked me. I had to defend myself. Look at the mess we created. I'm tired of this battle, Jace. Revenge doesn't matter to me anymore."

Chad coaxed Leigh into taking a private walk. When they were out of sight, he stopped and asked, "Are you sure you're all right?"

A glowing smile filled her blue eyes. "I'm perfectly fine, Chad. I'm sure it was nothing. It probably won't happen again."

"If it does," he insisted, "I think we should return home."

Leigh didn't want to leave this country where her love was exiled. "And let Jace Elliott win my bet? No way. If I have to remain in camp every day, the rest of you will have fun. Today was the worst, so I think it's over. It was probably one of those brief attacks people get when they visit unfamiliar areas."

Chad caressed her cheek and smiled. "You do look better. You had me scared and worried. I don't want anything happening to you. My ward has become very special to me."

Leigh feared that someone was trying to harm her. She wanted to make certain it wasn't her guardian. Then she would check out Louisa. To test him, she ventured, "If I decide to sell Webster International, would you like to buy it? I would make it easy and painless for you to obtain the firm."

Chad was stunned. "Sell the company? You can't, not even to me. You'll be good at running it, and I'm eager to work with you. We'll make a good team, Leigh. That firm's been in the Webster family for a hundred years. Don't consider a sale too hastily. if you don't want to run it, I'll do it."

She looked at him. "You don't want to purchase the firm?"

"Of course I do, if you are determined to sell. I love that company and helped enlarge it. But I hope you aren't serious and you won't sell it. We can do great things with it, together. I'd like us to get closer, Leigh. I'm very fond of you."

She was relieved that he appeared honest. He seemed to want both the firm and her but did not appear to crave the business in a threatening manner. She smiled. "And I'm very fond of you, Chad."

The call came that dinner was ready. Leigh and Chad returned to camp, smiling and chatting.

"You'd think one man was enough for that greedy girl," Louisa muttered to Jace. "I wonder what she's planning to do about her fiancé in Texas. Poor Tyler Clark is pining away while she's chasing Chad."

Jace glanced at the annoyed redhead. "Who is Tyler Clark? I didn't know she was betrothed. Chad didn't mention it to me."

"He's the foreman on the ranch her aunt owns in America. Leigh told me and Cynthia all about him, several times. She said she hasn't decided if she wants him to move to London or if she'll return to Texas. From the way she's carrying on with Chad, Tyler might have lost her."

Jace eyed Leigh and mused on what he'd learned today . . .

Chapter Fourteen

The following day, Chad suggested they remain in camp to rest and relax, and to make certain Leigh was all right before their trek continued. Everyone agreed, because they were satisfied with their successful hunt for leopard yesterday. As with the rhino head, the leopard's was sent downriver to Mombasa, along with its exquisite hide.

Seeing such a beautiful creature slain to mount its head on a wall and to use its skin for a cape took away part of Leigh's enjoyment of the safari. She was glad the British government had placed controls on how many leopards could be slain and was trying to halt poachers, as it would be a crime to see them vanish from existence one day.

Three-fourths of the bearers packed up extra goods and supplies, and everything the party could do without for a while. Chad helped Leigh gather her unneeded items and placed them before her tent. The sleek, dark-skinned carriers headed for the next campsite, to clear the area and prepare it for use, and to avoid the slower pace of the safari group. The hunting party was to leave early the next morning.

While Leigh and the others enjoyed a cooling swim, Jace searched his lover's tent once more to find the bottle of powder gone. While one of his men stood guard, Jace searched the other tents, finding nothing.

When Johi returned to camp, he told Jace, "The animal walked strange. He was weak, thirsty. He slept in danger. It is bad sign."

Jace was puzzled and unnerved. "I looked in her tent, Johi; it's gone. She doesn't have to lose her bet on purpose to have me. But if she got sick and had to be taken home, or pretended she was, what could I do? I have to question her. I don't like the fact she's to marry someone and hasn't told me. And I don't like how friendly she is with Chad." His green eyes were full of conflicting emotions.

"Jace ana wivu sana," Johi hinted.

Jace scowled. "No, Jace is not very jealous."

"We hunt *nyati, simba, tembo,* soon. Must clear head."

"I'll be ready to stalk buffalo, lion, and elephant, my friend. First, Leigh has some explaining to do. It could be someone hid that bottle there for me to find, so I'd blame her and doubt her. Or figured that was the last place I would search. That sneaky redhead is mighty jealous of Chad and Leigh. Watch her closely. As for my old friend, I know how deceitful he can be."

By nightfall, Leigh hadn't mentioned the missing bottle to Jace, so it wasn't medicine she needed. Nor had she mentioned the sweetheart awaiting her return in America. It was clear she did not suspect Chad of mischief, because she was too friendly with her guardian. Jace was disturbed. He couldn't forget the incidents in London, at the fort, and with her unloaded weapon. Yet they could have been all accidents.

Jace didn't want to panic Leigh, but he was worried about so many "accidents" atop this one with her canteen, which was clearly intentional. He had ordered Johi to make sure he handed Leigh her canteen as soon as it was filled, allowing no time for tampering. If Leigh was to blame, why? If not, who was framing her, and why? And was the motive potentially lethal? All he could do was wait and watch.

Chad noticed how tense Jace was, and knew why. While helping Leigh pack, he had recovered the tiny bottle from Leigh's boot to realize part of the powder was missing. He had hidden it there each day because it should be the last place Jace looked if his suspicions were aroused. To make certain Jace could not confront Leigh and the others with the bottle, he had discarded it in an abandoned termite mound during a private walk this morning while Jace, Johi, and the others were busy. If Jace made a fuss, he had no evidence. Besides, the drugging powder had affected Leigh so strongly, especially yesterday. Too, he could expose himself by pressing her to go home, as Jace had hinted accurately at his guilt and motive. All he needed to do was be patient, persistent, and charming. If Jace or Leigh became a problem, he could use the altered contract to—

Louisa nudged Chad and asked a second time, "Don't you think Leigh's better today? I was worried about her."

"Really?" Chad chuckled and taunted.

"Of course I was. If anything happens to your ward so soon after William's death, it might look strange to the authorities. It's to your advantage and safety, lover, to see that she stays alive and well."

Chad looked at her. "I hadn't thought of that, Louisa," he remarked, "but I've always tried to take good care of her. You didn't have anything to do with this odd illness, did you?"

Louisa glared at him. "Don't be absurd. As your . . . lover, I could be considered an accomplice if she died suspiciously. We had better make certain little Leigh returns to London in excellent health. I think Jace is responsible for her troubles."

"Why would you think that?"

"I'm not blind or stupid, Chad. You two hate each other. And Jace does have that silly wager with Leigh, and that large bet with you."

"I told you it was to trick Jace into working for me. But if you get jealous and tattle to Leigh about it, love you or not, I'll have to squash you like one of these pesty insects."

As if teasing, Chad laughed as he mashed the bug into bloody pieces, but Louisa knew he was serious, and dangerous. "I only meant that I doubt Jace views it as a joke. A lot of money and his pride are involved. Whether or not you realize it, lover, Jace is wooing Leigh. I tried to ensnare him as you requested, but he spurned my charms. He said it was to prevent trouble with you and Leigh. Sorry, but I can't distract him from his goal. That bruises me something awful."

"Don't worry about it. You did your best. Thanks, Louisa."

"Our best isn't enough, Chad. From the way I see it, she owes him a thousand pounds for being unable to take the hardships of this safari. Would Jace pull this deceit to win a meager bet with her? Or use it to score points with her by playing her concerned friend and fearless protector? Would he try to spite you by harming her?"

"Seduce her, if he could; but harm her, never."

"Aren't you forgetting he's a dangerous criminal?"

"*Alleged* criminal," Chad corrected.

"You can't argue he's a desperate and resentful

man."

"But a fair and honest one. Don't worry. She's fine now. I'm sure Jace wouldn't endanger Leigh's health and life for either or both bets. Just don't get edgy when it looks as if I'm wooing her. It'll only be a pretense to safeguard my bet with him."

"I asked Cynthia to sleep in Leigh's tent tonight and to keep an eye on your ward. She'll call us if Leigh has any more problems. I'm sure Reid won't miss her tonight. They aren't getting along well."

"That's a shame. We make a good foursome."

Louisa didn't know why Chad was defending Jace, or which man was responsible for Leigh's spells. Maybe Chad was getting anxious about his wager with Jace and was using a way to get Leigh out of the jungle man's reach. Or maybe, Jace was to blame for making Leigh lose their private wager, or to win Chad's. True or not, it gave her the opportunity to point a guilty finger at Jace Elliott for what would happen next. During the episodes, she had been careful with her words and expressions to make herself appear innocent when Leigh had her next and last accident. Chad didn't know it, but Jace stood to gain a lot more than a thousand pounds from Leigh Webster. Louisa knew she had to get rid of the blonde before they left Africa, because it was easier here. "Since Leigh's better, we won't have to return home early. That's good."

"Are you finally enjoying yourself?"

She smiled and licked her lips. "Yes. It took a little adjusting, but it's wonderful. Of course, today wasn't the best, not with so many of our nice things taken ahead. When do I get me a trophy?"

As the redhead skillfully caressed and aroused Chad, he replied, "Soon, my sweet. We're aiming for cape buffalo at our next camp. We leave in the morning, so we should get to sleep."

As she trailed her fingers over Chad's shirt, she felt the scars underneath and wondered if Jace was involved in that painful mystery. With their cots gone and sharing a bedroll, Louisa murmured, "We should take advantage of this last night of privacy for a while."

Chad seized her and agreed, pretending she was Leigh . . .

Restless, Chad left Louisa's embrace without disturbing her. He found Reid outside, a cup in one hand and a bottle in the other. The campfire was aglow as usual to chase away darkness and predators. Chad approached his friend and asked, "Couldn't sleep, either?"

"Not tonight. I'm worried about you, Chad. You're too charmed by your ward to think clearly. If I were you, I'd be worried, too."

"About what?" the dark-haired man inquired in intrigue.

"About your wild plan and Jace Elliott."

"Everything's going great, Reid. What has you troubled?"

"I don't agree that you're winning. Leigh offered to sell the business to you, not marry you. It sounds to me as if she doesn't plan to remain in London. I find it strange and unsettling that she changed her mind after meeting Jace. If I didn't know you were behind those drugging incidents, I would think Jace was up to mischief."

"You worry too much, Reid. The bottle's gone, and I've been keeping our contract in my pocket lately so Jace won't find it and see what I added above his signature. He's been doing fine, no problems."

"That's my point, Chad. Considering your entwined

past, Jace's suspicions about you and William, and what you two wagered—doesn't it strike you odd that he's not making any trouble or any overtures to Leigh? They were alone most of the day, and she was bathing when we returned. While strolling around, I made a curious discovery. Her tent, just hers, has a secret entrance at the back corner. For all we know, Jace has been sneaking in and out during the entire trip. I've been observing their behavior. I think he's already won the bet, and he's just waiting for the best moment to cram it down your throat."

In the dense jungle, their second temporarily permanent camp was ready upon their arrival. They had traveled through bushed grassland and thicket, journeying northwestward along the Tanzania border for several days before halting there. They had crossed the Amboseli Plains near the Chyulu Range. Eight to ten days' walk to their north lay the foothills of the Great Rift, and Nairobi.

Jace hadn't been given a chance to talk privately with Leigh. They had slept on bedrolls beneath individual tents of mosquito netting, instead of using the time and energy to set up and break a large camp each day. During their walks, Chad had kept Leigh close to him, laughing and joking and talking with her. It seemed to Jace that Chad was making a stronger move on his love. Jace was getting edgy with the new situation and with the denial of her company. Yet Leigh hadn't had any more problems. For that, he was glad.

Two hours after reaching camp and settling in, Jace and Johi left to scout the area for game: buffalo haunts.

* * *

Louisa and Cynthia returned to camp with wet heads. The area was safe, so the group had been told they could have more freedom in this location. Reid and Chad were playing chess, drinking, and listening to music on the gramophone. Leigh had been resting and reading, but came outside to join the others for hot tea at four. The head servant, Mkwawa, served it with tinned sweetcakes, and left.

"That was wonderful, Leigh," Louisa said. "You should have gone with us. There's a marvelous rock-enclosed pool not far away. Jace marked the trail with rags tied to bushes. It's so cool and clear."

Leigh watched the woman put away her rifle and rub her curry-colored hair with a drying cloth. Having been drinking for two hours, Reid and Chad separately excused themselves into the jungle for a time. Cynthia took a chair at the table and began to comb her hair. This site was hot and steamy. To Leigh, a bath sounded nice, especially if Jace sneaked a visit later. "I'll go after I finish my tea."

When Chad finally returned, he asked his ward, "Do you think you should take a bearer to guard you? They're camped in the next clearing. Mkwawa can assign one."

Leigh didn't care to have a stranger nearby during such a private moment, and the other women had encountered no trouble alone. She smiled at him. "I always keep my derringer in my bag. I'll fire a shot if danger strikes. Be back later."

"Just follow the marked trail, to the right when it forks. It's simple to find," Louisa told her. "Do you need to borrow anything?"

"Thanks, but I have everything I need." Leigh entered her tent.

Reid and Chad went to a small crate to select another bottle of wine. "It's odd she didn't go with

324

Cynthia and Louisa," Reid hinted. "You think she's secretly meeting Jace? He is out of camp, and he's been watching her mighty intently. I think something's going on, and it'll cost you everything if it isn't stopped."

Chad looked at Reid. "No, it won't. I've taken precautions."

"Flirting with her won't change matters if it's too late."

"Wooing isn't what I have in mind, old friend. Wait and see."

When the men rejoined the women at the table, Chad grinned at Louisa and suggested, "Why don't we sneak inside while she's gone?" Chad glanced at Reid and Cynthia and remarked, "You should relax, too. Maybe a little . . . recreation will do wonders for both of you."

Reid nodded and Cynthia shrugged, and both agreed to comply.

Leigh gathered clothes from her packs and lifted her grooming bag with her bathing supplies. Through the net-covered entrance to her tent, Leigh saw the two couples go inside. She decided to give them plenty of time for privacy. She surmised that Chad couldn't be too eager for her and her holdings or he wouldn't continue carrying on with Louisa. Unless, of course, the virile lord needed appeasement badly and frequently; she had heard that some men did.

She left camp and walked the verdant trail, its foliage heavy on both sides and above her. She hummed music from the gramophone and halted here and there to look at unusual flowers and plants. She was distracted by worries. She wanted to be totally honest with her love, but felt that was impossible at this time. She was certain Jace didn't know about the codicil and, even if he did, he wouldn't be a threat to her. She trusted Jace Elliott, but he did have secrets. She didn't know how facing prison or execution affected a person or what it compelled one to do for exoneration and survival; yet, she felt safe with him.

Leigh prayed that her grandfather was blameless for the Elliotts' troubles. She hoped that William had made out the codicil to lessen Jace's resentment and suspicions. But to enlighten her love at this early date would have the opposite effect. She couldn't guess how he would react to such a discovery. She didn't want him to feel duped, which he might. She didn't want an angered man to end the safari before she could expose her good intentions. Jace didn't seem impulsive or rash or vindictive, but he had suffered a lot and was in peril.

Leigh needed more time and closeness with Jace before that stunning revelation. She did not want to damage their budding relationship by inspiring him to doubt her reason for coming to Africa and for yielding to him. William had a reason for including Brandon's son in his will, and perhaps Jace would unknowingly reveal it. Her grandfather obviously knew Jace was trustworthy, as William would not tempt a dangerous man to harm her for revenge and greed. If Jace came to love her and staked a marital claim on her, he would understand and forgive her protective silence. Jace already mistrusted Chad and her grandfather, and had mistrusted her in the beginning, so enlightening him soon was too much of a risk. Jace needed time to get to know her better and want her even more, and to get reacquainted with his old friend. By the time the safari was over, her love would know she could be trusted, and hopefully she would find her guardian could be, too. It would be wonderful if the two men could bury their pasts and become friends again.

In time she would explain everything to Jace. For now, silent observation seemed best. Her curious ill-

326

ness had passed and she was feeling marvel —

The bushes wiggled to her left. Leigh glanced that way and saw ferns and other greenery trembling. No growl reached her ears, but something of size was disturbing the location. Perhaps someone was playing a trick on her. Thinking of Jace and time alone together, she grinned. "Who's there?" she asked, trying not to laugh aloud.

There was no response. Bushes and plants moved again. Leigh's smile faded as she scanned the area. Goosebumps danced over her body. Instinct warned of danger. She fumbled for her derringer. It wasn't in the bag, and her anxiety mounted. She always kept the weapon there, so she hadn't brought a rifle. How foolish she had been, and where was her gun? Leigh tossed the bathing bag aside and grabbed a broken tree limb for protection. It was short and weak, but anything was better than being unarmed. "This isn't funny. Who's there?" Still no response: no voice, no growl, no lunge at her. Leigh began to back away with caution, gluing her eyes to the suspicious location. Lush green leaves moved again, closer to her, but she couldn't see anyone or anything. Maybe, she thought, it was one of the bearers hunting or strolling. But no, she reasoned, they would answer.

"Who's there?" she demanded. Surely an animal would have fled or attacked by now. She was vexed and frightened. She dared not plunge into the ocean of green to remove her fears. She stood tense and still. The movement ceased. Leigh assumed it was a small animal and she had frightened it; yet she remained apprehensive. An eerie silence encased her; even the wildlife was strangely quiet and motionless. She realized she couldn't hear the gramophone. She must have walked too far. She should return to camp for a weapon and perhaps a guard. As she turned in the narrow path, there was brisk movement in that direction, cutting off her retreat. Watching that area closely, she began to back away again. Something was out there and it was a threat to her. Suddenly her feet gave way and she slipped. To her horror, she realized why: quicksand.

Leigh screamed, "Help! Chad! Reid! Help! Jace! Mkwawa! Help! I'm in quicksand. Hurry!"

There was no response. The engulfing foe sucked greedily at her entrapped body. Jace's words came to mind: "Don't struggle; it pulls you deeper. Stay limp and get control. You can float on your back in quicksand, but working slow is vital."

Once she forced herself to calm down, she didn't sink as fast. There was no need to waste energy screaming; she doubted she could be heard. She was too far from camp and the music was probably still playing. How could she have made such an error? Where was the fork? She scolded herself for not realizing how far she had walked, as the pool couldn't be this distant from camp, and she hadn't noticed a rag marker in quite a while. It had been rash not to bring a rifle or a guard. Jace had warned them about such precautions, and about quicksand being nearby. He had told them to never leave camp alone, and her Sir Lancelot was off in the jungle somewhere.

Hindsight was too late. Leigh saw a vine dangling in the hungry mud. She stretched her hand and tried to reach it. She prayed. She willed it to move closer. Her fingertips touched bark. The vine moved, the other way. Tears rolled down Leigh's cheeks. She was going to die, she feared, and Jace would blame himself for her carelessness.

She struggled again for the live rope, quicksand to her shoulders by now. Miraculously her fingers captured it. With all her strength, she pulled and worked until she was on the bank. Leigh rolled to her back, exhausted, still holding the vine in a tight grasp. Her breathing was labored. Her heart pounded. She was covered in clingy muck, but alive. She cried in relief, and from tension.

Jace appeared and snatched her into his arms. He didn't have to asked what happened. "That was stupid, Leigh!" he scolded, his temper getting the best of him from anxious relief. "I told you not to leave camp alone. What are you doing way out here?"

Leigh's frightened gaze locked with Jace's panicked one. She explained what had taken place, and noticed Jace's odd stare. Giddy from her shock and his soothing presence, she quipped, "How did you find me? Sir Lancelot to the timely rescue again."

"This isn't amusing, woman. When Johi and I returned to camp, Reid and Cynthia told me you were at the spring alone. I followed your tracks. You didn't even bring a rifle with you. How many tim—"

"I thought I had my derringer," she interrupted. "I told them I would fire a shot if trouble struck."

"Why didn't you?"

"It's gone."

"No, it isn't. I found your bag spilled back there. It's right here," he said, pulling out and holding up the little weapon.

"I didn't see it. I suppose I was too scared. I got lost."

"On a marked trail?" Jace scoffed. "You're more skilled than that."

Leigh had calmed enough to be miffed. "There was no fork."

Jace lifted her and the bag and headed down the trail. He stopped at one point and said, "This fork, Leigh."

The wide-eyed blonde gaped at the other trail to the

right, several rags tied on both sides of the path. Jace carried her down it to a beautiful spot where an underground stream bubbled up into a deep crevice to form a pool. He lowered her legs to the ground.

"I didn't see the fork. I guess I was looking up at the monkeys playing in the trees, then the bushes moved." Faintly she heard music coming from the camp, and realized it wasn't far away.

"That's when you should have screamed for help. Why did you keep going without a weapon and getting farther from camp?"

"I had a limb, and I didn't think," she admitted. "I'll bathe and change, then we'll talk. All right?"

"Fine," he concurred, knowing what *he* wanted to discuss.

"Want to join me?" she enticed, smiling to soothe him.

"The others could come looking for us. I'm sure Chad won't like the idea of us being alone in such circumstances. Get cleaned up. I have something to discuss with you," he remarked, sounding mysterious.

"Were Chad and Louisa in camp?" she inquired.

"Yes. In his tent having fun," he added. "Cynthia and Reid were quarreling and drinking. Why did you ask about Chad and Louisa?"

She was aware of his odd gaze and tone. "You didn't mention them earlier. I just wanted to make certain we're alone."

"We are. Johi is up ahead, guarding our privacy."

Despite that remark, Leigh didn't ask why it wasn't safe to make love. After her near-death experience and days of denial, she yearned to be with Jace again. But clearly he did not feel the same, and she wondered why. She stripped and bathed, then dried and dressed. Jace kept his back to her, an action she found curious. She was also surprised that the keen-witted man hadn't teased that she owed him an extra wager day for getting into danger, giving him five points. He was angry with her, she reasoned, but over an accident. There was no one to blame but herself. The gun was where it should be, and so was the marked trail. Jace had told her the others were in camp, so it must have been an animal in the bush. Everyone was accounted for, except Jace, who had been off in the jungle with Johi.

When she joined him, Jace asked, "Who is Tyler Clark?"

Leigh looked stunned. "Who told you about him?"

As she wrapped a drying cloth around her head turban style, he replied, "Louisa."

"I might have known," Leigh remarked with annoyance.

"Are you engaged to him?"

Her shock increased. "Heavens, no! Is that what she told you?"

"Yes. Why?" he probed, not taking his green eyes from her.

"I led her to believe we were sweethearts to stop her from worrying about me and Chad," Leigh answered. "I detest Tyler."

"Does she have reason to worry?"

Leigh didn't know if he was serious or not, but he certainly appeared to be. Vexed by his attitude, she scoffed, "Don't be ridiculous! How could I want Chadwick Hamilton when I have Jace Elliott?"

"You two have been very cozy lately," he accused.

"Jealous?" she teased, unaware of his real turmoil.

"Should I be?" he questioned, his tone demanding and cool.

To settle him down, she explained, "He's my guardian, stepuncle, business associate, and friend."

"I don't like him being any of those things to you."

"None of them can be changed, Jace."

"Why did you fake those spells on the trail?"

Leigh squinted her eyes and gaped at him. "What?"

"I found that tainted water in your canteen and that drugging powder in your tent," Jace divulged. "What happened to it?"

Leigh came to full alert. Something was afoot. "I don't know what you're talking about. Are we back to riddles, Sir Lancelot?"

Jace explained, and Leigh's eyes grew wide and large. "You've been searching my tent? Spying on me?"

"If you didn't pull those acts to help me win our wager, then who did? You do seem to be having a mighty lot of 'accidents.' "

"Where is this notorious powder?"

"As I said, it's gone. It was in your spare boots."

"I see, the evidence is now missing?"

"You have my word it was there," Jace vowed, "and your canteen was tampered with three times. Your gun, too, on the rhino hunt. Johi told me it wasn't loaded when he checked all the guns that night. Did you forget to reload after practice or did you remove the cartridges?"

Leigh didn't like this conversation. "Certainly not. That would be stupid and dangerous. Why didn't you tell me about it?"

"I didn't want to scold you, in case it was a one-time oversight. When you were having those curious spells, I didn't want to scare you until I had proof. I should have kept that bottle when I found it, but I thought it might be medicine, until Johi checked it out by drugging an animal that last day in camp. I ordered him to check your gun and canteen every morning. Nothing's happened to them since that last day you were ill. What did you and Chad discuss that night on your walk? Either it scared him, pleased him, or warned

332

him to watch out."

She caught his meaning. "Are you implying he's a threat to me, and I said something clever to halt his plan?"

"I think somebody on this safari is after you, besides me."

"I see," she murmured again. "I suppose you think this incident today was another false accident. I assure you it wasn't." She pointed out the facts to him. "So, you see, it was my fault. As for the powder and spells, that could be Louisa's mischief. She is jealous."

Jace was aware that she didn't mention the other episodes. "If Louisa was to blame, she got rid of the evidence to avoid being caught."

Leigh deliberated his words. Her father had taught her to use logic on problems, which she did now. It was illogical for Chad to harm her. It was illogical for a villainess to conceal her bane — her weapon and means to her downfall — where the victim could find it. By the same token, why would Jace lie? It had to be a mistake. It must have to do with him being suspicious of an old enemy, and perhaps wary of her and their wager. "Don't you think this alleged plot is a little melodramatic, Jace? Chad would kill Louisa if she harmed me."

"You're Webster's heir. What about Chad harming you?"

"I'm more than positive he wouldn't," she stated.

Her confidence riled Jace. He could not stop himself from taunting, "Because he loves you and wants to marry you."

Leigh was worried about this change in the man she loved. She did not like him keeping secrets and acting sneaky. "You could be right, but that doesn't matter to me. I'll tell you something private that might put your mind at rest. Lord Chadwick Hamilton doesn't inherit

333

if I die. If death befalls me before I marry and produce an heir, William Webster's estate is divided between two of his best friends." Leigh wanted to stop this nonsense, so she didn't mention Fiona as an heir. "For Chad to get his hands on any Webster money and property, he has to marry me. I ask you, would a man burn the only bridge across an impassable canyon to hid dreamland? That is, *if* I am the object of his greatest desire, as you believe and claim," she hinted. She observed the effect of her disclosure, and noted disbelief.

Leigh continued. "I've read Grandfather's will many times, and discussed it with a London lawyer. So has Chad and his mother. There are no loopholes. None, Jace. By the same token, why would Chad's lover, who knows all his secrets, harm me and cause Chad to lose everything? He would hate her and discard her, and she's smart enough to know that. So, that leaves me to suspect any deception. I ask you, why would Laura Leigh Webster beguile Jace Elliott?"

The instant those words left Leigh's mouth, she knew she could not now tell Jace he was one of those two heirs. That would supply the motive her love was seeking! She berated herself for not telling him the truth sooner. She must hold silent with him staring at her with a mistrustful gleam in those narrowed green eyes. As much as she hated thinking it, Jace was the only one unaccounted for earlier, and he had so much to gain by her death. He was always around when she had accidents. No, she argued with herself, he could never harm her. It was distress playing tricks on her dazed mind and battle-weary body.

Jace turned and took a few steps from the distracting beauty. This news was most unexpected and befuddling. It explained why Leigh didn't fear a threat from Chad. And it revealed why Chad was desperate to win

334

William's heir. Chad couldn't be trying to harm her. Jace finally turned and asked, "Do you think Louisa is capable of plotting to kill you?"

Leigh pondered his serious question. Louisa Jennings was a spoiled, vain, spiteful, and impulsive—yes, she admitted—bitch. But committing cold-blooded murder to chance getting Chad . . . The redhead knew of Chad's womanizing, knew she might never capture the handsome earl, knew another woman—besides Leigh—could steal him. Louisa could not go around murdering every female who caught Chad's roving eye. She disliked and distrusted Louisa, but thinking the woman able to kill seemed unconscionable. "No. Louisa is capable of pulling mischievous tricks to scare me off or to prove she's superior; but murder me, I think not. We both know ruses can get out of hand, as ours did in Mombasa. If she was responsible for any of those stunts, or all of them, obviously she's been frightened into stopping."

Jace was alarmed to discover that Leigh felt she was in no danger when his deepest instinct told him she was. "Will you at least keep your eyes and ears open, and be extra careful?" he entreated. He walked to her and gazed into her troubled eyes.

When Jace's hand lifted to caress her cheek, Leigh pushed it aside. "Strange things have happened to me since I left America, Jace. I find it odd that you're always around when they do. You were the only one not in camp today. You marked the trail I missed. You found my missing gun. Your friend prepares my canteen and weapon. We have a bet you want to win. The fort is in your territory. You were in London when I was attacked. You constantly accuse a man who can't possibly want to harm me. You try to create doubts and fears in me so I'll trust only you, yet you have no evidence. If we didn't pull those tricks, there's nobody

335

left but you."

Astonished, Jace stared at her. "You doubt me?"

Leigh needed to clear the wits of her confused lover. "No more than you doubted me when you searched my tent and asked me about those incidents. I'm hurt and disappointed. Why don't we keep a little distance between us for a while? You're already five points ahead. If I'm not careful, you'll win our wager. I plan to do everything I can to make certain you don't. Besides, you've already received the prize I wagered, and I've covered any extra nights you've won. You're five points ahead, Jace, so your plantation isn't in jeopardy. We both know rule three is a joke, so if you believed for one minute that I took staying with you for a year seriously and that I would fake an illness to entrap or elude you, you don't know me at all."

Jace halted Leigh's departure. He had to explain, make her believe the truth. "Listen to me, woman. I guess I handled this talk all wrong. I'm too upset to think straight. I could have lost you to that quicksand. That could have been poison instead of a dazing drug in your canteen. That rhino could have charged you when your gun was empty. Those Arabs in Mombasa could have you far away in a harem by now. Those false sailors could have raped you and killed you in London. I didn't do any of those things, Leigh. You must believe me. I'm sorry if I made it sound like I doubted you. We still have a lot to learn about each other. Everyone does impulsive things once in a while. I had to make certain you didn't want me to win badly enough to take chances and be sneaky."

"That's fair enough, Jace, as long as I can also make certain you won't be sneaky and desperate. I don't believe you want to harm me or trick me. I only wanted to point out facts you missed. As you see, we both have valid reasons to doubt each other and to be cautious in our relationship. I do think you're right about one important thing: we don't know each other very well. I think it's best if we get better acquainted before anything happens between us again."

Jace was vexed with himself. He knew Leigh was honest, fair, and innocent. He had let his fears and worries cloud his thinking. Without panicking her, he had to discover the truth and protect her. He knew what must be done soon. "I've messed up things between us, haven't I?" he asked.

She couldn't lie. "No, but it does make us stop and think. This has taught us a lesson, Jace—not to judge too quickly and rashly. If you make real peace with Chad, it might help you get over this bitterness and mistrust of everyone. As long as you cling to the past, you'll never be free of its demands. Let's get back to camp before the others start thinking wild thoughts," she hinted.

In camp, Jace revealed Leigh's "accident" with the quicksand and watched the others for clues. "From now on, nobody leaves camp without a guard and a weapon. Tomorrow, we're going after buffalo, so I suggest you all get a good night's sleep after we eat."

Chad grasped Leigh's hand and asked, "Are you hurt?"

"Just my pride. It won't happen again. I'm being too careless and having too many accidents lately. I'll be extra alert in the future," she remarked, knowing that would please Jace.

"It wasn't my fault, Chad," Louisa said. "I told her to take the path to the right. Didn't I, Cynthia, Reid?"

The sullen couple who had not enjoyed their afternoon did not get a chance to back Louisa's claims.

Leigh smiled at the almost frantic redhead and told her, "It was my fault, Louisa. I was looking the other way and missed the fork. Then I couldn't locate my gun to fire a signal."

Louisa eyed Jace's quicksand-soiled clothes and Leigh's freshly scrubbed look. She wondered if Chad noticed the implication in their appearances and realized how long they had been together in the steamy jungle. "Thank goodness Jace returned and rescued you."

"I didn't," Jace reminded the woman. "Leigh pulled herself out."

"You could have been killed," Louisa wailed in guile. She wondered where Chad had been while she was getting ready to make love. Her lover had excused himself first and hadn't joined her in their tent until sometime later, and in a strange mood. Was it possible . . .

"I'm fine." Leigh wondered why the woman was so concerned about the accident. Was Louisa afraid Chad would blame her as he had done with the attack in London? Had the handsome earl discovered his lover guilty of drugging his ward, as Jace believed, and threatened her again? Perhaps, Leigh mused, she had dismissed Jace's warnings too quickly or too lightly . . .

It was extremely hot and stuffy that night, so everyone slept with their tent flaps tossed aside and only mosquito netting covering the entrances. A large fire blazed in the clearing to discourage predators from strolling into camp. Nocturnal insects and birds were on the move during darkness. Floral odors clung to the heavy air, as did smoke from the flames where brush crackled as it was consumed.

Leigh tossed and turned for hours, plagued by this unexpected breach between her and Jace. Perhaps he did have valid reasons to think and say what he had, but it distressed her. Not only his behavior, but the fact he truly believed someone was a threat to her. It *was* possible, and that reality alarmed her. She hadn't told him about Fiona being in line for the inheritance to halt his suspicions about Chad. She had gone over and over the matter, but still felt that Chad wouldn't try to harm her to get half of an estate that would be years in coming. Nor would Chad want it split with anyone, especially with Jace Elliott. Perhaps, Leigh reasoned, she should tell Jace about her grandfather's strange codicil. Maybe he could understand the inducement behind it.

No, she decided, because Jace was keeping secrets from her. If she disclosed that fact, there was no telling how he would react. In view of his suspicions, he might think worse of her.

What if Jace knows about the will and the motive behind it? she fretted. *Or knows of the codicil and wants to learn the reason for it? If he loves and wants you to stay with him, why not propose or lose the wager to you? Yet he's trying his best to win only a night or two. Why? Are you ready to take that risk? What if you don't know him at all? He told you he was after Grandfather and Chad. Could love or desire change him so completely, so quickly?*

The safari had weeks to go, and civilization was far away. She wished she were somewhere alone with Jace, getting to know him better. That had to wait. Just because he claimed she was in peril, that did not mean she should flee to safety with him as he had coaxed several times.

Leigh left her cot and washed perspiration from her face. She saw Jace standing near the edge of the clearing with firelight flickering on his body. She realized he couldn't sleep, either, and that touched her. She was tempted to join him and talk, but anyone awake could see them and suspect the truth. She couldn't forget what Jace had told her about how much power her guardian had over her estate. No, she refuted — over her and her entire life.

To be fair to Jace, she didn't know Chad very well, either. Did her guardian crave a profitable marriage? He hadn't done more than a little flirting so far, and he was still dallying with Louisa. Would her stepuncle get rid of her and settle for half of everything, rather than get nothing, as half was still worth a fortune? Would Fiona Webster allow her son to control her share until he inherited it? But what if something happened to her *and* to Jace during the safari?

It's just hot and miserable tonight, Leigh scolded herself, *and you're thinking crazy. Both our deaths would look too suspicious to the authorities. Chad isn't stupid or reckless. But what about that deceitful redhead? Does she know about the will? Chad certainly tells her plenty for someone he intends to discard soon! Would she plot one or two deaths so her lover could inherit and then marry her? Stop it, Leigh!*

Leigh watched her lover as he took a walk. He was so tall, handsome, and virile. He knew so much about this land, possessed alluring prowess in all areas. His brown hair was mussed and his khaki shirt was hanging open and revealing a hard chest. His stubble looked dark against his tanned face. She loved him and wanted him deeply. She had to stay near him as long as possible. She had to win his love and trust. Would cruel fate let her? It was always stealing her loved ones, and maybe that was why she feared doing or saying anything to lose him.

Oh, Mother, how I wish you were here to counsel me, she thought with sadness. *I can do such terrible damage if I make the wrong moves. Does he love me as much as I love him? Does he love me at all, or only*

desire me? Is there a dark side to my golden hero? How
can I tell? What should I do?

Jace felt Leigh's gaze on him, as he had hoped and
intended. He knew it was an underhanded thing to do,
but he had to win back her trust, respect, and affection. She had proven she desired him as much as he
desired her, so he had to use all of his skills to tempt
her. He was unsettled by the distance that he had
placed between Leigh and him. There were so many
matters troubling him: his hunger for Leigh, the threat
to her, the charges against him in England, his beloved
father's murder and losses, Chad's motive for this
safari, and his old friend's odd behavior.

Only if Chad stood to gain from harming her would
a deadly threat from him be possible. Leigh had
revealed there wasn't one. As for the lustful redhead,
surely everything that had happened to Leigh was too
complicated for her wits. Jace admitted that some
women were as smart, brave, cunning, and daring as
men. But women too often allowed emotions to rule
their senses, to cloud their judgments. It wasn't logical
for Louisa Jennings to risk losing the object she desired most to spite—or to slay—a rival, as Leigh had
said. Joanna Harris had proven his biased—he admitted—theory about women to him; Leigh had proven to
him there were exceptions.

Chad had wanted, and had taken, Joanna. He had
ruined her. Jace could not let him do the same with
Leigh, even if he lost her through his foolishness this
afternoon. He and Chad had been so close long ago.
Chad's treachery had destroyed their tight bond. At
one time, Jace had wanted to slay him with his bare
hands. Now, he didn't know what to think and feel.
Chad was within reach for revenge, yet he couldn't

341

bring himself to do anything about it. He could have allowed that rhino to end the matter; yet something had stopped him. Perhaps Leigh's importance to him stayed his vengeful hand and lessened his hatred and bitterness. Good memories of the past and the old relationship with Chad had returned to haunt him. If only Chad wasn't right about him looking guilty years ago. If only he himself wasn't afraid to trust the man who claimed he wanted a truce. If only so much wasn't at stake.

It rained for two days, keeping everyone inside. They listened to the gramophone, played games, talked, and waited. The two men drank almost continuously, against Jace's advice. At times Leigh tried to read, but it was nearly impossible with the annoying Cynthia Campbell underfoot. Quarreling with Reid again, the brunette — at Louisa's secret request — had moved into Leigh's tent.

During their hunt the following day, Jace instructed the group about the buffalo. "We'll be able to locate them by egrets flying overhead. They perch on the animals to eat lice and pests. Buffalo usually feed at night and wallow in marshy spots during the day. They favor tall grass; that's why we look for the birds to give away their presence. You'll be amazed by his size. A full grown male weighs two thousand pounds. His horns are as thick as my arms, and the tips are sword sharp. They're mistrustful, violent tempered, and clever. They charge at the first sign of a threat, so we have to be quiet and careful. They gore their victims, trample them, kick dirt on the body, then trot away with head high in victory."

When the quarry was sighted, Leigh was indeed amazed by the creature's menacing size and apparent strength. Their hides were dark and their formidable horns were black.

Jace went on. "Even the largest and most skilled predators fear the buffalo. Lions respect them and keep their distance, unless they sight one that's sick or wounded from a battle. Those horns can rip open a lion's underside with one sweep. Animals are quick to learn their own strengths and weaknesses, unlike humans."

Leigh was glad they moved upwind toward the truculent creatures, allowing any breeze to carry their scent away from their quarry. She sighted numerous buffaloes resting in the tall grass, and a few grazing nearby. Egrets flew overhead or dined on huge carcasses. She saw yellow-billed oxpeckers seeking their own prey upon the enormous beasts. She walked close behind Jace and followed his silent signals. The others trailed gingerly behind her.

Jace halted the hunting party and turned for final instructions. "We'll take that big bull over there by himself. He's far enough from the others to prevent trouble. Everyone make certain you're ready. If the herd charges after we fire, do exactly as I say."

Jace and Johi started to move out first. Everyone checked their weapons. A gun discharged, the blast sending Louisa to the grass. Leigh screamed and hit the ground. The herd scrambled to their legs, bellowed in rage, and began an earth-rumbling stampede.

Chapter Fifteen

With speed and keen wits, Jace took in the situation. Leigh was fine, just shaken. His reflexes were quick at work. Over the din he shouted, "Everybody fire into the air and keep firing until I say halt. We need to scare off that herd."

Louisa had been knocked to the ground when her gun misfired. In surprise and fear, she had tossed the uncontrollable weapon aside. Her gaze had gone to Chad's, the startled look vowing her innocence.

Leigh gaped at the redhead for a moment. She jumped from the grass unharmed, just unsettled by the near miss. She began discharging rounds to help the others frighten off the menacing buffaloes.

The herd halted at the roaring of guns, bellowed and pawed, then trotted in the other direction to disappear into thickets.

Jace seized the Ross automatic to examine it. He had little time to decide how to handle the near fatal episode. If Leigh hadn't leaned over to scratch an insect bite, she would be dead. If he revealed the gun had been tampered with, Chad would end the perilous safari and take Leigh into danger in London. Johi checked Leigh's gun each morning, but not the others'. He also cleaned and checked all weapons after each hunt, so this deed had been done after gun reassignment and practice last night. Whoever did it knew Louisa Jennings would carry the rifle today . . .

"When Louisa threw it down so hard, it broke the mechanism," Jace explained. "I can't tell what caused it to misfire. Louisa is lucky it didn't explode in her face, or she didn't shoot off her foot, or shoot one of us in the back. I'll have this rifle checked out when we get back to Mombasa. This has never happened before, and I don't like it."

Chad glared at his fallen mistress, who had not gotten up or been helped to rise.

"It isn't my fault, Chad," Louisa declared. "When I slid the bolt forward, it fired. I didn't have my finger on the trigger."

"This is a new model, Chad, just came out this year," Jace explained. "Perhaps it has a defect. The gunmaker is Charles Lancaster in London. I'll ship it to him and let him figure out the problem. I can't use weapons I don't trust," Jace remarked, knowing the well-made gun was not to blame. If Louisa was responsible, his words should scare her into being more careful with her own life. With this foiled attempt, she wouldn't dare make another move any time soon. And if it wasn't Louisa, the guilty bastard would have to lay back for a while until everyone relaxed. That was all Jace needed, time to put his own play into motion. "You want to head for camp or track those buffalo?"

"I think they're too dangerous for us to challenge. I'm more interested in lions and elephants. Let's get on with our safari. Why don't we head for the next camp in the morning? This area is dangerous."

Jace was delighted with Chad's suggestion. He had intended to make the same suggestion tonight. Their

345

next location would place them within a few days of Nairobi, and closer to his plantation. "That's fine."

After reaching camp, Leigh went into her tent to be alone. Reid fetched a bottle of Scotch and went to work on it. Cynthia paced the clearing, unnerved by Jace's words. Johi began checking all of the weapons. Jace went to alert the bearers about the change in schedule. Louisa and Chad walked to the pool to relax and talk. Jace skirted the campsite to eavesdrop.

"Are you trying to get rid of me so you can get at your little ward?" Louisa asked. "You heard Jace; I could have been killed."

"Your imagination is running wild again, Louisa."

"Is it?" she challenged. "It would be profitable and vengeful for you to frame Jace for my death, then marry Leigh. Is that your plan? Get both of them?"

"Are you daft? Jace wouldn't be arrested for an accident, and I'm not trying to lure him back to London to get arrested for those other charges. I'm not after Jace. We've had problems, but I wouldn't try to kill him. As for you, I was planning to ask you to marry me when we returned to London. But, if this is what you think of me, I'd be the daft one."

Louisa was stunned. "What do you mean? Are you serious?"

"Don't play ignorant with me, Louisa. You know how I feel about you. Would I have stayed with you so long if you weren't special to me? I've tried to get you to be nice to my ward. You haven't been, despite your little pretense of friendship. As long as you

346

make Leigh want to avoid you, I can't tell her about us. I have to assure my friendship with Leigh before November. If we married or became betrothed, she could get rid of me to be rid of you. She's talking about selling the business to me. If I'm careful, she will. Hear me good, woman, if you're behind any of these accidents, stop them now."

Louisa was wary. "What about your wager with Jace?"

"What about it?"

"You told me you'll owe him fifty thousand pounds if he gets Leigh during this safari. You asked me to distract him. I tried, but he wasn't interested. He's too busy working on Leigh. If he wins, it'll cost you a lot of money and a great deal of pride."

"Don't worry about that silly bet. He would have charged me that much anyway. Actually, it saved me an extra twenty-five thousand by not having to double his salary. I don't have to marry her, Louisa. She just has to leave here with me, and alive, to sell out in London. I told you, it was only a trick to provoke Jace into working for us. He required an irresistible enticement and Leigh was my bait. I was hoping to get truly close to her during this trip, but my jealous lover keeps causing trouble and rifts. Even if she doesn't sell to me, I still need a way to control the firm and her."

"What if Jace does win her?"

"He can't. Leigh would never fall for Jace Elliott, never."

"She already has," the redhead disclosed, "and he's fallen for her. He was in her suite a long time in Mombasa, and left grinning ear-to-ear. I know a satisfied look when I see one."

"He was making that thousand-pound wager with her."

347

"Both times? He visited her twice." Louisa revealed how Jace had gone to Leigh's room one night and had remained a long time. "It was that day she was attacked at the fort, and I rented another room to ensnare him for you. I bet he planned that trouble just to weaken her toward him. How can a girl resist a man who's saved her twice? I was glued to my door, Chad, so I know when he left, very late and very happy. I bet they've been sneaking around during the safari. You know they were alone on the trail and in camp during our leopard hunt. I bet there was no quicksand accident. I bet they were meeting in the jungle. And I bet Jace is behind those incidents just to make Leigh cling to the Great White Hunter and that he's convinced her you're after her money and to blame. I bet they're having an affair!"

Chad's gaze was cold. "That's a lot of wagers, Louisa."

"I bet all I own that I'm right, and telling you the truth."

Gunfire sounded in the camp. Jace left his hiding place to rush to the clearing, where Johi was standing over a dead predator. The jackel had sneaked into camp after meat waiting to be cooked.

Chad's head jerked toward camp. "What was that?"

"Gunshots. Johi is probably testing the weapons. I'm not using that Ross again. I'm lucky his little trick didn't get me killed. One more thing, Chad, do you know about the bet between Leigh and Jace?"

"Of course I do. I suggested the thousand-pound wager."

348

"I mean the second one," Louisa divulged.

Baffled, Chad asked, "What second one?"

Louisa took great delight in revealing what she had discovered in Leigh's tent. If Chad was duping her, this news would change matters. "Do you believe me now, love? With all that's happened, you and Leigh have both lost your bets to Jace. That's why I think he's behind all these curious events, just to win. If Jace marries Leigh, you'll lose everything, Chad. I've tried to interfere by making Cynthia sleep in her tent, but I can't do it all the time. They've been making a fool of you behind your back. I bet Jace is licking his lips in anticipation of revealing the truth to you. I've never liked or trusted that little witch. You're so smitten by her that you can't see through her pretense. She's smart and selfish. She fools everyone with her angelic face and false behavior. I was so afraid she'd take you away that I've been acting badly."

Louisa glued her gaze to Chad's. "There's another clue you missed, lover: if Leigh lost her locket at the waterfront, how was she wearing it that day she had lunch with me and Cynthia? She wore it beneath her dress, but I saw it when she tried on a gown. How, when, and where did Jace return it, *if* she only saw him once? I bet he sneaked into her London suite and they got real acquainted."

Chad narrowed his glacial blue eyes. "That deceitful bitch! That bastard! They won't get away with tricking me. Jace will never marry Leigh and get her inheritance. I'll make certain of it. As for me, you don't have to worry about me loving that guileful bitch. I'm marrying you, Louisa, just as soon as I get control of the firm. Until this safari ends, we'll be the best friends Leigh has. Understand?"

* * *

Leigh had hurried from her tent to investigate the commotion. She watched Jace drag the daring but reckless animal from camp. She lifted the tea kettle and poured herself a cup. As she sipped it, Jace returned. They exchanged probing looks.

"How are you?" he questioned.

"Better now, thank you." She had withdrawn from Jace and now all she wanted to do was run away with him. Would he marry her if she sold out to Chad and agreed? How would he feel about the sale to his old enemy, a sale including all he had lost to her grandfather? What would Chad do and say about such an event? According to Jace, and she believed him, Chad had full authority over her and her actions until she was twenty-one. If only those two men didn't distrust each other, everything would be fine. How much did each want vengeance? Where did she fit into their puzzle?

"That was close, Leigh," he remarked.

"It was an accident, wasn't it?" she asked, watching him.

Jace knew his answer would control her emotions. "I plan to find out as soon as possible," he replied with caution.

Their talk ceased as Chad and Louisa returned. Chad and Jace looked at each other. Louisa poured the couple a glass of wine.

"How about you, Leigh? It'll calm the nerves," she remarked.

"No, thanks. Hot tea is fine. Are you all right? That must have been a terrible scare." From the redhead's reaction after the incident, Leigh felt it hadn't been intentional, not on Louisa's part.

Louisa inhaled deeply, then released the spent air. "It was terrifying, but it's over now. I'm glad you're

350

safe, Leigh. And the others, too. I could have wounded someone badly. Did you examine the rifle, Jace? We heard gunfire."

Jace related the killing of the marauding jackel. "That doesn't happen often. He smelled fresh meat and thought he could sneak off with our dinner." Jace hadn't been given time to deliberate what he had overheard. He wondered how Louisa knew about the fort incident. He wished he could have taken in the whole conversation.

Cynthia and Reid, who had been in their tent, joined them. They were smiling at each other, and everyone noticed the change in their moods. They, too, poured wine.

"The bearers are packing up," Jace informed the group. "We'll move out in the morning. I know a good place for elephants."

"I'd like to speak with you privately, Jace," Chad said.

"Fine. Let's take a walk."

All the while they walked along the jungle trail, Chad was wondering if Jace was behind some of those incidents, as Louisa suggested. To provoke information, he asked bluntly, "Is there anything serious between you and Leigh? Are you plotting and using these so-called accidents to get my ward into your arms? I don't like her being endangered just to win a bet."

Jace stared at the man. He knew why Chad was angry and suspicious: because of Louisa's accusations. He had to stay away from Leigh in private. He knew Chad had lied to his mistress and used the redhead. But Louisa's charge about getting both of them with one scheme sounded logical. Yet what had him worried was Chad's firm belief that Leigh would never be won by Jace Elliott. He had to be careful. "Whatever I answer, old friend, you wouldn't believe me. But I'll respond anyway. No, nothing has happened between me and that beautiful creature. Not that I haven't tried or wanted it to, but she's too innocent to charm quickly. Since we're being honest for a change, I'll tell you what I suspect. I think you're responsible, and you're questioning me to throw me off guard. I think you're trying to find a way to end this safari and our bet before I have time to win it. I think you want to get Leigh out of my reach and back to London, where only you can work on her. I warn you, I won't let her be killed or hurt."

Chad exploded like a short-fused stick of dynamite. "You think I'm trying to harm Leigh Webster? Are you crazy?"

Jace used his skills and wits to explore this perilous territory. "Harm her and kill her, no way, old boy. You just want to scare her into your arms and away from me. You want her to believe I'm plotting against her. She told me you can't inherit even a sixpence if she died, that Webster's holdings will go to two friends. I bet that shocked you and your mother. No, you don't want her dead; you need to marry her to keep all you have and to get the rest. You aren't fooling me with that redhead. If your jealous mistress is playing deadly games, you'd better stop her, or neither of us has a chance of winning our wager. I'm warning you, Chad, don't try to sneak out on me."

"What will you do? Track us to London for revenge?"

"Is that why you dangled that tasty bait before me? You hoped I'd be so ensnared I'd lose my wits and follow her home where the law would get final revenge for you. It won't work, Chad. If I don't win the bet here, I'm not leaving. If I do win her heart, will her guardian give us permission to marry after the safari?"

"No. If Leigh chooses you over me, it'll be November before you can collect. Until then, I'll do and say all I can to change her mind."

"I thought as much, so what good is our wager to me?"

"If Leigh says she wants to marry you in November, you'll be the winner and I'll pay off before leaving here. If she doesn't, you haven't won. Did Leigh tell you she's planning to sell me the business?"

"No, but why should she? She only told me about Webster's will because I was hinting at you being behind her accidents. She was really defending you, old boy. You really have her fooled good, don't you? Is she planning to return to America?"

"I don't know her future plans, but I'd be crazy to let her get hurt. I prefer to win her and the firm, but that might not be possible."

"Because of Tyler Clark, her fiancé in Texas?"

"Leigh isn't betrothed. Did she tell you she was?"

"No, Louisa said Leigh told her. Obviously your lover lied. What else has that redhead done, old boy? She does want you badly."

"I'll make a deal with you, Jace."

"Another one?" Jace teased.

"Don't be stupid. Let's both watch Leigh closely and make certain nothing happens to her. All of this trouble could be coincidental. If it isn't, and one of us isn't to blame, we have to make sure Leigh doesn't get hurt again. We'll both keep a sharp eye on my clever mistress. Agreed?"

"Agreed." And Jace revealed a few things that Chad, from his agitated reaction, didn't seem to know.

As Leigh and Chad played chess and talked, after dinner, Louisa watched them from a distance and fumed. She whispered to Jace, "Look at her working on him with those blue eyes and sweet ways. You'd think having one man snared was enough for her, but Tyler isn't around to hold her attention."

"Leigh isn't engaged, Louisa," Jace dared to reveal. "She only said that to stop you from worrying about her stealing Chad."

Louisa was shocked and angered. She eyed Leigh and scoffed, "That little sneak. I should have known she couldn't be trusted, but the trouble is, if she doesn't turn his head, another conquest will. Chad doesn't keep any woman around very long. I can't blame him for being tempted by Leigh; she does have a lot to offer him. It wouldn't surprise me to learn she's behind all her own mishaps just to catch his eye, and yours, Jace. She loves attention. We shot skeet on the ship, so I saw her working with guns. She knows a lot about them. She probably broke mine so she could make Chad think I'm after her. As for that quicksand episode, I don't know how she pulled off that trick. That little creature is up to something. I'm certain of it. If I were you, Jace, I'd watch her closely."

The group traveled for many days, sleeping again under mosquito nets suspended over bedrolls, which allowed no privacy for Jace to approach Leigh. He and Johi observed everyone closely, but nothing unusual occurred.

The third large camp was reached on the fifth day

354

around noon. While the bearers and servants labored with the preparation of tents and meals, the group went for a walk. They saw a variety of animals, prey and predator and scavenger. As Jace had promised, numerous elephants inhabited this area. With a love for acacia, many of the trees in the scattered woodland were destroyed, eaten and mauled into ruin. Yet it changed woodland to grassland, creating more terrain and food for the creatures who favored grazing.

They decided to hunt for a time. "Don't shoot high on the skull," Jace instructed. "It doesn't even slow an elephant, much less drop him. These creature have humanlike traits. They mourn dead mates and friends, even bury them and visit their graves occasionally." He educated them about the lumbering giants, then pointed to a bull that was standing away from the others. "That's the one you want, Chad."

Leigh eyed the enormous animal. Its hide was saggy, like an oversize garment. It was caked in mud and dust to ward off pesky insects and the heat. He uprooted a small tree, tugging on it with his powerful trunk and kicking at it with his large foot. The grayish-brown beast devoured his success, then searched for another, moving farther away from the clustered herd. His prized ivory tusks were as tall as a man, telling his advanced age, Jace revealed, and its skill in avoiding poachers and perils. Leigh wanted him to survive longer.

A mother strolled and grazed with her baby, the female's bulk dwarfing the calf. She gathered tuffs of grass and stuffed them into her mouth, and the baby followed her lead. When the calf rested on the ground, the mother's trunk hovered over it as if caressing her infant.

355

The sky behind them was an azure blue. The grass was a vivid green from recent rains. Their positions on the lush emerald landscape and against the rich blue horizon evoked a feeling of tranquility and wild beauty. Other elephants feasted in a grove of trees. A lion passed them, keeping its distance. The herd appeared gentle and affectionate. Their life was one of leisure, close to each other and to nature.

Leigh's eyes scanned their picturesque surroundings. It was alive and active this close to dusk. Warthogs routed near a waterhole, their tails flicking back and forth to discourage flies. The moment they became nervous, the tusked creatures backed into nearby holes until they felt confident enough to venture forth again. Impala, zebra, and wildebeest grazed far beyond their hiding place and stayed clustered for protection. Gazelles with their ringed horns browsed as if they were dainty ladies. Elegant giraffes dined on solitary acacias, their rough tongues curling around the supple leaves to yank them free. One towering giant spread his legs wide apart so his long neck and mouth could reach the waterhole, putting him in his most vulnerable position.

Predators—mainly lions—watched the same scene, but looked content to wait until tomorrow to attack and feed again. Birds landed here and there, mostly egrets and ox-peckers and tick birds who lived with, and on, the larger creatures. A group of vultures circled overhead seeking their next meal. Hyenas did the same on the ground.

Mosquitoes and flies were heavy today after the recent rains, and near this location where animals roamed and left droppings. The day had not started to cool yet, and perspiration beaded all over Leigh and the others. Leigh was glad Jace had cut a square from mosquito netting and had attached it to her topee. The net covered her pith helmet and grazed her shoulders like a veil, protecting her face and neck from hungry insects. Her long-sleeved shirt did the same for her arms, but insects sneaked under her skirt to feast on her damp legs.

Jace motioned them closer. He ordered caution, as they could not get upwind in this crowded and busy location. The bull elephant caught a whiff of danger, or perhaps an instinct came into play. His ears flattened against his body, a sign Jace had said to look for to indicate a charge. The beast lifted his trunk and trumpeted a threat to his attackers and a warning to the herd. He shifted menacingly on his front legs, legs that could trample a person into the ground. Its stance revealed power and confidence.

Chad had a good shot, and took it. He fired a second time. The animal dropped to the ground. The herd perceived death and danger. Quickly the mothers summoned their young, and all ran into thickets.

The group went forward and examined Chad's victory. Louisa took pictures, as she did during each hunt. Reid complimented his friend. Leigh stared at the dead giant and wanted to cry in mourning.

Jace realized this was his last safari. These animals were part of the land he loved, and he was helping to destroy them and it. At first, it had been a natural way of life. It had been exciting and stimulating. Now, it didn't seem the same. Watching an enemy get such enjoyment from killing suddenly had a strong impact on him.

"The bearers will handle it," Jace said. "Let's get back to camp before dark. I don't want any big cats jumping us." Jace glanced at Leigh, then Chad. "Predators sense when someone is encroaching on their territory. It makes them real nervous and irritable, and very dangerous. They'll attack just to scare

357

you away to protect their terrain."

Extra men went to work preparing the trophy to be carried to the river for hasty transportation to Mombasa. Jace had asked for most of the hunting to be done in this area, because it was easier and quicker to get the prizes to the Mombasan preserver from this camp. Certain men were trained and skilled in pretreating heads and hides to prevent their loss to scavengers, heat, and deterioration. The bloody and smelly task began as the safari party left the scene.

The next two days were busy, bloodthirsty, and successful ones for the two couples. Cynthia and Louisa killed zebras. Reid got a leopard and elephant. Chad got his cape buffalo, giving him four of the "big five" trophies he craved. Now he was eager to go after a lion.

Leigh didn't shoot anything, and that pleased Jace. He was also pleased, and slightly baffled, that no peril endangered his love. He wanted desperately to be with her, but open flaps at night prevented it. Too, Chad was sticking to her like a second skin.

As for Leigh Webster, she was relieved that the incidents had ceased. She missed Jace. He was nearby but so far out of reach for the present. Chad was on his best behavior, as were the others. She was enjoying the scenery, but she was miserable. She wanted Jace; she needed him. She longed for privacy and his touch. Not even a kiss or an embrace had been possible lately. If only they could find a way to be alone, to talk, to hold each other.

Jace realized how odd it must look to Chad for

him not to be pursuing Leigh. Of course, he laughed and joked with her in camp and on the trail, but he hadn't made any romantic gestures. Perhaps he should. Jace approached and asked, "Leigh, would you care to take a walk? The sunsets here are breathtaking. There's also a family of hyrax nearby that you might enjoy seeing."

Leigh turned and looked at her lover. "I'm sorry, but Chad just asked the same thing, Jace. Perhaps later or tomorrow?"

"That's fine," he replied, disappointed.

Reid prepared himself to do as Chad had ordered, to keep Jace and Johi in camp so neither could spy during the stroll. He knew what Chad was going to do, and he concurred. It was about time Chad got back to important business, he fumed, and rid them of that blond obstacle. Now that Chad knew he had lost, it would be easy for his friend to get rid of Leigh. Yet, Reid was worried. It was as if the girl lived a charmed life, escaping every snare set for her. After this talk, she would be vulnerable, susceptible, and helpless, because Chad would make her turn against her intrusive hero.

"Leigh, I have a terrible confession to make," Chad began when they were a safe distance from camp. He had guided them into an open space where no one could sneak up and listen, in case Reid failed in his task. For days he had been charming her so she wouldn't realize he intended to crush her. His first and only true love had to be punished for her betrayal. Before he took her life, he had to hurt her as she had hurt him. "I did something awful, and I'm sorry. I believe it's the reason behind everything that's happened to you."

Leigh's blue gaze focused on her guardian's. Her pulse quickened. Her heart pounded in dread. Her throat felt tight and dry. She sensed something horrible in the air. "What is it, Chad?"

Chad frowned and said, "I don't know where to begin, or how to make you understand and believe me. I know you haven't had any accidents for a while, but I'm still worried. I want to get this safari over with, so we can get out of this dangerous land. As soon as I get a lion, we'll have a reason to leave without arousing Jace's suspicions."

"I don't understand," she murmured, her heart pounding. Was he suspicious and trying to separate them?

"After I explain, if you think I'm right, I'll call off the safari today and we'll go home. I'll pay Jace his full salary, so he'll have no reason to object. It'll cost me a great deal, because I had to double it to coax him into taking this job. But I made a stupid mistake in judgment. He was so reluctant to become our guide that I made a crazy wager with him." He related their contract terms. "Whichever of us wins you in marriage gets you, the money, to share your holdings, victory, and revenge. That's why Jace Elliott accepted this job."

Chad watched the stunning effect of that disclosure on her. "I never intended to play our game for real, but I suspect Jace is doing so. I never believed he could catch your eye, and surely not your hand. The problem is, I love you and want to marry you. But I can't begin to woo you until I get rid of Louisa, earn your trust and respect, and get you away from Jace's threat. Those incidents at the fort, with your unloaded gun, with Louisa's rifle, those spells, and that quicksand. I think Jace is responsible. I also think he wants to turn you against me by hinting I'm to blame so he can win that foolish wager. He sees it as a way to get revenge on me and William and to get his hands on the woman I love and on your inheritance. That isn't the worst part. He insisted on adding an additional five thousand pounds for every night either of us slept in your tent. You know I haven't tried to seduce you to win, but I'm afraid he will."

Despite her horror at all he was telling her, one sentence stood out the most. "How do you know about my gun and the fort?" she questioned. "I told Jace not to mention them and worry you. Why did he tattle?"

"Jace told me when we took that walk at our last camp. I asked him face forward if he was trying to harm you or trick you. He denied it, of course. He tried to point the finger at me and Louisa. I'm not saying Louisa didn't pull any of those tricks, but not all of them. I know she's jealous and spiteful, and I shouldn't have brought her along. I knew I was falling in love with you, and that scared me. You're a tempting treasure, Leigh Webster, but I'm used to freedom. I also knew it would scare you for me to start acting lovesick. Jace told me what you said about the will. Why did you lie to him?"

"We agreed not to reveal it to him, so I haven't. When he kept making hints about you being a threat to me, I used it to silence him. Why are you telling me all this? Why should I believe you?"

Chad withdrew the cleverly altered contract from his pocket. "Can you recognize my handwriting and Jace's?"

She had seen both during the safari, when notes were made or licenses marked. "Yes."

"Read this, and don't judge me too harshly. I swear I never meant for it to go this far. I'll even pay

Jace the fifty thousand to get you out of here safely. I was trying to make peace with him, and I thought for a while I was succeeding. I was wrong, Leigh. He still doesn't trust me or forgive me. He hates me and wants revenge, through you. I told him I was in love with you and wanted to marry you. He charged it was because of the firm, as I was afraid you'd believe if I started after you too soon. If you'll marry me, I'll sign a legal document that will deny me any right to the company should anything happen to you. It's the only way you'll know you can trust me completely. Even if you don't love me, I can't allow you to get entangled in this mess between me and Jace."

After Leigh read the contract, Chad burned it. "Now, when you leave with me, I have no legal proof of his wager, nothing to gain. The bet isn't and never was important to me, Leigh. I only made it to get Jace to work for us. To prevent trouble, I'll pay whichever amount he demands. You can hate me, disrespect me, and reject me, but let me help you get away from him before he makes another attempt to beguile you. When we return to London, you can fire me and avoid me. You can sell the firm and return to America, if you desire. I won't try to stop you, even though I have the power to do so. I love you, and I only want you to be safe and well. I swear it."

As Leigh stared at him, Chad said, "I honestly don't know if Jace is trying to harm you or trick you, or if he's fallen in love with you, as I have. These incidents make me nervous and wary. I thought you should know the truth so you can watch yourself."

Leigh decided to test this man with her own stunning revelation, if Chad didn't already know about it. She needed it to appear as if she trusted and liked him enough to confide in him. Upon return to camp, she would destroy her contract, too. "You aren't the only one who made a foolish wager with him. Jace and I have a bet you don't know about." She revealed the terms of her secret wager and she watched Chad's blue eyes enlarge. "That's right, Chad, me against his plantation. Of course, like you, I wasn't serious, and never believed I'd lose. If it weren't for all those curious incidents, I would be safe from him. No matter, for I would not take his plantation and I wouldn't spend a single night with that greedy criminal. As with you, Jace insisted on a valuable wager before he would take the job. The thousand pounds weren't enough to entice him, and I knew how eager everyone was to go on the safari. He was so damn cocky I was provoked into signing an agreement. Besides, I wanted to study him, see what I could learn about that codicil. At the time, it seemed harmless and amusing. As Jace is a wanted criminal, after I return to London or America, what can he do to collect? Nothing. He's so proud that I figured he wouldn't tell anyone I had outsmarted him, so my reputation seemed safe."

"Heavens, Leigh! He's a clever and dangerous man, a vengeful one. I know from experience. You shouldn't have been so reckless."

"Neither should you, Chad. It appears he outwitted both of us. When I realized he was playing seriously and I was losing to him, I knew I had been a fool. That's why I couldn't cancel the safari when I became ill. I didn't want Jace telling everyone about our deal and humiliating me. If I lost, I planned to escape him before he realized I had sailed. Currently, we're even in points. I promise you, it'll be a draw, or he'll be left fuming after my deceit and departure."

"You mean you won't honor the agreement?"

Leigh sent him an insulted look. "I wouldn't sully myself for any man or reason," she scoffed convincingly. "You're right about him being suspicious of you and Grandfather, but I told him he was crazy. I told him you don't inherit if I die, so you have no reason to harm me. He didn't believe me. There's something else you should know."

Leigh seized his full attention with that hint. "I saw Jace twice in London, but he never revealed his identity, and we both know why. That night at Lord Salisbury's, I slipped outside for fresh air. Jace sneaked up on me and returned my locket. I told him you were my guardian and you wouldn't like a stranger chasing me. He said he wanted to get to know me; it's clear now it was because of my connection to you. To discourage him, I mentioned we were leaving on safari. That's why he was in Mombasa; he was lying in wait for us. I think he paid Mr. Hanes to fake an injury so you'd have to hire him. I didn't know who he was until he confronted me at the party here. That's also when he learned who I am and got these crazy wager ideas."

When Chad frowned, Leigh said, "I didn't tell you about our second meeting because I didn't want to worry or anger you. That's the same reason I didn't tell you about my rash wager. There's something I don't understand. Jace didn't tell me his name, but he was very romantic at the wharf, until he learned I was meeting Lord Hamilton for dinner. When I told him in the garden I was your ward, he became romantic again. But after he discovered I was a Webster, he backed off. Considering his wager with you, why did he halt his romantic pursuit? A man can't catch a woman if he doesn't chase her. True, he's been flirty and attentive, but nothing more. That's odd, unless those wagers were tricks to get

364

this job to spy on us. I made my bet to test his motives and knowledge, but he refused money, property, or marriage to me. I suppose he needed me to think he didn't want those things from me."

She took a breath and continued her ruse. "What I can't figure out is, if he needs to marry me to win or to get my holdings, why not woo me or lose to me? Unless he doesn't trust either of us to honor our wagers. On the other hand, perhaps he can't lose to me because he's guilty and can't clear himself. Or he assumes one night with him will soil me so much that you'd never want me and he'd have revenge on you and the Websters. I don't grasp his motives. I think it all hinges on how much he hates you and Grandfather, and on how far he'll go for vengeance. And on whether or not he knows of that codicil. I've watched him closely, but I haven't uncovered any clues. He also told me about your claims of love and marriage," Leigh added, "and he's hinted that you and Louisa are trying to get rid of me."

Chad grasped her hands and gazed into her eyes. His voice carried a pleading note as he said, "Surely you didn't believe him."

Leigh withdrew her hands. "Frankly, I don't know what or whom I believe. Both of you have tricked me, and tried to use me for your own gains. I can't understand why you would do such a thing to me. I'm a stranger to Jace Elliott and he could have just cause to beguile me, but you didn't. I'm hurt and disappointed. We'll complete the safari, then see what happens." Leigh turned and left him standing there.

Chad feared that Jace and Louisa had misled him. He realized that Louisa shouldn't have known about the fort attack. He had dropped his new plan too swiftly and rashly. Perhaps there was still a chance of winning Leigh and the bet with Jace. He should have known this sweet and innocent angel couldn't be wicked and devious. It was incredible, but he truly loved and desired her. Chad rushed and stopped her at the edge of the clearing. "Leigh, I love you. Please let me prove it. I'll do anything you say. You can test me and punish me, but forgive me. Please love me and marry me. Before the ceremony, we'll get a lawyer and I'll sign away all rights to everything you own. I swear it. Let me prove myself to you, prove it's you I want, not the money."

Leigh observed her handsome guardian. No matter how much Lord Chadwick Hamilton had lied to her, she was certain he was telling the truth at this moment. That astonished her, swayed her broken heart, and convinced her dazed mind. Jace should have told her about that awful contract. If she confronted him, he would give a logical explanation that she could not disprove, or believe, at this late date. Jace had deceived her in the worst way. She looked at Chad. "All I can promise is to think seriously about your proposal, Chad. I believe you, and I'm very fond of you. No matter what happens between us, you'll always be a part of Webster International, if I don't decide to sell it to you. Just remember your promise to keep the truth from Jace, as I have. It's been difficult at times not to tell him everything and get the past cleared up, but I don't know how he would deal with such facts. We came here to study him, and we have. He doesn't know anything, so we're safe. Let's keep it that way. Agreed?"

"Agreed, my love. I'm going to guard you, Leigh. I swear I won't let anything or anyone harm you. I'm relieved that you've kept what your grandfather did a secret. If he knew, Jace would kill us both."

"Perhaps, and perhaps not. He trusts me and

desires me. Mr. Jace Elliott isn't hard to fool. As I told you, I have no intention of honoring my secret wager with him. If he tries to follow me back to London to collect, he'll be arrested. Let's go. I need a drink."

Jace kept his seat on the ground behind the bush near where they had halted. As soon as he could get away from Reid Adams's questions, he had tried to sneak up on Leigh to see what he could learn. He had been too distant for listening, until they had paused nearby. What he had discovered staggered him, and he wished he knew the rest of their conversation. Pain knifed his heart, and fury burned hot and destructive inside his head. A ravenous hunger for revenge chewed at his tormented gut. As first suspected, he was the target of a cunning plot. But Leigh Webster was pulling the strings to her puppet Chad. He had never seen his old friend behave this way before. Obviously Louisa was being duped and framed to hide their guilt. All of those incidents had been to ensnare him. Leigh had lied to him. She had gone too far to beguile him. She had won his love. She had lowered his guard and dazed his keen wits. He had let her get to him and enchant him, just as Chad had done. She would pay!

In camp later, darkness engulfed the site. After finishing the strong Scotch, Leigh's anguish numbed a little. Knowing she couldn't trust Jace hurt deeply and intensely. Knowing she couldn't trust Chad, or the others, alarmed her. She just wanted to get out of this steamy jungle. She wanted to go home to her aunt Jenna. She wanted to exchange her new problems for her old familiar ones. She left the table and walked to loosen taut muscles. Jace swaggered to her and grinned, a sly and devilish expression.

"I'm seven points ahead, Miss Webster," he murmured. "It looks as if I'll win our little wager. You owe me one passionate kiss and six extra glorious nights. Maybe the ship will need repairs again to give you time to pay up. If not, we'll figure something out. Maybe I'll sneak into London again and you can help me in two ways."

Leigh was astounded by his words and mood. "You've been eating loco weed. I'm not an animal in one of your traps. You've been paid plenty for any honest debt I might have incurred. As for the rest, I can't be blamed for accidents or for carelessness on the parts of others. This wager is a farce to get at me. It's over, Jace."

"I'm afraid it isn't, my golden lioness. That wasn't our deal. Until you lose the contracted bet, points can't be tallied and payments can't be made. You owe me one kiss and six nights so far."

"You're a deceitful beast, Jace Elliott. I haven't lost fairly. As you said, I'm not paying for a crime I didn't commit."

"That isn't my fault, my wild beauty. A bargain is a bargain. I warned you to think hard and long before giving me your word. You'll have to stick to it. I'll be watching you closely to make certain you don't turn coward or traitor on me. Just so the others won't get suspicious, I'll keep my distance until the safari is over. Maybe you'll be hungrier for me by then and be a tigress in bed. Good night, love."

Leigh gaped at him, glad her back was to the camp so the others couldn't see her expression. She was also glad they were preoccupied in a card game so no one would interrupt or overhear. She couldn't get Jace's wager with Chad off her mind, but she thought it unwise to mention that knowledge. She couldn't understand how he could sign such a wanton wager, even if done before their love affair. The man that she loved was suddenly a mystery to her, and possibly worse. "You're only two points ahead, Mr. Elliott. You've endangered my life five times, so that's five points in my favor."

The handsome guide looked her up and down. "How do you figure that, Leigh? I know how I've earned my score: one scream during the rhino hunt for a kiss, three nights for being endangered by drugs three times, a night for quicksand peril, two nights for being endangered during the buffalo and rhino hunts to equal six extra nights and seven points in my favor. Where did your score come from?"

"You didn't tell me about the powder in my canteen three times, so my life was imperiled by your careless oversight and lack of defense. My gun was unloaded or mishandled during a dangerous hunt, putting my life in jeopardy, since you're in charge of all weapons. The same applies to my last point: your carelessness with a broken weapon nearly caused Louisa to shoot me. Since Johi is your hired man, you're responsible for any mistakes he or the others make. That's five points for getting me into trouble or peril, as per your rule two, Mr. Elliott."

Jace grinned and shrugged. "That's very cunning, Miss Webster. But I'm still two ahead and I will win. By the way, since I broke rule two five times at five kisses each, when do you want to collect those twenty-five tasty tokens? Just let me know. I'll be obliging."

Leigh watched him stroll away, whistling. He had won another battle with his quick and keen wits. She was unnerved again. *We'll see who wins our final battle, Jace,* she vowed to herself. *It could have been so wonderful between us, if you were honest and really loved me. Maybe you do and don't even realize it. Maybe you're too controlled by hatred and resentment to see what you've done to us. God help us both, because I love you and want you and I believe you feel the same way.*

Chad approached her. "What did Jace want? He looked annoyed."

Leigh had to fool her guardian to prevent any problems with him, so she replied, "He was just teasing me about our secret wager, playfully warning me to watch my step or I'd lose more points to him."

"I'm glad you trust me enough to discuss the matter with me."

Leigh sent him a convincing smile. "We have to stick together until this is over. I don't think it would be a good idea to let Jace know I told you about our real bet, or to let him discover that I know about his wager with you. We can't confront him with his duplicity. We burned our proof. I was afraid someone might find my contract, and I'd be humiliated. If we expose his game and demand to leave, it might cause big trouble. We don't know this jungle, Chad. If we angered or challenged him, there's no telling what he would do. He could lead us around in circles for weeks." She frowned. "I can't decide if Jace is dangerous or not. Every time I try to relax him enough to trust me and open up to me, he gets skittish. Are you sure he's serious about his wager with you? He's certainly not trying to win me."

"Jace never was a woman-chaser, so maybe he doesn't know how to charm and woo one. Or maybe duping you comes hard for him. Or maybe he realizes he can't collect on our bet even if he won your heart. You can't marry a criminal and exile yourself, and I guess he knows it. If he fell in love with you, he couldn't ask you to share such a fate; no proud man would. He probably knew all along that neither of us could win such a wager. But I'm sure he wishes he could. I do."

"Until this matter is settled, Chad, I can't think beyond friendship. We need to get to know each other better."

His eyes glowed from more than moonlight. "I understand, Leigh. First, we have to get Louisa and Jace out of our lives."

"Louisa will be easy to discard, but I'm not so sure about Jace Elliott. He's too suspicious of you, Grandfather, and me. If we tip our hand, we've got big trouble. If Jace knows about the will and is behind these accidents, he might be willing to settle for half of Grandfather's estate rather than pursue me for all of it."

From knowing Jace for years, and suspecting Louisa was the real culprit, and not wanting Leigh to panic into a slip, Chad said, "I honestly don't think you need to fear Jace. Even if he's behind these curious happenings, I'm sure it's only to compel you into his arms. Don't worry, Leigh; I'm here to protect you from all harm."

"We've been spying on the wrong person, my friend," Jace told Johi. He related what he'd overheard earlier. "Look at the two of them over there with their heads together plotting more mischief. She duped me. Lordy, she was so sweet a temptation. The craziest part is that Chad really loves her. He'd do anything for her, even confront an enemy again so she can study me. I only wish I knew what she really wants and needs from me. It must have something to do with her grandfather and those crimes. I'm a fool. I've been working on Chad for evidence when she's the boss, the one with all the answers I need. Damn her! She's a Webster through and through. Did you give Jomo and Buha my orders?"

"They are ready to obey."

Jace sighed in anguish. Once more his world was inside out; again, Chad Hamilton and a Webster were to blame. "Good. As soon as Leigh's dead, I'll guide the others back to Mombasa, then we'll return home, Johi. I'm tired, really tired."

Wanjohi knew the man meant in spirit, not in body. He would help his best friend exact revenge on those who had harmed him. Soon, the African sun would set on their deceits, and payment would be taken by force. Soon, this savage safari would be over forever . . .

Chapter Sixteen

On the fourth day of safari, at their third campsite, Jace and Leigh received a curious surprise: Louisa moved into Cynthia's tent, and Reid Adams moved in with Chad. Jace and Leigh surmised it was because of the talk late yesterday between Chad and Leigh, during which Chad had proposed. What both found strange was the fact that Louisa did not seem upset by the change in quarters. Since Chad had behaved little differently to his ward at breakfast, the blonde and the handsome guide concluded that Chad was somehow duping Louisa, and the redhead did not as yet realize she had been discarded.

They rested and relaxed that day following their long trek and several hunts. Music played on the gramophone. Chad and Reid enjoyed chess. Louisa and Cynthia chatted. The servants did chores. Jace cleaned his guns. Leigh read. Johi observed everybody.

It became hotter and steamier as the hours passed. Lunch was over, and the two men were drinking steadily. Sweat bees, flies, and mosquitoes pestered all of them today; and no one wanted to use the smelly repellent Jace offered. The air was still and heavy, and the sky was clear blue. Birds and monkeys chattered in the surrounding trees. Sweet scents of tropical flowers reached their noses. Louisa suggested a swim for the three women. Jace came to alert, and decided to be their guard. The four left camp and headed for the river.

Chad and Reid were at either end of a table, a chess board separating them, in the center of camp, with nothing between them and the tents to use for concealment.

When they began to whisper, Johi could not hear their words or get closer. Jace's friend was annoyed, but helpless. He did not believe the white girl was tricking his friend and he doubted Jace, too, mistrusted her deep inside. Something strange and perilous was going on, Johi concluded, but Leigh Webster was not to blame. He had studied enough creatures in the wild to know which ones were good and bad. Once Jace cleared his wits, his friend would know that, too. But he would obey Jace's orders no matter what they were.

"You said you would explain things, Chad. What's going on? Why did you kick Louisa out? And why isn't she mad?"

Chad looked at Reid. His brown hair was mussed, he hadn't shaved in two days, and his grayish-brown eyes were narrower than usual. His friend looked worried and puzzled. "Relax, Reid, old chap. Everything is fine. It's a good thing I haven't killed her yet, because I was wrong about Leigh. You were wrong about her, and Louisa was wrong. There's nothing between Leigh and Jace, nothing. She's considering my marriage proposal; that's why I had to dupe Louisa and get her away from me. It's a damn good thing those drugs didn't harm her. Of course they were not intended to kill her, only to make her sick enough to be taken home. I don't know if any of her accidents have been either Louisa or Jace's doings, but I'll make certain nothing else happens to my future bride."

"What are you telling me, Chad?"

Chad revealed what Louisa, Jace, and Leigh had told him. "It's a mighty big puzzle, but I figured it out. All the pieces fit, Reid. I haven't lost her or the bet, but Louisa and Jace wanted me to think I had. That sly traitor is damned lucky. I'm going to forget about my revenge on him. I'm not taking a chance of messing things up again. There's no way Jace can bind me to those crimes in London, so he's no threat anymore. As for that trouble years ago, hell, he might be telling the truth about trying to save me. I'll be generous and give him the benefit of doubt. If I keep things stirred up between us, I'll never be free of him. I'm going to let my whole past die, and begin a new life with my ravishing ward."

"You're talking crazy, Chad. She has you so charmed you're not thinking clearly. You'll lose them both . . . everything."

"Leigh Webster is going to marry me; I'm sure of it. Check," Chad said with the gleam of two impending victories in his blue eyes, putting Reid's king under attack with a white knight. "Take your next move wisely, old boy, or this match is mine, too."

As Reid Adams pretended to consider which ebony piece to move on the chessboard, his mind was troubled by Chad's swings in mood and behavior, which could get them both into trouble. And Reid didn't want to be incriminated in this lethal affair. He was angry with Chad for succumbing to Leigh's charms and altering the plot, not once, but twice. That was hazardous, as Jace and Leigh might al-

375

ready be suspicious of them. A smart man—which Chad usually was—should recognize the perils of being indecisive and emotionally distracted, but the besotted man was irrational these days. It would serve Chad right, Reid fumed, if Leigh coldly rejected him and surrendered to Jace Elliott. Chad had become a lovesick fool.

As Reid moved a castle on the chessboard to take Chad's knight and to defend his king, he reasoned, "What if she's lying? How do you know Leigh and Jace aren't on to your plot and duping you?"

"They couldn't be. I got rid of the drug, so there's no evidence. If Jace suspects anybody, it's Louisa, or Leigh. If I'm wrong, I have a pawn and plan in reserve. Checkmate, old boy," Chad remarked, placing a queen within striking distance of Reid's king, adding to the threat by one of Chad's bishops whose path had been cleared by the same move. The grinning champion hinted, "Another game?"

"No, thanks. Let's take a walk and loosen these stiff bodies. Do us both a favor, though. Keep a tight and clear eye on them."

While Louisa and Cynthia were in the bushes being "excused," Leigh was lying on her stomach on the grassy bank. She trailed her fingers on the surface and pondered the men in her life. A quote by Lucretius came to mind: "It is more useful to watch a man in times of peril . . . to discern what kind of man he is; for then at last words of truth are drawn from the depths of his heart, and the mask is torn off." She was doing exactly that.

Leigh's clothes and hair were almost dry. Yet it was so hot and humid that perspiration glistened on her body again. She wriggled forward and splashed cool water on her flushed face.

Jace bounded from beneath the surface, seized her, and pulled her into his slippery arms. She didn't have time to scream before he covered her mouth with a soul-blistering kiss. When he released her, he teased, "I still owe you plenty, so don't forget the count."

Leigh was aching for peace and truth, but he was being devilish. "Damn you, Jace Elliott, I hate your little tricks."

Jace smiled and chuckled. "Temper, temper, my tawny lioness," he taunted. "Retract those claws and get that kill glint out of those lovely blue eyes. I was only teaching you a lesson. You had your eyes closed. What if I had been a man-eating croc? By now you would have lost your head and your life. He can snap it off with one crunch. What a tasty meal you'd make for any creature, including this one. I can hardly wait for my feast to begin."

Leigh perceived something different about Jace, and it alarmed her. His smile was feigned. His kiss had been almost punishing. A curious glint was in his jungle-green gaze, a mysterious and predatory one. She studied him as he watched her. His jawline was taut, as if his teeth were clenched, as if he was keeping a demon imprisoned behind those white bars. His grasp had been tight and rough. He was pretending to be playful and seductive, but he was making an intimidating point. To draw him out, she remarked, "I believe you're supposed to be on guard against all perils, Mr. Elliott, including my notorious guide. I'm not in the mood for rogues and games. Just keep away from me, as you promised last night."

As they heard Louisa and Cynthia returning, Jace grinned and said, "Fine, for now. Later, never." He

377

swam away with long and graceful strokes.

Leigh forced her eyes to leave the enticing sight. *What are you up to, Mr. Jace Elliott?* she fretted.

Louisa called out, "You two having fun?"

Jace yelled back, "It's wonderful, Red. Come on in."

Cynthia and Louisa glanced at each other, giggled, and swam to him. The three began to frolic, laugh, and talk. And flirt with each other. Jace did not summon Leigh or look her way.

Leigh was riled by Jace's actions. She was also upset by what Chad had exposed to her. She couldn't get the two secret wagers off her mind. Jace was winning theirs, if she honored their deal. He had won part of his and Chad's: fifteen thousand pounds for spending three times in her tent. Twenty, if that night in Mombasa counted as part of the safari, as Jace had already been hired and contracted by that night. Would Jace demand payment for those romantic moments? Would Chad pay the fifteen or twenty thousand for her seduction as agreed? What would Chad do when Jace revealed that shocking debt to her guardian? Leigh didn't even want to imagine that distressing event. One point was odd: If Jace was willing to bet marriage to her with Chad, why had he refused wedlock in their wager when she proposed it? What was Jace's motive and plan?

Chad and Reid arrived. Reid stripped off his boots and shirt, and went for a swim. Chad sat down beside Leigh.

"Having a good time?" he asked, sending her a blazing smile. He noticed how her soaked shirt and pants clung to her shapely body. A camisole, alas, protected her breasts from visual attack. He watched her squeeze water from her golden hair, his loins burning for her.

She nodded toward the merry scene in the river and jested, "Perhaps you should warn our hired hand to behave himself, bossman. Some bulls can't be trusted around cows, even with fences around them. He's after the entire herd, flirting with all of us. Actually, I think he's trying to make me jealous."

"Is it working?" Chad teased, then winked.

Leigh used a sultry smile on him before she quipped, "What do you think, my handsome guardian? Louisa and Cynthia might be in danger of capture and branding, but I'm wary of that fierce jungle predator. He's as cunning and clever as a wolf on the prowl, and I don't want to be ripped apart. Jace Elliott isn't trustworthy."

Cynthia took Louisa's hint and swam to Reid.

Louisa grasped Jace's shoulders and scoffed, "Look at those two. Chad's twelve years older than Leigh. She's nothing more than an innocent girl. What does he see in her, besides money?"

"She's rich, beautiful, desirable, charming, witty, educated, seductive, sweet, innocent, good company, well-mannered, enchan—"

"Stop! That's enough," Louisa wailed, placing her wet fingers over Jace's grinning lips. She snuggled her body against his. "I'm all those things and more, Jace. When are you going to give me a chance to prove it? Everyone's busy. We could take a walk in the jungle. I promise, within ten minutes, you'll forget she exists."

Leigh realized that her guardian never removed his shirt, not even while swimming or on a hot day around camp. She wondered if that action was to conceal a disfigurement. "Why don't we return to camp and you challenge me to a game of chess?" she asked Chad. "Perhaps with a little wager?"

Chad leapt to his feet. His hand extended to assist

Leigh to hers. With his arm around her waist, they disappeared from sight.

"Despite your many charms and talents, Miss Jennings," Jace told the redhead, "the answer is still no. I have my eye on Leigh, for lots of reasons. If I played around with you, I'd be no more appealing to her than Chad is with you locked around his neck. Thanks, but sorry." Jace disengaged the woman's arms and swam to the bank. "Take over as guard, Reid. I'm heading for camp and a stiff drink." He left.

"What's wrong with you, Reid," Cynthia asked. "You've been a bore, and an old man in bed."

"I'm worried about Chad. He's determined to win Leigh, and I doubt he can succeed. If he does . . ."

"You mean he's lying to Louisa? He isn't going to marry her?"

"Where are your wits, woman? What do you think?" Reid hinted.

Leigh wondered if Jace would come running to prevent what he surely suspected from her provocative behavior with Chad at the river, and how soon? She hoped it was fast, because she allowed Chad to kiss her before reaching camp. She needed to let Chad believe he had her duped. She must observe both men during these perilous times, discover the truth and secrets in their deepest hearts, and remove their rivalry masks. She had to learn what they wanted from her. As soon as possible, she needed to escape both deceitful men, but until she did, she must find ways to delude and control both of them.

The kiss was pleasant, but Chad was a master at seduction. When it ended, she smiled at him and said, "Let's begin our game before the others catch

380

us. Perhaps a second kiss is a good wager."

Chad beamed. "That's fine, my beautiful ward, but I'd prefer marriage as an incentive, or even a betrothal."

"You're much too eager and disarming, Chad. You do have a reputation as quite a womanizer. I wouldn't be just another conquest, would I?" she jested, caressing his passion-flushed cheek.

"You're the only woman I've met of any importance and value. I would do anything to win you, Leigh."

"Anything?" she echoed, and laughed as if pleased.

"Name it, my love," he coaxed. "I'll be your slave for life."

"I'll have to give it serious thought. Let's go."

Jace witnessed the kiss, and Leigh's enticing manner. Something didn't seem right in her voice and behavior today. At the river he had seen such pain, such mistrust, such yearning in her gaze. Why? Her own words had exposed her as a liar and a cheat, but . . . But what? he agonized. It was almost as if she had been turned against him. Yet, if Chad had told her lies, why didn't she confront him and give him a chance to defend himself as he had with Louisa and Ka'arta? The words he had overheard the other day from behind the bush plagued him. Jace hated to imagine that Leigh knew that her grandfather was behind his troubles and had held silent to protect William Webster. But, he asked himself, what else could she have meant?

Jace grimaced. He despised the fact she had a powerful secret with his rival and was so close to Chad. He suddenly realized he had thought of Chad as his *rival,* not enemy. He knew why. His war with Chad no longer mattered if it cost him Leigh, or the woman he had thought she was. Johi was on her side, and the African's instincts had never been wrong. Too, rarely had his own led him astray, and his whole being shouted she was innocent or being coerced. If so, why didn't she seek his help? Perhaps for the same reason Joanna hadn't when Chad had entrapped her. Jace knew he must uncover both Leigh and Joanna's reasons. The truth, he scoffed. Why was it always so hard to find? This tormenting matter had to be settled soon, or he'd go crazy.

Leigh won her chess game with Chad, as her father had taught her well, and her uncle Colin had practiced for hours with her. She glanced at him, shrugged, and smiled. Chad then fetched a drink. She was suddenly aware of Jace's close proximity and potent gaze, and the untypical Scotch in his grasp. She dared not look his way, as that green gaze could be her undoing. She had to conceal her warring emotions from everyone. In a few days, she would find a way to get him alone, then force the truth from him.

Dinner was served using items brought from London: china, crystal, silverware, and a tablecloth from one of the Webster mills. While they dined, the gramophone sent forth strains of Gilbert and Sullivan's *Ruddigore* and Strauss's *The Gypsy Baron*. The conversation was light, mostly about past and future hunts. They were served a combination of British and African dishes. Roasted meat was topped with *piri piri*, a sauce of chopped chilis, grated coconut, and dried coriander. With it, they devoured yams and *chapatis*, a thick and large skillet bread. To drink, the servant poured cups of *chai masala*, a tea flavored with sweet spices, cardamom, and pepper to give a palate-tingling finish to the Swahili meal. For dessert, they enjoyed a mixture of tropical fruits sprinkled with a variety of spices and nuts.

Leigh fingered the fine linen tablecloth as she reflected on her grandfather and the business he had left to her. She was convinced Chad was honest about his affections, but she feared that her inheritance had inspired them. No matter if he swore she was the most important thing to him, she did not believe him. Perhaps he was so caught up in his desperate deception that he believed his own lie.

Where Jace Elliott was concerned, she was at a total loss. She was positive her love did not know about the curious codicil. She suspected that Jace had made the bet with Chad to give him justification for taking Chad's offer, as he had implied in her Mombasa suite. But why hadn't he explained the shocking matter after they became so close? Several times Jace had said he would tell her everything later. Was the secret wager part of what he planned to divulge? He had said that, if he revealed everything, she would turn against him. Surely he had believed Chad would never expose such information for the same reason. Perhaps Chad had done so to obtain an advantage.

Everything was so mixed up. And, she felt, there was a missing clue to this riddle. There must be more between the two men than either had related. That clue held their real motives.

Jace hadn't needed Chad's wager to win her. She was entrapped by her own emotions and desires, by her surrender and her wager. Even after making that offensive bargain with Chad, Jace had given her several opportunities to refuse the safari. Yes, she reasoned, Jace had practically pushed her away by making outrageous demands. She had persisted with the trek, his employment, and their bet. Jace had held silent to Chad about his two victories, despite her behavior of late. That realization warned her to be careful how she treated him.

"You're awfully quiet tonight, Leigh," the man in mind teased.

Leigh glanced at him and murmured, "I'm pleasantly fatigued, Jace. That swim, the heat, and this wonderful dinner have me relaxed. While I'm feeling so mellow, I think I'll turn in. Good night, all."

"Good-night, Leigh," said her guardian, and watched her leave.

"I think I'll follow Leigh's example," Reid told them, and headed for the tent he now shared with Chad.

Louisa and Cynthia left the table, too, to talk inside their tent.

Chad looked at Jace. "It's you and me, just like old times. Care for a hand of cards and a drink? I don't cheat anymore."

"Is that a fact?" Jace taunted as he observed Chad's genial smile and mood. It troubled Jace that his rival was actually trying to make peace and to win Leigh. Perhaps Leigh was accurate in her speculation that Chad had changed since their last conflict. If so, it was that tawny lioness's influence on the wicked beast. Time would tell. "Maybe tomorrow night. We should get some rest. We need our wits alert. Dulled senses get a man into trouble."

"You're right, old friend." Chad stood, stretched, and left.

Jace fetched an item from his tent and walked to Leigh's. "You awake, Miss Webster?" When she came to the entrance and lifted the mosquito-net covering, he said, "I have something belonging to you. It was mixed in with my clean clothes. Mkwawa should know it isn't mine." He held up the cotton, lace, and ribbon camisole and sniffed it. He grinned. "I recognized the size and scent as yours. It's been washed, but you have a nice fragrance that still clings to it."

Leigh frowned, then pulled the undergarment from his fingers. "Thank you for returning my possession, Mr. Elliott. Too bad you can't return all of them."

"Do you really want back what I took? Rather, what you gave?"

She eyed the grinning rogue. "Part of it, yes."

His playful grin faded. "Which part?"

"I'll let you decide my meaning. By the way, would you back off a mite with the taunts and flirts? You told me Chad was a threat, so I'm working on him to discover the truth. Your recent behavior isn't helping matters, and it isn't a good way to entice or to hold a woman's affections. Good night."

"What does that mean? What are you up to, woman?"

"I'll explain later, when I get the answers. Good night, Jace."

"Get plenty of rest. We go hunting early in the morning."

Jace decided to give Leigh one last chance to be honest with him. He sneaked into her tent and awakened her. "I wanted to apologize for being so asinine lately. Blame it on jealousy and tension. I also want to warn you to be careful with Chad. He isn't a fool, Leigh."

Leigh made the same decision Jace had, one last chance to tell the truth. She loved him, and couldn't give up on him until she was certain her love was in

385

vain. "That also applies to me, Jace, jealousy and nerves. If there was any peril, it seems to be over now. Soon we'll be alone and we can forget this mess; you are winning."

Jace recalled her words to Chad about fleeing their bargain, and it pained him. "I promise you won't regret losing to me. I can hardly wait until it's the two of us alone." *Please, open up to me, love,* his heart and mind—his very soul—urged.

Leigh needed to coax him to confide in her. "I know, Jace." She murmured. "It won't be long." She drew his head down and kissed him.

Wounded hearts, troubled minds, yearning souls, and hungry bodies craved contact and solace. They clung together in urgent need. They kissed until both were breathless and aflame, then yanked off their garments and sank to the bedcover on the jungle floor.

Jace worked skillfully and leisurely to arouse her, to dispel her tension and doubts. His tongue darted into and out of her mouth and across her lips. He nibbled at her earlobes, his hot breath enlivening her senses. His mouth slipped down her throat, halting at her pulse point to absorb her reaction to him. His lips brushed her collarbone, then moved down her cleavage to encircle the base of each firm mound. With tantalizing and stimulating slowness, he traveled up one breast to moisten and arouse the rosy-brown peak. When his mouth relinquished the taut point, his forefinger and thumb caressed it while he labored at the other peak. One hand drifted down her stomach, caressing every inch of her quivering body along its journey.

Jace's fingers stroked her inner thigh, moving closer and closer to her womanly domain. He felt her trembling in need, suspense, anticipation, and pleasure. His mouth recaptured hers as his hand covered the center of her desire. There, he intoxicated her until she moaned and writhed. His searing kisses and artful caresses drove her wild. She willingly and eagerly surrendered herself to him. He was determined to become her only reality, to make himself unforgettable, irresistible. He was resolved to titillate her fierce yearnings and to kindle her smoldering desires until her body pleaded for appeasement and her heart loved only him, until she was unable to never part with him.

Leigh's mouth fused with his, exploring and tasting the sweet desire within him. He held her so tightly that she could hardly breathe, but she didn't care. Her fingers played in his hair, across his back, along his arms, and down his neck. Every inch of her body tingled and burned. She let her responses tell him she was willing to be conquered and claimed by him, and him alone. She was enslaved to him. Her hand slid down his side and her fingers grasped the prize that could drive her mindless. She stroked it, relishing its warmth and smoothness. "Please, Jace," she entreated him to continue.

Jace moved atop her, and she greeted his arrival with blazing surrender. Her hands wandered up and down his strong back, savoring the feel of his rippling muscles as he labored to sate them. The stimulating sensations were overpowering and wonderful. By instinct her body responded to him. Engulfed by fiery desire, her mouth almost savagely meshed against his and her tongue danced provocatively with his. Her body arched upward over and over, and she seductively wriggled closer to his enticing frame. Wanting and needing him as close and deep as possible, she wrapped her legs around him and clutched him possessively.

Jace increased his pace and force, driving them onward toward rapture. He expertly guided her through the tangled jungle of desire, up the summit of pleasure, and carried them down the other side of the blissful mountain. As he trekked, he was patient and gentle, passionate and tender, taking and giving, pushing his self-control and stamina to their limits. His mouth rested upon hers, then his lips roamed to her neck. "You're mine, Leigh, all mine," he murmured into her ear at the height of their joy. He clasped her to him and rolled to his back, carrying her atop him. His mouth continued to savor her kisses and his fingers stroked her wet back and drifted into her damp hair. In time, his heartbeat returned to normal.

The staggering climax left them weak and shaky. They were exhausted but content. It had been a journey beyond description, beyond comparison, beyond any previous pleasure. Sweat rolled down their sides. The scent of lovemaking hung heavy in the imprisoned air.

Leigh nestled her face to his chest, uncaring that it was soaked from his exertions and the tropical heat. Heavens, she loved this man. She never wanted to be parted from him. She wanted to be his wife, the mother of his children, his partner, his friend, his lover.

"You don't know what you do to me, Leigh," he whispered.

She hugged him tightly. "I know what I hope I do to you; I hope I make you want me more than anything else in your life."

"Is that how I affect you?" he asked, his voice hoarse and husky.

"Yes," she admitted, then kissed him with yearning.

Neither asked probing questions, and neither offered answers to unspoken ones. Neither wanted to force a confrontation now; each wanted trust and a commitment to come willingly. Perhaps all they needed was more time together. Yet each felt hurt and denied, as they had failed to touch completely tonight.

While the safari party was concealed in tall grass, a band of hyenas raced by on their way to seek sleeping cover after their night of feeding on carrion. The carcass eaters reeked of rotten flesh and the stench of death.

Leigh felt queasy and held her nose for a time.

"They trail lions mostly," Jace whispered, "cleaning up after them. Sometimes they shadow pregnant animals so they can gobble up the newborn before its skin is dry from birth. Most people think the hyena is a coward, but he isn't. He can be ruthless and skilled on a hunt. You don't want one to bite you. His jaws and teeth can devour bone as easily as tender flesh. Some tribes leave their dead out at night for those scavengers to bury in their bellies, especially if the person died of a terrible disease and the natives don't want to touch the body. By allowing the hyenas to devour the dead, some natives believe a person's spirit can inhabit the animal and be reborn."

Leigh knew there were scavengers in the human kingdom as well, people who would consume other people, particularly the weak and helpless. Jace had teased her once to beware of "predators like me." She hoped and prayed that's all he was, and not a skulking scavenger.

The trek for lion continued. At the edge of the last

savanna before it swept into foothills, they saw numerous herds of migrating wildebeest. Among them were the ever-present zebra and gazelles. Some herds seemed to stretch for miles on the grasslands, reminding Leigh of what the buffalo must have done long ago on the American plains. An occasional tree offered a few animals shade from the blazing sun. Although peril was never far away, the creatures seemed content to graze and browse peacefully. Yet predators had followed the herd from Tanzania into British East Africa.

A pack of spotted wild dogs—the wolves of Africa, Leigh was told—were closing in on a solitary wildebeest. To her, the wild dog favored the hyena. But, as Jace explained, he was very different.

He motioned to the pack. "There's a bloodthirsty killer for you. A pack will challenge a full-grown and healthy wildebeest. Usually there are five to twenty running together. The wild dog has speed, stamina, and intelligence. They take turns running their quarry to tire it. If the creature falters or doesn't get back to the protection of the herd, like that big boy, they'll rip his flanks and belly open."

Despite her revulsion, Leigh watched the tragic, but natural, sight. The mostly black-and-brown killers had white-tipped tails and broad muzzles. The dogs were sturdy and determined. Their large ears were cocked to catch all sounds of the area and signals from the group. As with a wolf pack, the dogs relentlessly pursued their large prey.

Jace continued, "They offer more danger to the migrating herds than lions, cheetahs, and leopards put together. Watch how they close in on that bull when he fatigues and is forced to make a stand."

Leigh witnessed the beauty, intrigue, and horror of nature. The pack streamed after the wild beast, nipping viciously at it. At last, it halted and challenged its attackers with ineffective horns.

"He's twisting and turning to protect his flanks and belly. Once a pack separates its quarry from cover and help, they usually succeed with the kill. Those teeth are like sharp knives; it'll be over soon."

Leigh wondered if one of the human male beasts with her was trying to separate her from the cover and aid of the other. Presently she felt like secluded prey, helpless and vulnerable and afraid. She felt as if two predators were nipping viciously at her flanks and innards. She had, as the wildebeest, grown exhausted and been compelled to take her last stand. If only her beloved Sir Lance—

"Let's move out," Jace ordered again, tugging at her arm to pull her back to reality. "Did that scene disturb you?"

"A little," she admitted. "Brutal killing should, shouldn't it?"

"I would be stunned if it didn't. Out of ignorance and hunger, that animal made the mistake of getting too far from safety. As you can see, risks and recklessness cause trouble."

Leigh knew his words carried dual meanings, so she listened with care. "Paying with its life seemed unfair for a mistake in judgment."

"That's the way it is out here, Leigh: swift and deadly. If you walk a wild trail, you often get lost or slain."

"I'm not certain I like your Africa, Jace. It's very cruel and unpredictable. I have trouble understanding its secrets and ways."

Jace locked his gaze on hers. "But it's very beautiful, intriguing, and enchanting. It steals your soul if you aren't careful."

"A thief, too?" she quipped, aware Chad had

391

moved closer.

"Is there a problem?" Chad asked as he eyed the two intently.

Leigh smiled and said, "No, just talking about Africa."

They sighted several male lions beneath a tree in the open space. The beasts had tawny manes near their faces that drifted into black hair around their necks. They appeared noble, and had a wild beauty. Their golden eyes had not seen the hunting party, nor had their broad noses detected it. The solitary tree amidst the honey-colored trio was partially de-barked by sharp claws. The large-bodied males were among the finest in Africa, or so Jace claimed. Lions were social creatures who consorted in prides for strength. The hunt was what bound them to-gether. Power, wits, and daring selected the leader.

A pride nearby consisted of five lionesses, cubs of various sizes and ages, and the three males lying in the shade. Each pride claimed a territory, marked by clawed trees and urine-sprayed boundaries. Jace told them how a male would kill the offspring of other males to assert his rank, to allow survival for his heirs, and to put the females in heat.

One male stood and strolled, moving closer to their hiding area upwind, and yawned. "His teeth are yellow and blunt," Jace whispered. "He's battle-scarred and old, so you don't want him. The others are too far away for a clean shot. Let's move on."

The next sighting was no better, as the pride was still too distant. With the beasts in the open, there was no way to sneak closer.

They walked farther, and came upon an attack. Several lionesses brought down a zebra. The hair and whiskers near their mouths were red with fresh blood. As two males approached the kill to feed, a fight took place. In a flurry of bites, growls, and claws, one lost ground and bled profusely. As a gesture of defeat and submission, the loser rolled to his back with his mouth agape. The victor roared, and the loser remained cowered. The big cat tossed its head, shaking its amber and black mane. He stalked to the kill, and all moved aside to relent to his rank. The leader's mouth seized a black-and-white flank and jerked, ripping open a spot where he could begin his feast.

"After he's gorged himself, the others can eat. When they leave to nap, the hyenas and vultures will take over. There won't be anything left in a few days." Jace glanced at the sky. It was getting late. The horizon would soon be blood-red with sunset. "We can't get near enough today. Let's try again tomorrow. We need to reach camp before other predators go on the prowl."

Jace saw Chad talking with two of Jim's men and not the first time, he realized. He worried that Jim and those men were Chad's hirelings. Had he been watching the wrong people? Those men could have easily pulled off those "accidents." If Chad had been spying on him and Leigh, he could know the truth about their love affair. Chad's wooing could be a pretense to fool him and Leigh. The bastard could be after them as originally suspected.

Whatever, he was certain Chad planned to get rid of Leigh because of what she knew. If she held secrets about him, that explained her lack of fear of Chad. But didn't she realize the bastard didn't like loose ends? Maybe Chad had set up him and Leigh from the start, and Louisa was to be his scapegoat. The situation was getting more complicated and he needed answers soon.

As Jace lay on his cot, he reflected on this day of torment and ignorance. He had watched Leigh remove her pith helmet to pour water over her face to cool it. Her wet hair had clung to her beautiful face before drying to a sunny gold. He had wanted to lick the beads of water from lashes surrounding alluring blue eyes. He had yearned to yank her into his imprisoning embrace and never release her.

Once, she had grasped the back of her skirttail, drawn it between her thighs, and tucked the edge over her belt for easier movement. He'd glimpsed her sleek, tawny legs and ached for her. Each time she had spoken to him or looked at him, he had wished he could trust her.

Mercy, that false angel had him so bewildered and flustered and aflame. His mind was in turmoil. Why couldn't he forget her treacherous words? Why hadn't she told him the truth, whatever it was? He had given her many chances to come clean. If she loved him and had nothing to hide, why hadn't she? The safari was almost over and he was no closer to understanding Chad's involvement in those London crimes than when the man arrived. Worse, Leigh now seemed enmeshed. The bet and his wages didn't matter, only exoneration and desire for Leigh.

Jace, Chad, Reid, Johi, and ten bearers departed early to stalk lion: their final quarry. The three women and remaining men were left in or near camp. Chad had worried aloud that the lion hunt was too dangerous for the females, and Jace had ordered them to stay behind today. Mkwawa was told to watch Leigh with his eagle eyes.

The hunting party had been gone for two hours when Louisa told Cynthia, "I'm going to Leigh's tent and get my vengeance right now before someone else does."

"You can't, Louisa; Chad will kill you if you harm her. Here, take your quinine tablet. You've hardly used any of them, and I see you sneaking unboiled water. You're being foolish in both cases."

Louisa pushed aside the outstretched hand with the bitter pill. "Relax, Cynthia. Chad will never know what I've done. It's past time to deal with that blond harlot. Stay here. I mean it."

Louisa peered outside. Mkwawa was working at the table, his back to the tents. She didn't want the head servant to sight her and report to the men, so she crept to Leigh's tent and slipped inside.

Leigh glanced at the hostile woman as she entered the tent and approached the cot where Leigh was reading. "Hello, Louisa."

"It's time you and I have an understanding, my devious rival."

Leigh looked into the woman's cold eyes and concurred. "Perhaps it *is* past time for us to clear the air between us." The blonde had expected trouble ever since the redhead had been put out of Chad's tent.

"You think you're so beautiful and desirable, don't you? You think because you're rich now you can do as you please. You think you can walk into my life and steal my man. Tyler Clark isn't enough for a greedy bitch like you, is he? You crave Chad, and Jace, too. But you won't want either of them after you learn the truth. Chad can rant and rave, but I'm going to tell you."

"What truth is that, Louisa?" Leigh asked, calm and vexing.

The redhead's malicious words wiped the taunting smile from her rival's lips and eyes. "It isn't about those stupid bets you and Chad have with Jace. Not even about the secret one you have with our handsome guide." When Leigh's eyes widened in surprise, Louisa scoffed, "Yes, I know about all of them. I do have ways of extracting information from men. I was hoping both Chad and Jace would realize they aren't the hunters and you aren't the prey; it's the other way around. They only thought they were winning you, but you're duping both of them. Would you like to know why they really made that wager? Why both of them are so eager to get their hands on you? It isn't your virginal body or huge inheritance, Miss Webster; it's for revenge. Has either of them mentioned Joanna Harris to you?"

Leigh came to full alert. "Who is Joanna Harris?"

The redhead glared at Leigh. "I see; neither of them told you about her. I'm not surprised; it would spoil their wicked sport. She's more beautiful and desirable than both of us put together, but she was gullible and weak. She's what happened between two good friends. She's the reason they hate each other. After that trouble in South Africa, Jace and Chad were at each other's throats and doing all they could to spite each other. Joanna Harris was supposed to move to Africa with Jace as soon as everything was prepared here. While Jace was gone, Chad charmed and seduced Joanna. The bitch moved in with Chad. When Jace returned to London, he was furious. They got into a fight. Jace was jailed for a month for nearly killing Chad. On Chad's orders Miss Joanna refused to visit Jace in prison and explain. When Jace was released, Joanna still refused to see him or to leave Chad. Jace left London swearing revenge on Chad. That's what this little wager is about, you blind girl, another woman! Jace wants to take Joanna's replacement and all she owns away from Chad. And Chad, he's flaunting you in Jace's face because he thinks he has you hooked and turned against Jace. Chad didn't consider Joanna's conquest and ruin enough punishment for what Jace had done to him."

Leigh was stunned. "You're full of lies and hatred, Louisa."

The redhead laughed. "You know I'm telling the truth."

Leigh knew such words could be checked out too easily for her to lie. She wondered if that woman was the missing clue to the mystery, as Louisa alleged. "Where is this Joanna Harris?"

"After Chad was finished with her, he discarded her, just like he'll do with you after you've served your purpose. Joanna was very special to Jace Elliott. It was quite a scandal. Jace wouldn't forgive her or take her back, so Joanna was forced to leave town. Jace hates Chad for destroying her. I wouldn't be surprised if Chad is responsible for those London crimes as Jace suspects. Frankly I don't care. I think William Webster either discovered or realized the truth, and it caused his heart to fail. Chad and Jace despise each other. This wager and safari were for revenge. That's all you mean to either of them. Oh, I know he's discarding me for you. I know Chad craves your wealth and the firm, but those are merely added benefits. What he's truly after is destroying Jace Elliott for trying to kill him in South Africa and for stealing his diamonds," Louisa charged, having learned that fact from Cynthia, who had gleaned it from a drunken Reid.

"You've never seen Chad without his shirt. Have you wondered why? I'll tell you. He and Jace hired out as guards for a peace mission to warring Matabeles. On a dare from one of the men, Chad stole a sacred knife from their leader. The natives tracked him and abducted him. Every morning and night, they used the ritual knife to carve one of their pagan symbols on his back and chest. They poured a stinging liquid over the cuts to make him scream and beg. When his torso was fully marked, they were going to sacrifice him to their god. Every night he was kept suspended from a tree. I'm surprised the insects eating on those wounds didn't give him a disease and kill him. Luckily those savages didn't harm his handsome face. Chad used it to charm one of the native girls into freeing him, the chief's daughter. She led him to safety, then he killed her to punish her father. You know the other details of that misadventure, or what each man claims is the truth."

"If Lord Chadwick Hamilton is so terrible, Lady Louisa," Leigh scoffed, "why are you trying to kill me to get him? What do you want with a wicked earl, and at such a risk and price?"

"Are you crazy?" Louisa retorted. "Don't you realize Chad and Jace are behind those incidents just to turn you in their favor? Don't be so blind and naive. What good would it do me to risk prison to kill you? Chad would only find another woman to conquer. Why don't you confront them when they return to camp? I dare you. If you don't, I will. I swear it. I'm ready for this game to end. Chad has used me and humiliated me for the last time. They should return at sunset. We'll both be ready to greet them. Chad told me he was going to marry me when we returned to London. He said I was a problem between you and him, that you would fire him to get rid of me. I moved out of his tent to appease you. After thinking it over and watching you two lately, I know he lied."

"Yes, he did lie to you. He asked me to marry him. I said yes."

"You *what?*"

Leigh enjoyed the look of shock, then fury on the woman's face. "I also told Jace I would marry him. I'm not as stupid as you all think, Louisa. It was only a trick until I returned home and got rid of both of them. You can have Chad or Jace, or both. I'm only playing with them to keep the peace, nothing more, you bitch."

"Are you telling the truth? I don't trust you."

"No more than I trust you," Leigh scoffed. "But it's the truth."

"Why did you lie to me about your sweetheart in Texas?"

"To shut you up and to halt your petty jealousy. You were so damned worried about me stealing Chad that you never realized I didn't want him. I never have, and I never will. There is one thing you should know, Louisa. This may have begun as a plot for revenge, but Chad is really in love with me. So is Jace. It seems both got snared in their traps for me. That's a real shame."

"Love doesn't change your mind about them?" she hinted.

"No," Leigh replied in a cold tone. "I could never desire or trust either of them. As with you, I don't like being used, duped, or entrapped. I'm selling the firm—but not to Chad—and I'm going home to America after the safari. Both men can simmer and suffer for all I care. As for you, you deserve a snake like Lord Chadwick Hamilton, and he deserves a bitch like *Lady* Louisa Jennings."

The redhead glared at the blonde, mentally vowing she'd be dead soon and trouble her no more, and left the tent unseen.

399

As Leigh lay on her cot with her eyes closed, she waxed between alarm, anguish, and anger. Another woman was not the missing clue she had expected to find. Her treacherous lover had duped her for the last time, and so had her devious guardian. She yearned to get far away from all of these hateful scavengers.

Leigh looked up as one of the men from the safari sneaked into her tent. She was seized, disabled, and forced to drink a bitter drug. As blackness engulfed her, she knew the ruse was over . . .

Chapter Seventeen

Later, Jace entered camp and greeted Mkwawa. Louisa and Cynthia left their tent to join him. "Where's Leigh?" Jace inquired.

"In her tent, reading, as usual. Where are the others?"

"Reid nicked a lion," Jace responded. "Wounded predators are dangerous to the natives, so the law says a guide must trail an injured beast and slay it to prevent trouble. We're supposed to meet back here. I guess they're still hunting with Johi and the men. I'll fetch Leigh for a nice walk before Chad returns. This is a lucky break for me. If you ladies will excuse me . . ."

Louisa followed the whistling male to Leigh's tent. Through the mosquito netting, she and Jace saw the blonde lying on the ground, with a decapitated reptile nearby. She grinned maliciously.

Jace yanked the thin flap aside and dropped to his knees. He examined Leigh and said, "Bush snake. They're deadly. It's been some time since she was bitten. See how the area's discolored. Damn! Hardly anybody survives such a bite."

"He's so big." Louisa stated the obvious. "Is she . . ."

Jace listened to Leigh's heart. "Not good. It's too

late to cut the wound and suck out the venom. There's a Kikuyu village a few hours away. If anybody can save her, it's the witch doctor there. It's probably a waste of time," he mumbled. As he worked, he fumed aloud, "How the hell did he get in here and why did she challenge him? Bush snakes normally avoid clearings, and they'll crawl out of your path if you give 'em time. She should have screamed and run, or stayed on the cot. Hell, at least she got him, too. I'll return or send word as soon as possible. Don't tell Chad but I doubt she'll make it. Let me handle him when I get back." He lifted Leigh, tossed her over his shoulder, and rushed from camp.

The servants, other bearers, and the brunette gathered around the clearing. "What happened?" Cynthia asked.

"Little Leigh was bitten by a deadly snake. Jace thinks she's too far gone to save. He's rushing her to a local witch doctor. I wonder how Chad will take this news."

Mkwawa shook his head and murmured, "Bwana Jace waste time. Bush snake fatal. See faces of men. They know she dead, too."

Louisa watched the natives toss the snake into the campfire and begin to sing with lowered heads. "What are they doing?"

"They destroy enemy. They pray for her spirit to find peace. She dead by now. Bwana Jace be sad. She good woman."

Hours later, the hunting party returned to camp with a large lion Reid had shot. The men were laughing and talking as they entered the clearing. The singing bearers carried the trophy suspended

402

from a heavy pole by bound legs. Its tawny-and-black mane swayed with their movements, and water dripped from his ears and tail. A heavy rain was falling, but the soaked and jubilant men did not care. The lion was to be prepared and transported after the rain ceased.

Unmindful she was getting drenched, Louisa hurried to meet them. "There's been a terrible accident, Chad. Leigh is—"

Chad slapped the redhead and shouted, "What did you do to her this time, you jealous bitch?"

Louisa rubbed her stinging cheek and glared at the man. "Nothing, you bastard! She was bitten by a snake."

Chad pushed his ex-mistress aside and rushed toward Leigh's tent. It was dark and empty. "Where is she?" he asked.

"Dead," Louisa informed him. "But I'm not to blame."

"Where is she?" Chad yelled again at the belligerent woman.

"Jace returned and took her to a witch doctor to see if the man could save her. Mkwawa and the others said such a bite was always fatal."

Mkwawa explained to the startled men what had happened.

"Where is this village? Take me there immediately!"

"Which one, Mkwawa?" Johi asked.

"I know not, Wanjohi. Three are near."

"We'll track him," Chad suggested.

"How can we? The rain leaves no trail."

"It's a trick," Chad shouted. "He's stolen my love!"

"No, it isn't," Louisa argued. "We all saw her. She had two bleeding holes on her leg. The area was

403

yellow and green and reddish-blue. She was unconscious, hardly breathing. The snake was killed and burned. The bearers said—"

"I don't give a damn what they said! I want to see her."

The rainfall was hard and heavy. It pelted noisily on the large leaves and tents. It beat upon the people grouped together. The campfire was extinguished. The clearing was saturated, making the ground soft and mushy. Mud splattered on everyone's boots. Daylight was vanishing in the almost blinding rain and impending dusk.

As water poured over him, Chad murmured, "She can't be dead."

"Why, because you think she was going to marry you?" Louisa scoffed, her curry-colored locks flattened against her pale skin. Water streamed off her hair and over her sullen face. She kept blinking her narrowed eyes to clear them. Her shirt and skirt clung to her body. "Or did you realize you'd lost her to Jace and had her killed? I know how desperately you craved her."

"You whore! Get out of my sight! You're nothing compared to her. If Jace has stolen her, I'll kill him. By damn, I'll kill him!"

"I'll get you a strong drink, Chad," Reid said, and fetched it.

Chad downed the Scotch with one gulp. "I don't believe this."

"They can't all be lying, Chad," the other man reasoned.

"They were fooled," Chad argued before the crowd of men.

"You're pathetic," Louisa sneered and ran inside.

Cynthia glanced from Reid to Chad, then followed Louisa.

"Let's get out of this downpour," Reid advised.

Drenched, Jace stalked from the jungle. He went straight to Chad and slugged the man across the jaw. The blow sent Chad to the muddy ground. "What did you do this time, old friend," Jace shouted. "Have a deadly snake put in her tent? I let both of you convince me you weren't a threat to her. I thought you had changed; you seemed to be returning to your old self. I should have known that was impossible. You sorry bastard, you didn't have to kill her to punish me again!"

"Where is Leigh?" Chad asked, looking behind Jace.

Fury and coldness exuded Jace. "Right where you sent her, to her grave. If you wanted her money this badly, she would have given it to you. Hell, I would have helped you get it so she could live." Jace's expression and tone altered to sadness, then bitterness. "You didn't have to kill her, Chad. She lied, didn't she? You do inherit, don't you?"

Chad did not get up, as if the grim news made him weak. Mud oozed between his spread fingers, and water pooled around them. Rain flowed in rivulets over his black hair and pale face. He lowered his head to protect his eyes and nose from filling. "No, my mother does. But I didn't harm Leigh. She can't be dead. What did you do with her? I'll have the authorities on your back tomorrow."

Jace looked surprised, then angry. "So that's why you came here! That's your plot, isn't it? Kill Leigh and frame me. Why, because your first frame didn't get me killed? How can you hate me this much and for so long? Dammit, man, I didn't betray you. I don't deserve all this torment. It has to end, Chad. Why don't we have a duel here and now to settle this destructive war for good?"

405

"This isn't a game, Jace. I love her. I want to marry her. Bring her back and I'll do anything you say. I'll give you all the money, and I'll confess to the crimes. I just want Leigh."

Reid pulled Chad to his feet. "Can't you see he's tricking you into confessing to anything? It's your grief talking, Chad. She's dead. Nothing you say or do can bring her back. Stop this nonsense."

Chad looked at Jace and glared. "She's dead, and you're using that to get revenge on me. You're the one trying to frame me. You killed her and I know why!"

"If this wasn't a setup to look like another accident," Jace reasoned in a tight voice, "why did she have a bush knife in her hand? Did you hire some of Jim's men to do your dirty work for you?"

A servant shook Jace's arm and said, "I give her the knife. She asked. Little gun gone. She was afraid. It was kindness."

Louisa returned. "You're both fools. After you left camp this morning, Leigh said she wanted to 'clear the air between us.' She didn't trust either one of you . . ." she began. Then, without revealing her side of the conversation, she told them what Leigh had related. "You're both fools. She was duping both of you."

Chad asked Jace, "She agreed to marry you, too?"

Jace gaped at Louisa. "No, she didn't. I never proposed. I don't know why she would tell Louisa such a tale. Maybe for the same reason she lied about that beau in America. That doesn't change anything, Chad. You're to blame for this. I would have persuaded her to marry me. Everything was going fine until recently. You did or said something to turn her against me. What was it? Did you tell her about Joanna, tell her I was after her for revenge?"

406

"I never mentioned Joanna to Leigh," Chad yelled over the loud rain. "You're up to something. If Leigh's dead, I want to see her body."

Jace's jaw tightened and his eyes narrowed. "What do you think I did with her? Left her bound to a tree in the jungle?"

"I think you left her in that village, sick or captive."

"If it's proof you want, you'll get it at first light."

"How do I know you'll take me to the right village?"

Jace looked ready to strangle the man. "You'll know when we dig up her grave and you see her body. It won't be a pretty sight. You know what happens after a tropical snakebite."

"Why didn't you bring her back to camp?"

"And fight off hyenas and vultures all the way. You know what they do when they smell dead flesh. They would have attacked and devoured her. You couldn't want such a fate for her. In the morning, I'll take you to the Kikuyu village and you can dig her up."

"That's morbid, Chad," Reid said. "You know what condition she'll be in. Don't look at her like that. Jace is in too much trouble to fake her death. Besides, he wouldn't want you and your mother claiming her inheritance. She's dead. Accept it."

"Let him come with me, Reid," Jace almost demanded, "that's the only way he'll believe me. I tried to save her, so don't you try to pin another crime on me. I dare you to check her grave and body!"

In his emotional state, Chad concluded that Jace was too willing and eager to show him Leigh's bloated and discolored body for her death not to be real. Chad wiped the rain from his smarting eyes, but they filled again in the deluge. "Get me out of this damn jungle in the morning. Rain or not, we're heading for home."

"Can't wait to get back to spend her money?" Jace taunted.

"No, I can't wait to be rid of you for good. I'll pay you the twenty-five thousand pounds in Mombasa. Neither of us wins the bet."

"Losing yours doesn't matter. Losing hers does. I know the snake killed her, but I'm not convinced it wasn't slipped into her tent."

"Neither am I," Chad vowed, hatred gnawing at him. Distress filled the man's gaze. "Surely you didn't kill her because of my mistake with Joanna and your other crazy suspicions. How could you?"

Jace glared at him. "No, you sorry bastard, I didn't kill her." He fetched a bottle of Scotch and a metal cup. He dropped wearily into a chair and began to drink. "I almost had her. Damn you for intruding and getting her killed. I should never have left her in camp today. I knew she was in danger from you and Louisa."

"I had nothing to do with this, Jace," Louisa declared.

"But you had something to do with those other incidents, didn't you, bitch?" Chad accused. "That London attack, those gun problems, and that trouble at Fort Jesus. How else could you have known about them? You've been plotting against her the whole time! I'll kill you."

"You aren't going to put the blame on me; I won't be framed, damn you. Leigh told me about those incidents. I didn't mention them because I thought you and Leigh set them up to ensnare Jace's interest in her so he'd be our guide and so he'd lose the wager with you. I'm innocent, so I won't stand here and be insulted." She fled to her tent.

408

Johi touched Jace's shoulder and said, "Bwana Jace—"

"Leave me alone, Johi," Jace mumbled. "All of you, leave me alone. Lordy, she was too beautiful and gentle to die like that. Why couldn't that snake have attacked one of you?" He took the bottle and cup, and trudged through the rain and mud to his tent.

Johi watched, looked sad and worried, then shook his head. He walked toward the bearer camp nearby.

"It's over, Chad. Let's get inside."

Johi skirted the area and slipped behind Chad's tent.

The two men entered. Reid tossed Chad a dry shirt and said, "There's nothing we can do now but return home. It wasn't all wasted; you have Webster International."

Chad felt drained. "I wanted Leigh *and* the firm."

"You can't have her; she's gone. Don't let this loosen your wits and tongue, old friend. You were planning to kill her."

"That was before I met Leigh and fell in love with her."

"That's right, but you changed your mind again. You realized she was duping you, so you were going to kill her after we reached this camp. You changed your plan again because of what she told you during that walk. Don't you see how confused you've been?"

"She loved me and was going to marry me. She was fooling Jace."

"You only have her claims she was duping him."

"She didn't lie, Reid."

"Then why is Jace so crushed by her death?"

"He wanted her, too. We both lost this time."

"What are you going to do about him? He's still

409

after you."

Chad's mind and body were numbing fast. "Nothing. Revenge got me into this trouble. I was going to lure Leigh here, kill her, and frame Jace. That all changed after her arrival in London. I decided to marry her and forget about Jace. I didn't hurt her with those drugs in her canteen; I only did it to make her sick so I could cancel the safari and get her away from Jace. Then you and Louisa convinced me they were lovers, and I wanted to kill them both. I would have, if Leigh hadn't told me everything during our walk. That talk told me you and that bitch were wrong. Leigh would have married me."

Reid knew he couldn't reach Chad's deluded mind. "Do you think Jace pulled those other tricks? Or Louisa?"

Chad sank to his cot. "Yes, but what difference does it make now? My love is dead. Don't talk anymore. I'm tired."

At dawn, Chad left his tent and hurried through the rain and mud to Leigh's. He found Jace sitting on her cot, holding one of Leigh's shirts against his lowered face. "What are you doing in here?"

Jace lowered the garment and stared at Chad. He hadn't shaved and he looked exhausted. "I held her in my arms and I saw her die, but I still can't believe she's gone. We did this to her, old friend. If you hadn't insisted on leaving that last camp ahead of schedule, she wouldn't have been in this area yesterday. And it was your order to leave the women behind so you could kill your big lion. I should have been the one giving orders, but she had me too distracted to keep my mind on business. What do you want to do with her things?" Jace lifted a book and glanced at it. He picked up her brush, pulled blond strands from the bristles, and gazed at them. He kicked at the boots near the cot supports, then cradled the Leigh-scented shirt again.

Chad glanced around the tent, and anguish filled his eyes. "Burn it. Burn it all. I couldn't stand to look at this stuff all the way back, and nobody is touching or taking her things. When can we leave?"

Jace stood and flexed. "Mighty anxious to get to London, aren't we? We can't pack up and leave until the rain stops."

Chad looked outside. "When will that be? It's still pouring."

"By midday. This is our long rainy season. It's over in June, a week from today. You should have checked out the seasons before you planned this damned trip. If you'd waited until June . . ."

Chad hadn't slept, either, and his wits were dulled. It was as if the bad years between them slipped away for a time, and two old friends were sharing a grim moment. "I didn't think about it. I only wanted to get Leigh away so I could . . ."

Jace noticed the man's mood. Almost tonelessly he said, "You should have remembered. This isn't your first trip to Africa. That's when this whole mess started. If you hadn't stolen that ritual knife and provoked those Matabeles, none of this would have happened. You're lucky they left that handsome face of yours alone, but the women you've snared with it weren't so lucky. We've warred a long time, Chad. Look how it's ended. We're a fine pair of fools and losers. Joanna and Leigh are gone. We've been hating each other and battling for years. I really thought we could make a truce. Hell, I was stupid and gullible enough to believe you when you offered one. Sometimes I think about our years as best

411

friends, and I miss them. I still can't understand how this happened to us. It makes me mad. Lordy, I'm tired."

Chad looked the suffering man over. "You look terrible. Did you sit here drinking all night?"

"Most of it, but it didn't help." Jace stood and flexed. He rubbed his stubbled jawline and weary eyes. He finger-combed his tousled hair. "Why don't we rest and hunt here for another week while we clear our heads?" the green-eyed man suggested. "You still have three paid weeks of your safari. Leaving isn't going to change matters."

"I have to get home and forget this . . . accident. There'll be a lot of changes to handle. She would have been damned good at that firm. I took her around several days. She is so smart and quick."

"Was, Chad. *Was* smart and quick. Where is your mother?"

Chad sighed deeply. "In India. She went there with friends to get over William's death. This news will shock her. Of course she barely knew Leigh. But *I* knew her. What happened, Jace?"

"What do you mean?" Jace probed the weary man.

"To us. Here. Why did she have to die when everything was going so well? No woman has touched me as Leigh Webster did. We could have been so happy together. You and I could have made peace and become friends again. Her love taught me to forgive you. Why did fate hurt me again? I didn't do anything wrong this time. It's this land. Africa!" he accused in bitterness and mind-dazing grief. "I have to get away from here before something else happens to me."

"It's a hundred kilometers to the Athi River," Jace related. "I'll send two bearers ahead to hail boats.

Plenty of them use the river to transport goods close to Nairobi. Then carts take supplies on into town. Traveling by river will be easier and faster with all this rain to raise the water level."

"How far and long to Mombasa?"

"The Athi converges with the Tsovo and Galana. That'll put us two days from the rail line. We can camp there until the next supply load passes, then catch a ride." Jace murmured as he figured the time and distance, "About five or six days to the river, about the same to the Galana, two or three days to the rail line, half-day by train. That should get us to Mombasa by June eighth or so, about two weeks more or less. It all depends on the rains and stops."

"Lets get out of here as soon as we can."

"Would you like me to take you to that Kikuyu village to visit Leigh's grave?" Jace asked. "She had a decent burial. We can be there and back before everything is loaded."

"No, I want to remember her as she was, beautiful and vital."

"I'll leave Thiku behind. When this tent dries, he can burn it all. I never want to use it again. Since we've used a lot of supplies, we don't need as many bearers on the way back. I'll release some of them at the river to head home to Nairobi." As if that jogged his memory, Jace murmured, "I wonder how Jim Hanes is doing with his cracked leg. It's been weeks, so it should be almost healed by now. I may stop in Nairobi on my return home and check on him. Leigh might still be alive if Jim had been your guide; he uses different hunting locations. It seems that everything worked into cruel fate's hands this time. This safari was doomed from the start. But you and I were too caught up in our trouble to read the danger signs, and we had plenty of them along the way. So

413

many curious incidents should have warned us of peril. Dammit, why didn't I keep my wits clear?"

Those words jogged Chad's memory, and cleared part of his wits. Jim was supposed to be in Mombasa awaiting payment for his ruse. Considering the passage of time and easy travel on the river and train, Jace shouldn't be surprised to see the other safari guide in town. If he hadn't been determined to kill his old friend, Jim would have been their guide, and Leigh would be alive. Guilt chewed at Chad. He had to leave before his grief revealed something incriminating. "I'll go pack" was all he said, and left.

Jace sighed in relief and knew the hardest part of this scheme was done. His behavior and words had duped the distraught Chad. He relaxed his taut muscles and smiled in victory. He reclined on Leigh's cot, closed his eyes, and envisioned the scene in her tent yesterday.

While keeping a watch on the camp through the tent flap covering, Jace had smeared a greenish-yellow mixture onto Leigh's flesh, pinching the selected area hard to produce a reddish-blue spot. He used his sharp hunting knife to pierce two tiny holes in the unconscious blonde's leg. He watched blood seep from the round wounds and ease over her discolored calf. He wiped the sterilized blade and put it into its sheath at his waist, then poured antiseptic over the injury. He placed her on the ground as if she had collapsed, then laid the deadly bush snake, with its decapitated head and long body, that he had killed beside her. A bloody machete was placed near her right hand.

Jace gathered Leigh a change of clothes for the five-day trip to his plantation. He added one washcloth, one drying cloth, a bar of soap, and the extra brush he had brought with him for this occasion. He

414

couldn't take too many things or it would arouse the others' suspicions. Besides, he had left a note from "Leigh Webster" ordering her possessions to be shipped to America, to await her arrival there: that trick should confuse Chad. Yet his man was not to deliver her baggage to the ship; he was to take it to Jace's home as requested by Jace. Suspecting from the start that Leigh's life was in peril, Jace had made plans to remove her from jeopardy the moment he felt the situation demanded action. That time had arrived, thankfully in this advantageous location. When all appeared in order for his daring ploy, he brushed away evidence of his presence and sneaked out the back of Leigh's tent into the jungle.

Later he returned to complete his ruse in camp. He met Buha and Jomo at the assigned place. The men and supplies were ready. He stuffed quinine tablets and a note into her possessions. He washed the colorful deception from the injured area, tended the wounds with medicine to prevent infection, and rebandaged her leg. They talked a few minutes in Swahili, then Jace said, "You know what to do with her. You took care of the fake grave at the village in case Chad demands to see it? The chief will go along with our trick?"

The men nodded to both questions, took the lovely burden, and left the area. Jace sat down to rest. He would return to camp after dark with the grim news of Leigh Webster's death. Considering the legal charges that already existed against him, this could make matters worse. By faking Leigh's death, two people would take over her holdings, and he wanted to know those names. At least, it wouldn't be Chad or Fiona, he mused, and Leigh would be alive to straighten out the ruse later, if he ever released her. His scheme had worked so far. He had Leigh at his mercy or he had her safe, whichever proved to be true. She would be held captive at his plantation until he guided the others back to Mombasa. Then . . .

Jace halted the dreamy reflection. He got off the cot, glanced around the tent, then hurried to his. Thiku would be ordered to pack Leigh's remaining possessions and take them to the plantation not far from Nairobi. She should be delighted to have her belongings again. The books would give her something to do during the next three to four weeks before his arrival home. He knew the rain would halt soon. Then he could get these people gone, and return home himself. He hadn't learned anything from Chad about those London crimes, but he recalled how Chad—and Reid—had behaved last night.

Jace's green eyes narrowed and darkened as Johi joined him and gave a shocking report. He now knew the motive for Chad's trip, and the unexpected change in the man's plot. Leigh had been right about her guardian's love and innocence. The haunting question was, if Chad hadn't been trying to kill Leigh, who had, and why? With luck and stealth, perhaps he could get the answer during the return trip.

Leigh became aware of a bouncing movement. Her mouth was dry, her head cloudy. The sun was playing on her face through the trees and she heard birds and monkeys chattering overhead. A strange weakness assailed her body and she tried to force open her heavy lids, but they refused to work. She dozed again.

When she aroused, Leigh saw that she was being

carried by two brown-skinned bearers on a makeshift stretcher. The two men were loaded with packs. Her clothes and hair had dried, so she was unaware of yesterday's rain. The sun's position indicated it was afternoon. "Stop!" she commanded. "Where are you taking me?" She leaned to one side, glancing before and behind them. "Where are the others?"

The men spoke to each other in their language, and halted. They lowered the stretcher. One passed her a canteen.

Leigh stared at the water container. Images of Jace flooded her head. He had sneaked into her tent, pinned her down, held her nose, and forced her to drink a bitter liquid. Now she was alone with these two men, his men. "What's going on?" she demanded.

One man pointed to himself and said, "Jomo." He motioned to the other and said, "Buha." He untied a bundle and handed her a note.

Leigh took the paper and read it:

Dear Miss Webster,

Jomo and Buha do not speak English. They will take good care of you. Don't forget your quinine tablets every day. Drink only the water they provide. They will not harm you if you behave yourself, but they are ordered to make certain you do as told. Escape is impossible. They're taking you to my home to await my arrival. I should be there within three to four weeks. Abena will see to your needs. Don't try anything reckless or foolish. A few words you might need: *asante* is thank you, *ndiyo* is yes, *hapana* is no, *chakula* is food, *maji* is water, *kula* is eat, *lala* is sleep, *acheni* is stop, *bibi* is lady, and *iyoo* means you need to be excused.

Good luck. You'll need it, my golden lioness, my deceitful beauty. Soon all your secrets and charms will be mine.

Jace

Leigh eyed the two men and plundered through the bundle. Jace must have assumed Chad told her about their wager that day because he had started acting strangely afterward. If this was a trick to save her life or one to keep them together, why hadn't he told her and enlisted her approval and aid? His note was far from a love letter. Something was terribly wrong. She was astonished by Jace's boldness. She could not imagine how he hoped to get away with such a deed. Surely Chad was enraged by now and would have the authorities searching for her soon. Surely the first place they would look was the plantation. Jace would never kill all of them just to kidnap her!

Her mind was in a maelstrom. He could have faked an abduction by natives, particularly if he had an unshakable alibi this time, such as the others on the hunt not knowing he had sneaked away for a time. Farfetched though it was, he could have hired friendly natives to dress as savage warriors to fool Louisa and Cynthia into being witnesses to her false kidnapping.

Leigh knew that Jace wasn't rash or stupid or crazy. There had to be a way for him to carry out this treachery without endangering or incriminating himself. How, she fretted, and why? She noticed the bandage on her leg. She yanked it off and gaped at the injury that appeared to be a snakebite. More wild speculations raced through her mind. Even if he faked a bite, how could he fake her death? How could he get her "body" away from Chad? Even if he

418

pulled this stunt before the others reached camp, Chad would insist on viewing the evidence of her death.

Jomo brushed away mosquitoes and flies from the tiny wounds and rebandaged her leg to protect it. He offered her water again.

Leigh took the canteen and drank. It did not take long to realize it was not drugged, but Jace's wicked deed in her tent made her suspicious of those other drugging incidents. She could not help but believe he had been behind them. She had given him a last chance to be honest with her, and this was his response. She ate the bread and tropical fruit handed to her. All she could do was obey the men. As Jace's note warned, she could not escape into the perilous jungle. In a short time, she was feeling strong and healthy again.

The men gathered their burdens, placed Leigh between them, and their journey continued.

That night, camp consisted of a protective fire, three bedrolls under mosquito netting, a few supplies, and the three people. The two men talked to each other, but Leigh could not understand them. She wished she knew more African words than Jace had supplied. A lion roared in the distance. She clutched her cover to her neck and wished for a weapon. Despite her tension and doubts, she fell asleep soon, the walk having exhausted her.

They traveled for three days, trekking through the jungle and across grasslands without sighting anyone. Each night, Jomo boiled water and filled their canteens. Buha hunted small game and fruit for their meals. The two men shared camp chores. They allowed her to slip behind underbrush whenever she said, *"Iyoo."* They even corrected her pronunciations of their words and taught her a few more. If only she knew how to say, "help," "crime," and "reward for rescue." But even if she could, she doubted it would matter to them.

On the second evening, she had been permitted to bathe in a safe pool where water cascaded from a foothill. She had donned clean garments and washed the others, which would be dry by morning to pack. Leigh was glad Jace had sent along a few extra items.

On the third day, Jomo had whispered, *"Acheni."*

Leigh had stopped as ordered. Jomo had pointed to a leopard on early prowl. They had hidden until the spotted predator was gone. Leigh had been nervous, but the two men had carbines. She hadn't been tempted to steal or to snatch one to escape, as she knew she could never make it out of the jungle alone. She didn't even know which direction to take to civilization and safety.

During the trek, the two men called her "Bibi Leigh." They were friendly, protective, and kind.

On what she assumed was the fifth day since her abduction, Jomo pointed ahead to reveal Jace's home.

Leigh was amazed by what loomed before her wide eyes. There was an enormous clearing where coffee bushes covered the ground for a long distance. She noticed native workers amongst them.

Foothills surrounded the clearing, slopes with lush vegetation and trees. There was a huge open shed with equipment. A few hundred yards from it was a white wall that encircled the large home. Between solid sections, there was iron fencing. No doubt, she mused, to keep out wild animals while allowing for scenic views and air flow, and too high to scale for escape. So, this was Green Hills Plantation. She realized how aptly it was named.

Leigh followed the two men to a gate. It was open. They did not enter, but Jomo called to the housekeeper. She stared at what reminded her of a Spanish hacienda with its woodwork, style, white exterior, arched walkway, and red roof. The yards were clean. Floral bushes and tropical plants created a beautiful and tranquil setting. A swing for two was suspended from the branch of a large tree. A water-supply system could be seen over the roof: a giant container to catch rainwater, then pipes to let off the excess and carry it inside. She guessed the encompassing white-painted wall was ten feet high. She glanced through the decorative iron fencing that was located every ten feet or so along the wall. She scanned her surroundings again. Everything was breathtaking, incredible. She had difficulty believing she was in the middle of a jungle in Africa.

"*Jambo,* Abena. *Habari?*" Jomo greeted the stocky African woman who joined them and asked how she was doing.

"*Mzuri. Karibu. Habari ya safari?*" Abena told them she was fine, welcomed them, and asked how their journey went.

After the three Africans talked a few minutes, the older woman met the blonde's gaze and said, "Welcome, Bibi Leigh. You expected. I here to serve you. Come inside to rest."

"You speak English," Leigh murmured in surprise and relief.

"I speak good English, for many years. *Kwaheri,*" she told the two men good-bye. "Come. Must eat, rest, bathe."

Leigh observed the woman of about fifty who was

short and plump. Abena wore a colorful shift in native material. A matching bandanna concealed her hair. The woman smiled, exposing white teeth amidst a deep brown complexion. Her chocolate eyes sparkled with interest and friendliness. "Where is your daughter, Ka'arta?" Leigh tested Jace's words from that day in Mombasa.

"Ka'arta lives in village. She helps missionary speak to our people. She knows English more than Abena. When coffee berries ripe, she helps pick. She go Mombasa with Wanjohi for supplies. I work day for Bwana Jace. I go home night. I be close. No need to fear."

"Bwana Jace kidnapped me," Leigh charged. "That's against the law. He'll be arrested and taken to prison. You must let me go."

Unruffled, Abena asked, "Go where?"

"Home."

"You far from home. Must stay inside and be safe." The woman closed the gate, locked it, and dropped the key into her pocket. "Come," she coaxed, and walked toward the house.

Clutching her small bundle, Leigh followed the woman. "You must help me escape, Abena, or you'll be in trouble, too. What Jace did is wrong, bad. Lawmen will come after me and him."

Abena halted and turned. Displeased, she refuted, "Bwana Jace not bad, never wrong. He say keep you safe. He law here."

"You don't understand, Abena," Leigh reasoned. "Jace and I are enemies. He tried to hurt me, to kill me. He stole me from my family. I will not stay in his home."

The woman looked Leigh over and frowned. "No speak evil of Bwana Jace. No man good and kind as him."

"You don't know what he's like. He's mean and—"

The older woman backed away a few steps. She no longer smiled. "Say no more, Bibi Leigh. When comes home, you tell him such things. Abena his friend and servant. I cannot help you."

Leigh watched the woman enter the house. She realized the servant would not listen to her accusations or aid her escape. She glanced at the locked gate, the high wall, and the iron fence. Jail! she fretted. Jace had captured her and imprisoned her. She wondered why. If he intended to murder her, she would be dead by now. Perhaps, she worried, Chad had told him what she said about not honoring her bet. Louisa had learned about all wagers, so she could have told Jace with the hopes he would get her out of Chad's life. Perhaps Jace merely planned to force her to pay her debt to him . . .

Leigh was alarmed, afraid, and angry. There was no escape without help, and no one here would provide it. She must make friends with the housekeeper and workers. It would be a mistake to turn them against her. Perhaps in time . . . But how much time did she have before Jace arrived to collect?

Leigh was intimidated by doubts and fears. She decided to think about them later. She went inside the house, astonished by what greeted her alert senses. The living area was enormous, open and airy. The heavy furniture was in dark wood, and was spaced well in the room. The floors were polished and shiny and the high ceilings were beamed with dark wood, making a lovely contrast to the white walls and light-colored fabrics. Plants were here and there in various-size containers. Several paintings— all African scenes and animals—hung on the walls. Other African objects were placed at vantage points. A piano sat near one corner. Decorative oil lamps and candleholders were sources of light after dark. Drapes were pulled aside and belted. Mesh screens of a thin material covered the windows and doors to keep out insects. It was impressive and immaculate.

Leigh heard noises. She followed them through an archway into a dining room, then into a kitchen. There she saw a sink, working counters, a wood stove, cabinets, a round table with four chairs, and the servant. Abena was preparing food for her.

Leigh approached the woman and said, "I'm sorry if I upset you, Abena, but I'm upset. I'm scared and confused. I don't know why Jace drugged me and kidnapped me. He and my uncle are terrible enemies. Suspicious accidents kept happening to me on the safari. Jace kept threatening me. I don't know why I'm a prisoner."

The woman softened. "Bwana Jace have good reason. He tell you why when he comes home."

"When is he arriving? How did he explain my abduction? He'll be in terrible trouble for doing this. My uncle will have the law after him. I must go to Mombasa to show him I'm alive and well. Please have the men take me there. I promise to keep Jace out of trouble."

"He return soon. I not know answers to questions, but you safe. Sit, eat. I prepare a bath. Full stomach, clean body, clean clothes make you better."

Leigh gave up on the woman's assistance for the present. She took a seat and ate the hot meal. When she finished, she placed her dishes in the sink. She was amazed by the clever water system that made chores easier for any woman working in this kitchen.

Leigh went to look for Abena. Against the front wall of the house was a long hall. Leigh called out, "Abena?"

The woman's scarfed head appeared from one

room. "Come."

Leigh went to join her. Once more, amazement consumed the blonde. The spacious room held a large tub with a pipe over one end and a control valve. A drainpipe near the floor exited the house.

"Must keep plug in," Abena said. "If not, snakes and spiders get in tub. Mosquitoes and flies come in house."

Leigh glanced at the toilet. A water tank was suspended above it on the wall, with a long chain to flush it. She noted a smaller sink, shelves with linens and bathing supplies, a mirror, and lamps on the wall. The one window was high for privacy. Leigh's mouth was agape.

"How did Jace do all of this in the jungle?" she inquired.

"House built by other man. He sold to Bwana Jace. Bwana Jace do many smart things to house. Make it pretty and comfortable. He see many things sailing around world. He learn them and do here. He plenty smart. Good man, as Abena tell you."

Leigh noticed how the woman could speak good English at times or drop words in excitement at others.

"You want Abena to help? You want Abena to go?"

Leigh had never bathed before a stranger. She smiled and said, "Thank you, but I can manage alone."

"All you need here. I be in kitchen." She left the room.

Leigh stripped off the dirty garments. She removed her walking boots. Her eyes noticed the bandage. She removed it, staring at the clever wound and wondering again how and why Jace had faked the snakebite. She couldn't wait to hear his explanation.

The slender female climbed into the sun-heated water. It felt wonderful. She leaned back and relaxed. Leigh didn't know what kind of house she had expected Jace Elliott to have, but it certainly wasn't one this beautiful and efficient. What a surprising man he was.

After a time, Leigh took the washcloth and soap. As she lathered it, she realized the bar had a floral scent. Her brows lifted, and she smiled. After bathing her body and scrubbing her hair, she rinsed the tawny locks beneath the fill pipe.

Leigh stepped out of the tub. She dried herself and wrapped the large cloth about her. The polite girl bent forward and washed out the tub, being careful to plug the drain securely.

Her blue gaze touched on the medicine and a fresh bandage that Abena had placed on the sink. Suspicion and anger filled Leigh again. It was obvious Jace had planned this ruse from the start, and Abena knew all about it, else she would not have lain out such items.

As Leigh jerked a robe from a hook, she was shocked to discover it was one of her own, left behind in Mombasa. She donned it and went to find that sneaky housekeeper.

"Where did this come from?" she demanded.

Abena turned, looked at the robe whose front the girl was holding between her fingers, and said, "Bwana Jace sent for you. Have many things in your room. I show you."

"How did you know about this?" Leigh asked, lifting the robe and pointing to her injured leg. "Bwana Jace did that to me."

Abena frowned, creating creases on her forehead and between her brows. "Jomo tell Abena Bibi Leigh

426

hurt."

"Listen to me, Abena," Leigh demanded, then explained how she had been drugged and brought here. "I know that looks like a snakebite, but I wasn't bitten by anything. It's a trick. How can you defend a criminal and help him commit such a wicked crime?"

"I obey Bwana Jace. Come, I show you room." The vexed woman left the kitchen with Leigh trailing close behind.

There were four doors along the hallway. The woman guided Leigh to the third one, a bedroom.

"You stay here. Bwana Jace's room next; it locked. Office locked. I be in kitchen." The now-reserved African left her there.

Leigh fumed at the woman's stubborn behavior and her own mistake. She peeked out the door and heard noises from the kitchen. She checked Jace's bedroom and office doors; they were indeed locked. The vexed blonde returned to the guest room and closed the door; it would not lock without a key. She looked through the drawers and closet, stunned to find them filled with her own possessions.

"Is there no end to your boldness, Mr. Elliott?" she mumbled. "How did you get these away from the hotel? How will you explain their absence?" Reality engulfed Leigh. "You planned this abduction from the start. All the time you were romancing me, you were waiting to kidnap me. Damn you! You were lying and cheating the whole time. You were going to make certain I lost our bet and paid off immediately. You dirty, rotten bastard. You won't get away with this."

Three days later, Jace and the safari party reached

the Athi River. Two flat-decked boats were awaiting them, along with the men sent ahead to hail the cargo carriers.

One captain waved, smiled, and shouted, "Good to see you, Jace. You got trouble and need a lift?"

Jace went forward and shook his hand. "We lost a member of the safari to a bush-snakebite. The others don't want to continue. We only had a couple of weeks to go. Thanks for waiting, Daniel."

"That's too bad, but it happens. These English don't realize how dangerous the jungle is. They think it's all fun and games. They come here dressed and prepared for a tea party or afternoon stroll." Daniel hushed as Chad joined them and was introduced.

Jace looked sad as he informed the captain, "Leigh was his ward and niece. She was only twenty, beautiful and enchanting. We didn't find her in time to give any help."

"Wouldn't have done any good if you had," Daniel replied. "Bush snakes are deadly. We'll get you loaded and push off."

"I'll pay you in Mombasa."

"No charge, friend. You've done plenty of favors for me."

The extra bearers, those not needed for the last trek between river and train, were dismissed to head home. Jace's men trusted him and knew he would send their payment after he received his at the end of every journey. The baggage and passengers were put aboard the two boats and off they went. The river was high because of recent rains, so they made good time.

Jace sat cross-legged on the deck. He leaned his head against a support post and pretended to close his eyes but watched the others through narrow slits. Johi and the bearers were on the second boat; the two couples were with him. Everyone was silent and almost sullen. Chad drank heavily, and Reid stayed wrapped over the man like a cloak. Louisa and Cynthia kept to themselves, whispering and scowling.

To Jace, the redhead seemed to have given up on her pursuit of Chad. At first she had tried to repair the damaged relationship, but Chad had scorned and avoided the female as if she were a noxious disease. Observing the gleams of hatred and revenge in Louisa's eyes, Jace was glad he wasn't in Chadwick Hamilton's place.

Jace hoped the couples would relax and open up during the trip downriver. As it was perilous to travel at night, they would make camp each day at dusk. With others around, especially the amiable Daniel, perhaps the hunting party would settle down.

Jace thought about Leigh Webster ensconced at his home. He could hardly wait to confront her, to force the truth from those lovely and lying lips. He had to extract the secret she and Chad were withholding from him. No doubt the devious and delightful creature was plenty scared. That was good, he decided. It would make his impending task of extracting information easier.

Yet these days of separation had worked hard on him. Jace dreamed about her at night and thought about her all day. He couldn't forget how Leigh looked at him, how she held him and kissed him, how she made love to him. She did not do those things like a guileful woman. No matter her secrets and original plans, the woman seemed to love him. He couldn't get their last night together off his mind. She had been passionate but troubled. She had confessed to how much she wanted him. She had hinted at problems to be resolved later. Yet she had made love to him as if it were their last time. Something had her confused, frightened, and tightlipped. He had to unravel that mystery soon.

Jace reasoned that Leigh had to have good reasons for taking the actions she had. Whatever was troubling her, he aimed to discover it. Jace also couldn't forget what she had told him about investigating Chad. Perhaps Leigh had faked affection toward Chad to fool her guardian. That would mean she believed Chad was a liar and a threat and was afraid of the man. But how had Chad discovered their wager, if Leigh hadn't told him? Why would she expose such a shocking and damaging secret? And when had she done so? It must have been during that long talk at their last camp. Something Chad told her had provoked the exposure, and the change in Leigh.

On reflection, there had been almost desperation in her lovemaking and mood that night. It was as if she had been trying to prove her feelings, to test him, to entice something from him. Had she wanted to evoke a stronger commitment from him before baring her soul, and heart? Had she wanted him to confess, explain, deny something Chad had told her? What would she have said if he had revealed his love and had proposed? Since he hadn't responded as she needed him to, how had his stubborn silence affected her?

On the other hand, if she believed Chad loved her and wasn't a threat, who did she think was after her? Jace Elliott?

Chapter Eighteen

Leigh had been at the plantation for a week. She had halted her accusations and insults concerning Jace Elliott to prevent trouble between her and the housekeeper and to make a friend and ally of Abena. She had helped with the daily chores in the house and yard. The furniture and floors required frequent polish to prevent them from drying out in the equatorial heat. There were meals to be prepared, dishes to be washed, and laundry to be done. The cloth mesh screens were changed and washed when they were cluttered by the dead insects who had tried to get into the house.

Leigh had tried to help clean Jace's office and bedroom, but Abena always refused and locked the doors while doing her tasks there. Leigh knew one reason for keeping her out of the office: she had sighted a rack of weapons on the wall. Leigh hoped no incriminating papers or letters from Brandon Elliott or William Webster were present anywhere. She also hoped no copy of the strange codicil was in his possession. She wished she knew whatever truth lay behind those sealed doors. Yet perhaps nothing more than weapons and his privacy were being safeguarded by the stubborn housekeeper.

The yard demanded much attention to keep the

jungle vegetation from creeping into it and taking control. She had learned quickly that the jungle constantly attempted to recover any ground stolen from it. She enjoyed being outside and working in the area mostly shaded by large trees with persistent vines, colorful and melodious birds, and playful monkeys who chattered noisily when disturbed by her presence.

The same was true of the coffee fields. Workers from the Kikuyu village labored daily to keep back vines and weeds that would strangle the bushes if given a chance. Every week, the healthy shrubs required trimming and shaping. Leigh often watched the native workers through the iron fencing, as she was not permitted outside the high walls and locked gate.

She was eager to walk through the coffee fields and learn about Jace's business. She wondered why coffee beans were called cherries, and why a crop took years to produce. She wanted to know why Jace Elliott was intrigued by this time- and energy-consuming crop and by living in a secluded jungle. He had moved here long before his trouble with the London law. Didn't he find such an existence lonely and demanding? Was he still pining over the loss of Joanna Harris? Was more than the criminal charges against him imprisoning him here? Was he still tormented by that woman's betrayal with Chad?

That thought pained Leigh. Neither man had told her about Joanna Harris. Both men, as if a conspiracy, had held silent to prevent her from learning why they would battle over her. Was Joanna one of those secrets Jace had promised to reveal later?

Leigh did not want to think about the two devious men and their lies, or the woman who had broken Jace's heart, or Chad's vile seduction, or the possible peril—emotional and physical—she now confronted.

Leigh jumped from the swing where she had been cooling herself after yardwork. She went inside to take a bath and to change clothes. She prepared everything, then soaked for a long time.

One day she had traced the tub drain to learn the buried pipe crossed the backyard, passed under the towering wall, and dumped into the jungle. She reluctantly had admitted how clever Jace was.

As Leigh dried herself, she also confessed how miserable *she* was. Despite her anxiety and doubts, she was eager for Jace's arrival. She wanted to discuss everything with him. She needed to learn what he had in mind with this abduction. With her.

Leigh went into her room and found Abena there. Her possessions from the safari camp were being unpacked, sorted into clean and dirty clothes, items to be put away, and belongings to be repaired.

"Where did you get these?" Leigh inquired, lifting her brush.

"Thiku brought from Bwana Jace."

Leigh was stunned. "Why didn't you ask him to wait so I could speak to him? Where is Jace? What is happening?"

"Others believe you dead, buried at village," Abena revealed to the distressed female. "They on way to Mombasa to leave on big boat. Bwana Jace be home in two, three weeks."

"Did Jace send a message, a note, to me?" Leigh asked.

"Nothing. Others gone downriver. They believe Bwana Jace."

"But how could they believe I'm dead and buried?" Leigh argued with the housekeeper. "Uncle Chad is too smart to be fooled. He would demand to see my body. How could Jace pull off such a trick? I don't understand." Leigh was angry with Jace for not sending her an explanation.

Thiku had related most of the tale to the housekeeper, but the woman did not feel it was her duty or right to reveal it. Abena had been told of Leigh's perils and of Jace's feelings for the white girl. One of his most trusted bearers, Jace had exposed his daring scheme to Thiku, who had related it to the loyal Abena. Jace had sent word to the stout woman, telling her to take good care of Leigh but to watch the white girl closely for mischief and attempted escape.

Abena shrugged. To avoid a lie, she did not answer.

"Damn him!" Leigh declared. "He can't do this to me. If I'm believed dead, Uncle Chad will take over my business. He and his mother will get control of my money and possessions. They'll tell Aunt Jenna I'm dead. My friends will think I'm dead. This is cruel, Abena, mean and heartless. You cannot be a part of it. Please help me. I must get word home that I'm alive and well."

From blind loyalty and love for her employer, Abena refused.

In desperation, Leigh reasoned, "What if an enemy captured Ka'arta and convinced everyone she was dead? What if relatives took your daughter's money and belongings? Wouldn't her family and friends suffer? Wouldn't Ka'arta be terrified and angered? What if someone could help Ka'arta escape or send word home, but refused because she was loyal to the enemy who was holding Ka'arta prisoner?"

The woman did not change her mind, but did admit, "It sad, but must be this way. Bwana Jace not do evil. He has reason to steal you. When he comes home, he tell you."

"He doesn't have to tell me. I know why: half of my inheritance, and revenge." There was no need to ask the loyal woman about Joanna.

Leigh played the piano for a time and noted that it needed tuning. She was reminded of the hours her mother had compelled her to practice. She hadn't played in a long time, and her skill at the keyboard was impaired by neglect. Yet it soothed her tension and distracted her.

Suddenly Leigh wondered if the piano and music sheets had been purchased and brought here for Joanna Harris. That halted the blonde's enjoyment and fingers. She closed the key cover. After dousing the lamps she had washed and filled today, Leigh left the room.

She was alone tonight, as always after Abena went home. The gate was locked, and the brown-skinned woman had the key. Leigh dared not seek a way to climb over the high wall. It would be reckless and stupid to escape into the hazardous jungle, and Leigh Webster was neither. Nor did she close windows and doors, as the wall kept out wild animals. With the closeness of the metal rods and height of the iron fencing from the ground, no snakes or small creatures could get inside the yard to find their way into the beautiful house. For now, she felt safe. It remained to be seen if that was true when Jace arrived.

Several nights she had tried to pick the locks on Jace's office and bedroom doors, but without a proper tool, it was impossible to get inside. Since he had ordered them sealed against her nosing around, he must have something vital hidden there.

Leigh fetched the book she had been reading when Jace sneaked into her tent to drug her for this crime. She got into bed, needing the book to distract her from her loneliness and anguish. After finding a comfortable position, she opened it and saw two papers. One was his copy of their wager, and the other was a note from Jace. A very clever man, he had known she would reach for this book to finish it.

Leigh,

We're breaking camp and heading for Mombasa today. It should take about two weeks to reach town and two weeks more for me to get home. It's May 25, so expect me about June 25. Chad and the others fell for my trick. They're sailing for London as soon as I get them back. He's eager to get his greedy hands on the inheritance you said he couldn't claim. Naughty of you to lie to me. Do I get another point for you endangering yourself with that deceit?

Study our contract and add up my points. I'm eager to start collecting them when I reach home. I miss you, woman. This next year will be a pleasant one for me. You do realize I get a year because you couldn't finish the safari. Afterwards, you'll be released. You can go to London, shock old Chad, and recover your inheritance. You can explain to him how *we* tricked him until you reached twenty-one and were free of him. You can tell the law *we* were forced to fake your death to stay alive. Maybe in a year, Chad will earn you more money than he'll spend or waste. Besides, you were willing to bet me a third, so he probably won't cost you more than that.

Relax and get ready to enjoy me like I plan to enjoy you. We have a lot to clear up between us.

Jace

"You're damn right we have plenty to get straight between us!" Leigh fumed. "You're a fool if you think I'll be held captive for a year. I never agreed to rule three. I don't owe you anything. Your little tricks caused me to lose. That's cheating, you green-eyed monster! And you won't sweet talk me into becoming a willing partner in this foul deed. The repercussions are too serious. You'll be in worse trouble for this crime, and I won't take part of the blame and be sitting in jail with you."

Leigh wondered what day it was. She added up her trek to the plantation and her incarceration. It had to be during the first week of June. That meant the others were nearing Mombasa and departure, and Jace would be heading . . . Would be home in less than three weeks.

With this trouble between them, how could she enjoy him? How could she yield again? Would he force himself upon her if she refused to comply? He hadn't mentioned affection, only implied desire. He promised to release her after she served her sentence in this luxurious prison. Release her, Leigh accused, so she could return to London to snatch everything away from his hated rival. Chad would prosecute Jace for this crime and make a future together impossible.

Leigh wanted to cry in torment. It always came back to the men's hatred and their vengeful war. They would do anything to hurt each other, to

437

punish each other, to destroy each other. Did that mean Chad had committed those London crimes, as Jace had charged and as Louisa had remarked that last day in camp? Her guardian had ruined Jace's love, but could he destroy Jace's father? Could she be so wrong about the handsome Chad? Could her grandfather's death have resulted from agonizing discovery of such evil? Why had Chad told Jace she lied about the Hamiltons being unable to inherit? What was Chad planning to do about the codicil that included his bitter enemy as an heir? Did Jace know about it? Was Jace planning to collect half of her worth while holding her captive? So much, she scoffed, for her money meaning nothing to him! If he played this hand right, Jace could claim half and use her for a year . . .

Jace covered her mouth and kissed her. He held her in his arms, caressing her with great skill. He stimulated her senses and body. His lips and tongue worked magic upon hers.

Leigh returned her lover's kisses and caresses. It felt wonderful to be in his arms again. She stroked his tantalizing flesh and rubbed his hard muscles. She squirmed to get closer to him. It was as if she were starving for him and could not feast upon him fast enough. Her body blazed with desire, and ached to unite as one with his.

Jace trailed his fingers down her arm, up her side, and to her breast. His hand closed over it and gently fondled the firm mound. His fingers teased at the taut bud, and his mouth claimed it.

Leigh writhed in rising passion. She begged him to cease his enticing actions and to join his flesh with hers. As he parted them and rose to leave, she jerked upward to stop his curious withdrawal.

Leigh awakened with a start. She was alone in the dark. The bed was rumpled, her gown twisted about her body. She was drenched in perspiration. Tears rolled down her cheeks. "Damn you," she pleaded, "stop haunting me! What are we going to do, Jace? How can we ever settle our problems? I curse you for making me love you and want you this badly!"

Jace and the safari party reached the termination of their river journey that same afternoon. The goods from ships at Mombasa were waiting to be picked up and taken to Nairobi. Chad asked if they could travel to Mombasa with the returning men and carts.

"Yes, but it's much longer," Jace told him. "We can walk to the rail line in two days, then it's a half day back to town. With those men, it'll require a week. Whichever you choose is fine with me and my schedule. If we travel with them, you can do more hunting from camp each night. All of the licenses aren't filled."

Chad inhaled deeply and said, "No, I want to get out of Africa as soon as possible. How will the train know to come for us?"

"It takes supplies up the line every two days," Jace explained. "We'll camp by the tracks, hail it, and catch a ride on its return trip."

"Fine." Chad responded.

Jace ordered the bearers to load up and begin their walk. He watched Louisa and Cynthia bid the African man and Daniel farewell. Cynthia and Louisa had enjoyed the captain's attention and company. Chad had kept to himself downriver and in camp. Since no tents were set up each night, there had been no opportunity for Jace or Johi to eavesdrop. That irritated Jace, but he just wanted this trek over so he could get to Leigh. He was anxious and ready to learn the truth.

The train picked up the safari party on Tuesday, June eighth. They were in Mombasa by dusk. At the hotel, Jace told Chad he would report Leigh's death to the Colonial Office in the morning, then headed for his room to bathe and rest. The two women did the same.

As Chad spoke with the hotel clerk about sailing dates and arranging transportation of their stored possessions, the man revealed that Miss Leigh Webster's things had been shipped to America after their departure inland, as the woman requested.

"What are you saying?" Chad demanded.

"Miss Webster asked for us to ship her baggage to Dallas, Texas, in America. She was planning to return home immediately upon arrival. We did as she requested. Is there a problem, sir?"

"None," Chad stated with a dark scowl.

"See," Reid told him. "See, she was lying about returning to London and marrying you. She was planning to sail to America, then sneak back to Jace Elliott."

"If she was, she changed her mind during the safari. I changed it for her," Chad refuted. Yet he was riled by this news.

"What about Jace and the will?" Reid hinted.

Chad had decided how to solve that problem. "Before we sail Friday, I'll handle him. He won't get anything. I'll see Jim Hanes tomorrow and make him an irresistible offer, fifty thousand pounds and my silence if he doesn't let Jace reach home alive."

"How can you do that? You only have a little over fifty thousand in the bank here, and half's to pay Jace with."

A cold and evil gleam was in Chad's eyes. During his misery, all the hatred for Jace had resurfaced, and increased. In his crazed mind, Jace had lured him here with dreams of final revenge and had gotten Leigh killed. His old enemy had taken away his two dreams and had to die. "I'll give Jace and Jim twenty-five each tomorrow. Then Jim can take Jace's money when he kills him and drops the body in quicksand. I don't want any evidence left behind, and I want to be gone when he's slain. When Jace can't be found to claim his half of the inheritance, I'll get everything."

"Fiona will get everything, Chad." Reid reminded.

The handsome and cruel man scoffed, "That's the same thing. She wouldn't dare cross me. If she tries, I'll kill her, too."

Wednesday, Leigh saw crimson spots on her undergarment. It caused her to realize that during the safari she had missed "Mother's Misery," as her aunt Jenna called it. She was glad she hadn't noticed that absence, or she would have panicked, thinking herself pregnant.

Her female condition only lasted two or three days, and was always very light. She had experienced "Mother's Misery" during those last few days aboard ship. She had skipped her monthly flow in May, but it had returned on time in June. Yet it wasn't unnatural for a woman to skip a month here and there. Illness, extreme tension, medicine—and drugs—could delay or bring on the condition at times. She also knew that her mother, Mary Beth Leigh Webster, had given birth to only one child and Jenna Leigh Barns Hastings had given birth to none. Perhaps the Leigh women were not as susceptible to pregnancy as were most females.

She went to find Abena for help. Leigh touched her feminine area, blushed, and said, "I'm in my woman's way. I need cloth."

Abena understood her hints. The woman fetched old linens from a chest and helped Leigh make pads to absorb the red liquid. Placing a small wooden box in the bathroom, she told Leigh, "Put here. At night when I go, I bury deep and sprinkle with pepper. We not want to attract hyenas with smell of blood."

Leigh returned to her room to lie down. She had endured a restless and tormenting night. She wondered what Jace would have done if she had gotten pregnant. Surely he would marry her. Surely he realized such a complication was possible during a long and intimate stay with him. *Another trick to entrap you, Leigh?* she mused.

She propped on the bed to read herself into a sleepy mood. Before doing so, she murmured a quote from "Ode to Joy," "Sweet magic brings us together," then added a quote from "Lutetia," "Wild, dark times are rumbling toward us." Leigh told herself to calm down but she was unable to do so. *Wild perils brought us together, my love, she contemplated, your hunger for revenge—and Chad's. But sweet passion and magic nearly destroyed the past for you, Jace. Why can't you let the dark past be over? Why can't you let us have a bright future?*

* * *

442

On Thursday, after Chad paid him, Jace pretended to leave Mombasa for home. He concealed himself to make certain the two couples caught the steamer for London tomorrow. A telegram from Lord Salisbury revealed that Sean and Jaimie, the men who had attacked Leigh on the London waterfront, were stablemen for Marquise Cynthia Campbell. The two bastards had been killed while resisting arrest so no testimony from them was forthcoming. There was no news about the two men who had attacked Leigh at Fort Jesus.

Jace followed Reid Adams to the telegraph office late that afternoon. He also witnessed a meeting between Chad and Jim Hanes this morning. He noticed that Jim was walking fine on a leg supposedly broken in early April. He decided to have a word with Jim later.

On Friday, the ship sailed with the two couples aboard. Jace and Johi searched for Jim Hanes to question the safari guide.

"Come clean, Jim, your leg was never broken. How much did Chadwick Hamilton pay you to fake that injury so I'd take his job?"

Jim sent him a sly grin. "Ten thousand. He's gone now, so why lie about it? He really hates your guts, Jace, so I'm a little baffled by why he wanted you as his guide. He paid me twenty-five thousand to trail you homeward, kill you, and hide your body in quicksand. He said you'd be carrying another twenty-five I could steal. That's a mighty high price on a man's head. What did you do to him?"

"Not what he thinks. Why are you telling me this?"

"Why not? I'm not going to murder you or any

443

man for money, not even for fifty thousand pounds. I took the bastard's money because there's nothing he can do to get it back. If he learns I didn't carry out his orders and returns, I'll be long gone. I'm sailing for Australia tomorrow. He provided me with a nice stake."

"I'm glad you told me the truth. I knew he hated me, but not enough to murder me."

Jace waited until the man who worked in the telegraph office locked up and left to eat. He had been unable to sneak inside last night to steal a copy of Reid's telegram because the employee also lived in rooms attached to the office. When Jace located the handwritten page, he stuffed it into his pocket and slipped away unseen.

Before leaving town, he sighted the two men who had attacked Leigh at the old Portuguese fort. He and Johi raced them down and beat one man into answering his questions. He learned that a woman with "hair like fire" had paid them to abduct and sell the sunny-haired female into slavery. Jace turned the men over to the local authorities.

While riding on the train toward the river to catch a boat to the stop nearest Nairobi, Jace withdrew the paper and read it. He smiled, then frowned in rage. At last he had a piece of enlightening and incriminating evidence in Reid's handwriting. When he was confronted with it, Chad would be furious. Jace was eager to wave this stolen page in the guilty bastard's face.

At dusk, Leigh was washing her hair and bathing. Jace should arrive any day now, and she wanted to be ready to confront him at her best. She stepped from the tub and reached for the drying cloth.

"Still as beautiful and enchanting as ever," Jace murmured.

Leigh whirled, dropping the bath sheet from her light grasp. Jace was leaning against the doorjamb, grinning broadly with a devilish sparkle in his green eyes. She retrieved the cloth and wrapped it around her naked and dripping body. Her heart pounded from more than startlement. Her face glowed a vivid pink from more than modesty and anger. He had caught her off guard, and her wits scattered at his sudden appearance and close proximity. "Damn you, Jace Elliott! How dare you sneak up on me like that! Get out of here, and close the door!"

"You weren't shy or reluctant when you enticed me to join you for a bath after that quicksand incident," he murmured in a husky voice, and strolled forward. He yanked her into his confining arms and teased, "Is this any way to greet me after such a long and painful separation?" His mouth closed over hers.

When he released her, Leigh stared into his merry gaze. She felt weak and anxious. Her breathing was fast and shallow. Her cheeks were aflame, as was her body. Her pulse raced like a wild and unbroken mustang that was fleeing wranglers across the plains. Her heart throbbed in her chest and ears, and she wondered if Jace heard it, too. His allure was overpowering, his touch burning like a skin-searing tropical sun as his potent gaze and strong embrace held her captive. "Let me go," she ordered in a strained voice, her throat clogged with warring emotions. "This wouldn't look proper to Abena. Get out and let me dress. Then we'll talk. You and

445

I have a lot to settle, Mr. Sneaky Elliott."

"Abena has left for the night. We're all alone, my tawny lioness. She said you've . . . mostly been a good girl. That was wise."

Leigh gathered her wits and used them. "Stop playing these silly games, Jace. We both know why I'm here. I'm your prisoner."

"Partner, love," Jace corrected. "I won our wager, so you owe me your undivided attention and delightful company."

"I don't owe you anything!" Leigh argued. "You lied and cheated. I lost points only because you plotted and carried out devious incidents. You can't force me to honor a deal you won unscrupulously. I won't!" she stated adamantly. "I only agreed to rules one, two, and four. I never agreed to rule three to wager a year with you."

Unyielding, Jace persisted, "Our bargain is binding, Miss Webster, so you'll have to abide by the rules we agreed upon. You allowed me to include rule three and you signed the contract."

"As a joke, and you know it, you sneaky devil."

"Did you mark it out or change it and initial the revision? No, so it's part of our deal. I warned you to read carefully before signing. I won fair and square. Actually, under rule two, you owe me over an extra month because you were in trouble and danger every day. Why not admit you wanted rule three in and you wanted to break it?"

"I'll admit to no such thing, Mr. Lawbreaking Elliott. I did fine without your interference. You ended the safari, not me, so I win."

"Even if I agreed, the contract says if I terminate the safari for any reason, you get an extra prize: me, any way, any time, and any place you desire. Well, here I am: ready, willing, and able."

Leigh frowned at the grinning man. "I decline my extra prize."

"If you prove to me you won," Jace reasoned, "you can't refuse me. You can't change the rules. We had a deal. You gave your word."

"So did you," Leigh protested, "not to cheat. All right," she conceded with a taunting grin, "by the contract, I want you . . . in London, in prison, and for life."

Jace laughed. "There's only one catch, love; I never quit the safari. I finished it, but you didn't. Therefore, I am the winner."

"I didn't finish because you tricked everyone. Kidnapping and faking deaths are illegal, even here in the jungle. This is British territory, and under English law. We're both English citizens."

"But I'm a criminal, Miss Webster; they don't obey laws."

" 'Alleged' criminal according to what you told me." Leigh scoffed in frustration. "In light of this illegal action, I'm not certain you told me the truth. I didn't cancel the safari and wasn't given a chance to earn more points, so how could I lose?"

"Simple: 'prove unable to complete it . . . presence in my home for one full year . . . pay your debt immediately and in full.' Nothing was listed as a disqualifying reason for being unable to finish."

"Are you deaf? I never agreed to that! I can't stay here a week or a year. Release me and I won't press charges against you."

"I won, Leigh. You're mine, until I decide otherwise."

"You promised you wouldn't make me lose, or help me lose!"

"I didn't. With all those curious accidents happening to you, there was no way you could com-

447

plete the safari alive. I had to protect my interest and winnings."

"By abducting me? By faking my death? By terrifying me?"

Jace watched her blue eyes dance with fiery lights. Her wet hair looked darker and flowed down her bare back. The drying cloth clung to her enticing frame and beads of water stood on her silky skin. "You left me no choice. We both know," he mocked her earlier words, "you were lying and cheating. I kept my word. You will, too."

Leigh could not vow she had never misled him, so she didn't. He was so cocky, so handsome, so maddening. "I had no intention of breaking our agreement," she informed him in a haughty tone and manner, "so you should have won it honestly. You didn't. You planned this little abduction from the start. That night you rescued me on the waterfront, I told you I was meeting Chad. Your craving for revenge saw a way to get at him through me. That's why you trailed me to Lord Salisbury's and tried to dupe me with your charms. You wanted to get close to him, and I was your path. When I mentioned the safari and that Chad was my guardian, you saw an even better way to obtain vengeance, on him and Grandfather. You came here, lay in wait for our arrival, then pounced on me like a leopard. You were the one using me as bait in your trap for Chad, not the other way around like you accused at Mr. Johnston's party. The wager was just another beguiling trick by a clever seducer."

"At Alfred's party, I thought I was being set up, woman, and you know why I believed it. I was right all along. Chad did have a sly motive: marry you and get rid of me. I'll confess our wager began as a ruse, one to capture your interest. I was testing you

448

and probing for information about Chad's motives and your possible involvement. You were doing the same thing with me, so don't deny it."

She didn't. "There was no plot, Jace Elliott. You're mean, bitter, and devious. How did you pull off this stunt?"

Jace explained the snakebite ruse to her. "Reid only wounded the animal," he added, "because I tampered with the sight on his gun. Johi kept them out of camp long enough for me to fool the others and steal you. I had men hiding and ready to track whatever Reid wounded to spare me that task and time. Very clever, eh?"

"Very illegal and cruel," Leigh refuted. "Not only does Chad think I'm dead, but he'll tell my family and friends. You have to let me contact aunt Jenna before he does. That news will crush her."

Jace shrugged and nodded. "Fine. I'll handle it. I'm sorry I didn't think to send her a cable before I left Mombasa. Consider it done tomorrow. But we will have to swear her to secrecy about your survival. I don't want anyone to know you're alive yet."

Leigh stared at him. "You'll let me cable her?"

"I'm not a heartless bastard, Leigh," Jace said. "Though, at times, you tried your damndest to rip it out of my chest."

That accusation astonished her. He actually looked and sounded honest. "I tried to hurt you? Are you crazy? You're the one who had me terrified at the fort, unloaded my gun during a dangerous rhino hunt, put drugs in my canteen, lured me into quicksand, fixed Louisa's gun to almost kill me, then faked my death. You did all those wicked and dangerous things just to win a stupid bet, and you claim I—"

Jace straightened and stiffened. His hands moved

to her shoulders and shook her gently. "Shut up and listen, woman. The men who attacked you at the fort have been arrested. A woman with red hair hired them to sell you into white slavery. The men who attacked you on the waterfront in London are dead, killed resisting arrest. They worked in Cynthia's stables. I asked a man there to check out everyone around you. I knew they weren't sailors, and you told me they smelled of horseflesh. You also caught their names and gave their descriptions. I don't have to tell you who Cynthia's best friend is."

During the past few weeks alone, Leigh had come to realize how much Louisa hated her, and how suspicious she was of the redhead. Mention of the vixen who had flirted with Jace in Mombasa and in camp and who had said such horrible things that last day provoked her to scoff, "The same woman who shared old times with you! The same woman you were playing with in the river in an attempt to anger me."

Jace frowned and said, "I'm not going to deny that first charge again, because we both know it isn't true. But the second one *is* true."

Leigh moved from him, causing the hot hands on her bare shoulders to fall to his sides. His clothes were damp from contact with her. She lifted her robe and donned it, also leaving on the drying cloth. "Then why did you tell her about our wager? It was a secret."

Jace lifted one brow quizzically. "I didn't."

"How did Louisa know about it? I certainly didn't tell her. She confronted me about us and the bet that morning you pulled this stunt."

Jace mused for a moment, then surmised, "Perhaps she found your contract. It was hidden in your

450

tent, and she did remain in camp one day." He didn't want to suggest Chad had told Louisa about the wager, after Leigh had confided in her guardian. He would solve that mystery later.

Leigh had suspected Chad of revealing that news, but Jace's guess sounded more logical and probable. "You could be right."

Jace responded with confidence. "I'm sure I am. As for those drugs in your canteen, Chad was responsible. Johi overheard him mention it to Reid after your 'death.' " Leigh's eyes narrowed in impending debate. "But he wasn't trying to poison you," Jace quickly added, "just make you ill so he could end the safari and get you out of my reach. He was worried that all his lies and deceits wouldn't keep us apart. You were bait, Leigh, but not mine. The safari was his idea. He plotted it to get revenge on me. You were his tool to pry his way into my life again. Since that frame in London failed, he sought another road to victory. Chad told you about our past in Mombasa just to win your favor and to prevent anything from happening between us. He was playing on your tender heart and suspicions; he figured, by confiding in you, you would be fooled about him. I promised to reveal everything and I will, in time. I didn't want you to know about our quarrel because it would make me look bad before you could get to know me and judge the truth for yourself."

Leigh knew he hadn't talked about the wager, but she didn't broach that topic yet. "Even if that's true, none of it changes what you planned and did to me, Jace Elliott. You had my clothes and things sent here as soon as we left Mombasa. You prepared a tent you could sneak into and out of at your pleasure. Then, all those curious incidents

451

happened. After we got close, you should have trusted me and confided in me. You had plenty of time to expose the truth, and you owed it to me, but you held silent. That last night, I tried to coax the truth from you, so we could be totally honest with each other. You responded by kidnapping me! What am I supposed to think and feel, except you were duping me from the start?"

Jace grasped what she must be thinking. "I had your clothes sent here because I was planning to find a way to keep you here and safe until November. I suspected Chad would either slay you or ensnare you in marriage to get his hands on Webster's estate. I couldn't allow either to happen to you. I wanted you to have your things to use during your stay. I knew there was no way to get them up here after the safari. As for that secret exit, that tent is mine. Sometimes I need to slip out of camp at night, so it allows me to do so without being seen. After we . . . got close, I let you have it to conceal our relationship. Chad must have located it and gotten suspicious. That's why Louisa and Cynthia kept sleeping there with you. That's why he wanted to do us harm."

"After this imprisonment, I'm supposed to believe you and trust you?" she reasoned. "I'm supposed to accept your charges against nearly everyone on the safari? What did Chad do after my death?"

Jace walked to the door. He turned and said, "It's been a long journey to and from Mombasa. We're both on edge. Why don't you dress while I get something to wet my throat? We have more matters to discuss, don't we?"

Leigh's gaze met his troubled one. "Yes, we do." He left.

Leigh wrapped the colorful sarong around her

452

and secured it. Abena had given her several. It was hot most days, and the garment was cool and comfortable. She brushed her hair. The honey tresses were almost dry, again due to the African heat. She was nervous, wary, and a little frightened. She was baffled by Jace's words. She wondered if this ruse was for her protection and if it had been necessary. She quivered, thinking of the long night ahead.

Leigh joined Jace in the kitchen. He turned and smiled, looking her over with pleasure. His pulse quickened and his heart raced at the provocative sight. His loins burned and ached, aflame with desire and hungry with need. "Would you like juice? Abena makes it fresh every day from tropical fruits. Or would you prefer something stronger?"

Leigh noticed his reaction to her, and she felt the same. "Juice is fine. I'd like to keep my head clear."

Jace chuckled as he poured the tasty liquid. "Me, too," he said, handing her a filled glass. He lightly clicked his glass to hers and said, "To our time together and all the surprises it will bring."

Her somber gaze met his probing one. "Why are you hurting me to get back at Chad? Which one of us will suffer the deepest and longest? *Me,* not Chad. For a time, I really believed you and I had something special. Suddenly you changed. You became mean, snide, and mysterious. Everything was good between us, then you backed off and spoiled it. Why, Jace? Are you going to force me to . . ."

Chapter Nineteen

Jace stared at the woman he loved and wanted to trust more than anything in the world. She looked vulnerable and afraid. She looked beautiful and innocent. "No, Leigh; I won't force you to honor any of the terms of our wager, but I won't allow you to leave my plantation until I learn the truth and know you're safe. If you want to make it hard on us, I can't stop you. But I'm hoping you'll relent and tell the truth so we can clear the air. You don't have to worry about me assaulting you. I've never forced myself on any woman, and I certainly wouldn't do so with you because you're much too important to me."

"Why?" she asked, confused by his words. Her mind longed for an understanding. Her heart ached for a reunion of spirits. Her body yearned for closeness with him again.

Emotions had built so high between and within them during their separation that both needed to seek the truth and peace together. Both decided it was past time to be completely honest in order to solve the mysteries surrounding them, to tear down the barrier between them.

"Because I want you and need you. Because I

don't want you to hate me and reject me. Because I want you to trust me enough to tell me the truth." Jace walked through the dining room into the living area. He took a seat on the sofa.

The befuddled woman followed him and sat down on the other end. "Why do you keep saying 'truth' as if it has a special meaning?" she questioned. "What is it you want from me? I've already told you I don't know what goes on inside Chad's head. Revenge has you both suspicious of everyone. I tried to keep myself from getting entangled, but I obviously failed. That's why I'm here, isn't it? Somehow you think losing me will hurt Chad. Just when he gets used to the idea of having the firm, you want to release me to snatch it away. Do you ever think of anything except your next plot?"

"The only thing I want to get Chad for is framing me and my father, for murdering my father," Jace informed her. "I want my father exonerated. I want my family name cleared. I want Chadwick Hamilton punished. I know he's guilty; I just can't prove it yet." Jace fused their probing gazes. "You asked what Chad did after your death. At first he didn't believe my ruse. He was so distraught at losing the path to his dream that he said he would confess to those crimes if I returned you alive. Reid stepped in and made him hush, made him think I was using your death to evoke a confession. Then Louisa jumped in and claimed you and I were lovers, and we'd been duping Chad all along. I denied it of course and, for some reason, Chad believed me. He honestly thought you were going to marry him. We argued for a while, but I convinced him you were dead."

"How did Louisa know about us? We were very careful."

"I followed her and Chad into the jungle after she nearly shot you. I overheard them arguing. Louisa accused Chad of trying to kill her. She thought he had rigged her gun to explode. She accused him of trying to frame me for her death, thereby getting rid of two obstacles at once, then marrying you to get your money. He denied it, and he asked her to marry him when they returned to London. He claimed he was only being good to you to entice you to sell him the firm, or to prevent you from firing him. He told her you hated her and didn't want her around, so he had to pretend to push her away until he got the company. She also mentioned that she'd been helping him by trying to distract me. That's why she took that new room at the hotel and tried to lure me into her clutches. She planted lots of rotten seeds in his mind. Then I heard gunfire and rushed back to camp. It was that jackel stealing food, remember? I didn't hear what else they said. It's my guess she knew about the wager between us and told Chad. If you'll recall, he asked to see me privately that day."

"What did he want?"

"He came right to the point and asked if we were lovers. He also asked if I was behind those accidents. I told him there wasn't anything but friendship between us, but not because of lack of trying. I accused him of those incidents, of trying to get you away from me. I knew about that powder and the canteen. I believed what you told me about him being unable to inherit, so I thought he needed to marry you to get control. We both know he didn't. He taunted me about following you back to London and getting arrested. I told him you always defended him, and he loved that news. That's when I learned you weren't engaged to Tyler Clark. When

Chad discovered Louisa was lying to us, he was furious. He suggested we both safe guard you and keep an eye on his mistress."

"I know Chad didn't trust her fully," Leigh told him. "After you left the garden that night, I overheard a talk between them. He accused her of the waterfront attack, but she denied it, even blamed me. She's hated me since my arrival in England. I've never liked or trusted her. I told her about Tyler to settle her down about us being rivals for Chad. I only pretended to make friends to avoid trouble."

Jace was happy to find her cooperating. "Louise tried to cause trouble with Chad and with me. She hinted that you had tampered with the gun, said how much you western women know about them. She constantly tried to place suspicion on you and me to hide her guilt. She wanted to kill you, Leigh. She tried in London and she tried in Mombasa. But don't believe she rigged her own gun."

"Then who did?" Leigh asked, expecting him to say Chad.

"Reid Adams." When Leigh stared at him, he said, "That's right, Reid Adams. I'm sure he's the one who tampered with Louisa's gun. He's probably the one who unloaded yours before the rhino hunt, and he's probably the one who lured you into that quicksand. I think he sneaked from camp, concealed the trail, stole your derringer, then returned things to normal while you were fighting for your life. I'm going to London when it's safe and kill the bastard."

This revelation was unexpected and shocking. "Why would Reid want to harm me? Are you saying he worked for Chad?"

"Part of the time. The rest, for himself and Fiona Webster. I didn't tell you all Johi overheard the night of your 'death.' Their original plot was to lure you here, kill you, frame me, have Fiona get your holdings, and Chad control them until he inherited. When you arrived in London, Chad actually fell in love with you, and changed plans on Reid. Chad decided to marry you and get everything. He was going to forget revenge on me because he didn't want to take a risk of losing you and your inheritance. Chad mentioned the drugged canteens, but also that he didn't pull any of those other stunts. I have to admit, I believe him. Reid reminded him that he had changed his mind again after the buffalo hunt and was planning to kill you in our last camp because of what Louisa told him that day, something vital that I missed after the gunfire. I think it was about our secret wager, and it made him go wild with jealousy and hatred."

"This is crazy and complicated, Jace."

"I know," he concurred, "that's why I had trouble figuring out what was going on. After I was cleverly led to doubt Chad was trying to murder you, I knew it had to be one of the others. I was afraid to give the culprit another chance to succeed. I was afraid you'd never be allowed to get out of the jungle alive. I couldn't guard you every moment. That's why I faked your death, Leigh. But it wasn't the only reason."

Jace explained his meaning. "Even if I guarded you successfully during the safari, I couldn't let you leave Africa with Reid and Louisa determined to kill you, and I couldn't trail you to London to keep foiling their efforts. I couldn't even be sure they wouldn't find a way to murder you while you were in my protection. You had become angry and distant, and you refused to confide in me, especially that last night. I sneaked to see you hoping you vould open up to me. When you didn't, I doubted you would believe me and agree to this plan. I was even afraid you would sneak out of Africa with the culprits endangering you. You seemed as if you were telling me good-bye. I was worried and suspicious, and I couldn't allow you to make a fatal mistake. It seemed best to act then and explain later. Whatever you said to Chad that day you two took that long walk, it changed his mind about returning to his original plot. You told him something to make him doubt Louisa's accusations and Reid's urgings. You convinced him he had a real chance to win you. I think Louisa had him fooled by the wager between us. Yet you persuaded him it was meaningless. How?"

Leigh deliberated his words. "You're telling me that Chad, Louisa, and Reid were all trying to kill me?"

"For different reasons. Chad waxed back and forth. Louisa wanted Chad, enough to kill to get him. Cynthia was aiding Louisa. Reid wanted you dead so Fiona could inherit everything. They're lovers. I'm certain Chad doesn't know about them, or he would have grasped why Reid was so eager to assist his original plot and why Reid kept stirring him up against us. You see, woman, Reid was the one using Chad, not the other way around."

"Reid and Grandfather's widow? Where did you get such ideas?"

Jace pulled the paper from his pocket and said, "Reid sent this message to Fiona before he sailed. He was gone before I could steal it. If I had read it first, he would never have gotten on that ship alive. All the time I was watching Chad and Louisa, Reid was fast at work. I just didn't grasp how involved and how determined he was. Chad finally convinced me he loved you and wanted to marry you, so I was baffled. Johi and I started spying on the others. I suspected Reid of mischief, but I didn't have any proof or a motive. But now, we do."

Leigh took the page and read it. The message was from Reid Adams in Mombasa to Fiona Hamilton Webster in Bombay. Those words clarified the mystery, and corroborated Jace's accusations:

Business complete. Big success. Work over. L dead. J gone. You get all. May have C problem. Will handle. Leaving Africa June eleven. Leave India today. Meet in London. Come fast. Marry me. Love you. Miss you.

R.A.

Leigh was staggered by the multiple plots to . . . murder her. She recalled that night when she and Reid had talked about Fiona. She closed her eyes and mentally returned to that scene. Leigh knew the woman was beautiful, beautiful enough to be desired and loved by a younger man. There was fourteen years between them, but Fiona looked Reid's age. The man had tensed while discussing the widow. Leigh asked herself why she hadn't caught clues in his eyes, voice, or words.

"What are you thinking?" Jace inquired.

Leigh related her thoughts about Reid. "Why aren't you on your way to London to keep them from getting all the money?" she asked.

"I'm sorry they'll waste some, but that can't be helped. Your survival is worth a small loss, and you can recover the balances soon. When I thought two friends were joint heirs, I knew Lord Salisbury could use his power and position to prevent execution of the will until we straightened out this mess.

I dismissed my suspicions because you lied about the will. You did it to silence me, didn't you?"

"Yes," she admitted. Her head was spinning. What she was hearing was painful and alarming. She had underestimated Louisa Jennings. She had been fooled by Chadwick Hamilton. She had never suspected Reid Adams. Her ingrained nature had resisted accepting such evil. So many pieces to the puzzle fell into place, but others were still missing.

"I saw Jim Hanes in Mombasa." Jace revealed more shocking news. "Right now, Chad thinks we're both dead, so you're safe here. Once you're in control after your birthday and make a new will, none of them will have reason to kill you for profit. But that might not stop one or all of them from trying again for revenge. Frankly, I hate for you to ever return to London, but that's your choice. I wish my evidence could imprison them, but my word isn't worth much these days. And I can't protect you from here. If I trail you there, I would be risking my life and freedom. I hate feeling helpless and defeated. I'll have to think of something."

Those discoveries convinced Leigh he was telling the truth. "Chad was fooled because I told him our wager was a trick. He implied you were a threat to me. He said he loved me and he proposed. He offered to sign a legal document giving up any claim to my holdings. He sounded sincere, almost desperate to convince me of his love. I said a lot of things to fool him. I used my feminine charms, and I said bad things about you. I didn't trust either of you, and I was stalling you both until I could leave for America. He didn't get me on his side, Jace, but he did turn me against you, with good reason. He told me about the wager between you two. He made me read the contract, including the extra five

thousand for each night you spent with me. He
burned his copy to prove he wouldn't try to claim
any winnings from you. Did you collect the twenty
thousand pounds for your four nights with me as
you wagered with Chad? Twenty-five, if you count
that first time in Mombasa."

"What are you talking about? That wasn't part of
our deal. I would never agree to such a wicked
term."

Leigh related what she had read in Chad's contract. Jace fetched his copy, and the truth came to
light. Both were shocked and pleased.

"So, that's how he made me a bastard in your
eyes. I'm sorry you learned about the wager from
him. That clarifies a few things."

Needing an explanation, Leigh accused, "You lied
to me. You duped me, used me, and betrayed me. I
. . . trusted you. I gave everything to you. Why,
Jace? Why wasn't it enough? Why did revenge on
Chad mean more to you than I did?"

He gazed at her and said, "You were enough,
Leigh. I was willing to forget the past just to have
you. Until I discovered you were lying to me. That
day you and Chad had that long talk, I was spying
on you two, but I couldn't hear what was being
said. After you left Chad in the clearing, he raced
after you, and the two of you halted near my hiding
place. He swore his love and offered to do anything
to prove himself to you. You agreed to consider his
proposal. I heard you tell him to remember his
promise to keep the truth from me, as you had.
You said it had been difficult at times not to tell
me everything and get the past cleared up, as you
didn't know how I would deal with such facts. You
said: 'We came here to study him, and we have. He
doesn't know anything, so we're safe.' Chad replied:

'I'm relieved that you've kept what your grandfather did a secret. If he knew, Jace would kill us both.' You told him I trusted you and desired you, that 'Mr. Jace Elliott isn't hard to fool.' Those words were burned into my memory, Leigh. When we talked in Mombasa, and other times, you claimed you had no knowledge of why Chad came here, but your own words exposed you. Isn't it time for the truth between us? Was William Webster involved in those charges against me? Is that what you're hiding from me? You're condemning me to a life of exile and dishonor to protect a dead man's name and your inheritance?"

Leigh was astonished and dismayed to learn that Jace had heard those incriminating words, words used only to fool Chad. She had to make him understand and believe her. "If Grandfather and Chad were responsible for those crimes, I know nothing about it. We came here to enjoy a safari. At least I was led to believe so. But we did want to learn something from you. It's the same reason Chad wants you killed. Obviously there was a deadly plot against both of us, and I was too naive and distracted to see it or to believe your charges. Now I understand why you changed and acted so oddly toward me. I'll tell you the whole story. What I wanted to glean from you during the safari and our talk at the hotel was why Grandfather left half of his estate to Jace Elliott in case of my death. I wanted to know if you knew about such a strange codicil. Since my inheritance includes money and possessions taken from your family, I wanted to know if you would kill me to collect it."

She paused before stressing, "You see, Fiona gets half and you get half, and Chad doesn't inherit. At least, not until his mother dies. I didn't exactly lie to you about that part. That's why I was so shocked at Mr. Johnson's party to discover the man I had been dallying with was the Jace Elliott in Grandfather's will. That's why I wondered if you had been trailing me in London for criminal reasons. After I got to know you, I trusted you. By then, I was afraid to tell you. Every time I was going to be honest, something happened to silence me. I'm sorry, Jace. It was so confusing. What do you mean to my grandfather? What debt does he owe you? What was your connection to him? Did you know about the will? Are you planning to collect your half before I'm proven alive?"

Jace jumped up and stalked the room, clearly shocked by all she'd revealed. "You're serious?" he halted and asked. When she nodded, he declared, "This is crazy! What's going on?"

"As of my death, which you've already cleverly arranged and pulled off, Jace Elliott owns one half of my worth: the estate, the companies, the money, everything. So, you see, I'm very valuable to you dead. You don't even have to risk your life by going to England to claim your half. You can contact the law firm from Mombasa. Chad will be shocked to discover you're alive and demanding payment of your share. That's why he hired Jim Hanes to kill you."

"You can't let them get everything by allowing them to think you're dead, too," Leigh entreated. "Fiona goes through money faster than a bullet leaving a pistol. You must cable them you're alive."

Leigh had to settle another deception. She provoked the truth by hinting, "You have quite a decision to make. Do you truly get rid of me, claim half my wealth, and go after your true love? Or do you let me live and pay off my wager, then release me? Joanna Harris still haunts you, doesn't she? If you can forgive her for yielding to Chad, you might be able to win her back and live happily ever after."

Jace reacted by ceasing all movement and staring into her misty eyes. "Are you surprised I know about your lost love?" Leigh asked. "Louisa told me how Chad took Joanna Harris away from you. She said you bought this home for her, but she betrayed you and didn't marry you. She became one of Chad's conquests. He hates you for that trouble in South Africa, and you hate him for stealing your love. What a misguided and wicked pair you make. Louisa said you wanted to punish Chad for stealing Joanna by stealing me from him. Is it true?"

"When did Louisa tell you about Joanna?"

"That last day, during our little confrontation." Leigh repeated their entire conversation.

Jace was furious. "That bitch! She told us part of your talk, but she left out plenty. Lordy, what you must have been thinking and feeling all these weeks. I'm sorry, Leigh. I should have told you everything long ago. Yes, I loved Joanna Harris; I still do." Jace witnessed the anguish in Leigh's eyes. He went to sit beside her and held her hands in his.

"Joanna Harris is my stepsister. My father married Catharine Harris when Joanna was six and I was fifteen. She was a little sister to me. While I was working here on the plantation, Joanna's fiancé dropped her for another woman. She was crushed and humiliated. While she was in that vulnerable condition, the charming Chad seduced her. She moved in with him and became his mistress. She believed he loved her and was going to marry her. When I went to London to bring her here to recover, I found her living with that bastard. We fought, and I was jailed for almost beating him to death. He paid guards and prisoners to harass me every day and night. Joanna refused to see me. She disappeared right after Father's death. I think she knows Chad was involved. He's looked for her and I've looked for her. Catharine lives in Scotland now, but she doesn't know Joanna's whereabouts. I visited Catharine before I met you in London. If Joanna knows what Chad did, she's in danger, and she could help exonerate me."

"You think Chad wants to kill her to silence her?"

"Yes, but he can't find her. I can't either. The reason I was in London was to see Lord Salisbury. It's due to him I haven't been arrested. He's stayed the law and has men from Scotland Yard searching for my stepsister and trying to prove me and Father innocent. I told you before, the two witnesses against us are dead. Chad isn't one to leave loose ends. I know Joanna is still alive because she's written to me a few times over the years. Somebody mails letters for her from different ports, so I can't track her. She's hiding something, Leigh, and she's afraid. That night in the garden, I was waiting around to see Salisbury. He left town before I could reach him, and I had to sail the next morning to beat you here. That's why I didn't know about William's sudden death or who you were."

"What about Grandfather's will, Jace? I don't understand it."

"Neither do I. He and Father were friends, but he didn't know me. If he was involved in Father's frame—and mine—that could explain why he felt guilty and made retribution before he died. If he wasn't, and discovered Chad was, that would explain his curious decision, too. Since he's dead, we'll never know the truth. He could have left Fiona included because he didn't know about her and Reid, or to keep them from getting suspicious and angry. We don't have any evidence against Chad, except for what Johi overheard. It's Lord Hamilton's word against an alleged criminal's and his best friend's. I don't even know if we can have Reid and Fiona investigated and arrested. Hopefully that cable will incriminate them. Maybe we can unmask Cynthia and Louisa. I hate for any of them to get away with this." Jace looked at Leigh. He smiled. They had talked enough about such terrible matters. "Did I tell you how beautiful you look? Was your outfit supposed to appease my temper and distract me?"

Leigh laughed. "Abena gave me several sarongs. They're comfortable and cool in this steamy climate . . . I've missed you, Jace."

He pulled her into his arms. "And I've missed you, woman. After what you've been through, this isn't the best time to complete my confession, but I love you."

Leigh leaned away to look into his eyes. She smiled and refuted. "It's the best time in the world, Jace, because I love you, too. What a complicated mess we're in. How will we get out of it?"

"By getting married, if you'll agree."

Her pulse raced. "Marry you?"

"That is what I wanted to wager but realized it wasn't the right time. You know why. I was a fool not to tell you that was my intention all along. I wanted time to win your love and trust. When I feared I didn't have them and wouldn't have a chance to get them, I had to act boldly and rashly. I know I don't have the right to ask you to marry a criminal and exile yourself here with me, but I can't help myself. As long as Chad thinks we're dead, he

467

can't stop us. I wanted to clear my name before offering it to you, but that might be impossible. I love you, Leigh, and I can't imagine spending the rest of my life without you. As soon as I prove myself to you, will you—"

Her fingers on his lips halted his remaining words. "You don't have anything to prove, Jace. I believe you; I was only confused for a time. I don't care about the past or those charges against you. I don't care if having you costs me my entire inheritance. I love you, and I want to marry you. Name the date and place."

Jace beamed with joy. "Abena told me the Protestant missionary will be in the village in a few days. Is that too soon?"

"Not soon enough. What shall we do until then?"

Jace smiled and nestled her into his arms. "It's almost dawn. We've talked all night. You must be exhausted. What do you want to do?"

"I want *you* and need you, Jace."

"You have me, love."

"All of you, now. Do I need to explain my meaning?"

He chuckled. "No, Miss Webster, I hear you clearly, thank goodness. I love you and want you so much I might have broken my promise not to seduce you."

"What about Abena?" she queried.

"I told her not to return to work until I sent for her. I knew we needed privacy to talk."

"We're finished talking for now, aren't we?" she hinted.

Jace stood and pulled her toward him. He lifted her in his arms and carried her to his room. Beside his bed he lowered her bare feet to the floor. Dawn's first glow lightened the cozy room, creating a romantic aura. Jace loosened the sarong and let it flow to her ankles. He unbuttoned his shirt and removed it. His boots and pants followed the khaki garment to their feet.

Their gazes locked and revealed their inner emotions. They were alone in a dreamy world, safe and together. No longer were they strangers. No barriers were separating them. Their hearts beat as one; their spirits soared in tune; their bodies yearned to join. Neither moved nor spoke for a time, merely savoring their closeness, this special moment in their lives.

Their hearts pounded with intense love, and their bodies burned with passion's flames. It was strange how just gazing at each other and standing close could have such a powerful effect on them. They smiled. No modesty, reservations, or mistrust, were present.

Jace's hands captured her face and he lowered his head to hers. The first kiss was leisurely and soft. The second was long and deep. The ensuing ones were swift, urgent, and greedy. His mouth brushed over her face, exploring the tawny surface with delight. His mouth drifted to her ear. "I love you and need you so much. I was afraid I'd never win you. That would have been torture, Leigh."

His tenderness and desire aroused Leigh to a heady level. Her arms encircled his body and she leaned against him. "I love you, Jace. I was so anxious for you to come home so I could prove it. I wanted to teach you that our love is more important than revenge." She cuddled closer, adoring the contact of his flesh pressed to hers. She loved his smell. She loved his touch. She loved him with all her being.

Jace's mouth roamed her throat. He buried his

469

nose in her fragrant hair. His fingers traced over her skin. She was the one woman to complete him. He had no doubts, no hesitation, no fears.

They sank to the bed to kiss and caress. Their bodies pleaded for an immediate union, but they wanted to linger a while at the entrance to paradise. They wanted to stimulate each other, to whet their appetites until they were so ravenous that they feasted wildly.

Jace's touch was tantalizing, gentle and demanding. His naked body was splendid. Leigh longed to see, feel, touch, and taste every inch of it. His frame was hard and well-toned from physical labor. She felt her senses responding madly to him.

Jace's mouth journeyed down her throat, leaving fiery and tingly kisses along its path. His lips climbed one mound and claimed its peak. Slowly he traveled to the next one to pleasure both of them. His hands trekked lower and lower, exploring and teasing until she thought she'd explode.

Leigh responded in like fashion by capturing every sensation and by roaming his blazing body. Her hands stroked and enticed; her mouth kissed and enchanted. She knew how much he wanted her, and that sent thrills through her. Her heart overflowed with an abundance of love. It made her bold and brave. She felt hot all over, and couldn't wait to possess him. Leigh guided him over her.

Jace obeyed her mute request, as he was enduring blissful torment. Control was hard to maintain. His mouth returned to hers.

They breathed, thought, and loved as one. Their desires were so great and their emotions so intense that ecstasy claimed them quickly. Both shuddered and moaned, as they extracted every ounce of pleasure from this reunion. Rhythmically they fused over and over until contentment surrounded them. They snuggled and kissed as their bodies calmed. It had been the most wonderful experience they had shared, because love had been exposed, renewed, and strengthened.

Jace kissed her forehead and hugged her. "It feels so good to have you here with me," he murmured. "I love this house, but this is the first time it's seemed like a real home. We'll make a fine life together, Leigh."

She stroked his chest with her fingertips. "Yes, we will. I'm so glad I found you, Jace. We're going to be happy together."

Jace closed his eyes and sighed in rapture. He was relaxed, and drowsy, fulfilled in body and spirit. All else could wait.

Leigh felt the same. Happy and sated, she closed her eyes, remained in his arms, and fell asleep.

Leigh and Jace warmed some bread and prepared coffee. They sipped the aromatic liquid and ate bread smeared with jelly.

"Did you grow this coffee?" she asked. "It's very good."

"I'm afraid not, but you can enjoy our new crop by spring."

"I love that word," she murmured with a glowing smile.

"What word?" he asked.

"*Our.* I can hardly believe we'll be married soon. I never dreamed I would find a man as wonderful, handsome, and virile as you. I'm very lucky, Mr. Elliott."

Jace captured her hand in his. His gaze locked with hers. "I'm the lucky one, Leigh. I have you. If

Louisa hadn't pulled that waterfront stunt so we could meet before we discovered each other's identities, this romance could have been hard and long in coming."

Leigh nodded. "Bad as she was, she did one good thing; she got us together at the best time. When I had lunch with her and Cynthia in London, she made a toast: 'May the best woman bring home the best prize.' Well, I won the best trophy of the entire safari."

"Do you have any objections to making this our home?" Jace inquired. "It is secluded, and it can be dangerous."

"I love it, Jace. It's so beautiful and comfortable. You're a clever man. I'm impressed with your water system."

He beamed with pride. "I saw it during my travels. It certainly does make life easier and nicer. So do you, woman."

She nuzzled her cheek against his hand. "It's both tranquil and exciting here, Jace. It already feels like home. I hate to leave it to . . ."

He knew she had halted to prevent spoiling their tender morning. "I know, love, but they have to be exposed and punished. I've been doing a lot of thinking this morning and I have a clever plan."

"Let the law do it for us, Jace. Don't get into more trouble. I couldn't bear it if anything happened to you."

Jace rose, walked behind her, and kissed the top of her head. "I promise, no violence on my part. I'll let the authorities handle almost everything. But I will do whatever necessary to protect us."

Leigh looked up at him and smiled in relief. "I understand and agree. What do we do until November?"

Jace bent over and kissed her lips before answering. As he was taking his chair again, he said, "It'll take them three weeks to reach London. They should dock about July first. Fiona should reach home about the same time. If we sail as soon as we're married, we'll be five weeks behind them. With luck, Reid and Fiona will be together, proving our charges. I'll let Lord Salisbury know we're coming. We have to defeat them now, love."

"We can't go; you'll be arrested. If it means endangering you, I don't care about the money and firm, and I don't care about punishing them. Until you're cleared and safe, I can't let you go to London."

"Don't be frightened, love. This mess must be straightened out. The only way to do that is go in for questioning. Even if I can't exonerate my father or dispel all suspicions about me, I have to clear myself. I'm giving you a blackened name; I'd like to clean it up for both of us, and our children. You do want children, don't you?"

"Yours, yes. But I don't want you to take such a risk. What if our testimonies and evidence aren't enough to clear you and convict them? It's too great a gamble, Jace."

He reasoned with a tender gaze and gentle voice, "I have to try. I need to get the past behind me. If I tell the truth, and they can't prove I'm lying and don't have any fake evidence I'm ignorant of, they'll have to close the case and release me. What kind of future can we have with this black cloud hanging over us? We'd be exiled here permanently. We both have business interests in London. You have the firm and I have coffee to market. Too, Chad and Reid are still threats to us. Until they're arrested and imprisoned, we'll have to keep looking over our

473

shoulders. We don't want to live that way, love, and I doubt they'll wait long to make sure we're dead. Right now we have the advantage of surprise."

"You're right, Jace, but I'm frightened for you, for us."

"Now that we have each other, everything will work out fine. There doesn't seem any way to clear my father, so I might as well accept that fact. I have to think about us first. My father would understand."

Leigh realized how much Jace Elliott had changed. She smiled.

"What is that sly grin for, woman?" Jace asked.

"I'm so happy, Jace. I know everything will work out for us."

Jace put their dishes in the sink. "Would you like some fresh air and exercise?" he asked. "I need to check the fields. It's been months since I was home. Would you like to see them?"

"Yes," she replied in excitement.

"You'll need to change clothes, put on boots, and get your topee. It's hot beneath that sun. I don't want you suffering heat stroke."

Leigh hurried to don a shirt, long skirt, boots, and pith helmet. She joined Jace outside. The gate was unlocked and opened. She walked to him and teased, "No more prison, my tricky captor?"

Pulling her into his embrace, he replied, "Only these arms and my determination never to lose you." He kissed her.

Holding hands, smiling, and chatting, they walked past the towering shed where the coffee beans were cured and bagged. The area around it was cleared. Jace explained how the cherries were spread out beneath the sun and turned several times a day for even drying. It required more time than the "wet process," but sufficient water for that was unavailable. Afterward, the beans were graded, sorted, bagged, and stored until transported to Mombasa for shipment to England.

As they walked, Jace related all he knew about growing coffee, and Leigh listened with great interest. The bushes were tropical evergreens, and each flower contained two seeds, called cherries. Shrubs had to be planted at the right time, the beginning of the rainy season, and groomed frequently. They did not start producing until three to four years later. It required nine months between blooming of white flowers and maturing of the seeds. When reddish-purple, the fruit was gathered by hand, by his Kikuyu workers.

"Coffee from this protectorate is considered some of the best in the world. The man who owned this place before me only brought in one crop before giving up and selling to me. He didn't like the seclusion or the time involved. His wife hated the heat and dangers."

"I don't," Leigh said and squeezed his hand.

As they roamed through the fields that seemed to stretch for miles, Jace checked his bushes and spoke to workers. She met all of Jace's employees, including Kambu, the overseer of his plantation. He told her about the loss of his last crop to disease. Occasionally they cooled themselves beneath thatched sheds where workers did the same. It was vital not to overheat the body in this sultry location.

They encountered Abena who had brought food and water to her husband, one of Jace's workers. The woman exposed white teeth as she smiled at the loving couple. "You see, Bwana Jace good man."

Leigh laughed at her implication. She glanced at

475

Jace and said, "Yes, Abena, a very wonderful man, and I love him. Thank you for taking such good care of me. I was mixed up at times. I'm sorry."

They chatted, then Jace told the African woman, "I'm marrying her as soon as the missionary arrives. Tell Ka'arta to send him to me."

Upon return to the walled yard, Leigh and Jace sat in the swing. They savored their closeness and deep love while Abena prepared their evening meal. When it was done, the Kikuyu woman left for the night. Jace and Leigh ate, then washed the dishes.

"Where is Johi?" she inquired.

"He returned to the village. He goes on safari with me, then works around here when we're home. Maybe when he hears we're getting married, he'll take the leap with Ka'arta."

"That would be nice. I like Johi. Tell me something, my love; why were your office and bedroom doors locked?"

"Abena was afraid you'd get a weapon and try to escape, or go through my stuff. She's very loyal and protective of me."

"I know. I almost made an enemy of her by insulting you. I'm glad I was wrong, and you were, too. I'll see you in a little while. I want to freshen up. It's so hot." Leigh went to take a bath.

Jace entered the room. "Mind if I join you this time? It's a big tub, and you did invite me to share such a pleasure in the jungle. I don't have to tell you how many times that offer has haunted me."

Leigh laughed and moved inside. "Why not?"

Jace stripped and slid in behind her. His legs stretched out on either side of her body. Leigh leaned her head against his chest. His arms wrapped over hers. Her hair was pulled atop her head; its lengthy ends grazed and tickled his shouller. They relaxed.

When she spoke, it was with jest words. "At least you don't have to worry about your bathwater getting chilled here."

Jace lifted a cloth and soap. He lathered it and washed her back, neck, and arms. His hand rounded her body and moved the soapy cloth over her breasts, teasing the rosy-brown tips.

Leigh leaned her head backward and Jace nibbled on her ear. She turned her face to him to kiss him. Jace moved the cloth over her stomach and between her thighs. Leigh shifted to allow his stimulating action. Soon she was mindless with desire for him.

She twisted in the tub and rested on her shins. She took the cloth from him and lathered it again. She covered his neck, chest, shoulders, and arms with suds. As she rinsed them off, her gaze met his.

Jace's hands grasped her head and pulled her mouth to his. Leigh wiggled her legs on either side of him, between his hips and the tub. As they kissed urgently, she straddled him. With boldness and need, she positioned herself on his erect manhood.

Jace assisted her with eagerness. He was surprised and pleased. Her actions meant she felt totally at ease with him, that she was playful and sensual. It stimulated him to grasp that she was a sharer in lovemaking, not just a recipient of pleasure. She possessed daring and courage. She was the perfect mate to share his life and desires.

Imprisoned against the tub, Jace could do little to labor with her. His mouth worked at her breasts. His hands clasped her hips and he arched as best he could to be a part of the provocative movements.

It was a swift and passionate union. Leigh spread kisses over his face, then captured his mouth as the climactic journey ended. Breathing hard, Leigh rested her cheek on the top of Jace's brown head while his nestled against her chest.

Finally she straightened, and her glowing gaze met his merry one. They shared laughter and kissed. Leigh grabbed the cloth and finished her bath. As she was drying, Jace completed his.

When he stepped from the tub, Leigh took a large cloth and removed the water from his frame. As she did so, she eyed him and said, "You're magnificent. Every time I look at you, I feel funny inside."

"It's called love, woman, and I feel it, too."

The next morning, Leigh made the bed while Jace dressed. She walked up behind him and wrapped her arms around his waist. "What do we do today, my love? We could work in the vegetable garden."

Jace remained still, savoring the contact of their bodies. "I have trouble thinking when you're near me, woman. Or else, all I think about is making love to you. When I visited the Far East in my sailing days, I saw men addicted to drugs. I have that same fierce and helpless craving for you, my sweet Opium."

"Like you did in the tub, or in the middle of the night?"

Jace turned and embraced her. He chuckled. "Sorry about disturbing your sleep. When I stirred and felt you near me, I couldn't help myself. As for the tub, Miss Webster, I was seduced."

"Only because you provoked it, Mr. Elliott."

"As soon as the missionary arrives, I can't call you 'Miss Webster' anymore. You'll be Mrs. Jace

Elliott."

"Laura Leigh Elliott," she murmured. "That sounds nice."

"It certainly does," he concurred.

"What about a license? We can't get married without it."

"I got one in Mombasa. We'll tell the preacher our parents are dead, so you're signing permission for yourself, which is true. We won't mention you have a legal guardian to consult."

Leigh recalled what Jace had said about Chad's power and control. "If Chad causes trouble, will the marriage be legal?" she fretted.

"We'll tell the authorities we couldn't get your guardian's permission because he and I are enemies and because he wanted you for himself. We'll explain the dangers you experienced. Of course it'll be our word against his: a wanted man and a love-smitten girl against a well-respected and charming businessman. We'll need to prove he was a threat to you or we'll be in trouble." Jace grinned. "On the other hand, I haven't been charged, tried, or convicted yet; so you won't be marrying a proven criminal. Besides, it'll be too late for him to protest and change matters. We'll have been married five weeks or more by the time we reach London. What lawman would part such a loving couple? And we do have a powerful ally in Lord Salisbury . . . See, here's the license," he said, pulling it from a drawer.

Leigh looked at the paper. It was dated in April, and was good for one year. "You got this before the safari."

Jace sent her a broad grin. "I told you I was going to convince you to marry me. I wanted to be prepared when you said yes. I didn't want to give you time to change your mind. I wasn't sure how I

was going to pull it off while Chad had control o
you, but I figured I'd think of something clever.'
They shared smiles and laughter.

As she watched him put the license in his desk
she teased, "And you did. You're a wonderfu
sneak, Jace." Then noticing some other items in th
drawer, she asked, "Who is that?"

Jace lifted a handful of pictures. "My father and
stepmother right after they married in '79. This i
me and Joanna. She was a pretty little girl. And
was a handsome youth, don't you think? I really d
like that camera invention. I don't know how i
works, but I'm glad it does. I have yours from th
safari, so we'll have our first pictures of us together
Remember the one by the termite hill?"

"Yes, I do." Leigh pulled two pictures from th
stack. She studied the lovely woman in them. "Wh
is she? An old sweetheart?"

Jace glanced at the two she was holding. "That'
Joanna, a year or so back. She became quite a
beautiful woman. She sent me those to prove she'
alive and well. If only I could locate—"

Abena summoned Jace to speak with a visitor.
He told Leigh to stay hidden in his bedroom in cas
it was a hireling of Chad's or Reid's. Leigh paced
the room until her love's return.

"You won't believe this, but that was a cabl
from one of the detectives I hired to locate Joanna.
It's like talking about her made her surface. You
must be my good-luck charm. He found her."

"That's wonderful, Jace." Leigh giggled as he
lifted her, swung her around, and kissed her. The
moment her feet touched the floor, she asked,
"Where is she? What did she say? Does she know
anything about those crimes? Will she come forward and help us?"

"Slow down, love. I'll tell you everything. She's Joanna Marlowe now, Frank Marlowe's wife. They live on a ranch near Denver. As ordered, my man didn't approach her or question her."

"Is he certain it's your stepsister? What if he's mistaken?"

"He isn't. He had an old picture of her. Besides, Joanna can't be missed even in a crowd. She's English, a few years older than you are, auburn hair, hazel eyes, about your height and size. She's lived there with her husband since the winter of '94. The timing is perfect. She has a scar here," Jace said, motioning to an area below Leigh's left cheekbone. "Just like the woman in Denver. He traced her from place to place and name to name. It has to be Joanna. She got that scar from Chad's ring when he backhanded her one day. That's what started the fight when I nearly beat him to death with my bare hands. This is incredible, just what we need. Lordy, I'm glad she's safe and sound. I can't wait to see her."

"How did she get to America?" Leigh inquired. "To Colorado? Who is the man she married?"

"I don't know. I wish there were more details in the cable. He's watching her and awaiting my next orders."

"At last you know where to find her. I'm so glad, Jace. Will we sail to America first and get Joanna to betray Chad in London? Oh, my goodness! Aunt Jenna. I have to cable her before Chad tells her I'm dead. She'd be devastated by that news."

"We'll cable your aunt, Lord Salisbury, and Joanna when we reach Mombasa. It would take us months to get to Denver and more time to reach London. If Joanna is ready and willing to save me and help me, she'll respond to a cable. If her distress is so bad that she can't, I could never force her to testify. Do you understand, Leigh?"

She caressed his cheek. "Yes, my love, and you're right."

"We'll take Reid's message, the statements from those men who attacked you at the fort, and all we've put together. It's a start. I don't know if it's enough, but it makes our trip worth the risk."

"You have their statements?"

"I'm to pick them up on my return. I asked Jim Hanes to make out one about his dealings with Chad. If he decided to comply, Alfred should have it. That would make our case against Chad stronger. I was planning to send everything to Lord Salisbury and let him handle both matters until November. But now, I think it's best if we go and give our testimonies. With that evidence, if anything goes badly for me, Salisbury can protect you from Chad and the others."

"Don't even think such horrible thoughts, Jace."

"I must, love, because none of this evidence helpes the case against me. If Joanna doesn't come forward . . ."

Jace pulled Leigh into his arms. He hugged her tightly and kissed her. Going to London was a big risk for both of them.

Laura Leigh Webster and Jace Edward Elliott were married by a Protestant missionary in a short and simple ceremony the following afternoon. The wedding took place in the yard, with many joyous workers in attendance. Johi, Ka'arta, Abena and her husband, and Kambu were present. Leigh wore a lace pale-blue dress, and tropical flowers in her tawny hair. Jace wore a suit, and looked the perfect gentleman. A party followed with foods and treats prepared by Abena and her daughter. The guests drank lavishly from fruit juice and wine.

Using the one bottle of champagne Jace owned, he toasted his bride with the unchilled liquid saying, "To the only woman I've ever loved or ever will love, my beautiful wife."

Leigh did not give him her toast until they were alone. She said, "To the only man who has or can or will offer me wild perils and sweet passions. I love you with all my heart and soul, Jace Elliott."

On June twenty-five, Jace checked his crop one last time and left Kambu in charge again. Bearers had been summoned to get them to Mombasa. Johi went along to guide the men home afterward. Farewells were said to Abena and the others, and they departed.

The group reached Mombasa on July sixth, four days after Chad and his companions docked in London.

On the seventh, Jace picked up the written testimony of Jim Hanes from Alfred Johnston, to whom Jace explained the events. He went to the Colonial Office and was given copies of the Arab abductors' confessions. He placed those crucial papers with Reid's cable to Fiona, then sent a telegram to Joanna Harris Marlowe, telling her of Chad's threat to his and Leigh's lives, and pleading for her help. He asked his stepsister to meet him in London at Lord Salisbury's home. Then he cabled the prime minister.

Leigh sent word to her aunt near Dallas, also

explaining matters and requesting secrecy until her problem was solved. She did not go into detail, but told Jenna she would write everything soon.

On July ninth, Leigh and Jace Elliott sailed from Mombasa, British East Africa, toward London. Leigh was prepared for "Mother's Misery" which was due that day, but it never appeared . . .

Chapter Twenty

London, England
July 30, 1896

Leigh was in London once more; this time, it was under different circumstances. She was the wife of Jace Elliott, and they had come to settle the past. She and Jace had traveled under the names of Mr. and Mrs. Alfred Johnston. Upon docking, they remained aboard the steamer until dark, in case Lord Chadwick Hamilton was having the waterfront watched for Jace's approach. They were picked up in a covered carriage belonging to Prime Minister Cecil Salisbury and taken to his home. There they found Joanna Harris Marlowe, who had arrived two days ago.

The auburn-haired woman of twenty-three hugged her stepbrother and cried. Joanna begged Jace's understanding and forgiveness. When she was calmed, Jace asked for the truth.

Joanna's hazel eyes were red and dewy as she complied. "I never wanted you or anyone harmed, Jace; you must believe me. By the time I learned what was happening, it was too late; I was too deeply involved to expose Chad. After Father's death, I heard Chad say you could never return to England. He said he didn't want to kill you, that he wanted you to live and suffer, so I believed you were safe. When I received your telegram about his attempts on your life, I couldn't hold silent any longer. Whatever happens to me, this horrid nightmare must end. I would have told you sooner," she vowed, "but I wanted to protect Frank and little Jace, and myself. I have a wonderful husband and son. I told Frank everything, and he agreed I should come."

Leigh and Lord Salisbury remained silent and alert, but Jace asked several questions; "How did you meet Frank Marlowe? How did you run away? Why?"

Joanna sipped water to wet her throat and dry lips. "Let me tell you what happened here first. My journey started long ago, when our parents married. I've known Chad since I was six years old. I liked him and trusted him, Jace, just like you did and Father did. I was daft about him from the time I became a young woman. You know how he attracted and charmed all the girls. Chad had a powerful magic, an evil magic, about him that lured people to him; then, he consumed them like a voracious devil. All except you, Jace; you saw him for what he was and pulled free of him. I wasn't that strong or that lucky."

Her hazel eyes were haunted by memories. "If you'll recall, I was not in London when you visited in '92. I was with Mother's kin in Scotland. I didn't know about the trouble between you two." She pushed straying locks of chestnut from her pale face. "I was to marry Benjamin Carver in the spring of '94. He called off the betrothal and married another woman. I didn't truly love him, but I was

486

hurt and humiliated. Chad rushed to see me. He poured on that magical and irresistible charm. Before I knew it, I was enslaved to him in heart, mind, and body. He promised to marry me that Christmas, and he convinced me to move into his home. Father and Mother were ashamed and furious, but I was too in love to listen."

No one interrupted the painful confession, and no one spoke a distracting word when Joanna halted to sip more water.

"When you came home in June, Chad ordered me not to see you. I didn't want any trouble or to lose him, so I obeyed. When you came to his townhouse, you two got into that terrible fight. Someone summoned the authorities, and you were arrested. Chad refused to let me see you and explain about our love and marriage." She rubbed the scar on her cheek. "He told me he had struck me in the heat of your quarrel because I begged to speak with you alone. He told me what happened in South Africa. He was so loving and convincing. That's why I didn't come to the jail or see you after you were released. While you were imprisoned, he asked me to steal Father's knife. You know, the one you brought to him from South Africa with his name carved on it. I also stole a lantern from the company, marked Elliott's of London. Chad said they were for a harmless trick, and I believed him. Then Mr. Stokely was killed and his company burned, the very day of your release and departure. Those two witnesses lied about Father being there before the fire. His knife and lantern were found in the alley. Chad had asked me to invite Father to the townhouse to discuss how to make peace with my family so Chad and I could marry. Father was with me during the fire, Jace; he couldn't have been involved."

Jace concealed his rage and shock. "Why didn't you tell the authorities?" he asked, "Or tell me?"

"I was afraid and confused," Joanna admitted. "I didn't want to believe Chad was involved. I hoped Father would be proven innocent. I reminded Chad that Father was with me that awful night, at his request. I also reminded him about the knife and lantern I had taken for him. Chad told me they had been stolen from his office, possibly to incriminate him. He said people would think we were lying to save Father, and we might become suspects if we went forward. Chad promised to find the best way to handle everything; he swore to help clear him. It sounded logical, and I was so enthralled by him. When Father killed himself to avoid arrest, Chad said it was because he feared he couldn't prove he was innocent."

Joanna dabbed at tears. "When Webster International took control of Father's firm and most of his estate, Chad mentioned that both his business rivals were gone. The way he acted made me suspicious. Mother was left with very little, and Chad refused to help her or to discuss our marriage. He became cold and hateful. He started making hazy comments about how Father's death and the loss of your inheritance would hurt you. He boasted how my seduction had hurt you. He talked about Webster's having a monopoly, as if he was due the credit for such prosperity. They all tormented me. I had to discover the truth."

Joanna lowered her lashes. "I watched Chad closely. One night I followed him to a meeting with the two witnesses. He didn't pay them, Jace; he murdered them. Reid Adams was there, too. I realized what Chad had done, how he had used me, now he had destroyed our family as revenge on you. I realized he had lied about you. I even feared he had killed Father. I knew he would kill me to silence me. I hurried to his place, packed a few things, and sailed on a ship leaving for America at dawn. I left Chad a note saying I was with my grieving mother so he wouldn't search for me in time to halt my escape. I docked in Charleston, took a train to Atlanta, then several to Denver, using different names each time. I hoped the many changes of cities and names would prevent Chad from finding me and killing me. I thought he'd never look in that area of America. I was so distraught that I didn't think anyone would believe I wasn't involved."

Jace grasped her trembling hands and murmured, "You could have come to me. You could have trusted me. I would have helped you."

"You had sailed for Africa. I was afraid Chad would come after both of us. I knew you and Mother would be safe as long as I stayed away and remained silent. I didn't want to go to prison or be hanged, Jace. I couldn't face any more humiliation or endure more anguish. On the train, I met Frank Marlowe. He is such a good and kind man. He knew I was suffering. He spent time with me. He made me smile and laugh again. He had a ranch near Denver. He said all he needed was a wife, and he asked me to marry him. I was fond of him, and it seemed the perfect escape. But I came to love him, really love him. It wasn't infatuation as with Ben and Chad. When our son was born, we named him Jace. Everything was wonderful. I was happy, and starting to forget. Then your cable arrived. I knew if you had located me, Chad could, too. I couldn't run away from Frank and the baby. I

489

revealed the whole truth to him. He understood and believed me. He said I should help you convict Chad for his crimes."

"How did you get those few letters to me?"

"Frank's brother is a sailor. Frank thought I had run away from a bad home. He thought my scar was inflicted by a cruel father. He asked James to mail letters to my brother from ports he visited. I couldn't tell you the truth, but I had to let you know I was alive and well." Joanna looked at Jace. "I'll testify against Chad and Reid."

Jace hugged his stepsister. "Thank you for coming and telling the truth, Joanna. I know how difficult and painful it was." He stroked her damp cheek and curly hair. He noted the dark circles beneath her hazel eyes and he saw how pale and tense she was. "You look tired. Why don't you go to bed? We'll figure out what to do."

Joanna looked at Leigh and said, "It's so nice to meet you. I wish it wasn't under such grim circumstances. I'm glad you and Jace found each other and married. Please don't think too wickedly of me."

Leigh smiled and said, "I don't, Joanna. I know how charming and devious Chad can be. He fooled me for a long time. He would have killed me if it hadn't been for Jace. He'll pay soon. After this matter is settled, we can get better acquainted. We'll be good friends."

After Joanna left the room, Lord Salisbury revealed, "With these facts, it will be a simple matter to clear you and Brandon, but Lord Hamilton cannot be arrested and punished. He killed himself last week. He placed a pistol to his head and ended his madness. I thought it best not to upset Mrs. Marlowe with that news. After receiving your cable

I contacted Charles Nelson, my man at Scotland Yard. I asked him to begin a routine investigation. I surmise that Lord Hamilton became worried and suspicious when questioned so thoroughly about Miss Webster's sudden death so close to that time of a large inheritance. From Charles's report, Lord Hamilton behaved quite strangely."

"No, sir," Jace refuted, "I don't think he committed suicide. I believe Reid Adams killed him." Jace withdrew the cable from Reid to Fiona from Mombasa. He explained his suspicions to the startled prime minister and showed him the sworn statement of Jim Hanes and the confessions of the two Arab kidnappers. He related the talks that he and Johi had overheard, and the perilous incidents involving Leigh during the safari. "As you can see, sir, it's a complicated situation."

Lord Salisbury shook his head and ruffled his whiskered jawline. "Madness is never simple, Jace. It is apparent that the two cases overlap. It has always amazed me what some people will do for money and power. Greed and obsessions have destroyed many people. A life in politics has shown me countless dark hearts and minds. Charles Nelson will be given this information and evidence tomorrow," the heavy-lidded man added. "He will take down Mrs. Marlowe's statement. You and your father will be exonerated of all charges."

Jace sighed in relief, so did Leigh. Jace said, "I'd like to see Louisa Jennings and Cynthia Campbell tomorrow. I want their confessions and punishment, too."

"Scotland Yard has been unable to question them, as you suggested. Lady Louisa has been very ill since her return from Africa. She is at Marquise Campbell's estate. Charles did learn that both

491

women are facing financial ruin. That might explain their actions. As soon as Lady Louisa recovers, she'll be questioned and charged."

"As for Reid Adams and Fiona Webster," Jace added, "I have a plan to entrap them, with help from your Scotland Yard friend."

Saturday morning, Jace, Leigh, and Charles Nelson of Scotland Yard arrived at the marquise's estate. Cynthia refused to receive them, but Charles insisted. When Cynthia joined them in the parlor, she looked terrible. Her brown hair was dull and uncombed, her complexion colorless, her lips almost white. Her clothes were wrinkled and stained and her sunken eyes exposed fatigue and anguish. Her mood was a mixture of somberness and hostility.

With the drapes drawn, the house was dark and gloomy. Within moments, they learned why.

"I will tell you nothing about Louisa. She died Wednesday," Cynthia revealed, "died from an awful disease she caught in Africa. I warned her to stop drinking unboiled water. I warned her to take her quinine tablets. Why didn't she listen?" the brunette wailed in anguish. Her brown eyes chilled instantly. "Get out of my home. You did this to her!" she shouted at Jace, then glared at Leigh. Her gaze widened and she paled. "You're dead! Why have you returned to haunt me?"

"It was a trick, Cynthia," Leigh revealed, "a trick to save my life. We all know Louisa and Chad were trying to kill me."

"Don't speak evil of my friend," Cynthia cried. "You should be dead. Louisa should be alive and married to that handsome devil. It's all Chad's

492

ault. If he hadn't wanted you, we wouldn't have
one to that death trap. I hate you. I won't tell you
nything."

Recognizing the woman was on the edge of insan-
ty, Leigh motioned the two men to silence. In a
oft voice, she urged, "You must tell us the truth,
Cynthia. It can't hurt Louisa and Chad now. We
now your people attacked me on the waterfront.
We know Louisa paid men to abduct me in Mombasa. We have witnesses and evidence against both
f you. If you don't tell the truth, you'll be arrested
nd sent to prison. You'll lose everything and be
umiliated. Is that what you want?"

"I've already lost everything," the woman scoffed.

Leigh continued in her soothing and persuasive
one. "I can help you, Cynthia. I can give you
noney to pay your debts, and money to go some-
vhere—like Australia or Scotland—to begin a new
ife. You won't have to be humiliated. You don't
ave to be penniless. Why protect a dead woman
nd destroy yourself? Louisa was your friend. She
oved you. She'll understand you must save yourself.
We can't harm Louisa. We only want to know the
ruth. Please, let me help you."

Cynthia looked around the darkened room with
wild eyes. The creditors were coming Monday to
ake everything, to evict her, to shame her. She
would have nothing and no one. With money, she
could leave London, leave England. Louisa was
gone. The plot was dead. She glanced at Leigh and
sked, "Will you give me lots of money?"

"Yes, all you want. I have plenty. The money
neans nothing to me, only the truth. Will you let
ne save you?"

"What about him?" the brunette hinted, point-
ng to the man from Scotland Yard. "Won't he

493

arrest me?"

"No, Marquise," Charles said. "We simply want
to solve this case." With those promises, the grief-
crazed woman relented. She revealed how Louisa
had poisoned William Webster so Chad could inherit and marry her. When Leigh inherited everything, Louisa went after the blonde for the same
reason. She related how Louisa had pulled off the
London and Mombasa attacks, and how she had
removed the cartridges from Leigh's gun before the
rhino hunt. "We were best friends. I loved her. I
helped her because we needed the money. Louisa
hated you for messing up her plans. She would have
killed you if you hadn't died from that snakebite.
But you didn't die. My sweet Louisa did. And that
bastard who lied to her, I'm glad he's dead too."

"Did you or Louisa punish Chad?" Leigh probed
in a careful tone.

Defeated, the woman mumbled, "No. Louisa fell
ill on the ship. Chad refused to help her. The
doctor couldn't help her. I brought her home with
me. My doctor said it was blackwater fever. Louisa
suffered terribly. I tended her day and night. Chad
wouldn't even visit her. He's cruel and selfish. He's
been mad ever since he thought you died."

Charles Nelson wrote out the woman's statement.
Cynthia didn't even read it before signing it. "When
do I get my money?" she demanded.

"Monday, when the bank opens. We'll come and
take you there."

On Sunday night, August first, Leigh and men
from Scotland Yard were concealed behind machinery and stacked crates inside the main Webster company, and other men were concealed outside to

494

thwart any hirelings Reid Adams brought with him. Jace was standing in the middle of the floor, awaiting the final confrontation. One lantern was aglow nearby, casting about eerie shadows in the enormous room.

Leigh was frightened for Jace. She knew that men with drawn weapons were guarding her clever husband. Yet, something could go wrong. Reid Adams was an evil and unpredictable man, also a cunning one. Her pulse raced, and her heart pounded.

Reid arrived, alone. He stalked toward the light and Jace Elliott. His features looked sharper than usual in the near darkness. Malevolent shadows danced on his face and body. A cold sneer curled his tight lips upward. "I see you survived Chad's trap. What are you doing here? Why did you send for me? What do you want?"

"My half of the inheritance, old chap. I know about the will. Leigh told me before . . . her little accident," Jace hinted. "Too bad she got herself killed. I wanted to marry her and take everything, just like Chad planned. You helped him, Reid, so you're just as guilty. If you don't get me my half and help me escape London safely, I'll risk going to the authorities to take you and Fiona down with me. That's right, old boy," Jace taunted when the man reacted to his threat. "I know all about you and Chad's mother, and all about your little plot. Is that why you killed Chad? Did he add up the facts and confront you?"

Reid pulled a pistol from beneath his coat and pointed it at Jace. "That's right, but you won't tell anybody anything. I have men watching all the doors so you can't escape me. Nobody is spoiling things for me and Fiona. We waited too long to have each other and the money. Nobody, not even Chad, knew the truth about me and my beautiful Fiona. We were careful over the years to conceal our love, so nobody would suspect we had anything to do with those deaths."

"In the beginning, Chad was the one who wanted Leigh dead," Jace said to elicit evidence.

"You're right, Jace, but he got weak on me. The plot was devised cleverly and perfectly: Leigh was to die; you were to be framed; Fiona was to inherit; and Chad was to run the empire. But Chad didn't know we had additional plans. Fiona and I were going to marry, then travel wherever our spirits took us. It was five long years of terrible sacrifice, of annoying pretenses, of sneaking around, of having to dally with other women like that Campbell whore. I was miserable after Fiona left for India, but I had to prevent her from falling under suspicion in case anything went wrong with the plot."

"She's home now," Jace pointed out, "so you should be very happy. But how could you let the woman you love marry another man?"

"I hated for my sweet Fiona to wed William Webster and to sleep with that old man, but it was necessary for our future. I would do anything for my love, and she had wanted the Webster empire that her son dangled under her pretty nose. None of us expected the old man to leave everything to his granddaughter, or to die so soon. Then he thwarted us from the grave with his strange will. Chad should have stuck to the original plan, and everything would have been fine. Chad would still be alive, and very rich. I liked Chad. But when it came to a choice between having it all with Fiona or letting Chad have it all with Leigh, even a friend has to be sacrificed."

"You're right." Jace said. "How did you do away with him?"

"It was simple. He was acting crazy after losing Leigh. When the law started nosing around, he got worse. I got him drunk, put a pistol in his hand, and helped him pull the trigger. Have you ever read Tennyson's 'Lancelot and Elaine,' old boy? 'Sweet is true love though given in vain, in vain; and sweet is death who puts an end to pain.' That's all I did, put Chad out of his bittersweet agony. He was going to kill that blond witch until she enchanted him. I couldn't let her live. I couldn't let her and Chad take away my dream with Fiona."

"So, you were the one behind Leigh's so-called accidents. You were very clever, Reid. I finally caught on, but too late."

Reid laughed, a cold and menacing sound. "Yes, I tampered with Louisa's gun. You and Leigh were always in front of her. I hoped that redhead would shoot her, or get rid of the man who kept rescuing her. I needed a scapegoat. Louisa or you were perfect for that role. Chad shocked me when he fell in love with that girl and changed our plan, even dropped his revenge on you; that told me how enchanted he was. With Leigh leaning his way or with Chad believing she was, I couldn't provoke him into mistrusting and killing her. She really had him under a tight spell. I figured if you two began fighting over Leigh, you'd be distracted from my threat. Or from Louisa's. Since I couldn't get Chad to doubt Leigh and to carry out the original scheme, Leigh's death was up to me."

"But Louisa was after her, too. And Chad was also part of the crime."

Reid didn't seem to care what Jace learned now. "Yes, but he kept wavering. When Chad was drugging her canteen, that last time, I added an extra dose. I hoped she would fall or shoot herself or be unable to flee a wild animal. Somehow she always eluded my traps. She was one lucky bitch, until that snake solved everything for me. But the cleverest of all was the quicksand."

Reid bragged on how he had accomplished that "accident." "As soon as Leigh said she was heading for the pool after teatime, I excused myself to cut brush to pile in the right trail which would force her to take the wrong fork when I scared her later. I sneaked into her tent by that secret flap you two used for your lusty meetings and stole her derringer. While Chad and Louisa were playing around inside their tent, I left Cynthia in ours and sneaked into the jungle again. I scared Leigh right into my trap. Once she was in the quicksand, I tossed her gun into the pile of her possessions, cleared the trail, and hurried back to camp. I picked a fight with Cynthia so no one would realize I'd been gone. You see, old chap, I know a thing or two about tracks and trails, too. If you're as good in the wilds as you and others believe and you hadn't been so distracted, you could have been on to me that day."

Jace was furious with himself. Reid was correct. He hadn't checked the area because Leigh had convinced him of her error and he had been distracted by their dispute. Reid had lured her into death's jaws, heard her scream for help but sneaked back to camp. While the man's wits were dulled by overconfidence and his tongue was loosened by pride, Jace asked, "Did you know Louisa poisoned William Webster? She told me before she died."

Reid looked surprised. "She was so eager to get Chad and his money that I should have guessed. I'm certain Louisa was behind the London and

Mombasa attacks on Leigh, but I didn't tell Chad. I didn't tell him that Louisa's family was facing financial ruin. I needed that redheaded whore on the safari to take the blame when Chad wondered who was behind Leigh's accidents and then her death. I was very careful not to drop any clues to Chad, particularly after he fell for his ward and switched plans on me. I hated Louisa and Cynthia, and I didn't want those wanton bitches around me. But there was a possibility that Louisa would get rid of Leigh for us. She might have, if Chad hadn't duped her and halted her deadly schemes. Louisa was a prime suspect because of her reckless actions. I figured, if Leigh's death looked odd to anyone, she could be framed easily."

Reid sent forth evil laughter before revealing, "Every time she let up on Leigh during the safari, I provoked her again, or tricked Cynthia into doing so. I tried with Chad, but he loved her and wanted her as much as I do Fiona. I'm glad that bitch killed the old man. It ate me up to let Fiona sleep with that old bastard. After Chad pushed Sarah Webster down the steps, he convinced Fiona to marry William to get his money. Of course, that wasn't Chad's plan, either. He loved the old man, and he wanted them to be a family. He liked being William's son, but he was damned mad over that crazy will. Fiona and I agreed to wait five years before killing him, but he only lasted four. Now that Fiona's home from India, soon I can publicly woo her and marry her. Too bad her son got suspicious of us, but we couldn't let him spoil things. As soon as it's proper to marry and slip away, we'll be gone and happy."

"You mean as soon as the mourning periods are over? Why didn't you ask me to take Leigh Webster off your hands? I would have been delighted to hold her captive forever at my jungle plantation. I would have settled for her instead of half the money, especially since Chad wanted her so badly."

"Webster's the one who endangered his granddaughter by leaving it all to her. Fiona and I would have settled for half. After serving him for years, she deserved payment. She deserves every shilling."

"Before you pull that trigger," Jace coaxed, "mind telling me if Chad and Webster framed me and my father. Call it a dying man's last request. You owe me that, since my jungle killed her for you."

"William Webster a killer and arsonist?" Reid scoffed. "He wasn't involved. The old man didn't know anything about it. Chad burned out Stokely and killed him. He scattered around that evidence against Brandon, and made certain your father didn't have an alibi. Your ignorant stepsister did that little task. Chad had her duped. If she hadn't escaped, she'd be dead, too, just like those witnesses Chad and I got rid of. I'll tell you something else, old chap: before Chad killed your father, he forced him to write that suicide note implicating you. He told Brandon he was holding Catharine and Joanna captive and would kill them if he didn't. I guess your father figured you could get away or clear yourself, so he did as ordered. Chad planted that other evidence to make it look like a political murder."

"So, it was all for revenge aimed at me. Why did he warn me to flee years ago? I could have been captured and hanged."

"Chad didn't want you arrested and killed. He wanted you alive to suffer like he had. He was having you watched. He knew you didn't have an alibi. He forced your father to make that suicide note sound crazy on purpose. He wanted it to look like you knew about his crimes and you were connected to those Irish rebels. Chad knew that evidence would force you to stay out of England and keep you from interfering. Once you'd suffered enough, he was going to have your plantation burned, lure you here, then let you be arrested and executed. He got revenge on you and got a business monopoly with the same scheme. Of course, he passed plenty of business to me for helping him, but I only did it both times so my sweet Fiona could profit."

Jace had a hard time controlling his rage. He wanted to attack the man and beat him senseless, but he couldn't because he needed more facts while Reid was boasting. "Why did Webster leave me the money you won't let me collect?"

"Chad and I couldn't figure out that one. Chad suspected the old man discovered a clue about his actions. I guess it was a way to pay you back for losing your father and your inheritance. He must have left Fiona in to ward off suspicion and as a threat to Leigh. Something else, and it might ease your mind: Chad liked your father. He hated killing him, but it was the best way to hurt you and to profit."

"Are you telling me Fiona agreed to have Chad killed?"

"I pulled the trigger, but Fiona agreed. Chad didn't love his mother. He threatened to kill her several times. She married William to get his money, and we have. We're not letting anyone foil us."

Reid aimed the gun at Jace's heart, but Jace taunted, "Don't you want to know how I discovered the truth about you and Fiona? I doubt you'll pull

501

that trigger after you realize I have proof, proof that can get you two in big trouble. If you shoot me, the law gets it. Imagine your beautiful Fiona in prison or with a rope around her neck."

"What proof?" Reid demanded. "It's a trick. I was too careful."

"Not that last day in Mombasa, old boy. Your rash cable to Fiona in Bombay is mighty incriminating," Jace hinted, withdrawing a blank paper from his front pocket and waving it in the air. "It fell into my hands. How much will you pay for this evidence, old boy?"

"Hand it over!" Reid shouted. "Or I'll take it after you're dead."

"You could, if this was the cable copy. I'm not a fool, Reid. I have it hidden. Once I'm dead, my things will be searched and the real telegram will be discovered. I wonder what the authorities will think about it. Webster dead. Leigh dead. Chad dead. Fiona and you getting married. Then that cable shows up and inspires questions. I also have a confession from Jim Hanes that includes you, old boy. If I don't get money and get killed, so will you and your lover."

"What do you want, Jace? Name your price."

Jace scratched his head as he murmured, "About half is—" He brought up his knee into Reid's groin as hard as he could. As the man reflexively jerked forward, Jace landed a stunning blow across his jaw. When Reid was floored and the gun was sent clattering from his grasp, Jace pounced upon him and socked him several times.

The authorities and Leigh rushed forward.

Leigh grabbed her husband's arm. "Enough, Jace! It's over. Your plan worked. The authorities heard everything."

Jace glanced up at his frantic wife, his image reflected in her blue eyes. The animal instinct within him was mastered. He ceased beating the man who had tried to destroy him and everyone he loved. He inhaled, stood, and pulled Leigh into his arms. "You're right, love; it's finally over. We can go home now."

"We heard every word, Jace," Charles Nelson said. "You're under arrest, Mr. Adams. I'll have my men pick up your accomplice tonight. You're both facing a lot of very damaging charges."

Reid jumped to his feet. He gaped at the embracing couple. "You tricked me. You faked her death!"

"Of course. You couldn't expect me to let one of you kill the woman I love, the woman I married."

Reid was stunned. Reality flooded him, and terror filled him. "I was lying just to provoke you," he claimed in desperation. "Chad did all those things. He killed himself. I thought you were trying to blackmail me and Fi—Mrs. Webster. I was only trying to get information from you. We're innocent."

"It's useless, Mr. Adams," Nelson told him. "We have plenty of evidence. We have your cable from Mombasa. We have a statement from Jim Hanes, one from Joanna Harris Marlowe, and one from Cynthia Campbell. It's over. Come along quietly."

Leigh watched as the sullen Reid was taken away. His hirelings outside had been captured. Men were sent to arrest Fiona Webster. So many people had died for greed and money. So many people had been hurt. Each of them had wanted her inheritance, when only Jace Elliott meant anything to her. She wished her grandfather hadn't made her his sole heir. Yet she realized she would never have met her love, her husband, if that weren't true.

Too, she comprehended, Jace and his father were cleared of those crimes. Joanna was free of the past. Her grandfather hadn't been involved. Brandon Elliott and her grandparents could now rest in peace. She and Jace could return home and build a bright future. At least some good things had come from so much evil and suffering.

On Monday, Jace and Leigh went to see Cynthia Campbell and realized she'd finally lost all touch with reality and sanity. The pitiful woman would have to be taken to an institution for care and treatment, but the doctor they summoned said her recovery was doubtful. If she traveled the long road back, she would spend her life in sorrow.

The remainder of that day was spent with Jace's stepsister.

On Tuesday morning, Joanna Marlowe sailed for Scotland to visit her mother. With her, she took a document that revealed a large deposit Leigh Webster Elliott had made in a London bank for Catharine Elliott's support, enough for Brandon's widow to live comfortably for the rest of her life. From Scotland in two weeks, Joanna was sailing home to her family. Jace and Leigh promised to visit them and Jenna late next summer, after the coffee crop was in and sold.

During the day, Jace rode Leigh by his old home, and they visited the graves of their loved ones. He related his family history to his wife, who was delighted to learn all about Jace.

They went to Webster International and searched Chad's office to make certain no family possessions or incriminating evidence was left behind. Leigh bid the workers good-bye. She urged them not to worry, that everything would be settled soon. She questioned Jace to make sure he did not want to retain his father's company. Both decided they did not want to be in the textile business or to live in London.

At four, they had afternoon tea with Lord Salisbury. They thanked him for his past and recent help. All three were glad to have Brandon and Jace exonerated, and the case closed. For a while, they talked of Brandon Elliott and William Webster, then parted at six, with Lord Salisbury promising again to introduce Leigh and Jace to Queen Victoria on their next visit during the early summer of '97.

Over dinner in their hotel suite, Jace talked about Chad for the last time. "He really loved you, Leigh. In time, if you had loved him, I think you could have changed him back to the way he was before he was destroyed in South Africa. At least I'd like to believe that was possible. There are plenty of good times to remember. I'd like to forget the bad."

"He must have been different long ago, Jace, or you wouldn't have loved him so. I'm sorry about the pain both of you endured. Deep inside, I think he always knew you didn't betray him. I doubt he could have ever admitted it, not after the terrible things he did during his madness. Whatever happened to Chadwick Hamilton during his capture and torture by the Matabele warriors altered him inextricably. He couldn't accept the fact you couldn't rescue him from anything. To get back his manhood, he had to blame someone for his troubles; he had to use a powerful emotion to push him onward. It's sad that he chose hatred and vengeance."

"At least he's at peace now. I want that for him, Leigh. He was an important part of my life. When I thought he was dead years ago, it really hurt. When I discovered him alive, I was overjoyed, until he made us bitter enemies. The loss of our friendship created a vast emptiness in me. But you've filled it, and I'm at peace now, too."

On Wednesday, Leigh and Jace met with the Webster lawyers to unravel the shocking affair of her faked death. She ordered a sale of all her holdings in England except the ancestral estate, which she could not bring herself to part with yet. She told the lawyers she would visit there next year and make her final decision. Leigh couldn't help but think that perhaps one of their children might reside in England one day in that beautiful country setting.

Arrangements also were made for any further support of Jace's stepmother that ill health or such might necessitate. Money was allotted for a nice house for Catharine, who had been forced by Chad's crimes into the home of relatives far away. It would be the widow's decision to purchase a dwelling there or in London where she had once lived. With Brandon and Jace cleared, there was no reason she couldn't return.

Jace was happy to see his wife so concerned over his father's widow, and so generous in heart.

Afterward, the couple went to the Webster home, where Fiona Hamilton Webster had been arrested Sunday night, dragged away screaming and protesting and finally sobbing at her defeat. Leigh went

506

through her grandparents' belongings. Servants helped her pack the possessions she wanted to take home to Africa. Other items were given to the men and women who had served her family for years. The London home and Chad's townhouse were to be sold, along with the business.

Charles Nelson called to reveal that Reid and Fiona were incarcerated and awaiting trial, with no hope of escaping convictions. Charles revealed that he expected Reid to be sentenced to death for those murder charges, and for Fiona to get life in prison for her conspiracies. He coaxed Leigh and Jace to remain to testify, although it wasn't necessary for convictions, and their testimonies were on file. The couple said no, satisfied that justice would be meted out by the court.

On August sixth, Leigh and Jace Elliott sailed for Africa, to arrive on the twenty-eighth.

A letter from Jenna, which had been mailed in mid-May, was awaiting Leigh in Mombasa. It related how Jenna had nursed Carl Hastings back to life following a grave illness. From her aunt's words, the episode had changed her new uncle. Jenna wrote of how happy they were. She also revealed that Tyler Clark had been fired and was gone from the ranch.

Leigh was glad. She planned to write a long letter to Jenna soon and she looked forward to visiting her aunt and Joanna next summer.

Other delightful news awaited Jace and Leigh. Johi and Ka'arta had married during their absence. Abena was beaming ear to ear.

Kambu, the overseer, reported to Jace that the crop was heavy and healthy, and should come in

507

during March of next year.

As soon as greetings and news were exchanged and baggage was put inside the house, everyone left the couple alone.

Leigh strolled around the house, smiling as she touched things here and there. She was at home. She was with her love. Nothing could endanger or part them again. Looking forward to a sensual night with Jace, she took a long bath, and donned a yellow-and-red sarong.

She had missed two spells of "Mother's Misery," in early July and in August. She suspected she was with child, and it caused her to glow with delight and anticipation. She revealed her suspicion to Jace. "If I'm right, the baby should come in March. I know that's going to be a hectic month for you. I'm sorry I can't schedule it for a more leisurely time, Mr. Elliott, but you have only yourself to blame for seducing me the moment we were reunited."

Husky laughter filled the room. "You've given me everything a man could desire, Leigh. Abena will be happy to help tend a little Bwana Jace or Bibi Laura Leigh, if she isn't looking out after her own grandchildren. What a spring it will be—a big crop and a new baby. I'm a lucky man. We've endured a lot of wild perils. From now on, it's just sweet passions, my tawny lioness."

Leigh gazed at the gold band with its large diamond on her finger. "It's so beautiful, Jace, and so big. When and where did you get it?"

"I found it in South Africa when Chad and I were mining there. I knew it was special, so I saved it for the right occasion. Mr. Carnes did an excellent job of cutting and mounting the stone. It's the only diamond I had left. After my crop loss, I

508

feared I would have to sell it. I'm glad I didn't, because it looks perfect on this lovely hand," he said, lifting it to kiss its back, then her palm.

Leigh had never seen Jace look happier or more relaxed than he did at this moment. No shadows from a dark and painful past lingered in his lucid green gaze. No deceits controlled his tender smile. No trouble stalked his life and mind. No intrusive mysteries surrounded him. No doubts or anguish tormented him. He was free to love fully and to think of their life together. As she removed the provocative garment, she teased, "I won't be able to wear these much longer, so I better use them to entice you as long as I can."

Jace pulled her naked body into his arms. His fingers trailed over her flesh. His mouth nuzzled her ear. His nose inhaled her sweet fragrance. He was at peace, filled with pride and contentment. His predatory lips tracked across her face and captured her mouth. Intense joy surged through him.

They shared countless kisses, their lips and tongues tantalizing each other. They exchanged caresses, their hands stimulating and pleasuring each other's eager bodies. They hadn't made love since the steamer docked, and they were ravenous for each other. They wanted to savor this privacy, this unique moment; but fierce cravings demanded to be fed.

They hastily removed Jace's boots and garments and fell across the bed, clinging to each other and laughing. The two explored love's land with as much leisure as their yearnings allowed. They preyed on each other's weaknesses; they captured each other's strengths. They hunted for blissful satisfaction as they journeyed toward ecstasy. They came together to share love, desire, a special oneness. Their safari to a bright future was underway; their first hunt was a heart stirring success; and their most prized trophy was love everlasting.

Jace looked into his wife's eyes. "I love you more than life itself, Laura Leigh Elliott. Just as I will love the child you carry," he added, stroking her stomach.

Leigh smiled into his jungle-green eyes. She caressed his sun-bronzed face, playfully mussed his brown hair. "You're an excellent safari guide, my virile rogue. You gave me pleasure and excitement. You led me through dangerous territory, and brought me home safe. You helped me hunt down and obtain the best prize of all: you."

"Only so I could capture you for myself," Jace teased. "That night on the waterfront, I warned you not to tempt a determined man like me. You were stubborn and impulsive, and did it anyway. You left me no choice but to lure you into my trap. I told you I would win our wager, any way necessary."

Leigh rolled atop him. She shook her tawny hair in his laughing face. "We're both winners, Jace. We have each other."

Jace grinned. "That we do, my beautiful wife; that we do." He pulled her head downward and sealed their lips, forever.

Author's Note

I want to thank the staff of the American Museum of Natural History in New York City for their assistance and research materials on the Akeley Hall exhibit and for suggesting the purchase of a video about it called *Brightest Africa*. Carl Akeley made five trips to Africa to study, hunt, and collect specimens; his displays capture the animals and habitats down to the smallest detail.

The *Discovery* cable TV channel was a tremendous help and inspiration with its African features and safari programs each week. *National Geographic* magazine was also helpful with numerous stories and pictures.

I am most appreciative to the staff of the Augusta/Richmond County Library for assistance with research materials and for suggesting numerous books of great value. In one, I was lucky to find a list of laws and regulations by the IBEA Company for safaris in 1896. In another, I was inspired by William Holden's *Journey Through Kenya,* a wonderful book of large pictures in vivid color and with detailed text.

For a *Janelle Taylor Newsletter* and bookmark, please send a self-addressed, stamped envelope (long size is best) to Janelle Taylor; P.O. Box 11646; Martinez, GA., 30917-1646. Please print clearly.

Until next time, **GOOD READING** . . .

Janelle Taylor

THE BEST IN HISTORICAL ROMANCES

TIME-KEPT PROMISES (2422, $3.95)
by Constance O'Day Flannery

Sean O'Mara froze when he saw his wife Christina standing before him. She had vanished and the news had been written about in all of the papers—he had even been charged with her murder! But now he had living proof of his innocence, and Sean was not about to let her get away. No matter that the woman was claiming to be someone named Kristine; she still caused his blood to boil.

PASSION'S PRISONER (2573, $3.95)
by Casey Stewart

When Cassandra Lansing put on men's clothing and entered the Rawlings saloon she didn't expect to lose anything—in fact she was sure that she would win back her prized horse Rapscallion that her grandfather lost in a card game. She almost got a smug satisfaction at the thought of fooling the gamblers into believing that she was a man. But once she caught a glimpse of the virile Josh Rawlings, Cassandra wanted to be the woman in his embrace!

ANGEL HEART (2426, $3.95)
by Victoria Thompson

Ever since Angelica's father died, Harlan Snyder had been angling to get his hands on her ranch, the Diamond R. And now, just when she had an important government contract to fulfill, she couldn't find a single cowhand to hire—all because of Snyder's threats. It was only a matter of time before the legendary gunfighter Kid Collins turned up on her doorstep, badly wounded. Angelica assessed his firmly muscled physique and stared into his startling blue eyes. Beneath all that blood and dirt he was the handsomest man she had ever seen, and the one person who could help beat Snyder at his own game.

Available wherever paperbacks are sold, or order direct from the Publisher. Send cover price plus 50¢ per copy for mailing and handling to Zebra Books, Dept. 2912, 475 Park Avenue South, New York, N.Y. 10016. Residents of New York, New Jersey and Pennsylvania must include sales tax. DO NOT SEND CASH.